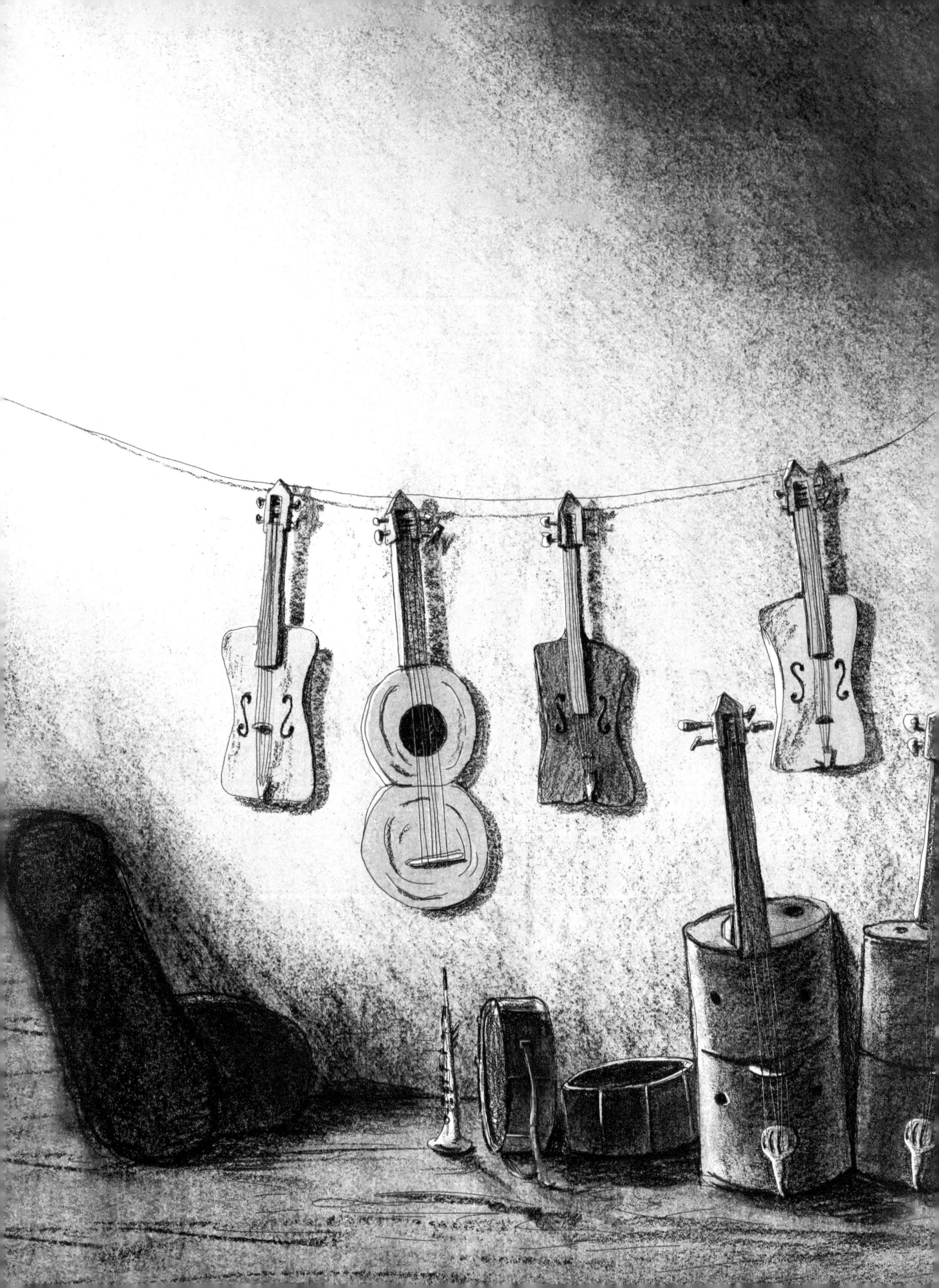

ANOTHER BAND'S TREASURE

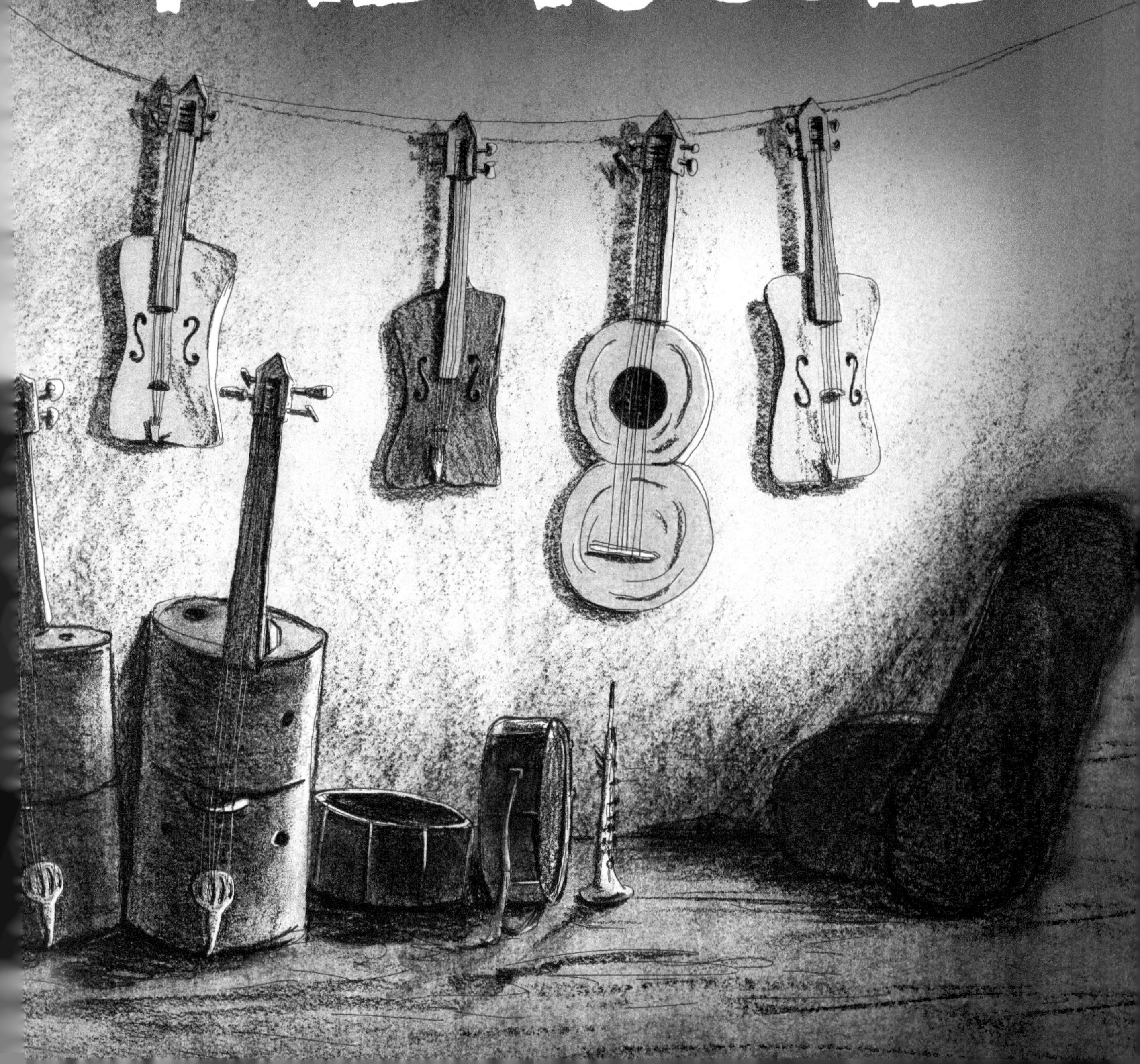

Thank you to Frédérick Mansot and Olivier Jouvray for their encouragement on this book.

Thank you to Qiang for lettering the original edition.

And thank you to everyone who helped and supported me while I was making it.

—HUA LIN XIE

Story and art by Hua Lin Xie
First American edition published in 2023 by Graphic Universe™
Translated from the French by Edward Gauvin

Sous les déchets . . . la musique copyright © 2021 by Steinkis

Graphic Universe™
An imprint of Lerner Publishing Group, Inc.
241 First Avenue North
Minneapolis, MN 55401 USA

For reading levels and more information, look up this title at www.lernerbooks.com.

Main body text set in Pencil Pete.
Typeface provided by JoeBob Graphics.

Library of Congress Cataloging-in-Publication Data

Names: Xie, Hua Lin, author, artist. | Gauvin, Edward, translator.
Title: Another band's treasure : a story of recycled instruments / Hua Lin Xie ; translated by Edward Gauvin.
Description: Minneapolis, MN : Graphic Universe, [2023] | Audience: Ages 8–12 | Audience: Grades 4–6 | Summary: "In Paraguay, teacher Diego and carpenter Nicolas look to a nearby landfill and see instruments in the making, and soon, they are building what they need to begin music lessons for local children." —Provided by publisher.
Identifiers: LCCN 2022023629 (print) | LCCN 2022023630 (ebook) | ISBN 9781728460376 (library binding) | ISBN 9781728478234 (paperback) | ISBN 9781728480534 (ebook)
Subjects: CYAC: Graphic novels. | Musical instruments—Fiction. | Recycling (Waste)—Fiction. | Teachers—Fiction. | Paraguay—Fiction. | LCGFT: Graphic novels.
Classification: LCC PZ7.7.X54 An 2023 (print) | LCC PZ7.7.X54 (ebook) | DDC 741.5/973—dc23/eng/20220713

LC record available at https://lccn.loc.gov/2022023629
LC ebook record available at https://lccn.loc.gov/2022023630

Manufactured in the United States of America
1-51492-50377-8/24/2022

ANOTHER BAND'S TREASURE

A Story of Recycled Instruments

HUA LIN XIE

Translated by Edward Gauvin

Graphic Universe™ • Minneapolis

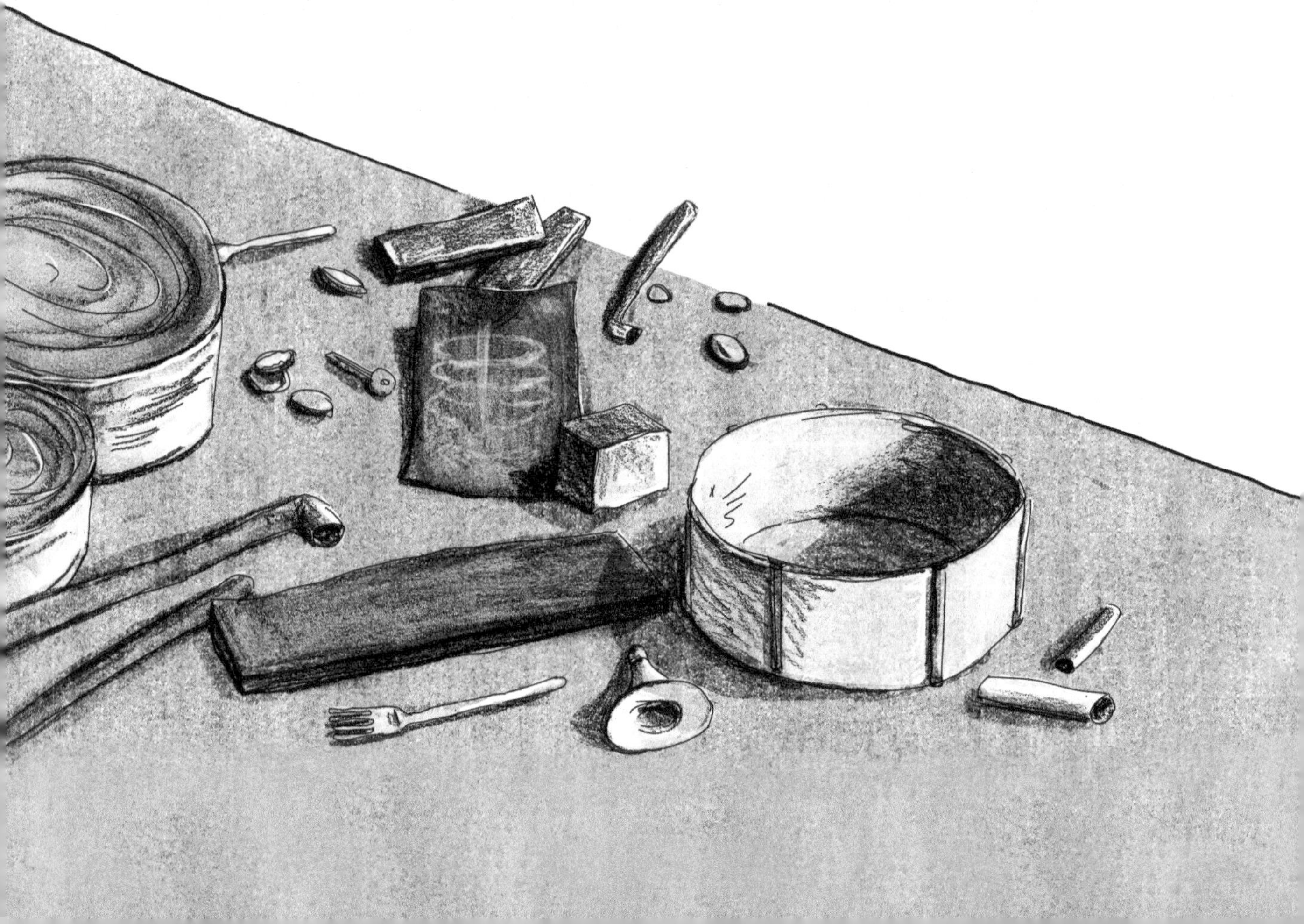

1

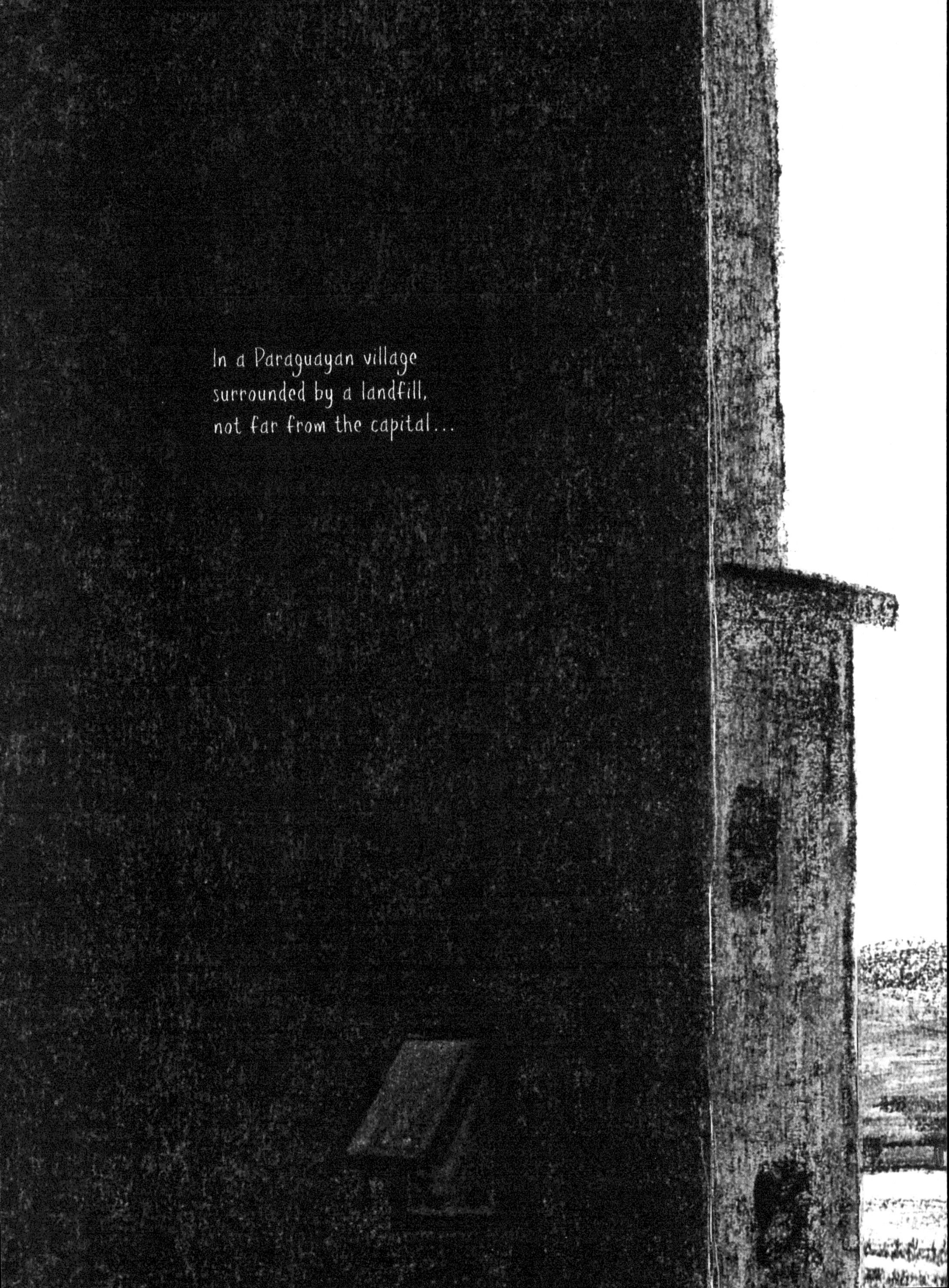
In a Paraguayan village
surrounded by a landfill,
not far from the capital...

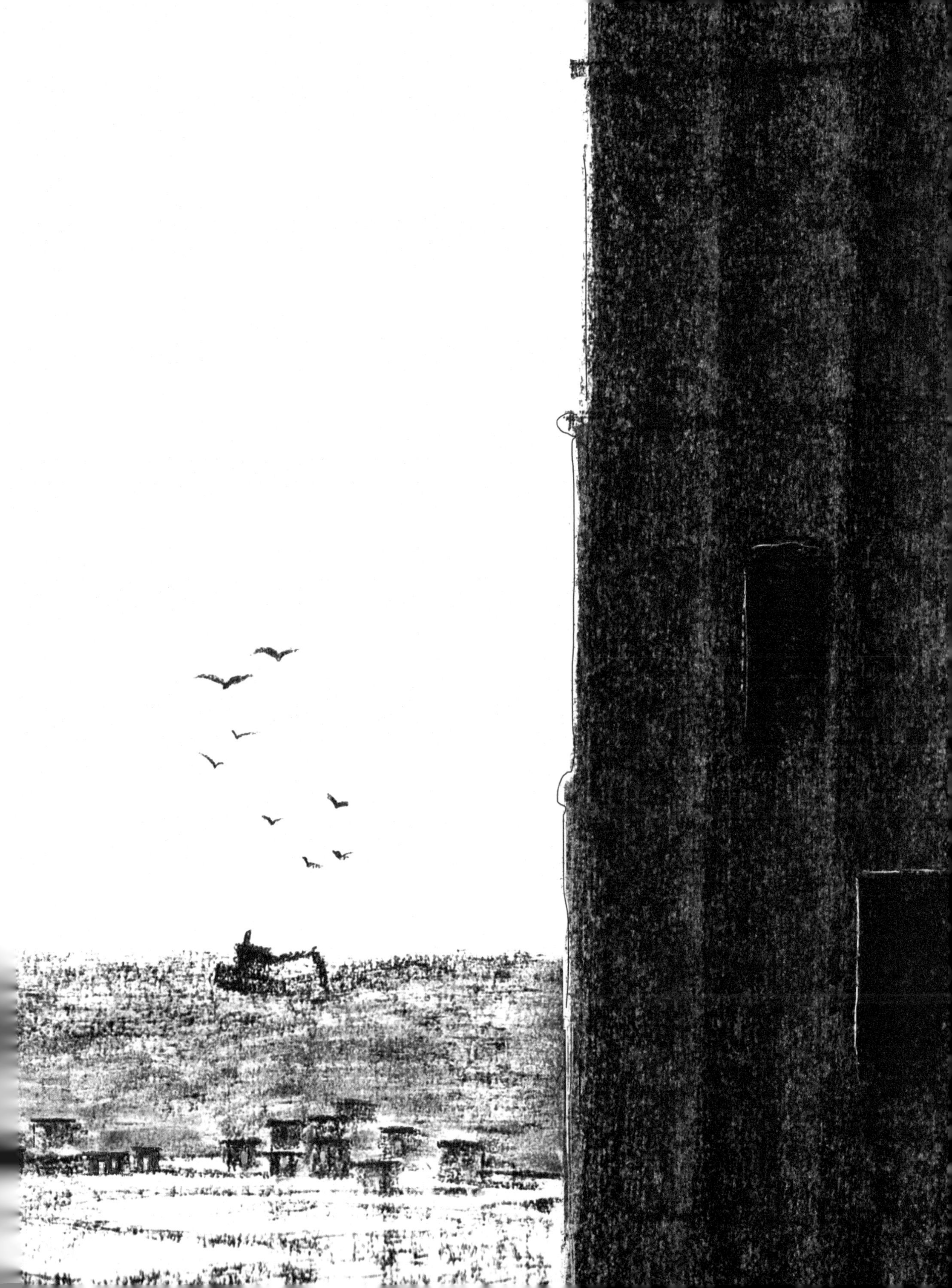

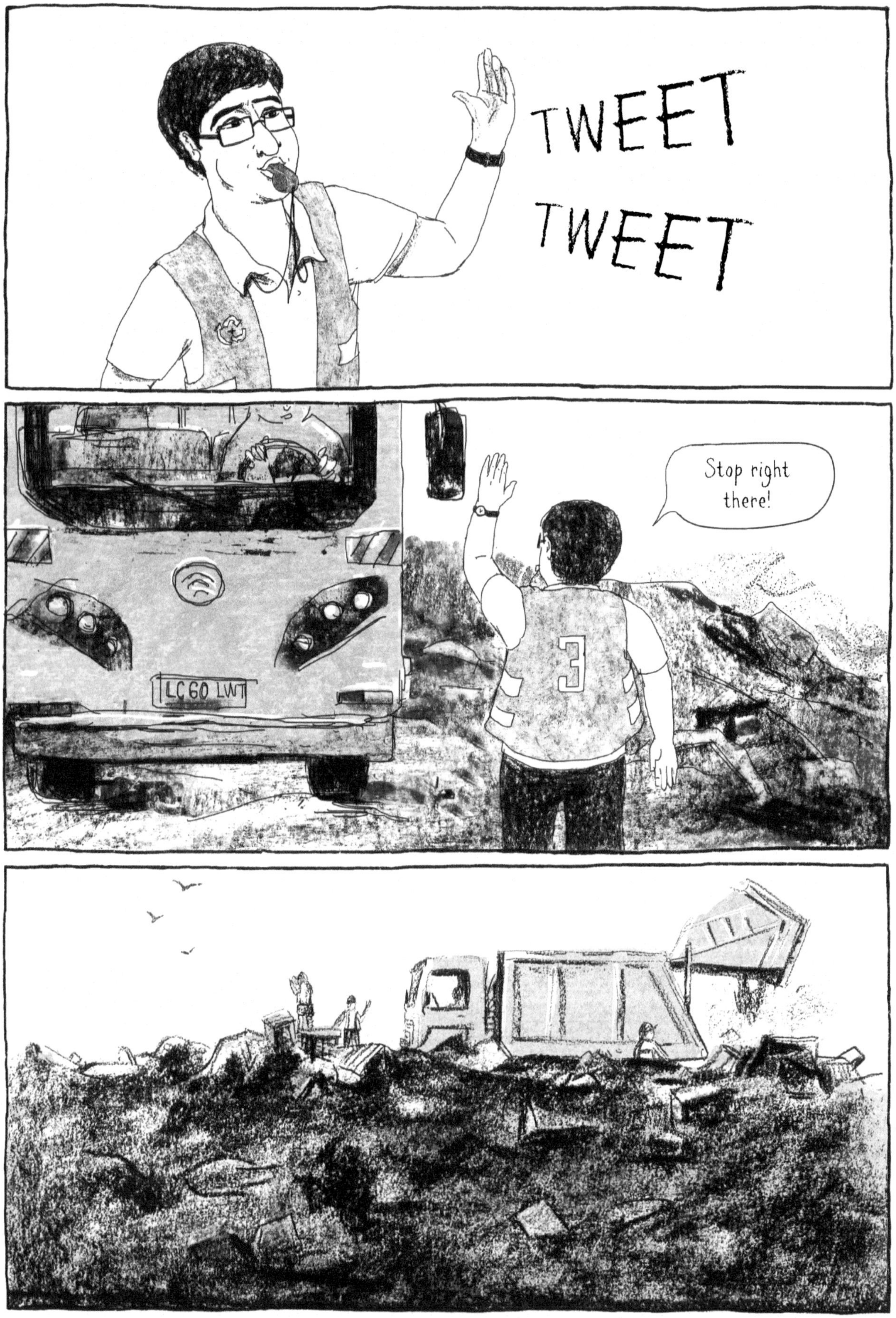
TWEET
TWEET
Stop right there!
LC60 LWT
3

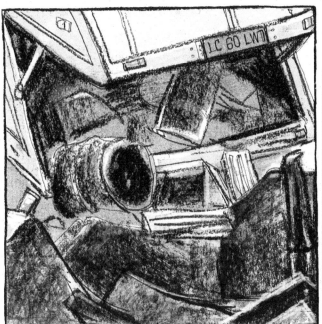

C'mon, Nicolas.

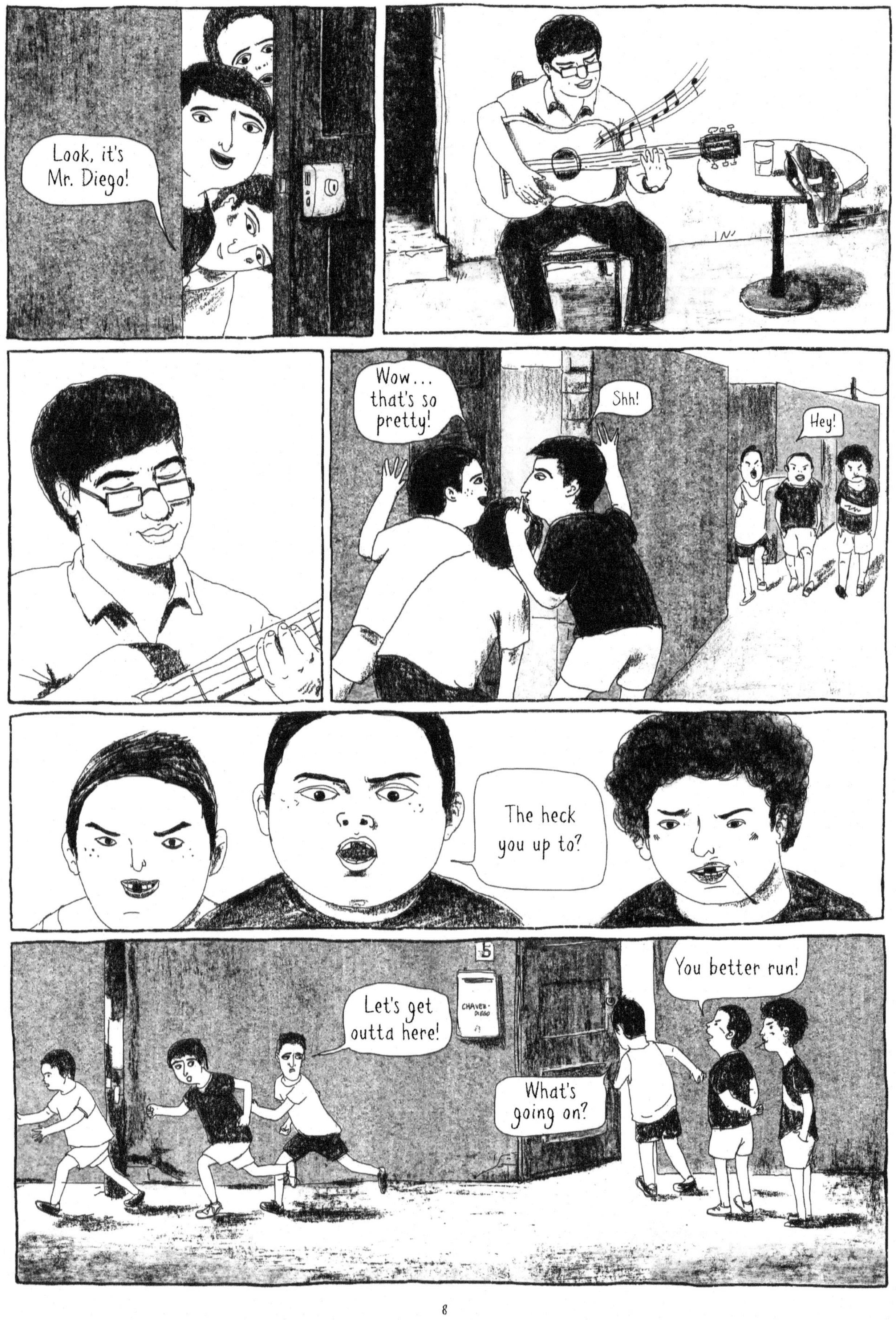
Look, it's Mr. Diego!
Wow... that's so pretty!
Shh!
Hey!
The heck you up to?
CHAVES · DIEGO
Let's get outta here!
You better run!
What's going on?

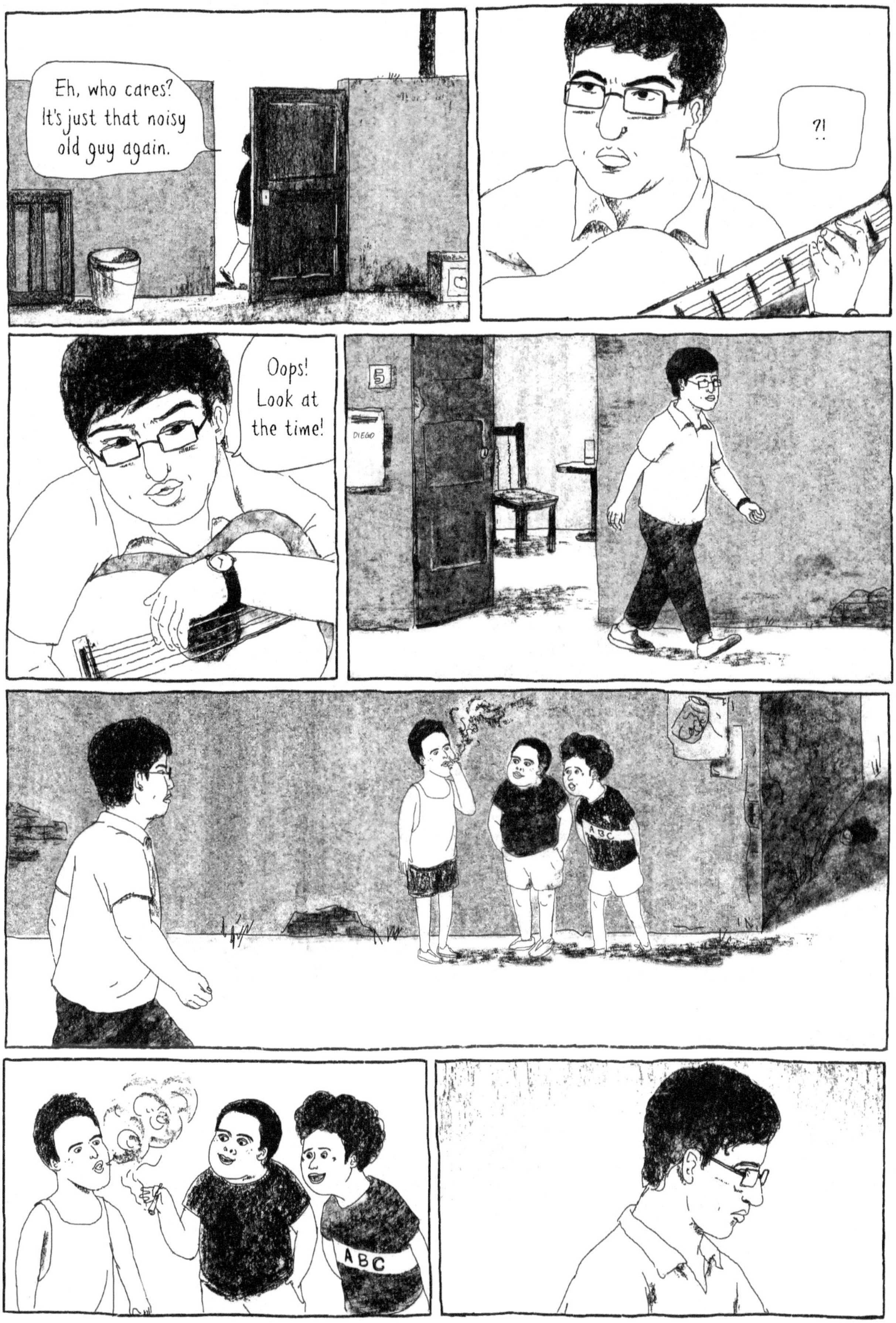
Eh, who cares? It's just that noisy old guy again.
?!
Oops! Look at the time!
5
DIEGO
ABC
ABC

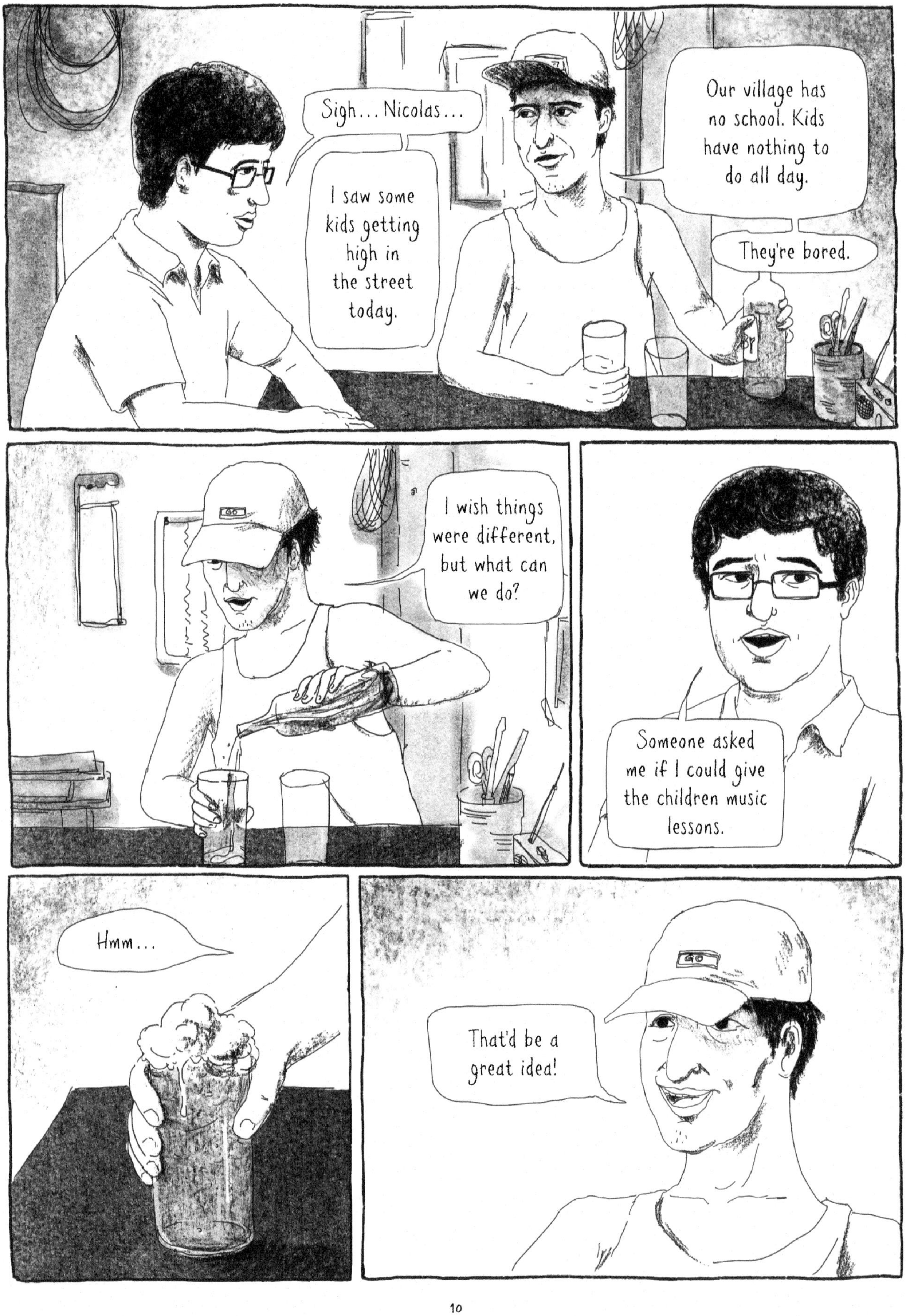
Sigh... Nicolas...
I saw some kids getting high in the street today.
Our village has no school. Kids have nothing to do all day.
They're bored.
I wish things were different, but what can we do?
Someone asked me if I could give the children music lessons.
Hmm...
That'd be a great idea!

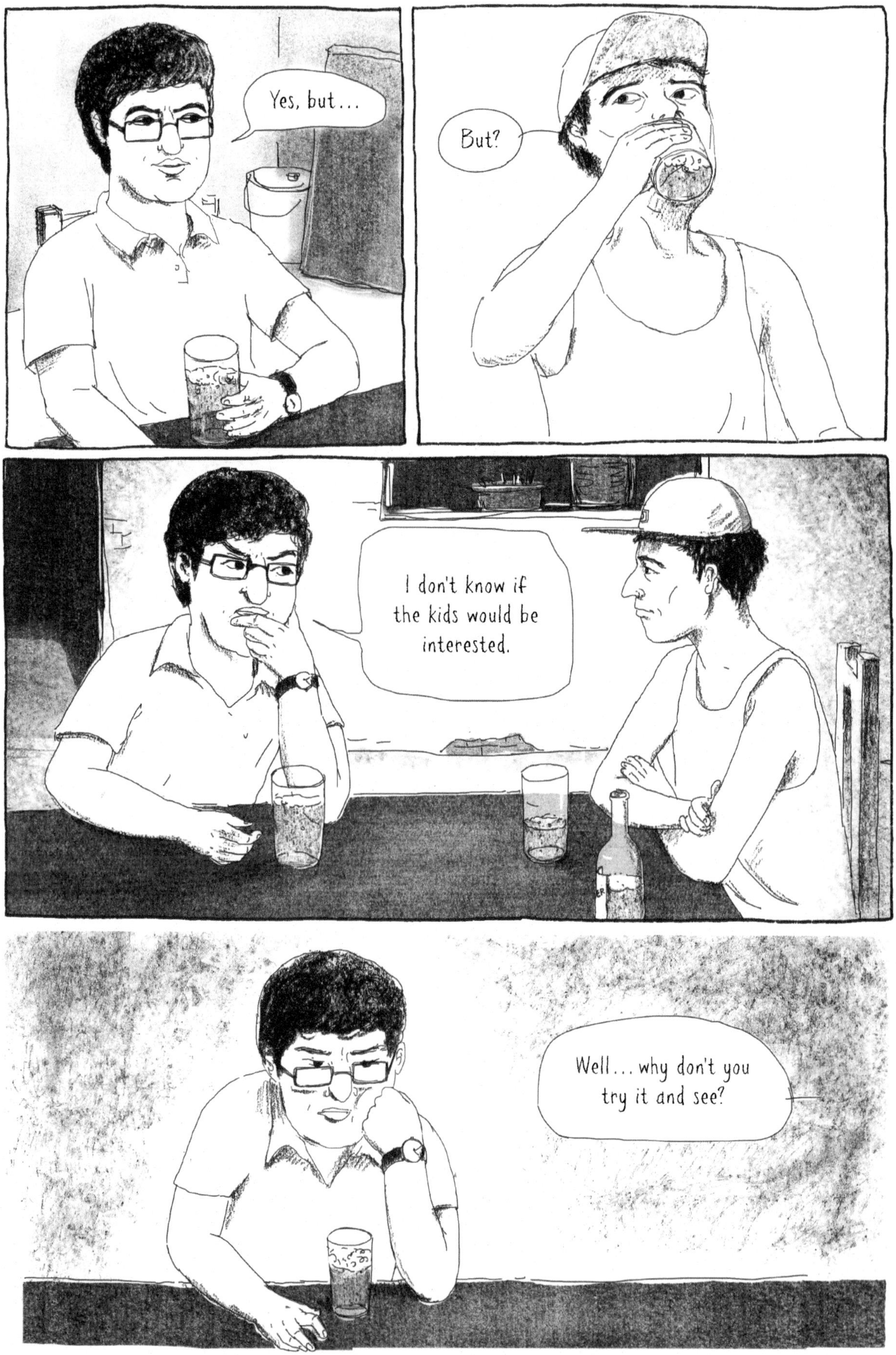
Yes, but...
But?
I don't know if the kids would be interested.
Well... why don't you try it and see?

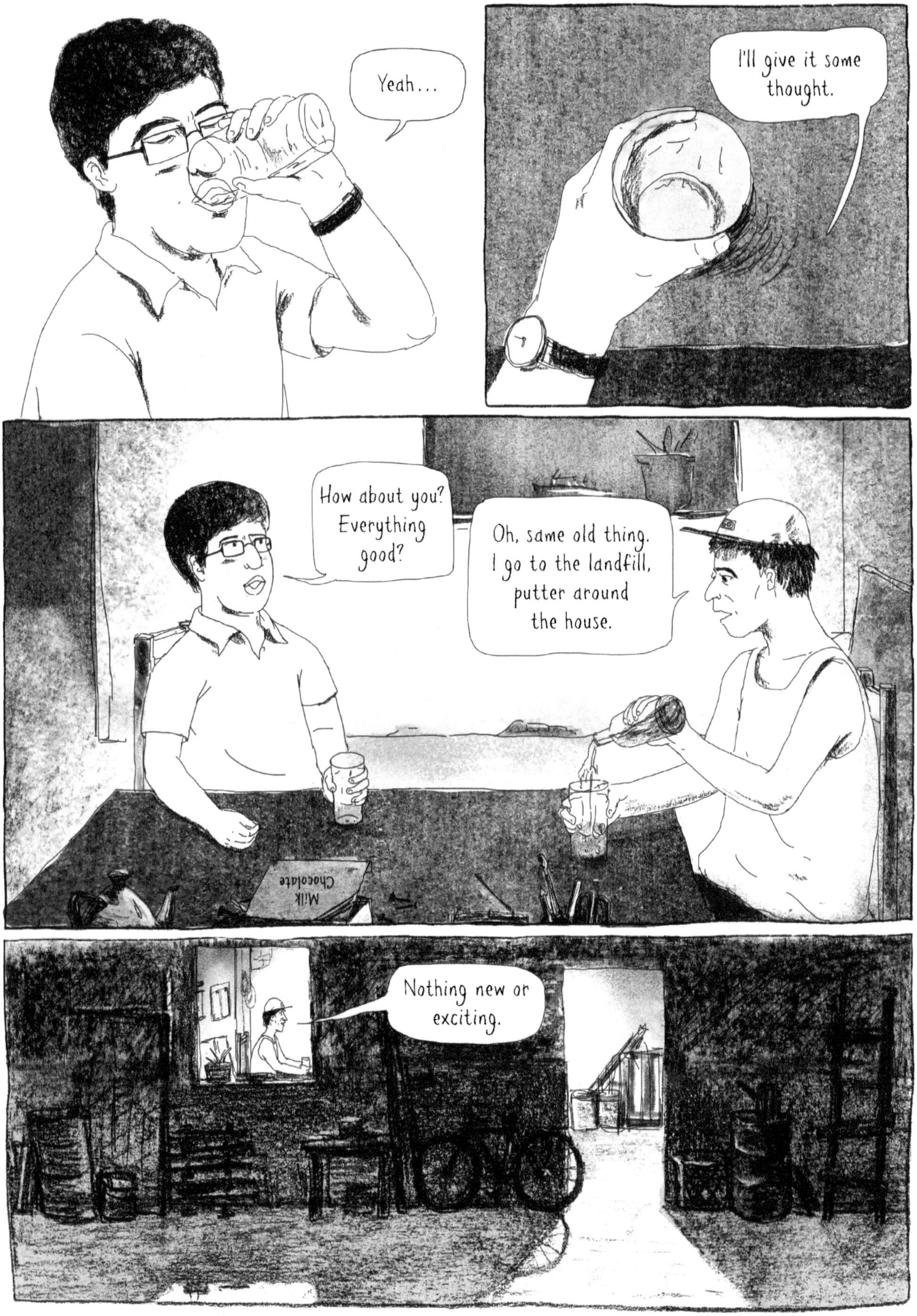
Yeah...
I'll give it some thought.
How about you? Everything good?
Oh, same old thing. I go to the landfill, putter around the house.
Milk Chocolate
Nothing new or exciting.

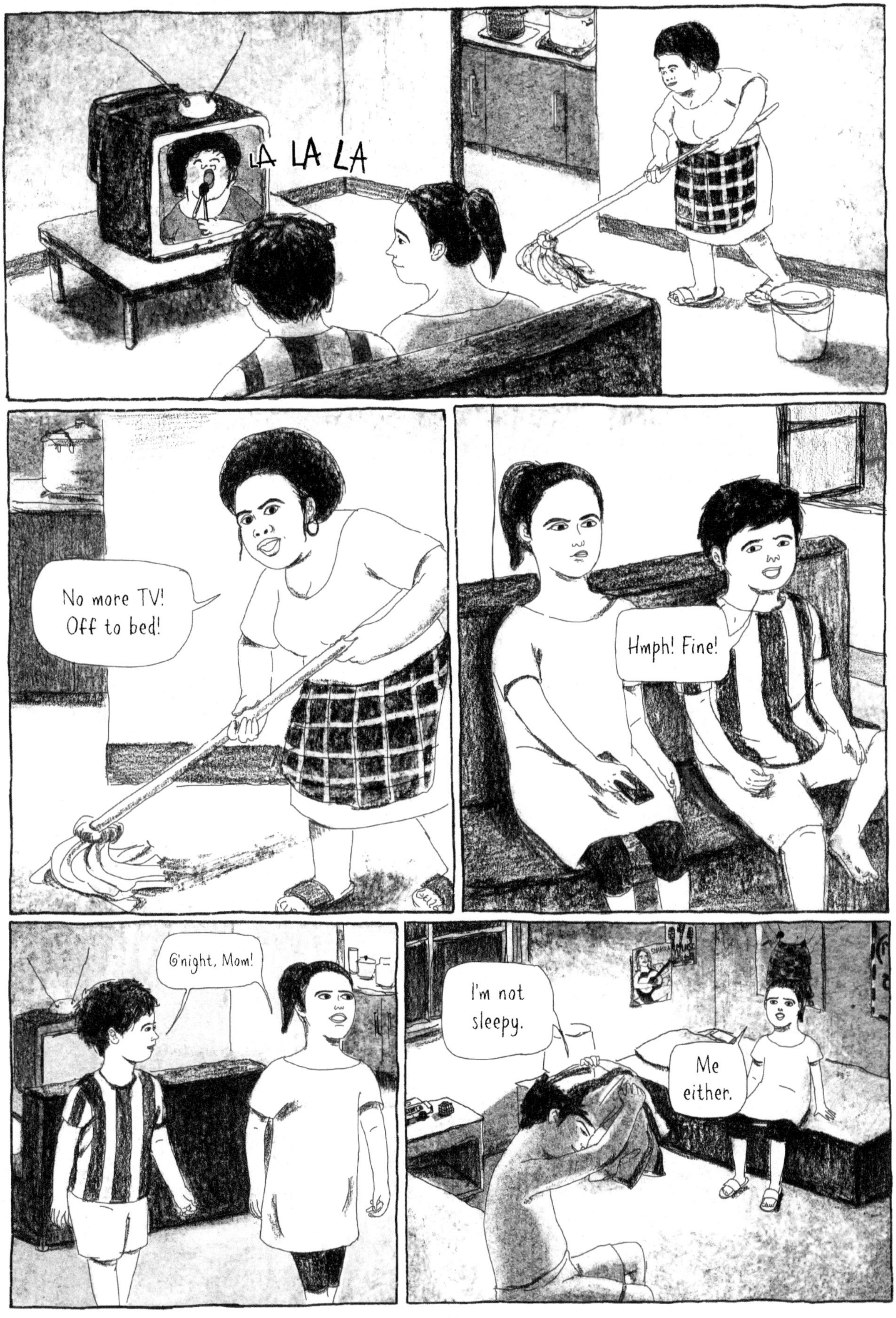
LA LA LA
No more TV! Off to bed!
Hmph! Fine!
G'night, Mom!
I'm not sleepy.
Me either.

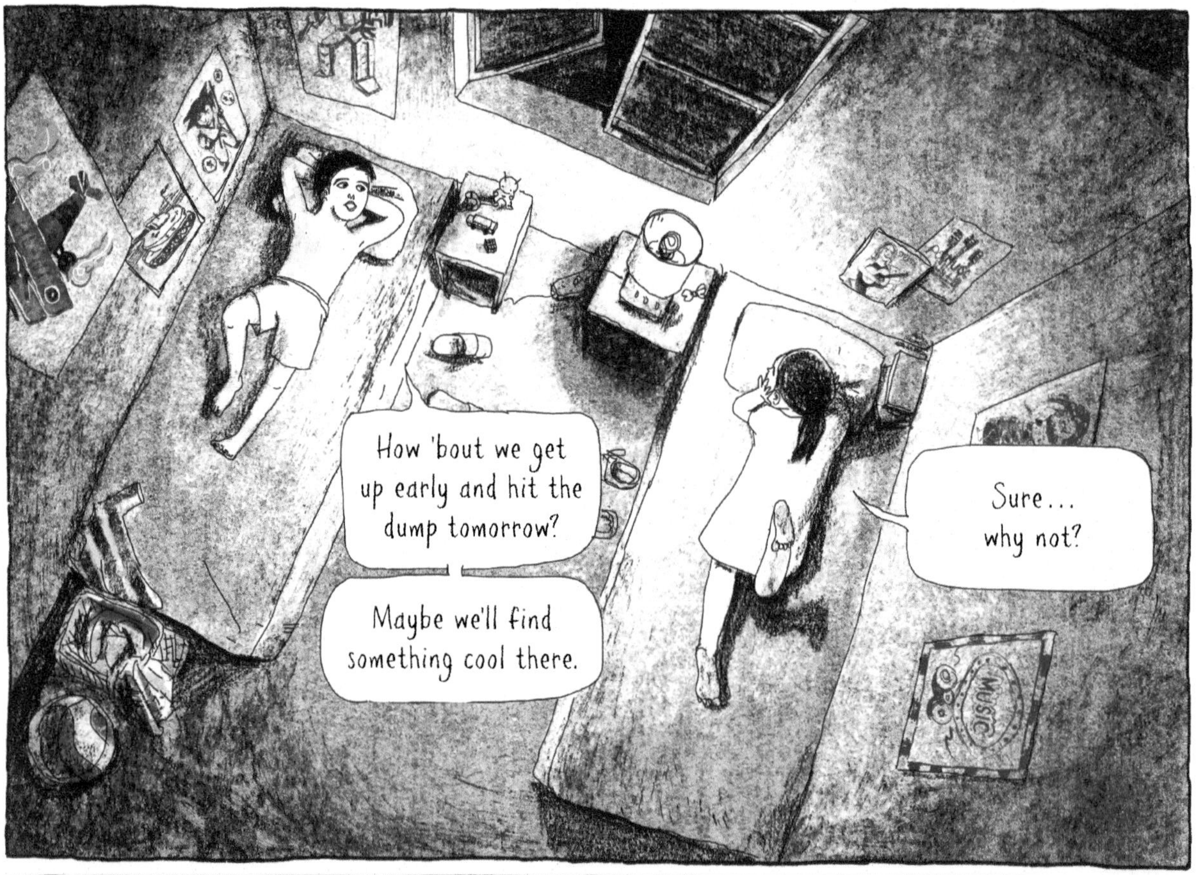
How 'bout we get up early and hit the dump tomorrow?
Maybe we'll find something cool there.
Sure... why not?

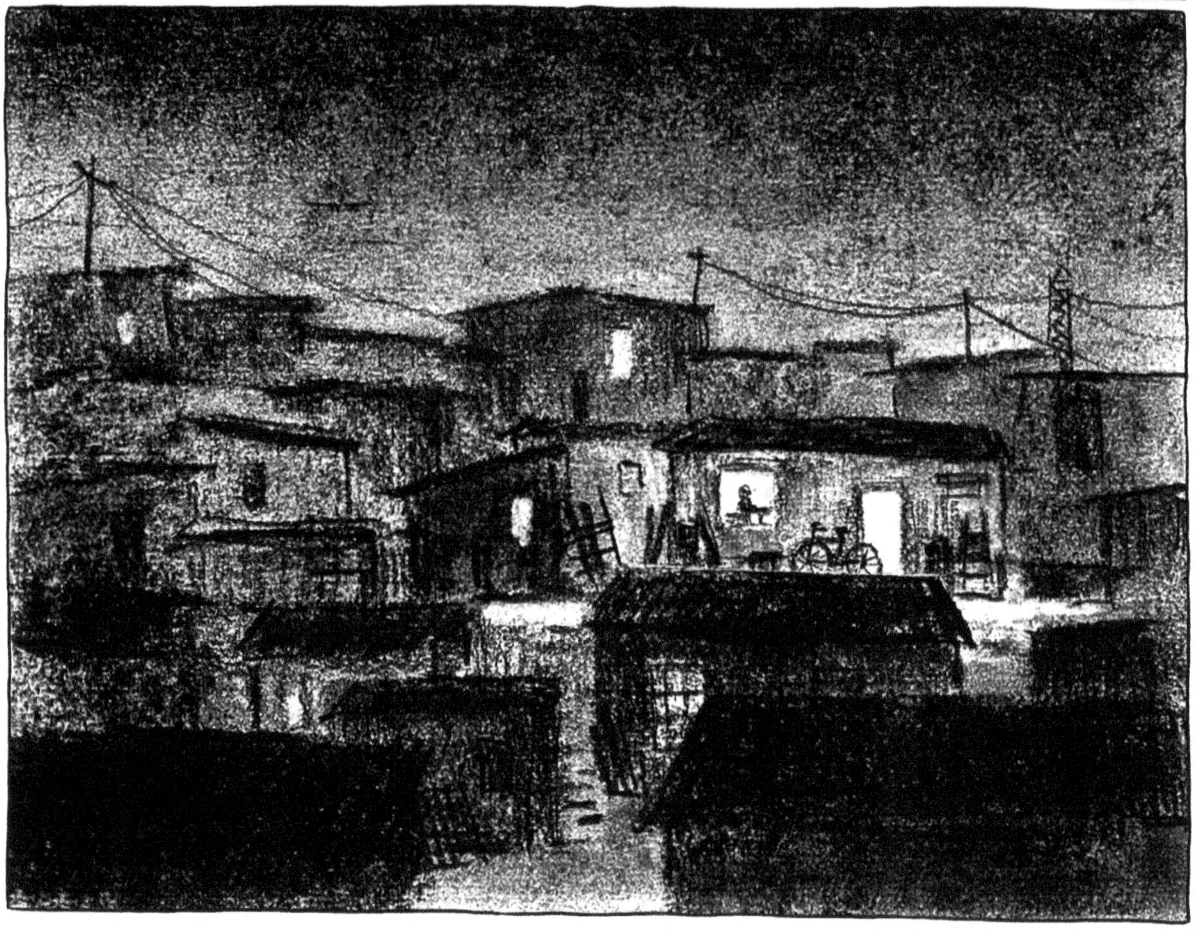

2

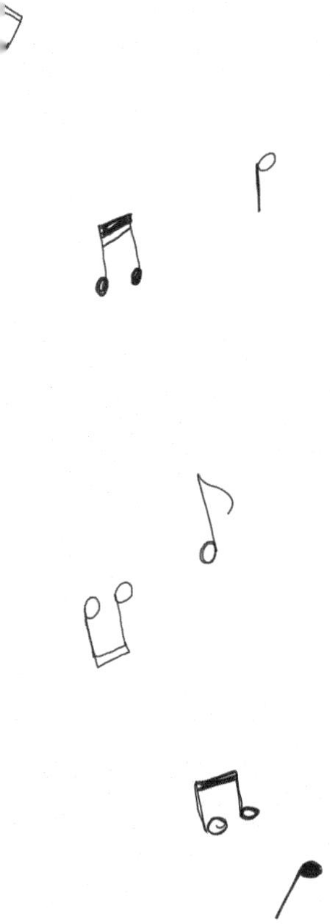

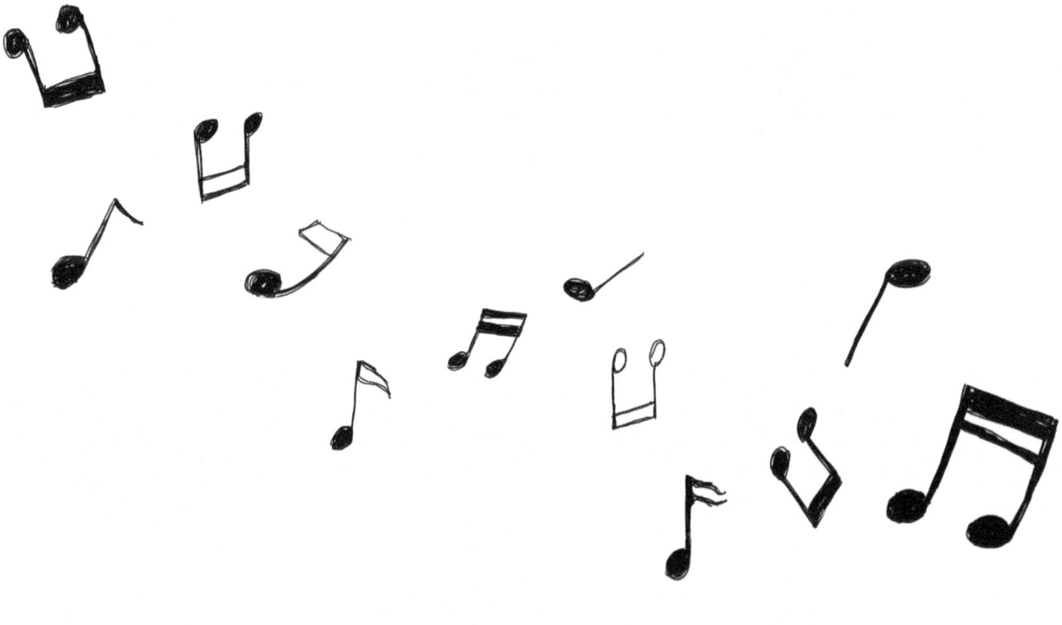

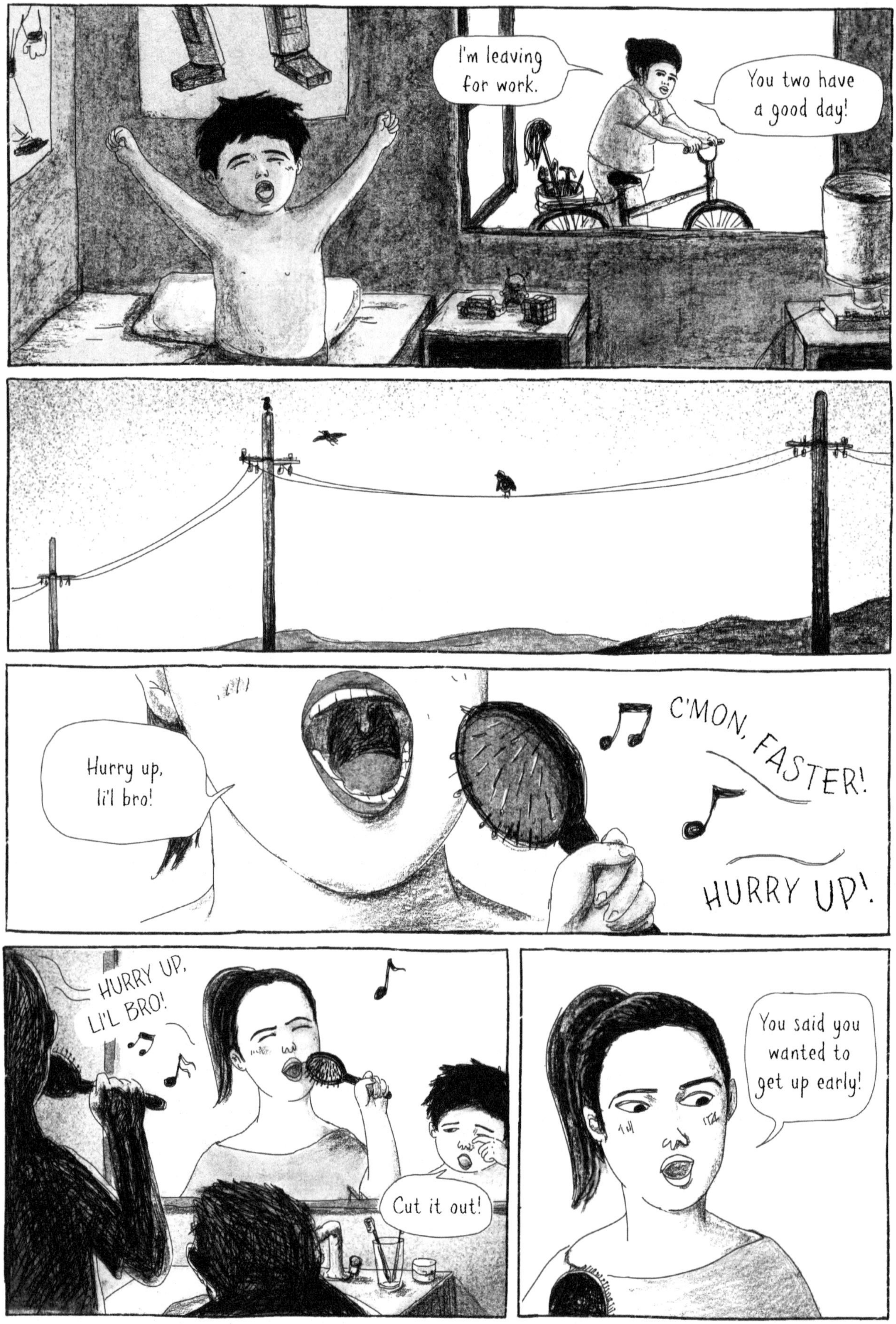
I'm leaving for work.
You two have a good day!
Hurry up, li'l bro!
C'MON, FASTER!
HURRY UP!
HURRY UP, LI'L BRO!
Cut it out!
You said you wanted to get up early!

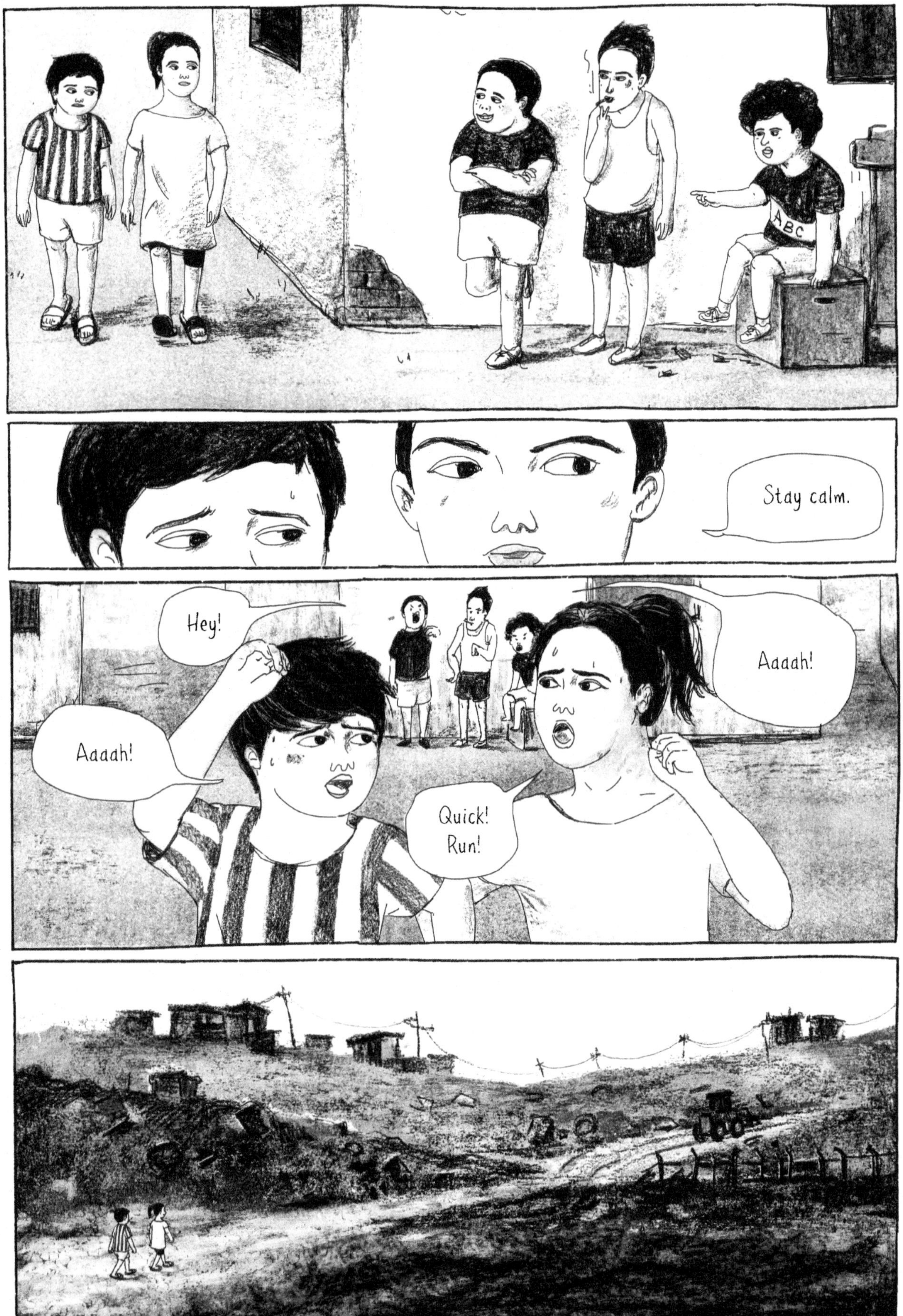
Stay calm.
Hey!
Aaaah!
Aaaah!
Quick! Run!

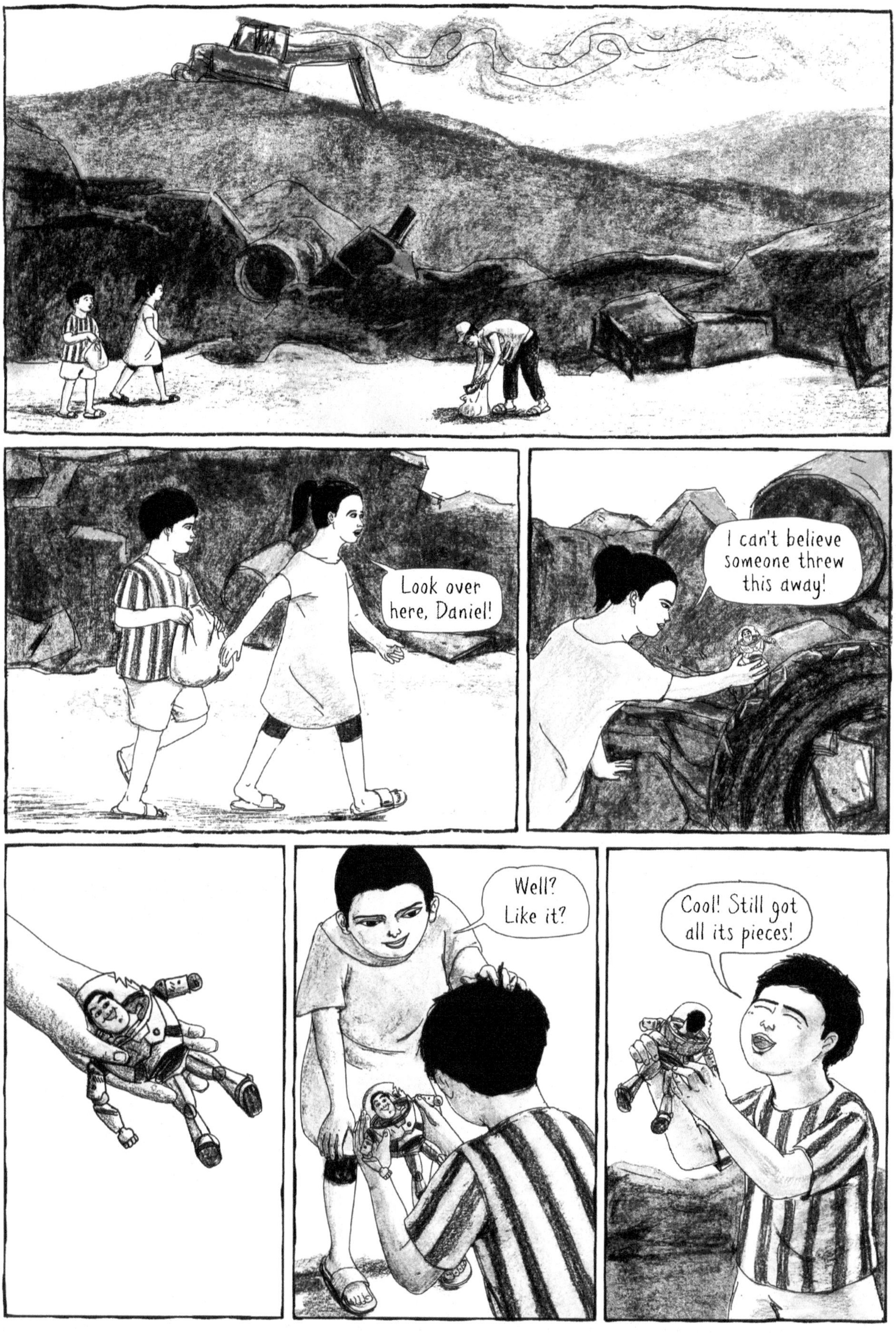
Look over here, Daniel!
I can't believe someone threw this away!
Well? Like it?
Cool! Still got all its pieces!

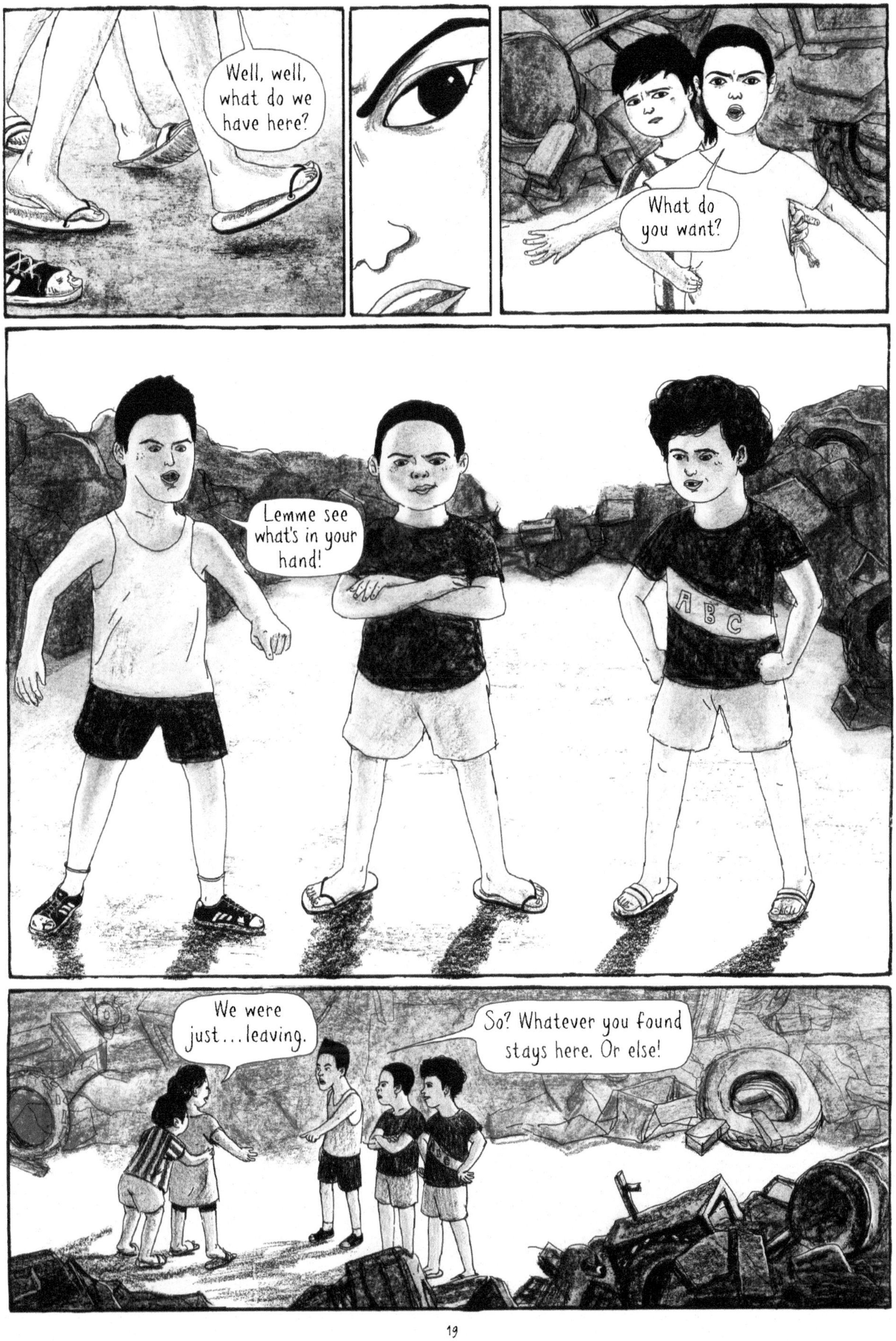
Well, well, what do we have here?
What do you want?
Lemme see what's in your hand!
ABC
We were just...leaving.
So? Whatever you found stays here. Or else!

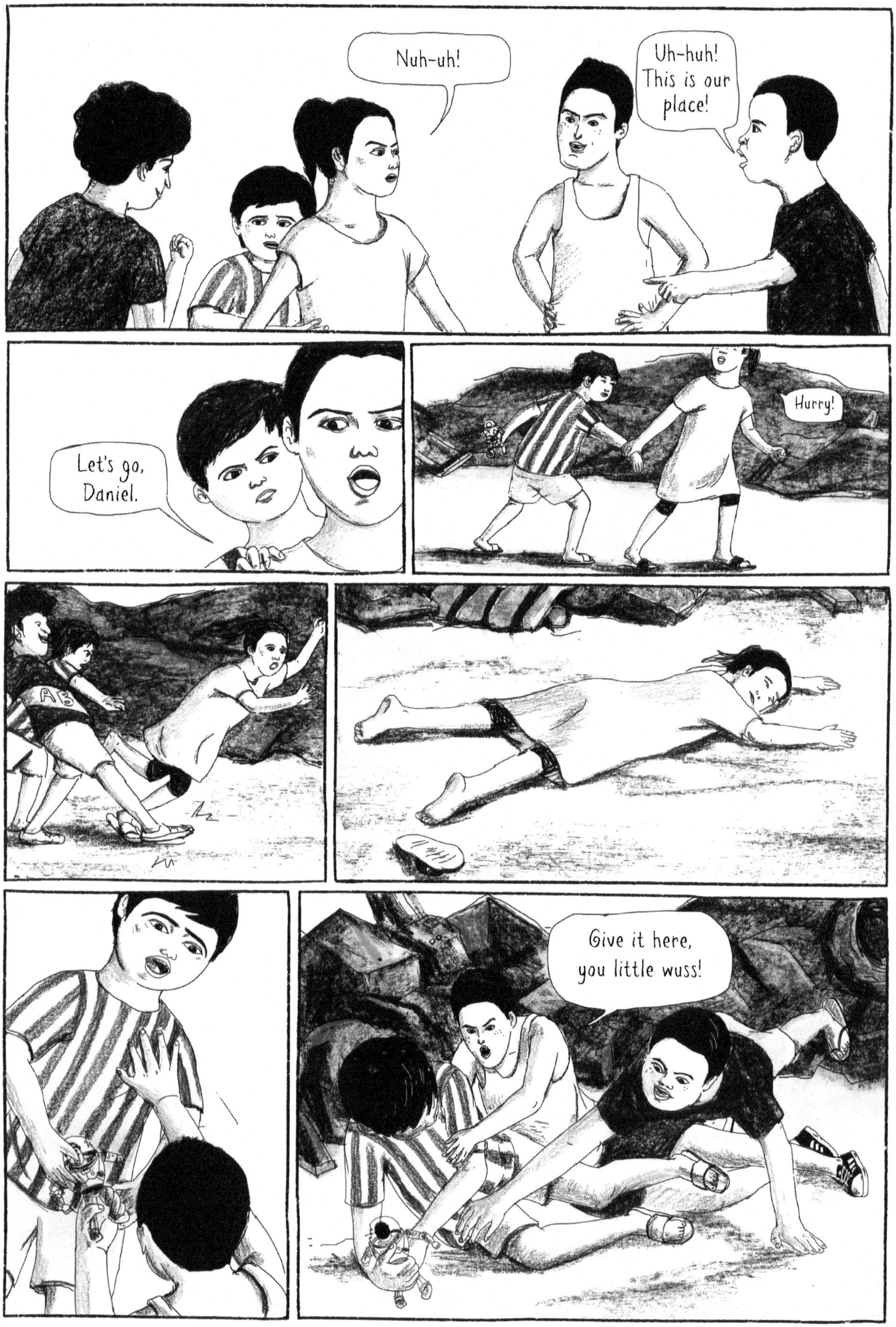
Nuh-uh!
Uh-huh! This is our place!
Let's go, Daniel.
Hurry!
Give it here, you little wuss!

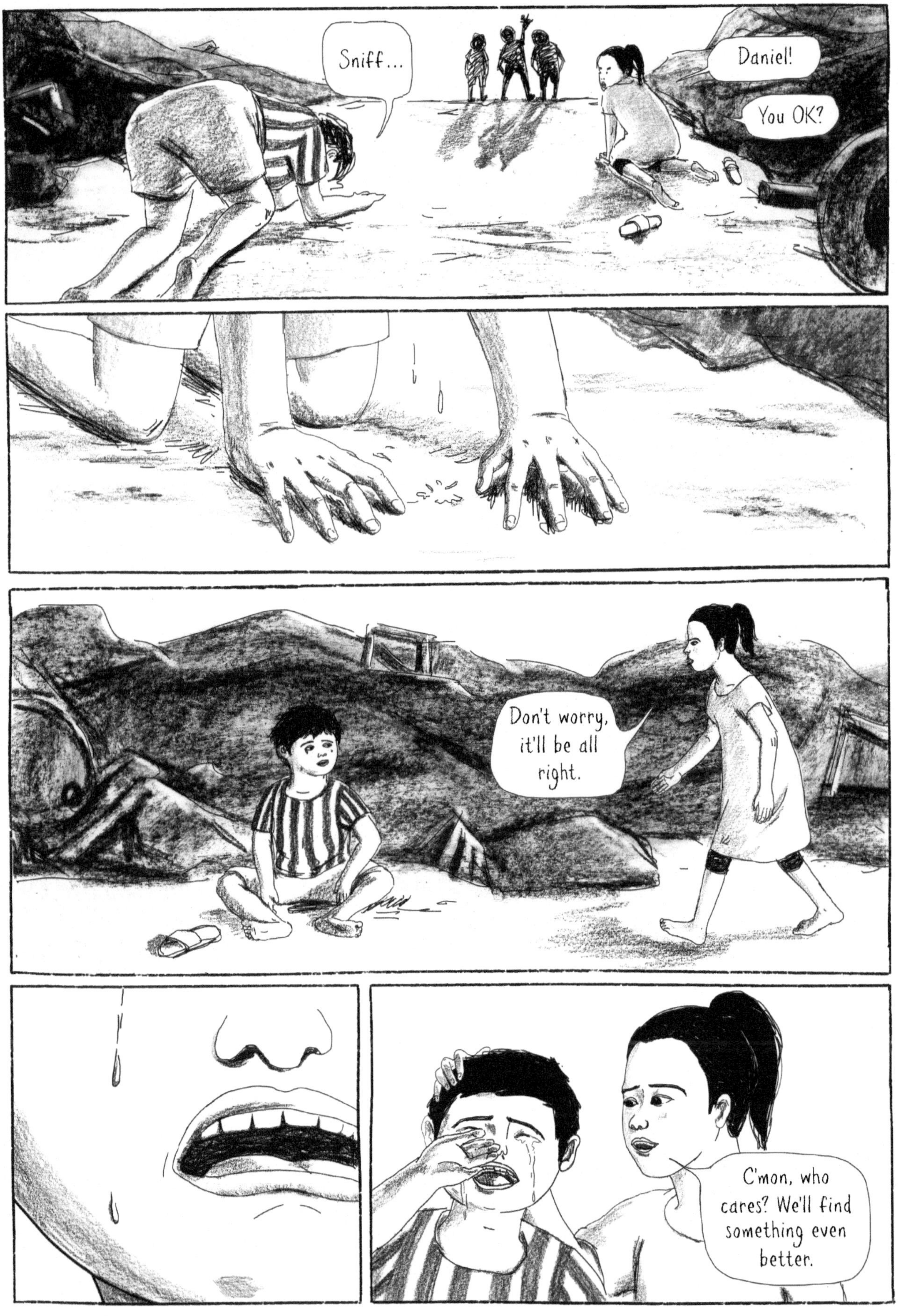
Sniff...
Daniel!
You OK?
Don't worry, it'll be all right.
C'mon, who cares? We'll find something even better.

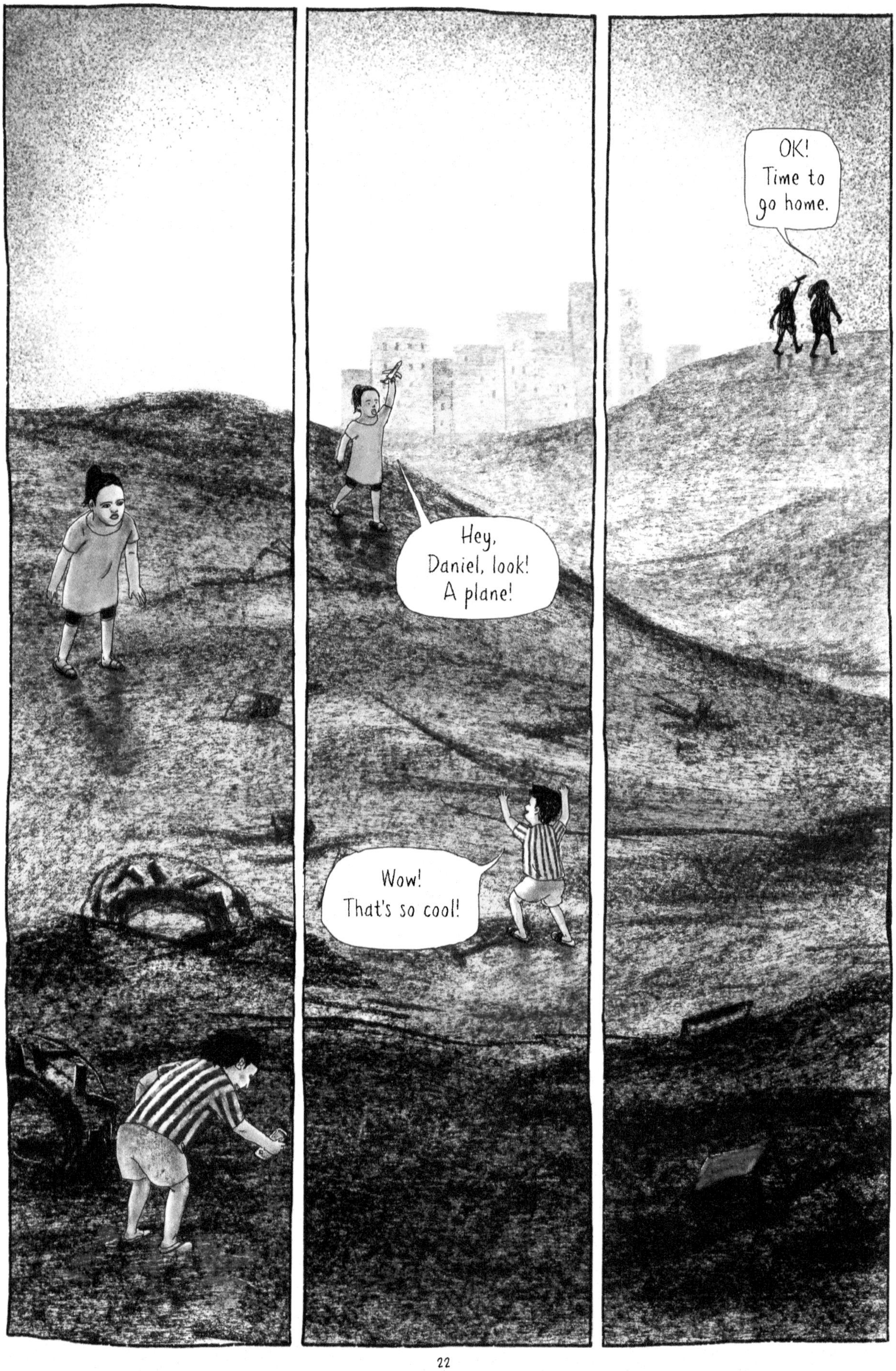
Hey, Daniel, look! A plane!
Wow! That's so cool!
OK! Time to go home.

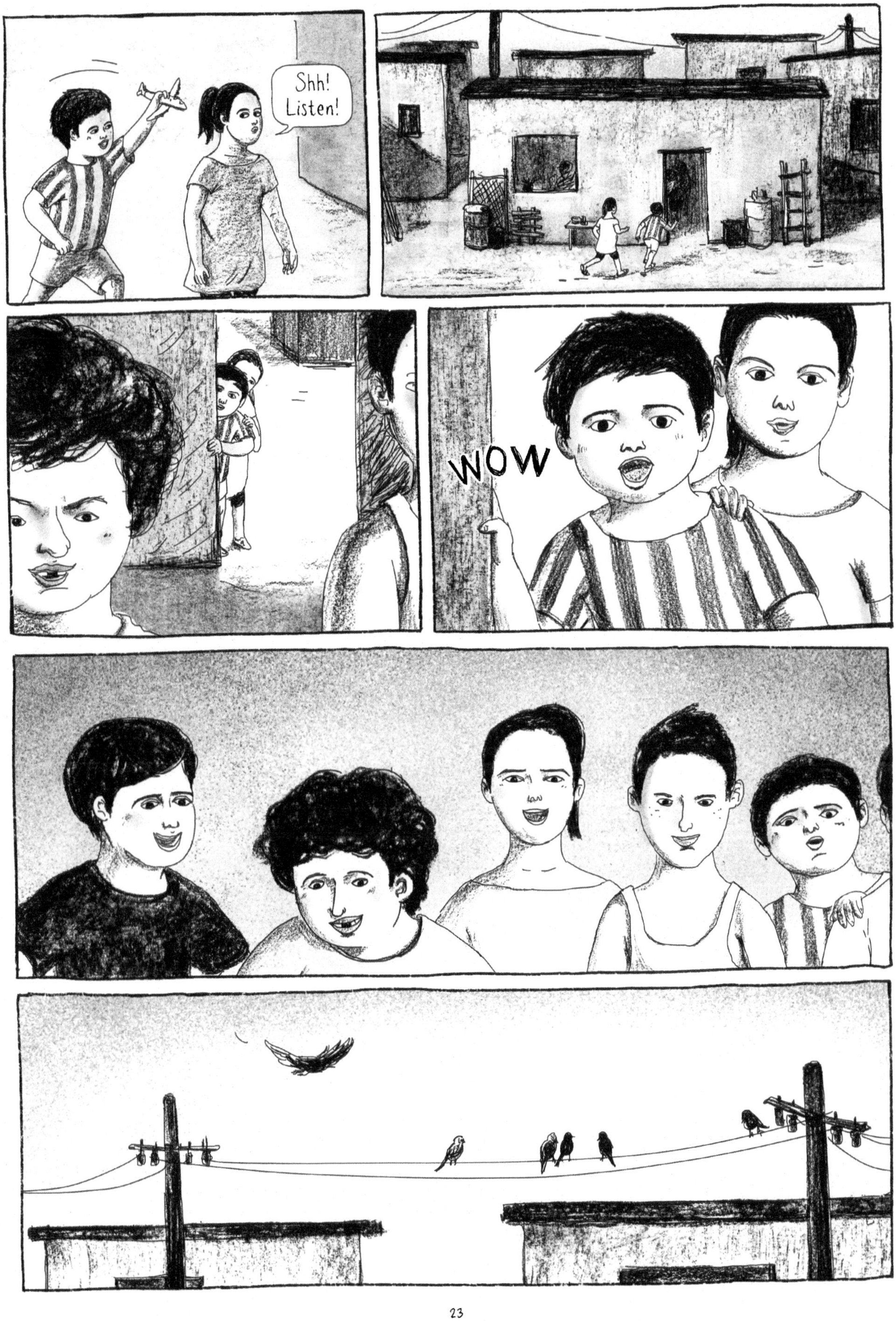
Shh! Listen!
WOW

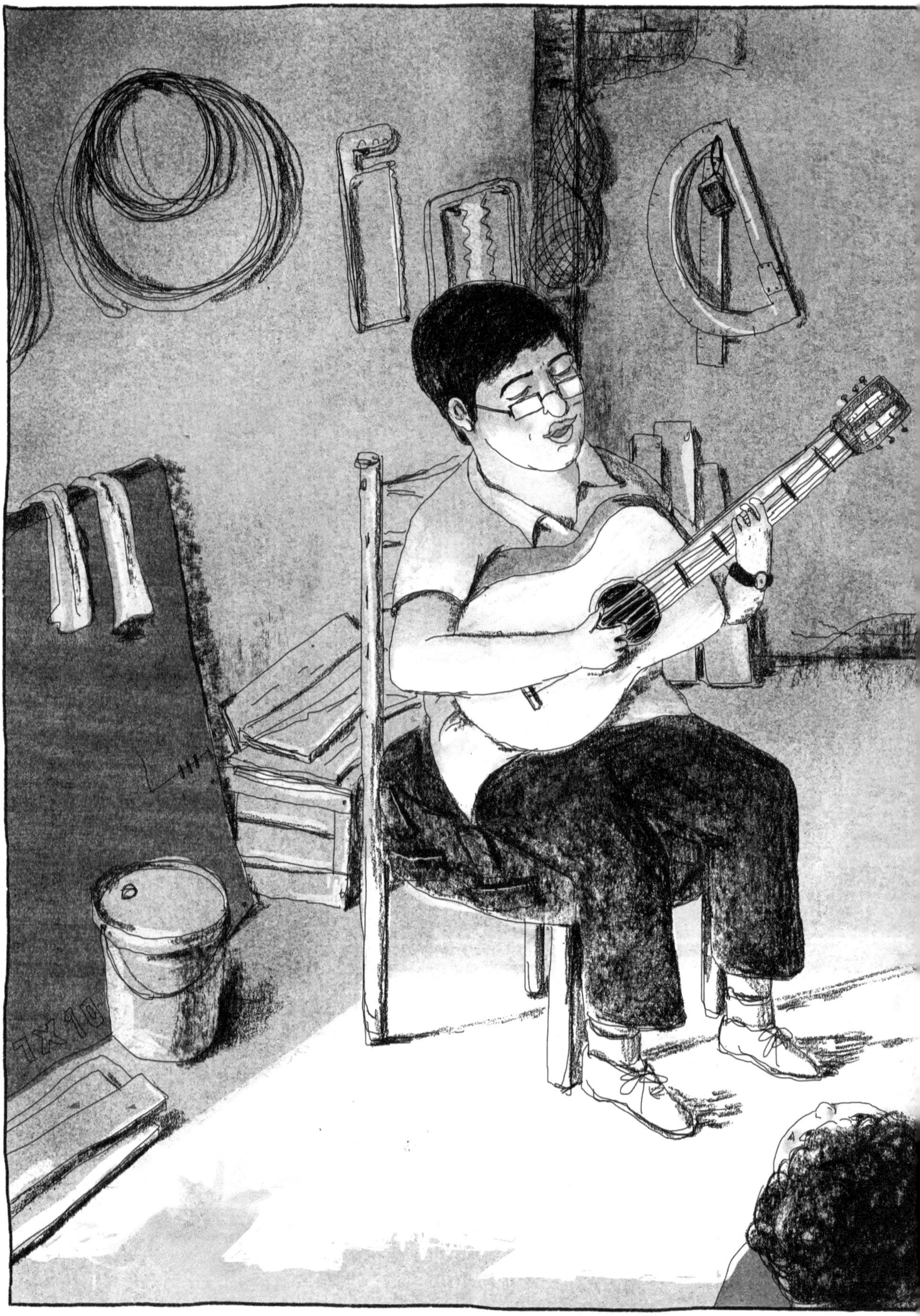

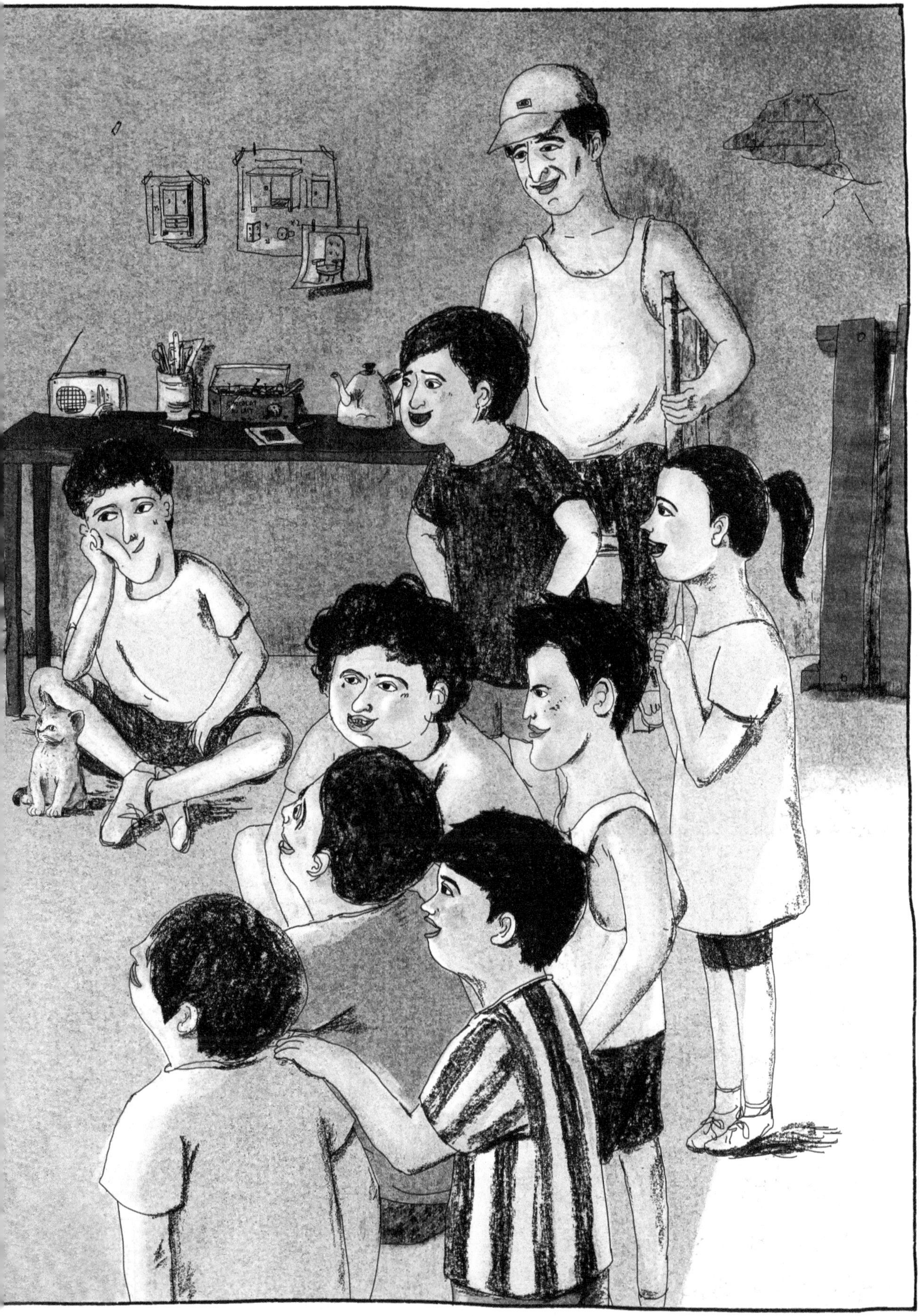

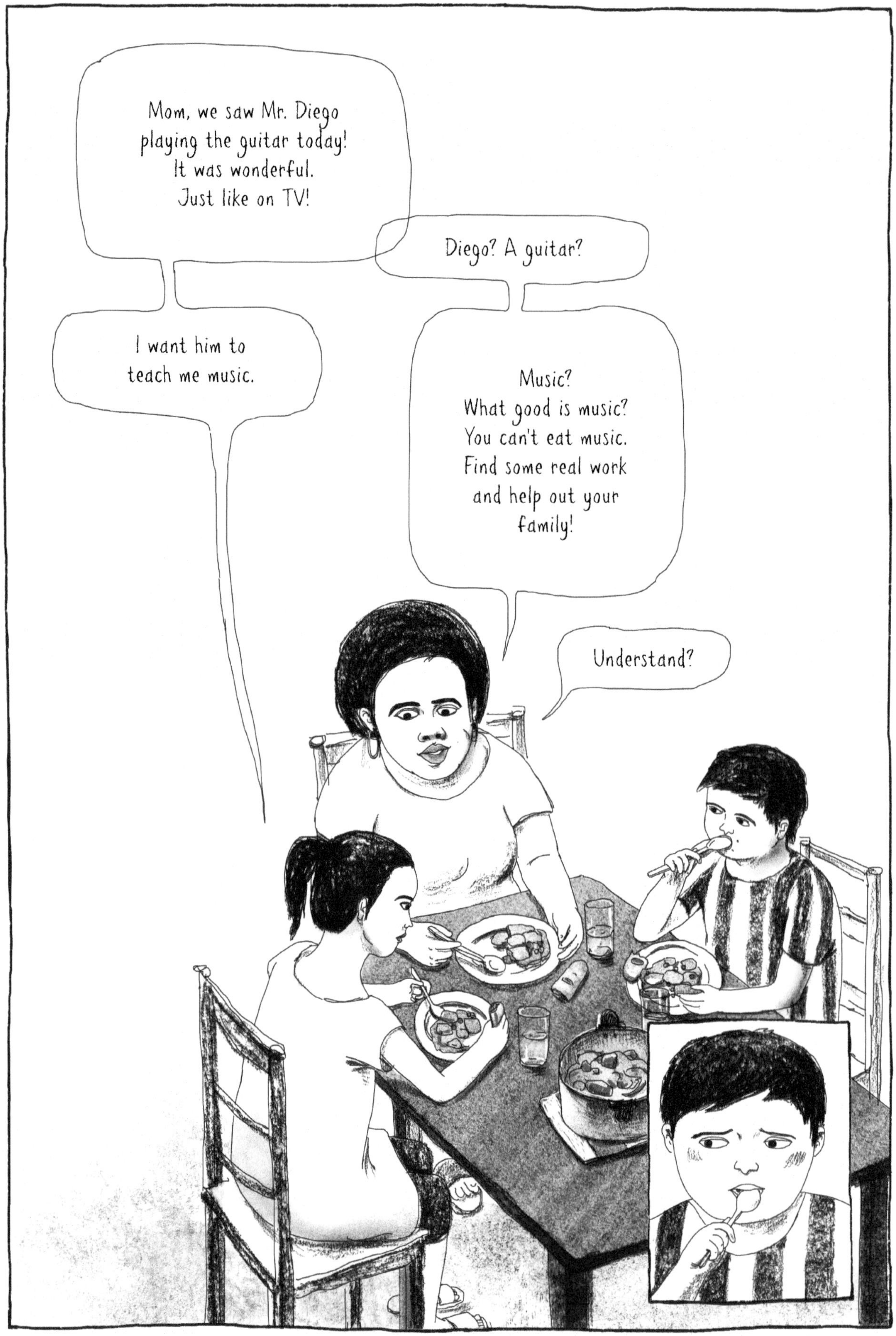
Mom, we saw Mr. Diego playing the guitar today! It was wonderful. Just like on TV!
Diego? A guitar?
I want him to teach me music.
Music? What good is music? You can't eat music. Find some real work and help out your family!
Understand?

3

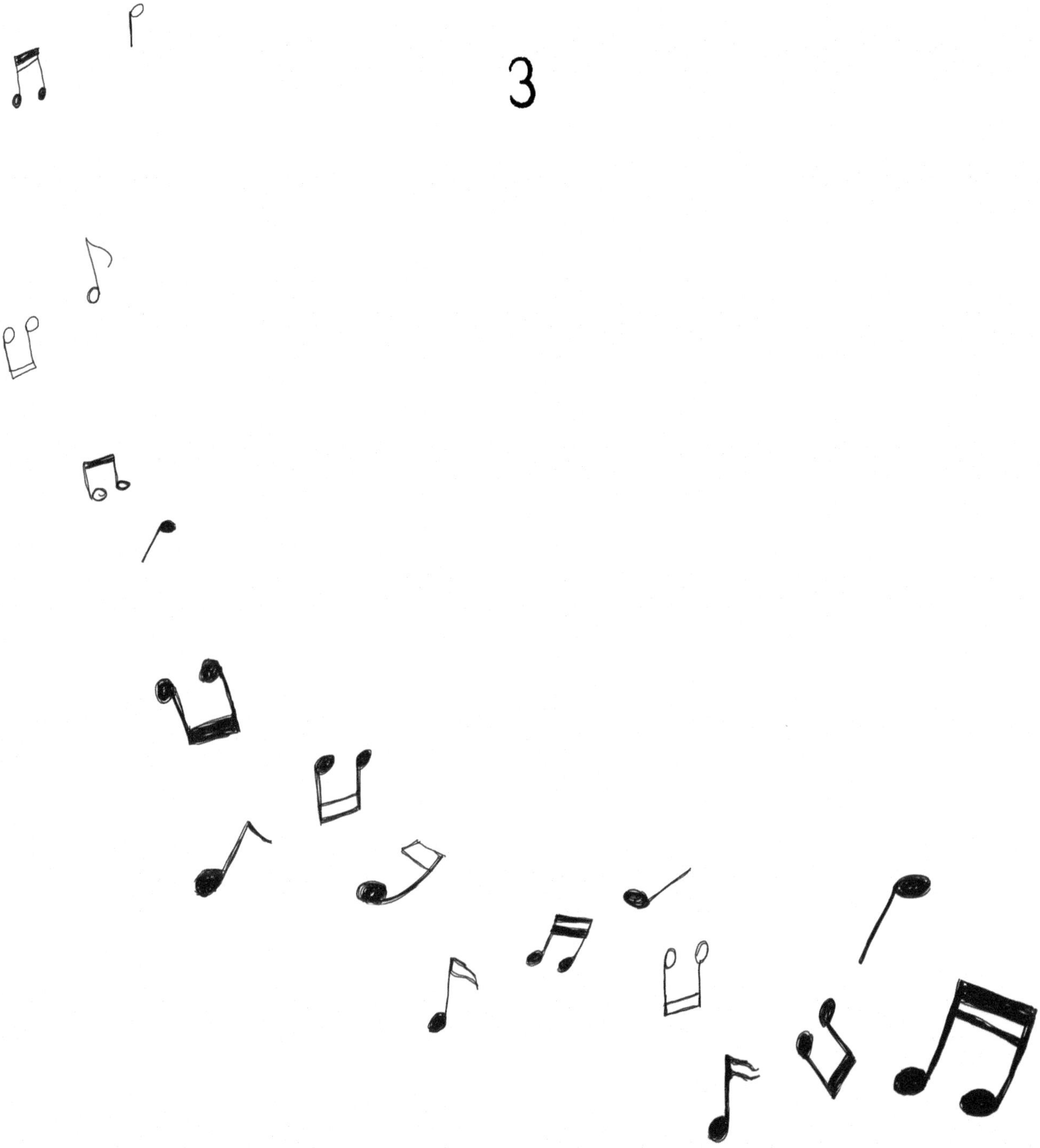

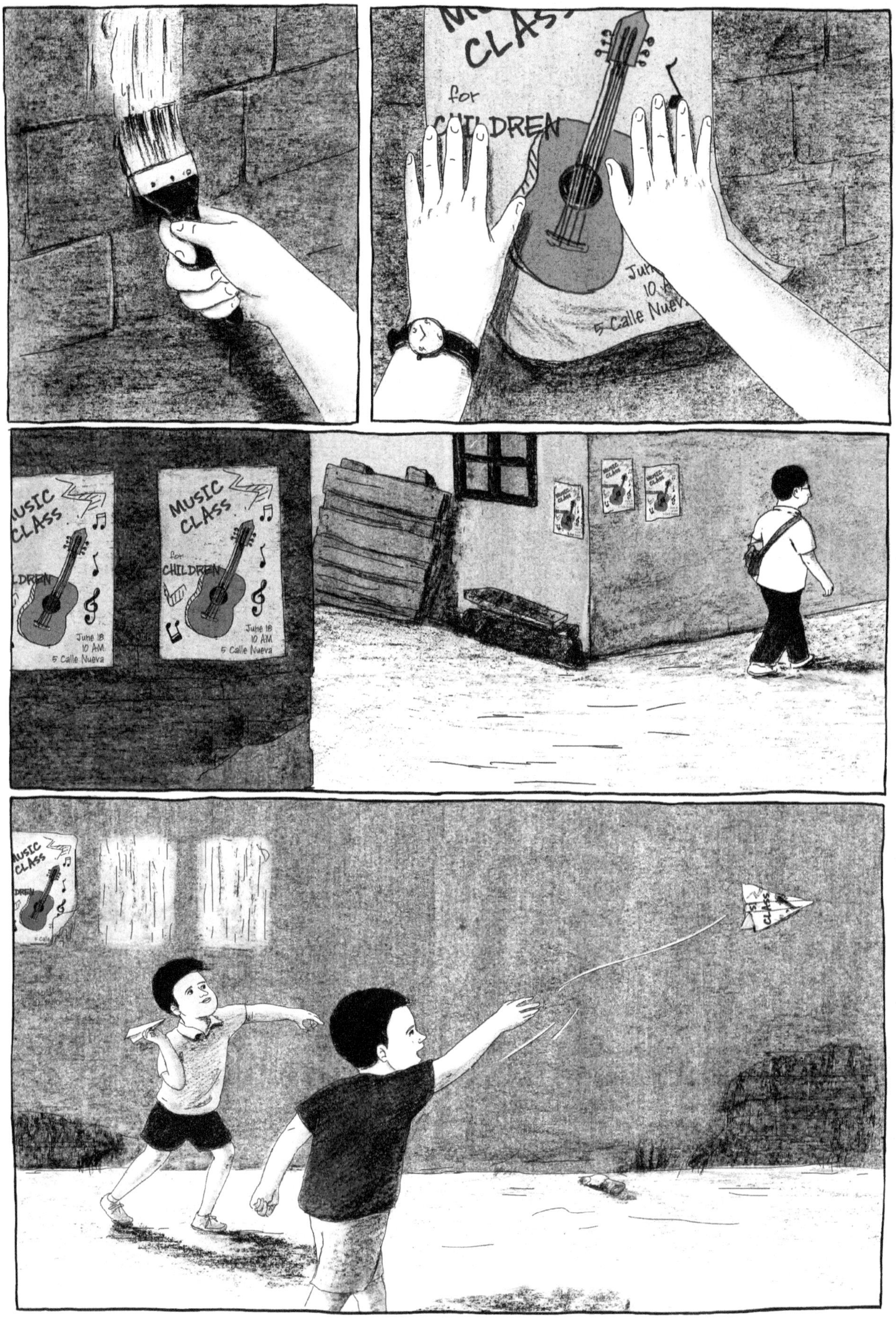
CLASS
for
MUSIC CLASS
for
CHILDREN
June 18
10 A.M.
5 Calle Nueva
MUSIC CLASS

MUSIC CLASS
MUSIC CLASS
June 18
10 AM
5 Calle Nueva
MUSIC CLASS
June 18
10 AM
5 Calle Nueva
MUSIC CLASS
for
June 18
10 AM
Calle Nueva

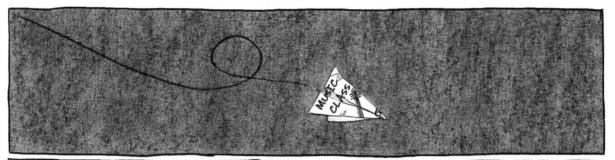

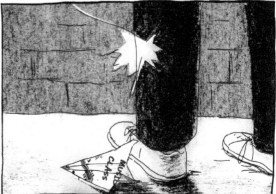

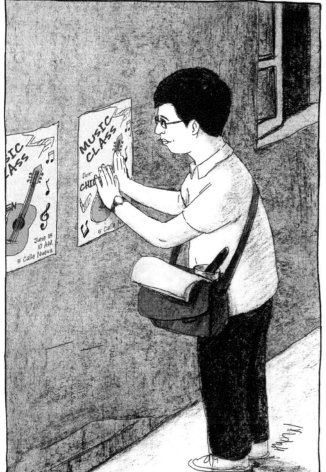

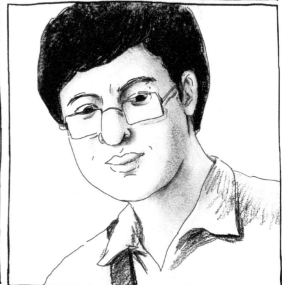

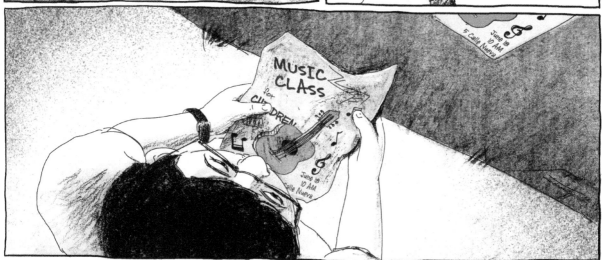

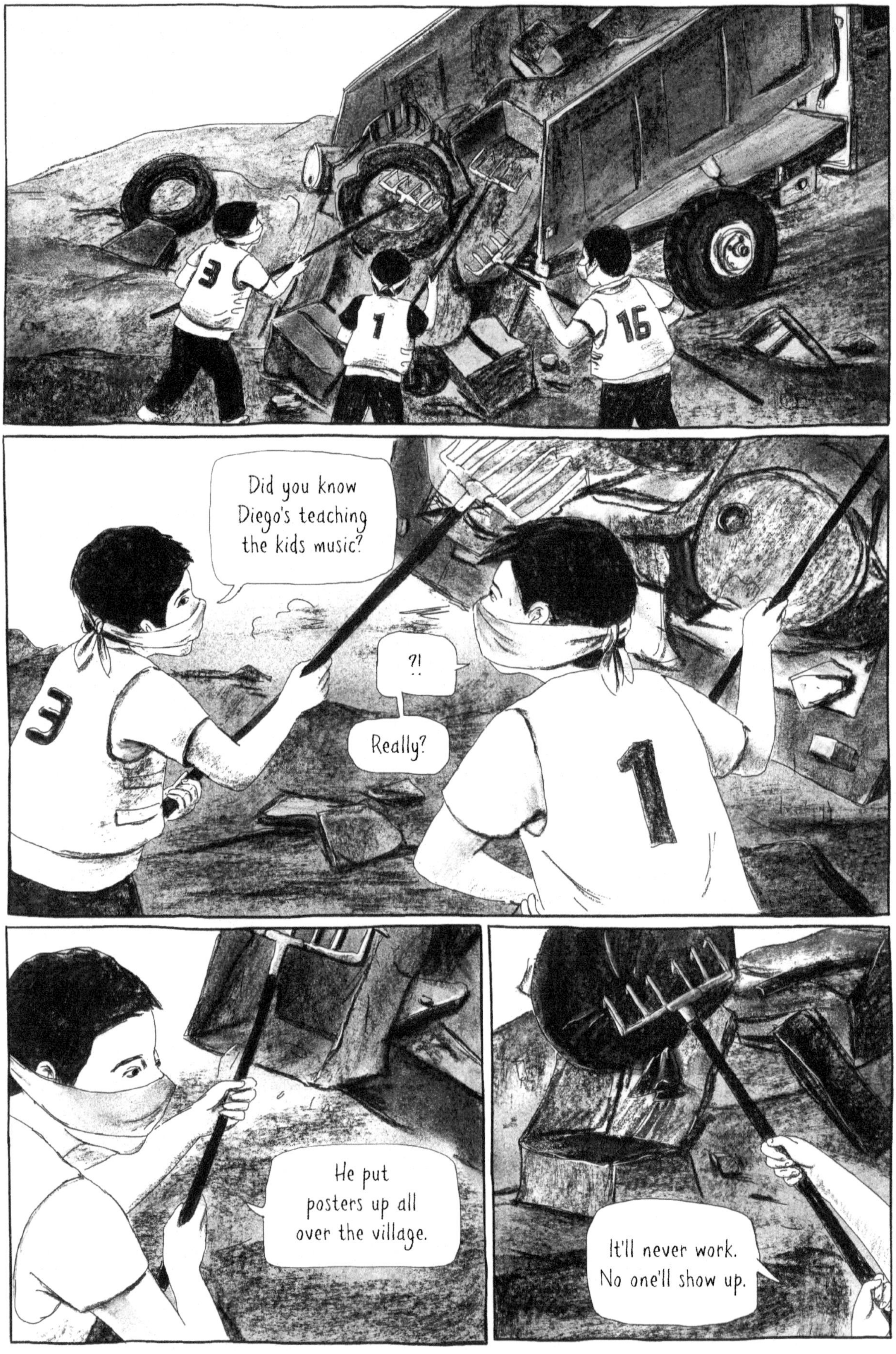
Did you know Diego's teaching the kids music?
?!
Really?
He put posters up all over the village.
It'll never work. No one'll show up.

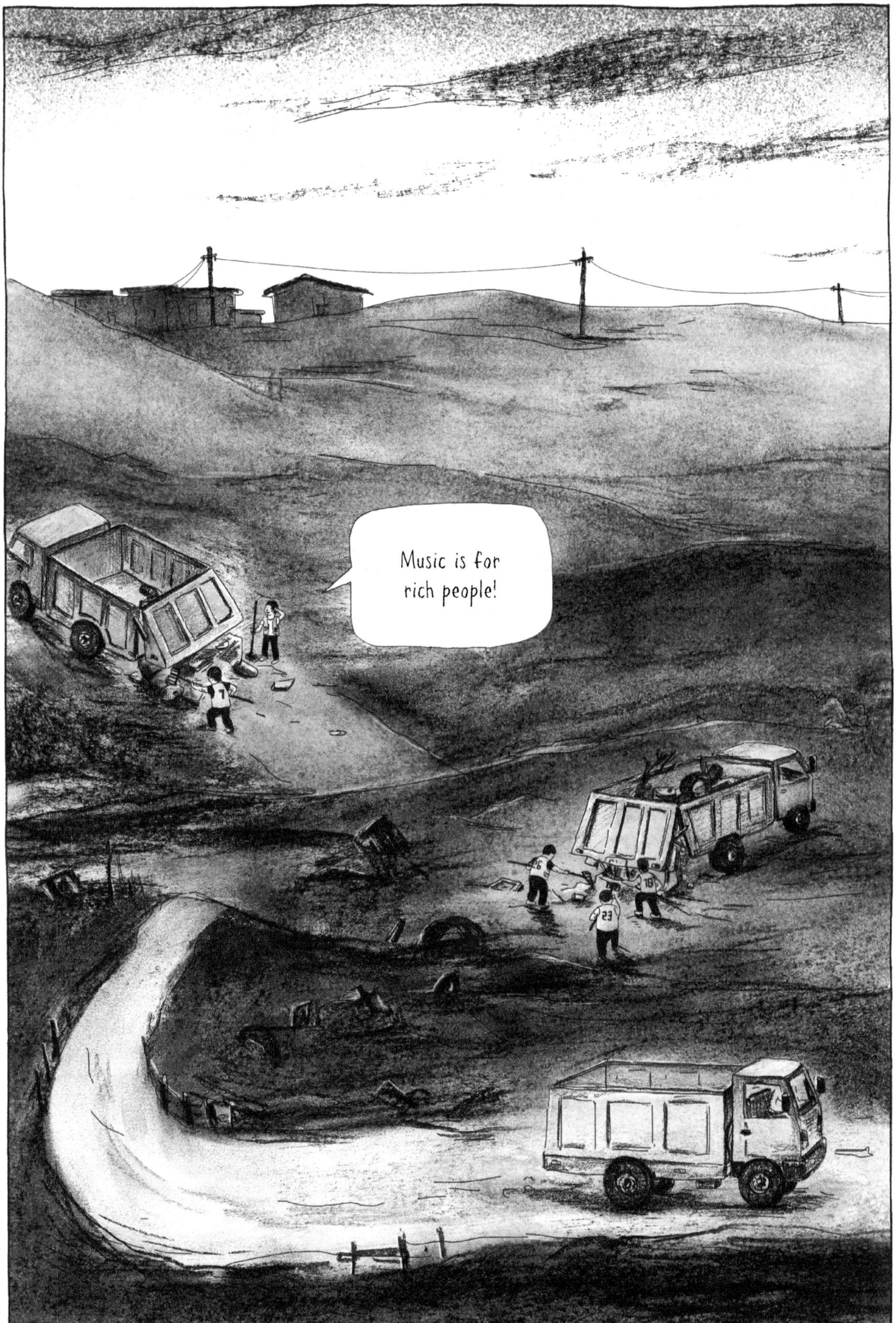
Music is for rich people!

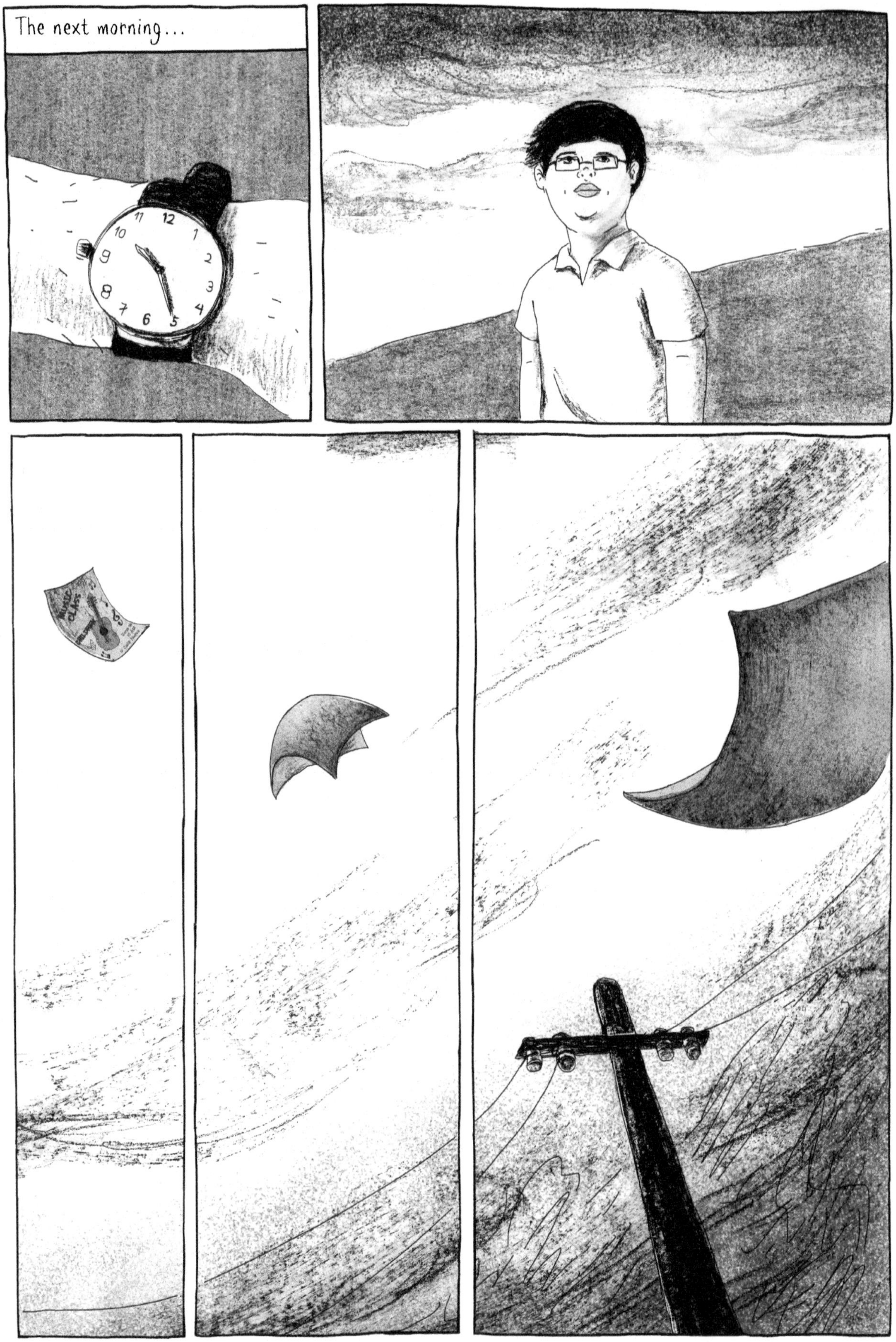
The next morning...

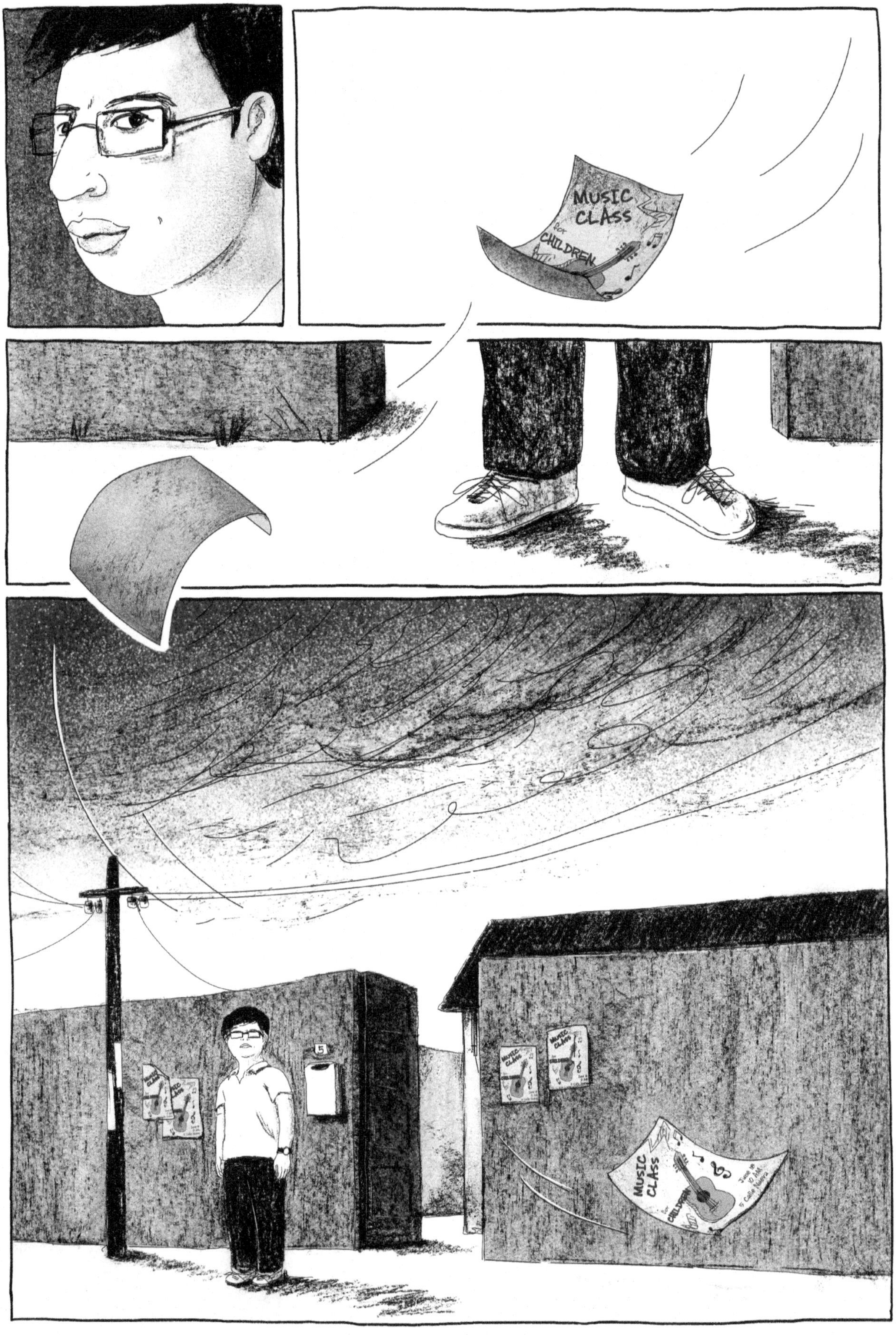
MUSIC CLASS
for
CHILDREN
MUSIC CLASS
for
CHILDREN
10 AM
5 Calle Nueva

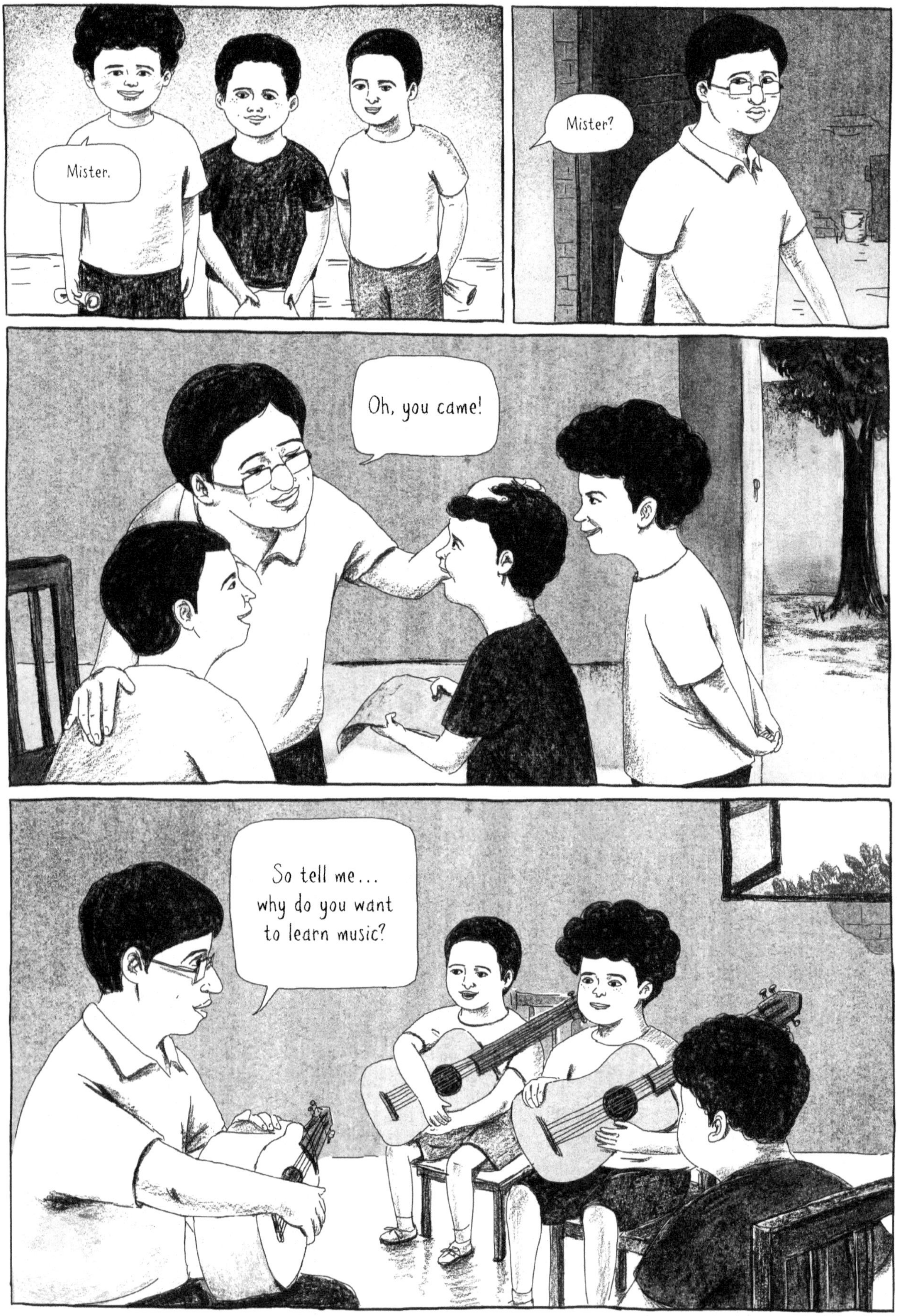

Mister.
Mister?
Oh, you came!
So tell me... why do you want to learn music?

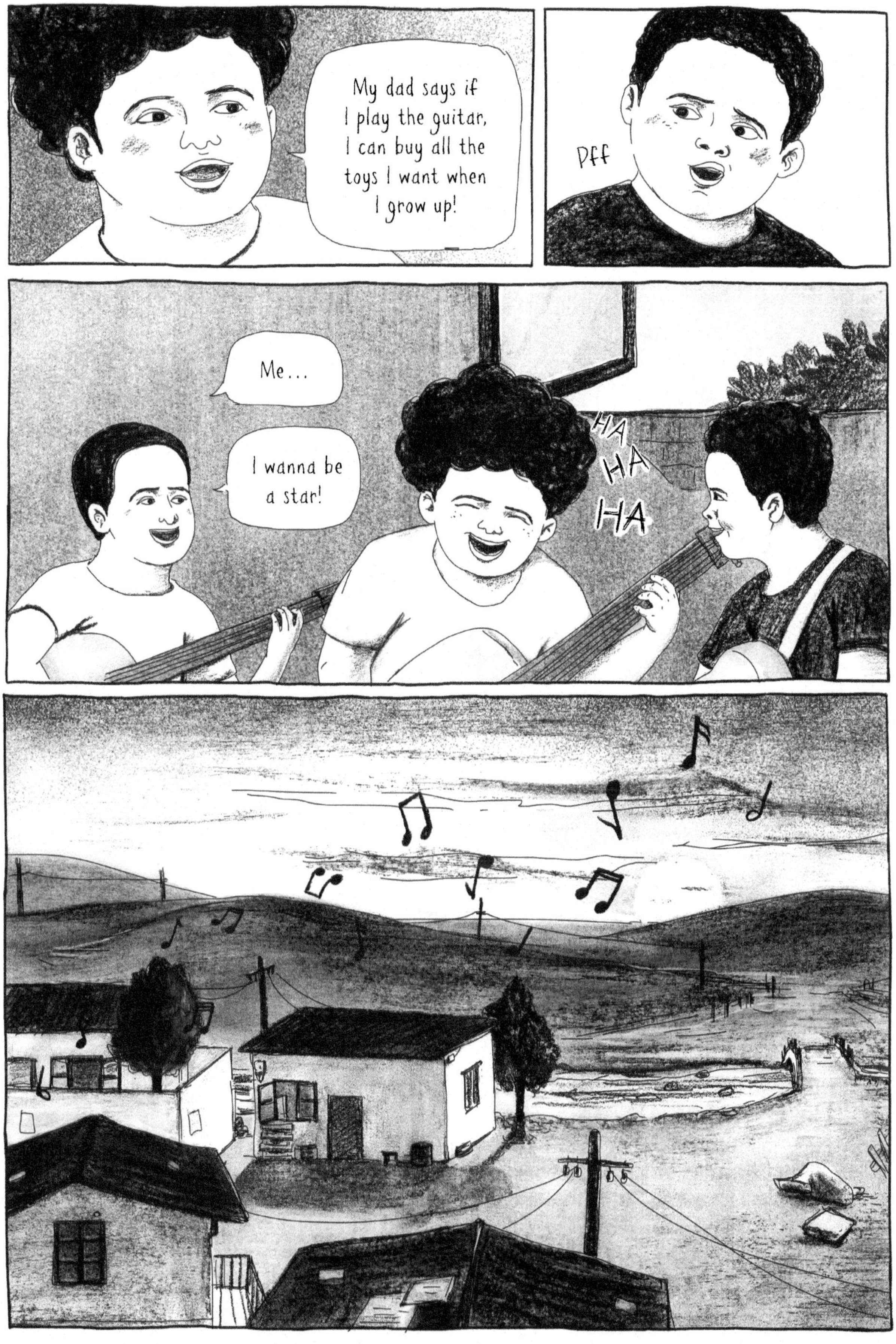
My dad says if I play the guitar, I can buy all the toys I want when I grow up!
Pff
Me...
I wanna be a star!
HA HA HA

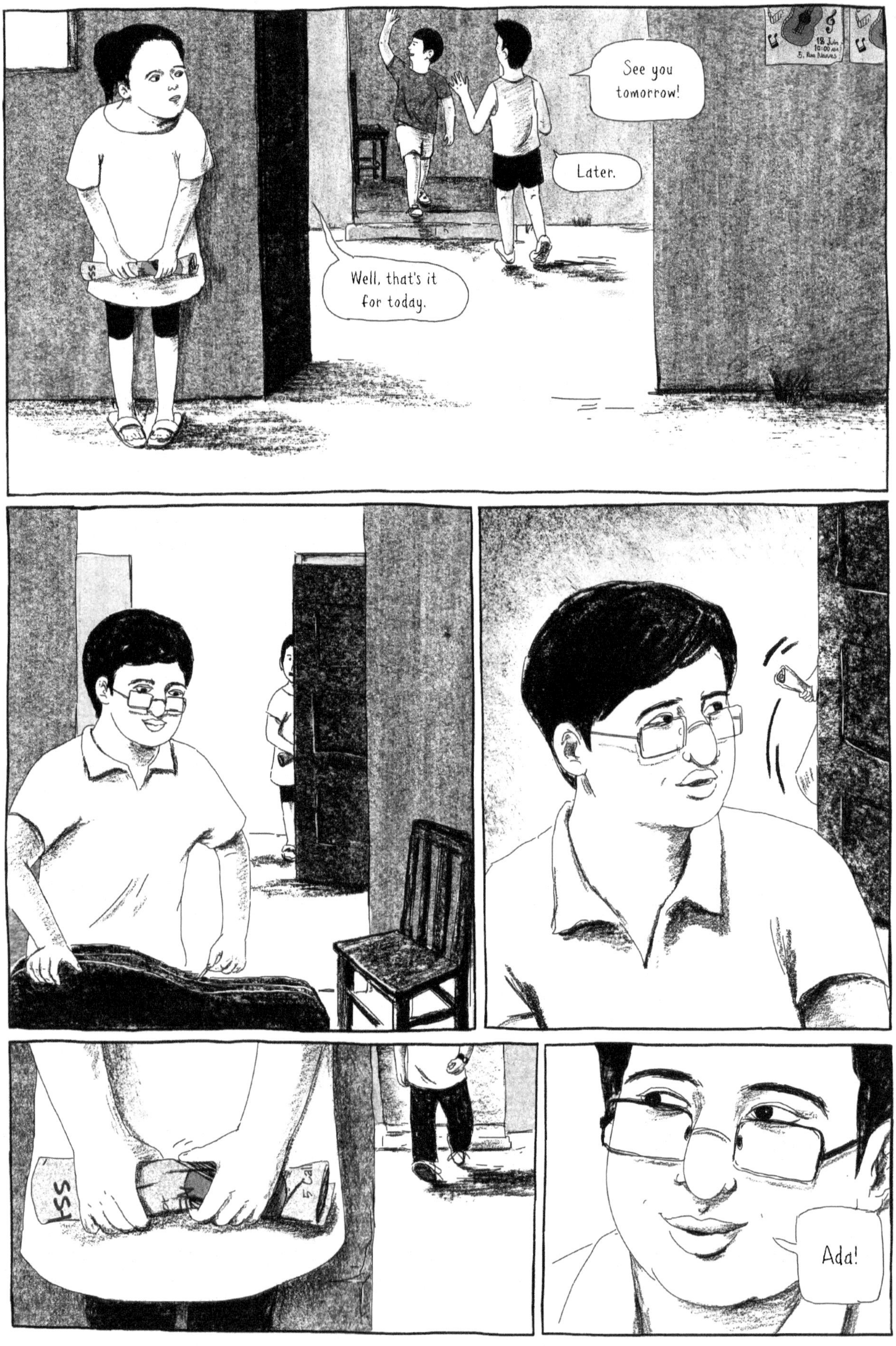
Well, that's it for today.
See you tomorrow!
Later.
Ada!

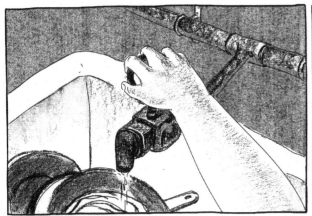

Ada! Come help me!

Where is she?

She went out.

Dunno where.

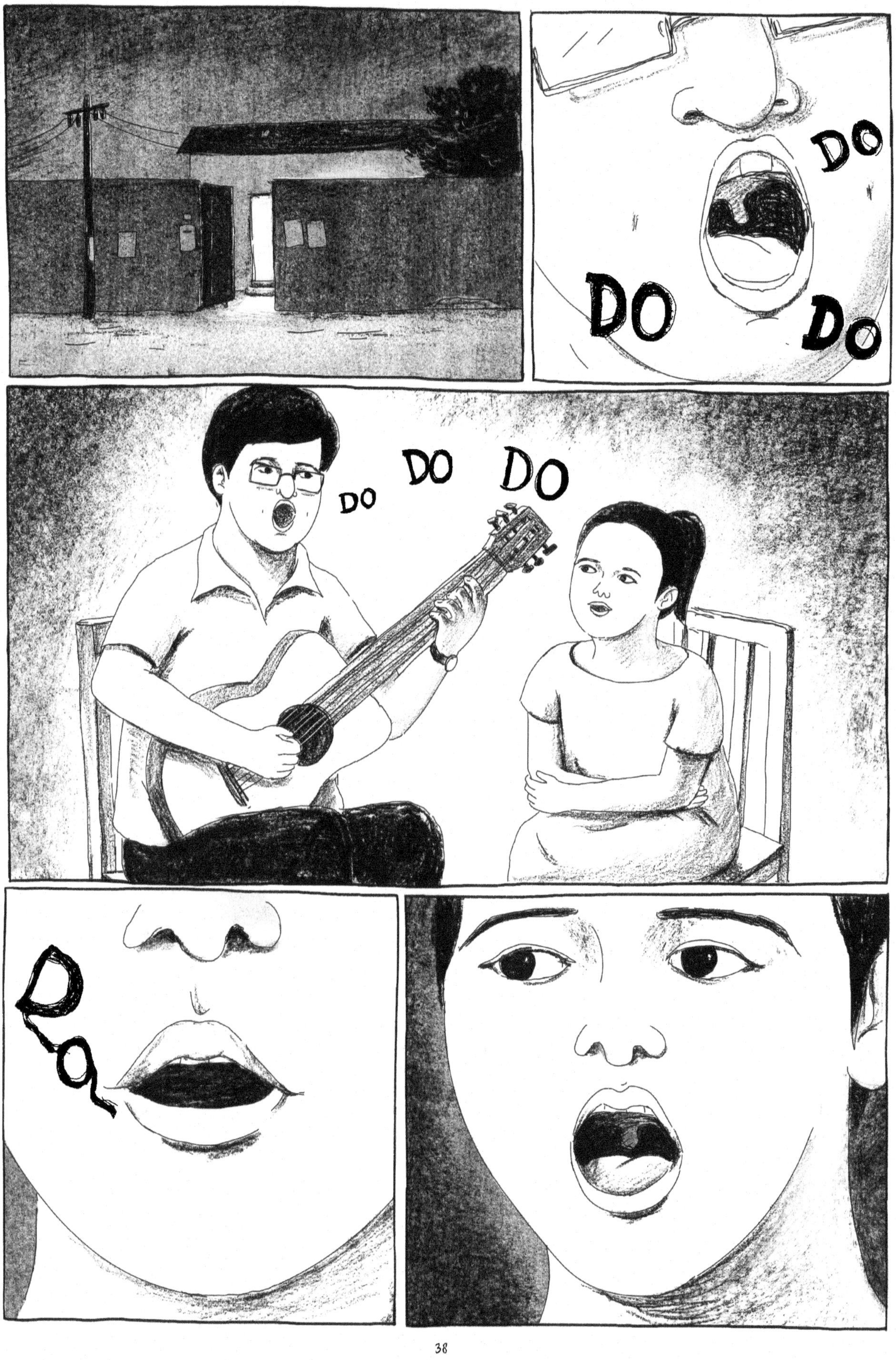
DO
DO
DO
DO
DO
DO
Da

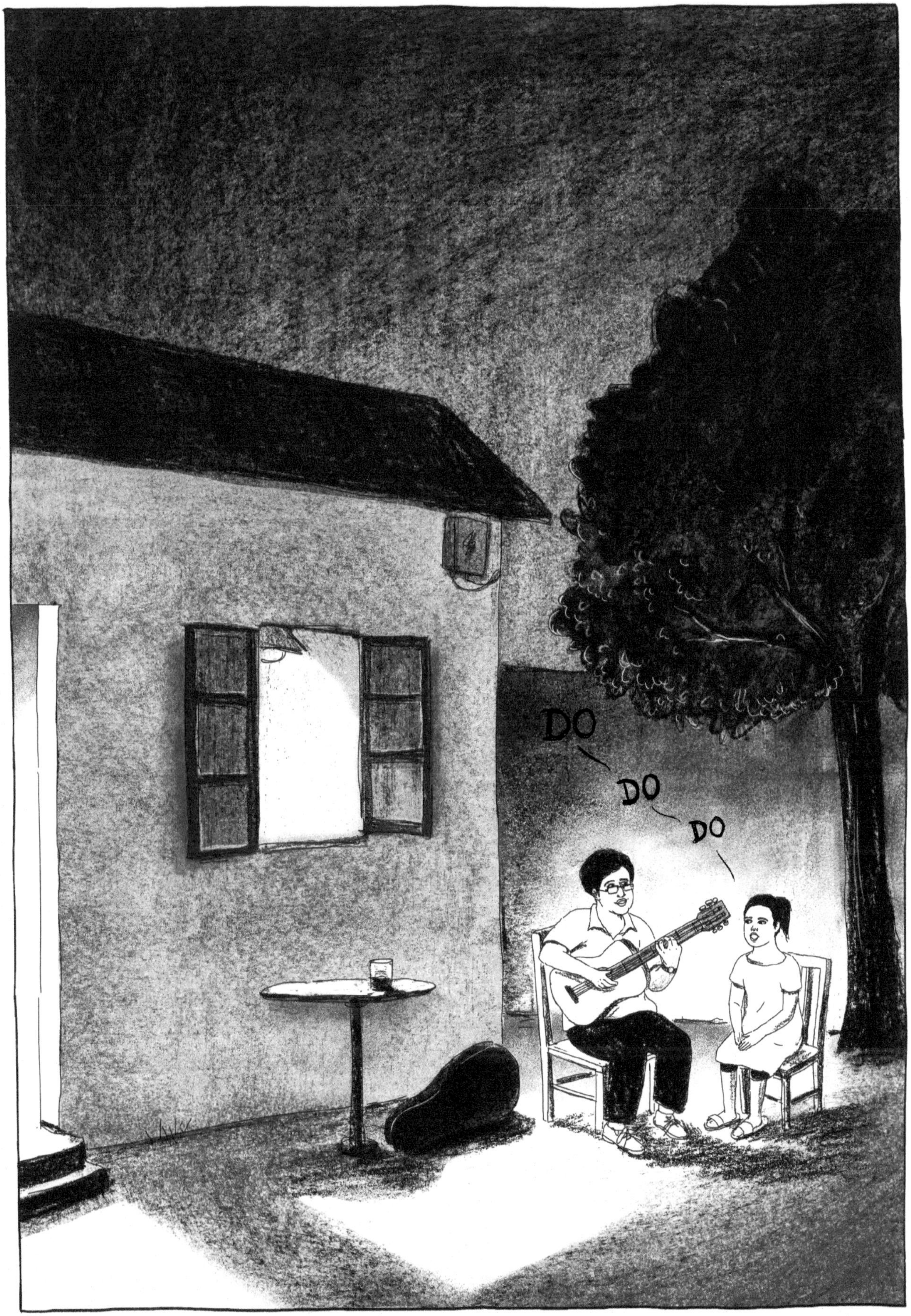
DO
DO
DO

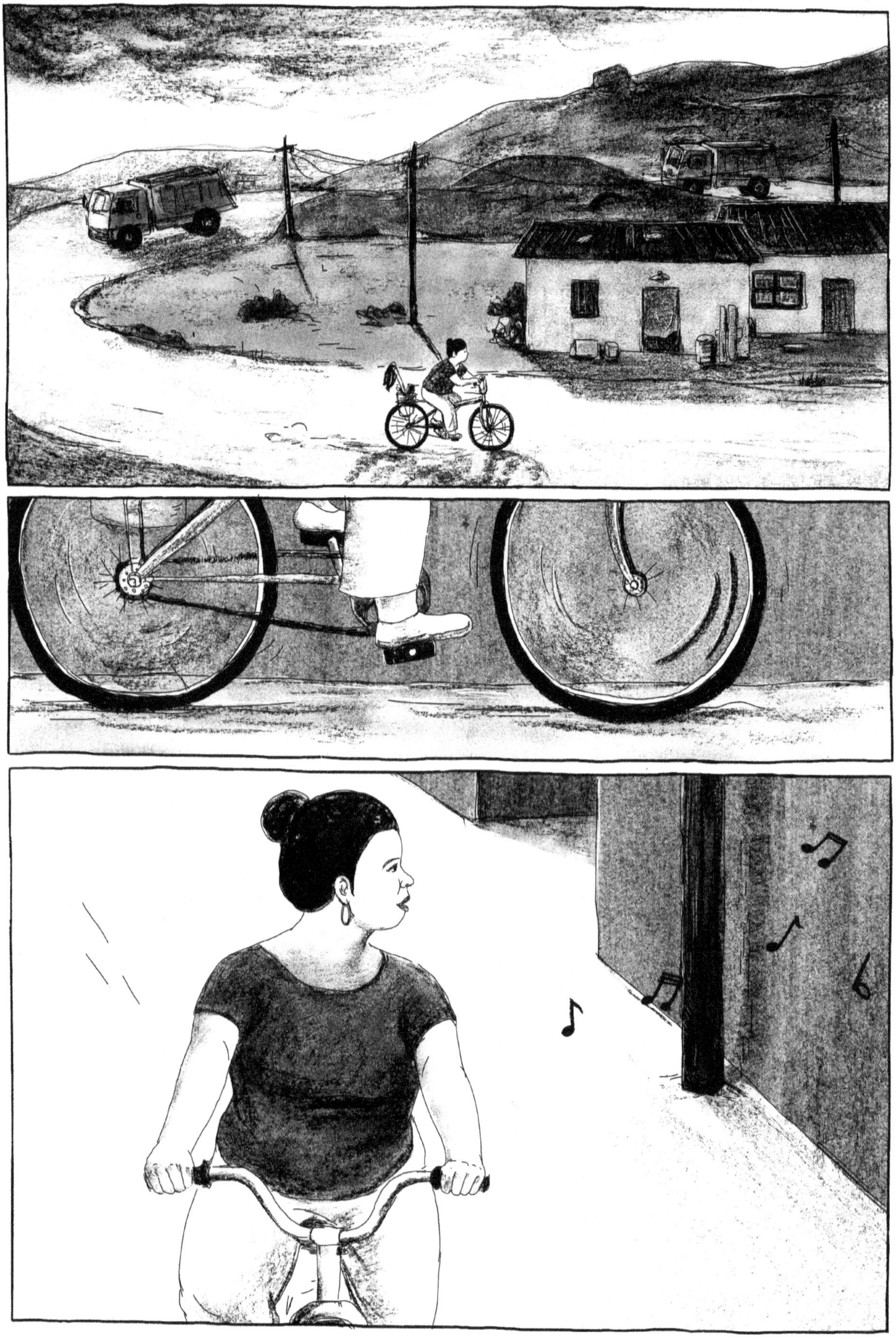

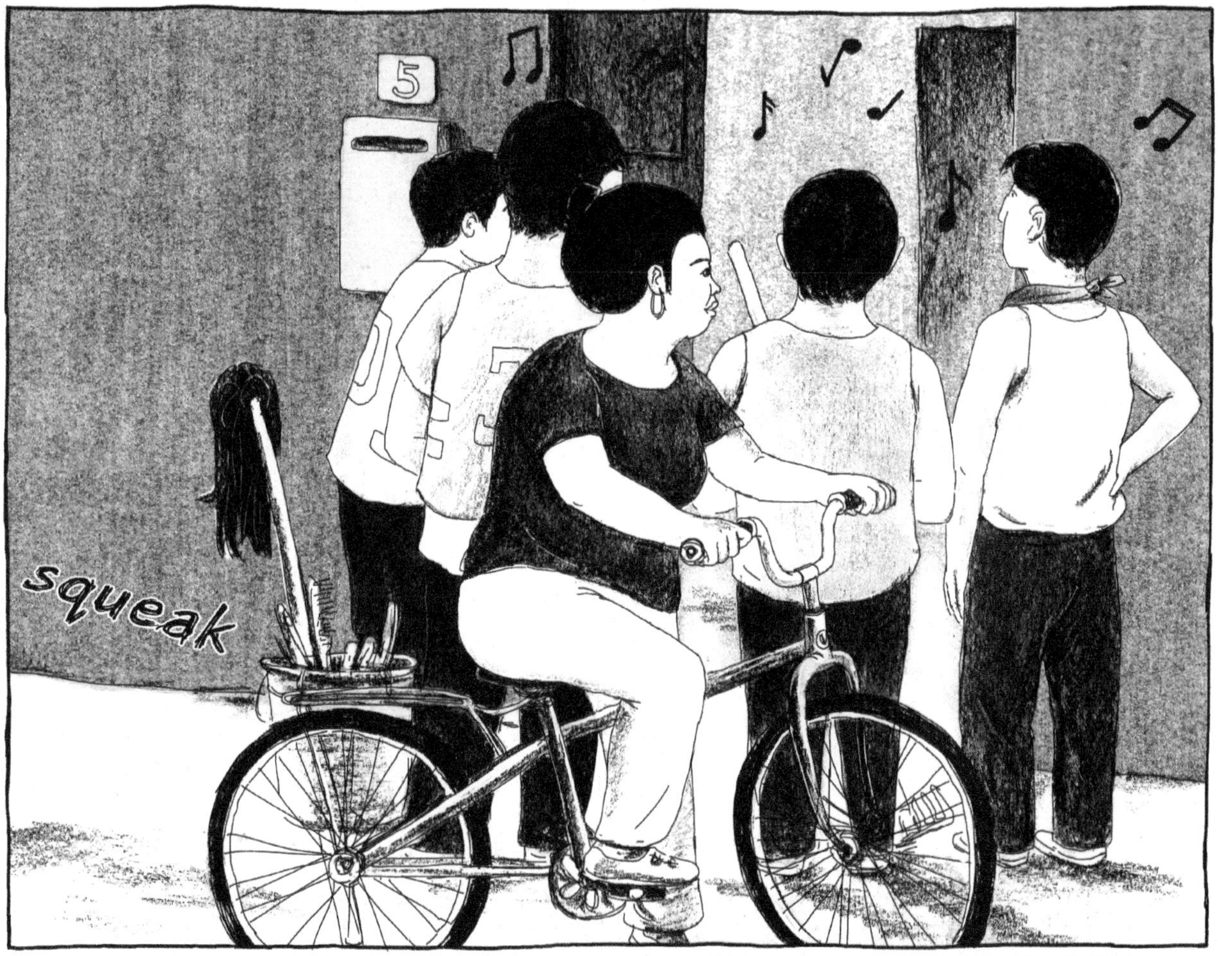
5
squeak

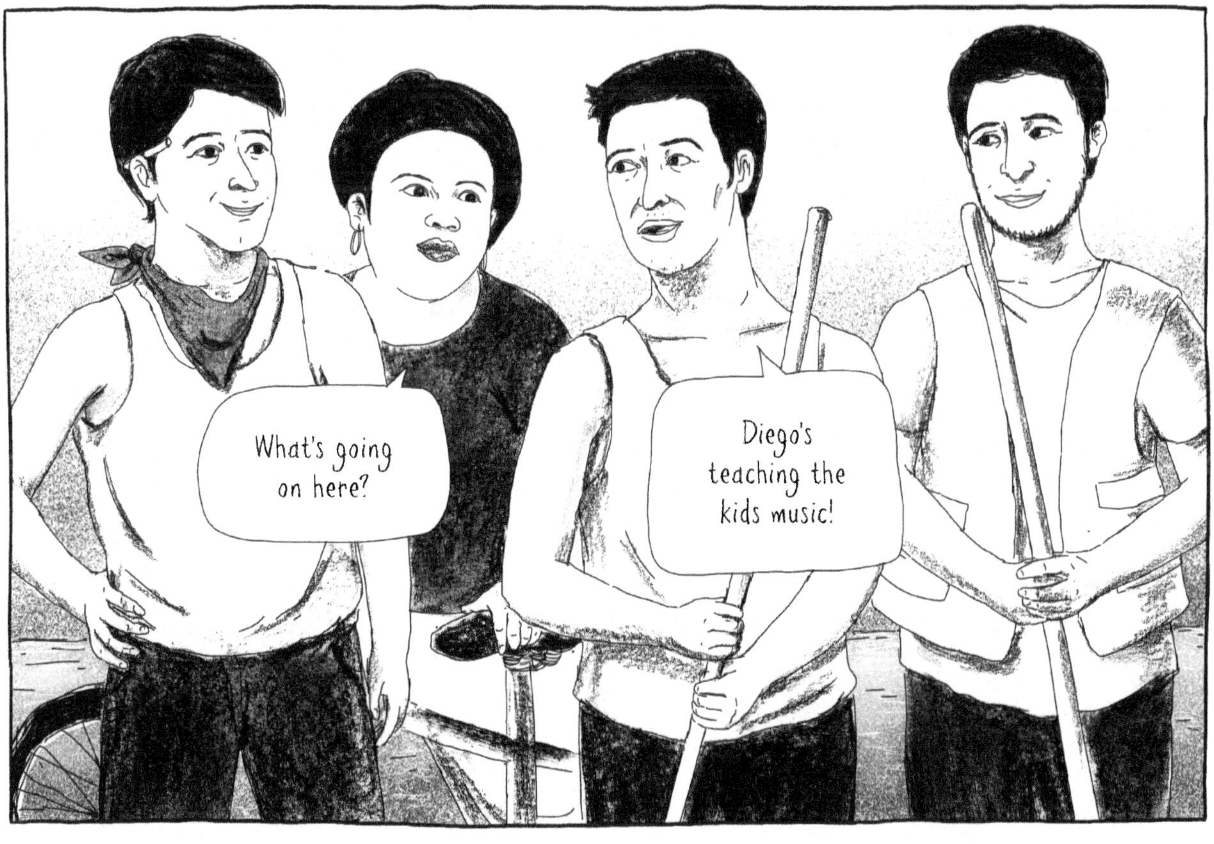
What's going on here?
Diego's teaching the kids music!

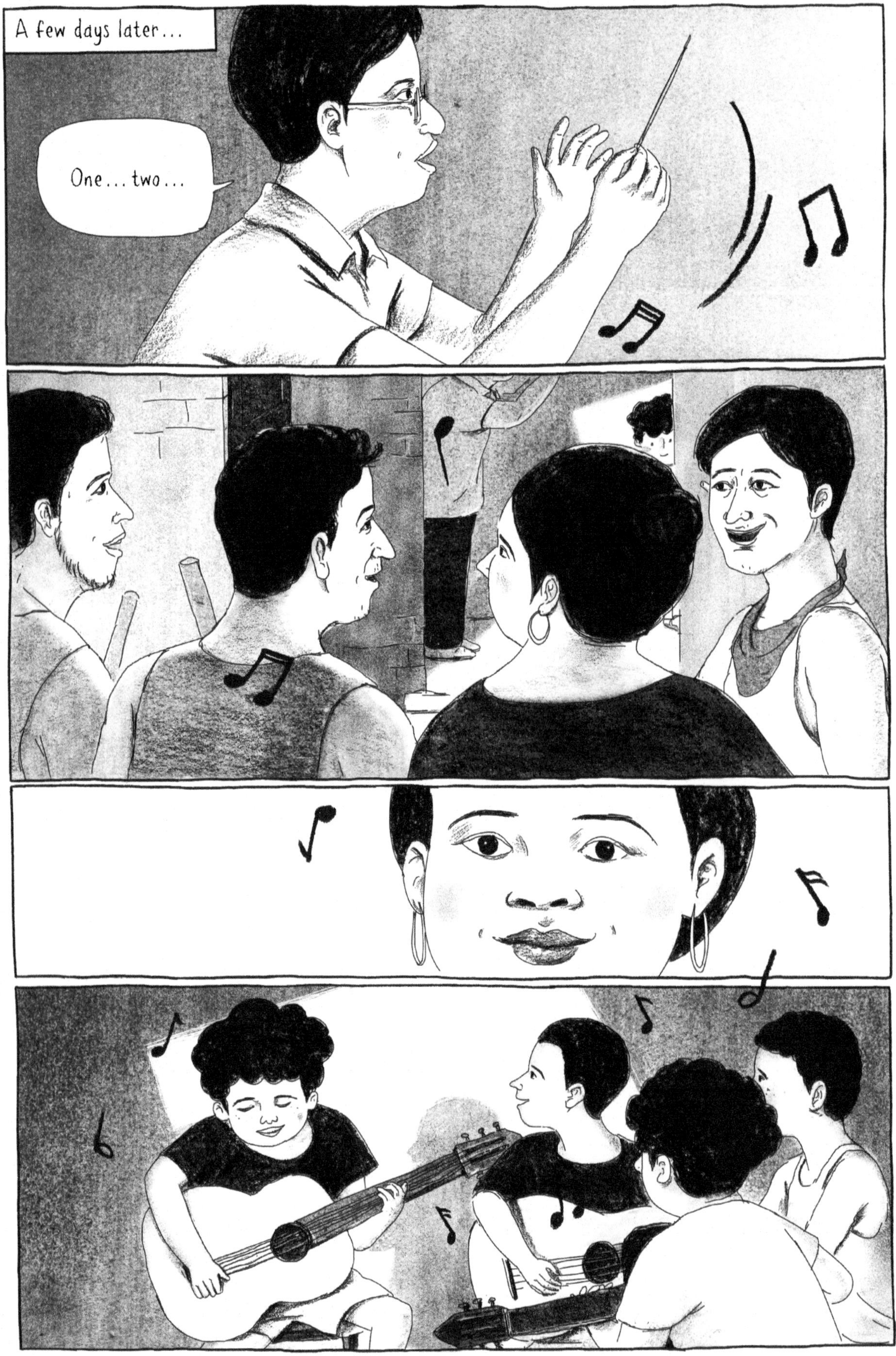
A few days later...
One... two...

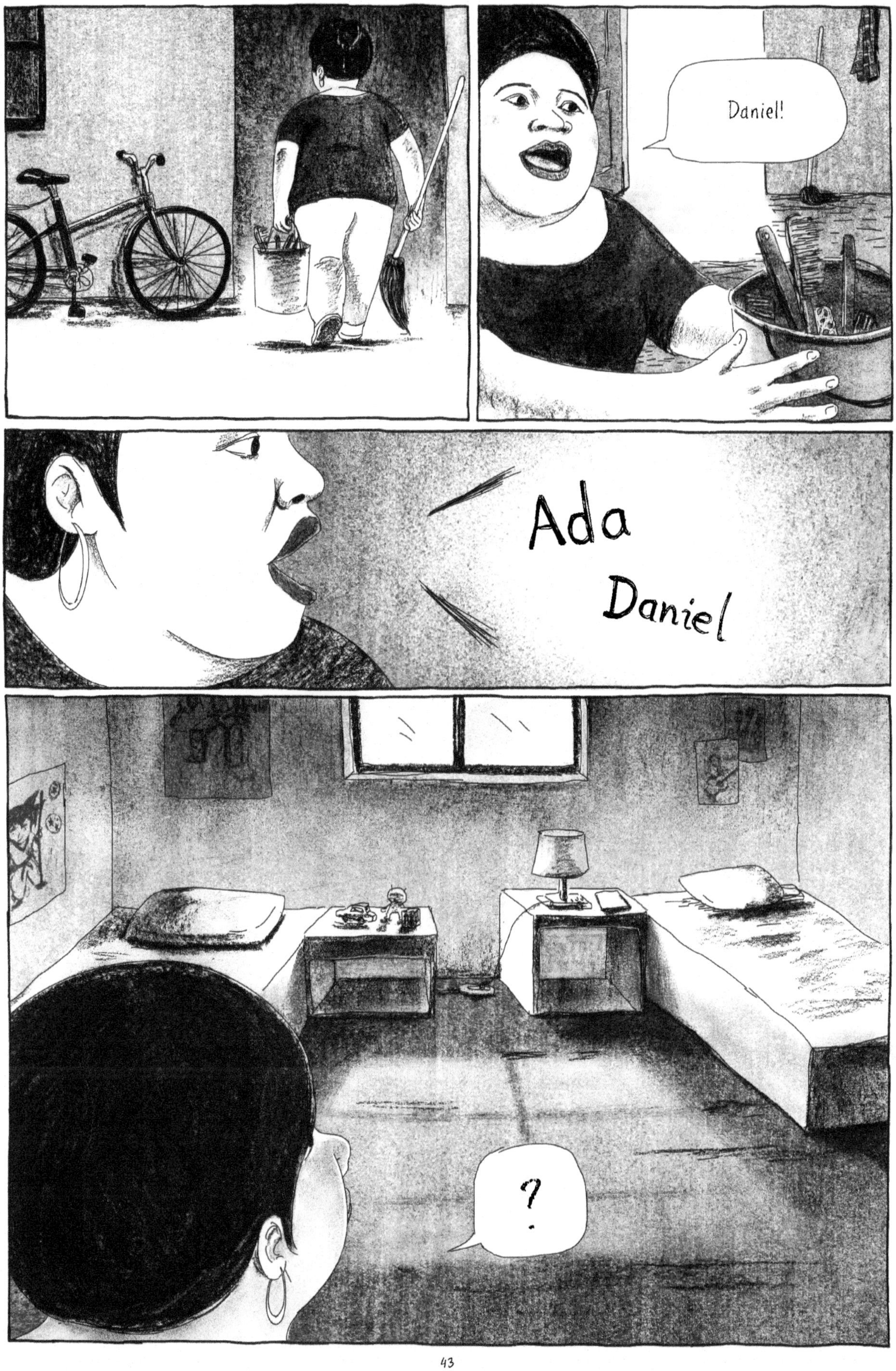
Daniel!
Ada
Daniel
?

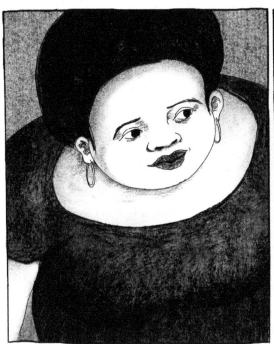

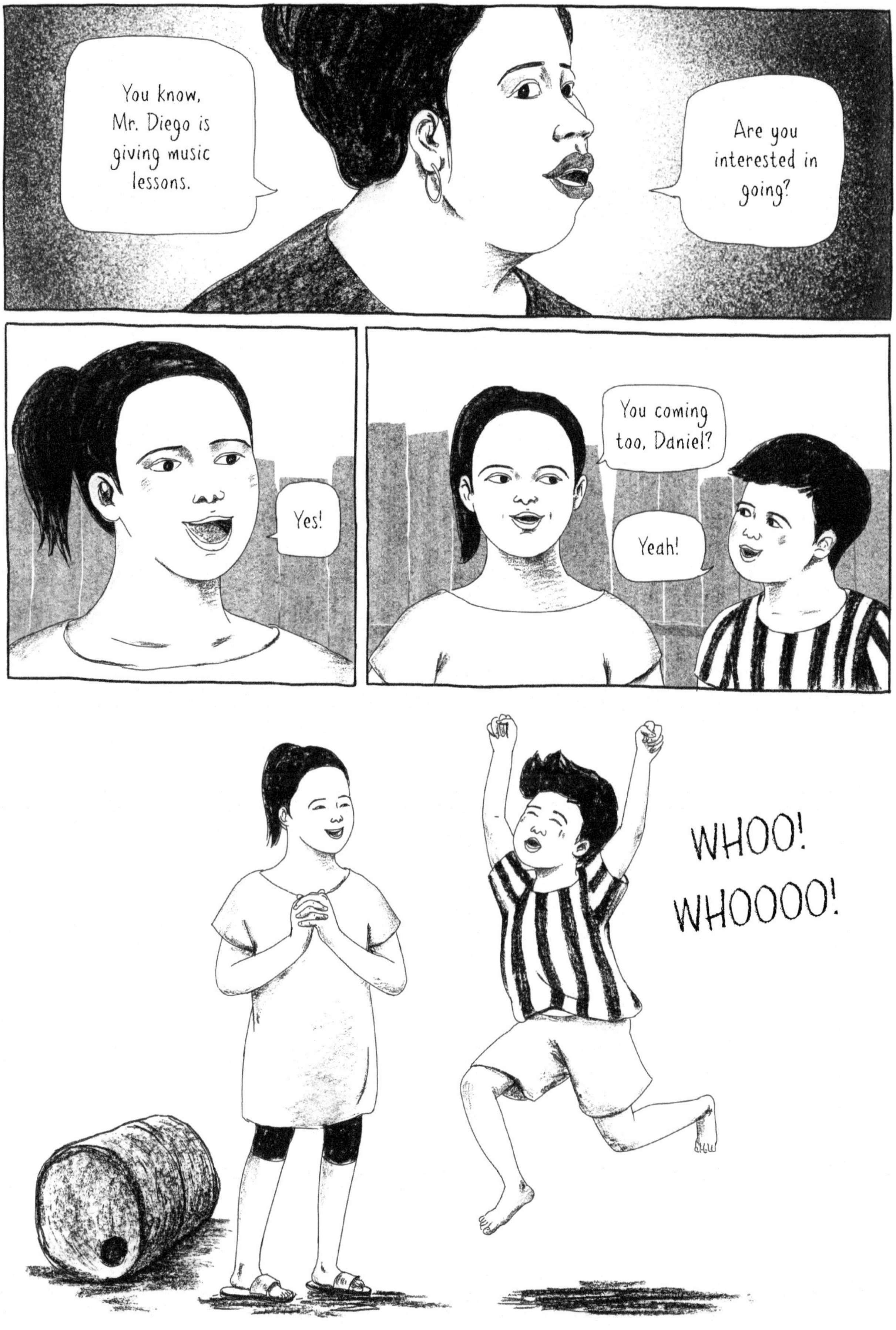
You know, Mr. Diego is giving music lessons.
Are you interested in going?
Yes!
You coming too, Daniel?
Yeah!
WHOO!
WHOOOO!

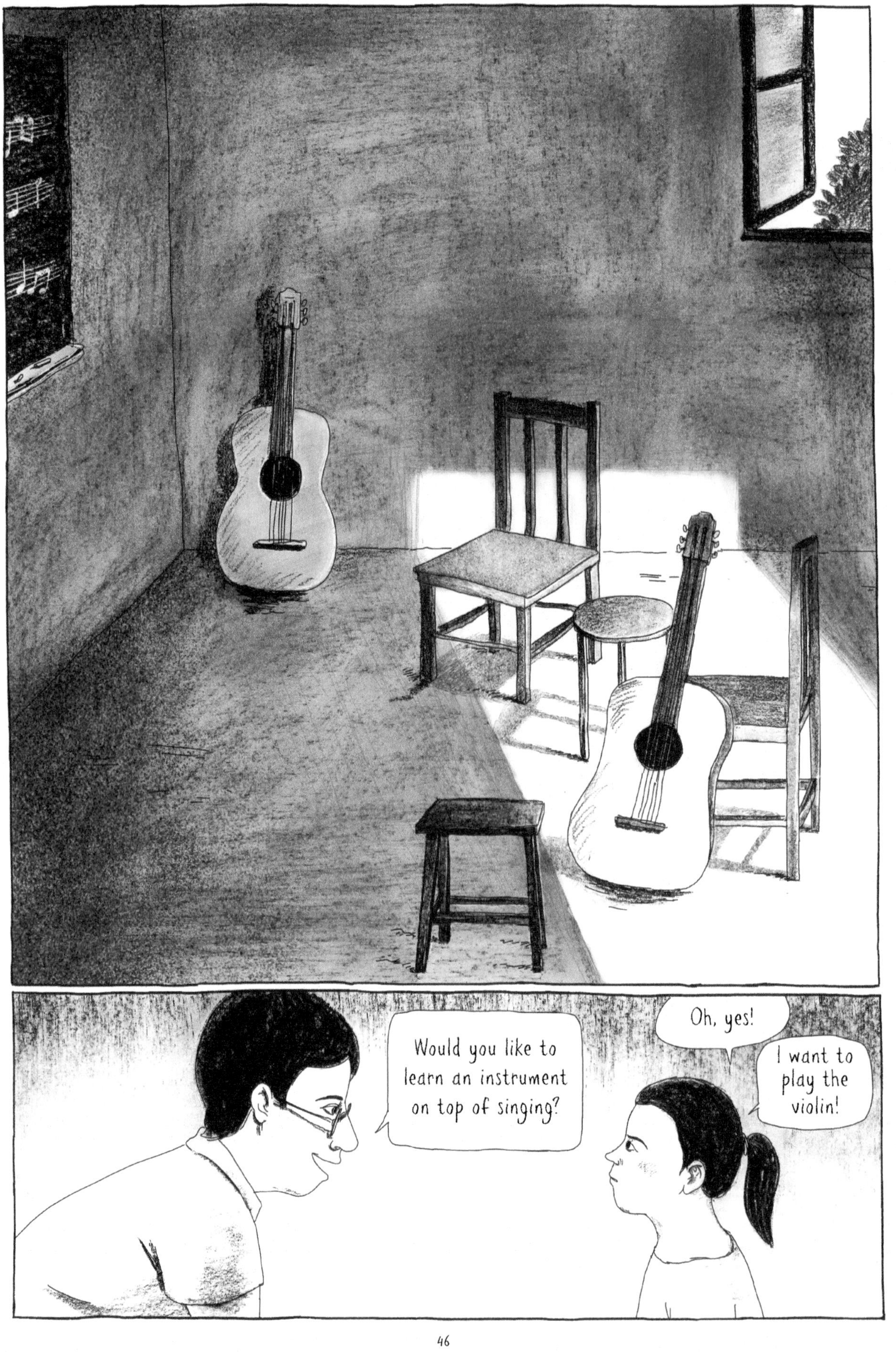
Would you like to learn an instrument on top of singing?
Oh, yes!
I want to play the violin!

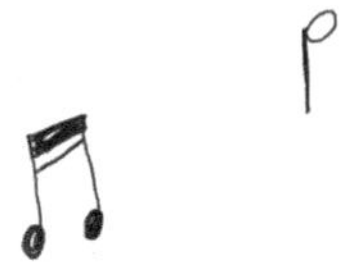

4

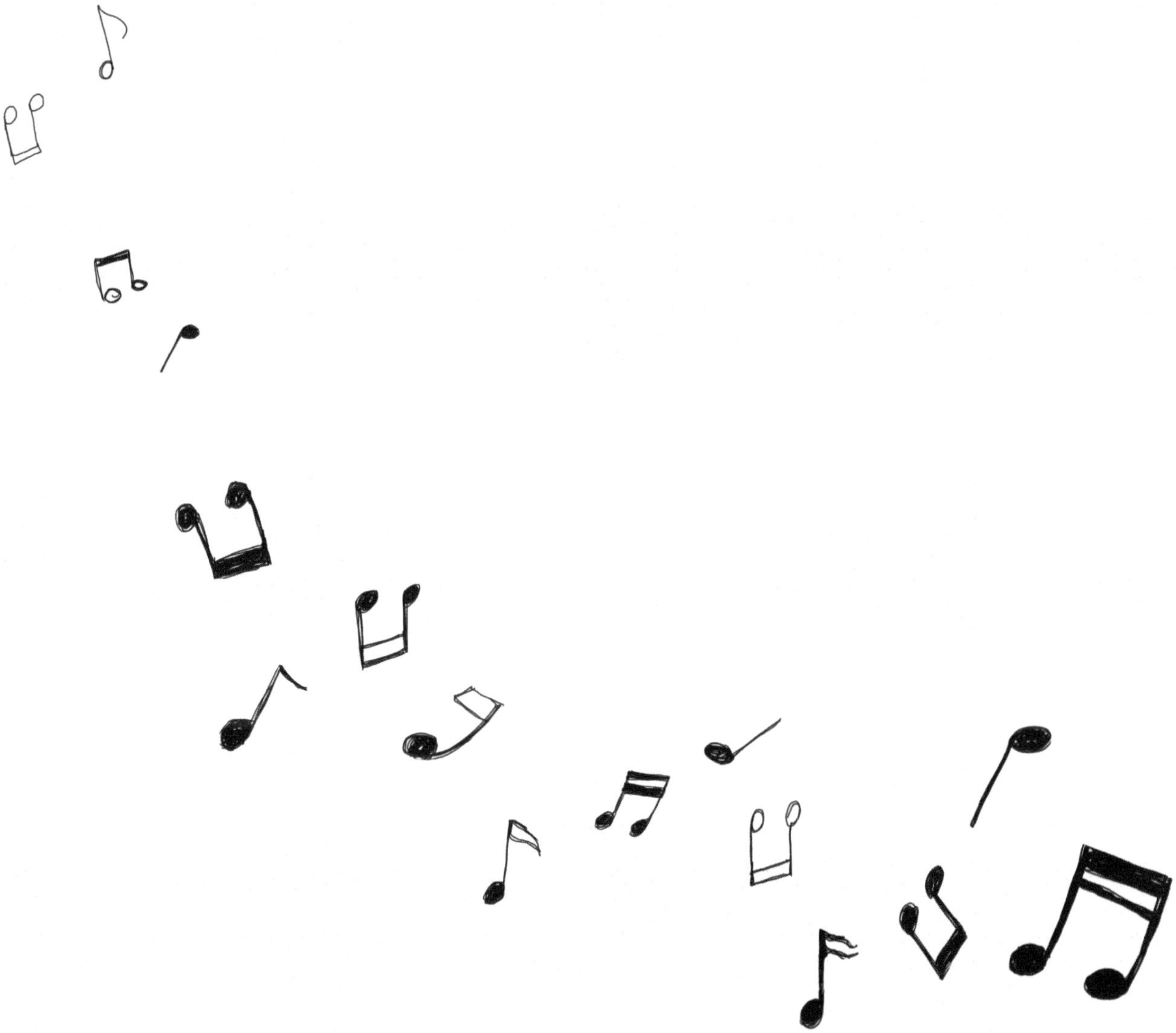

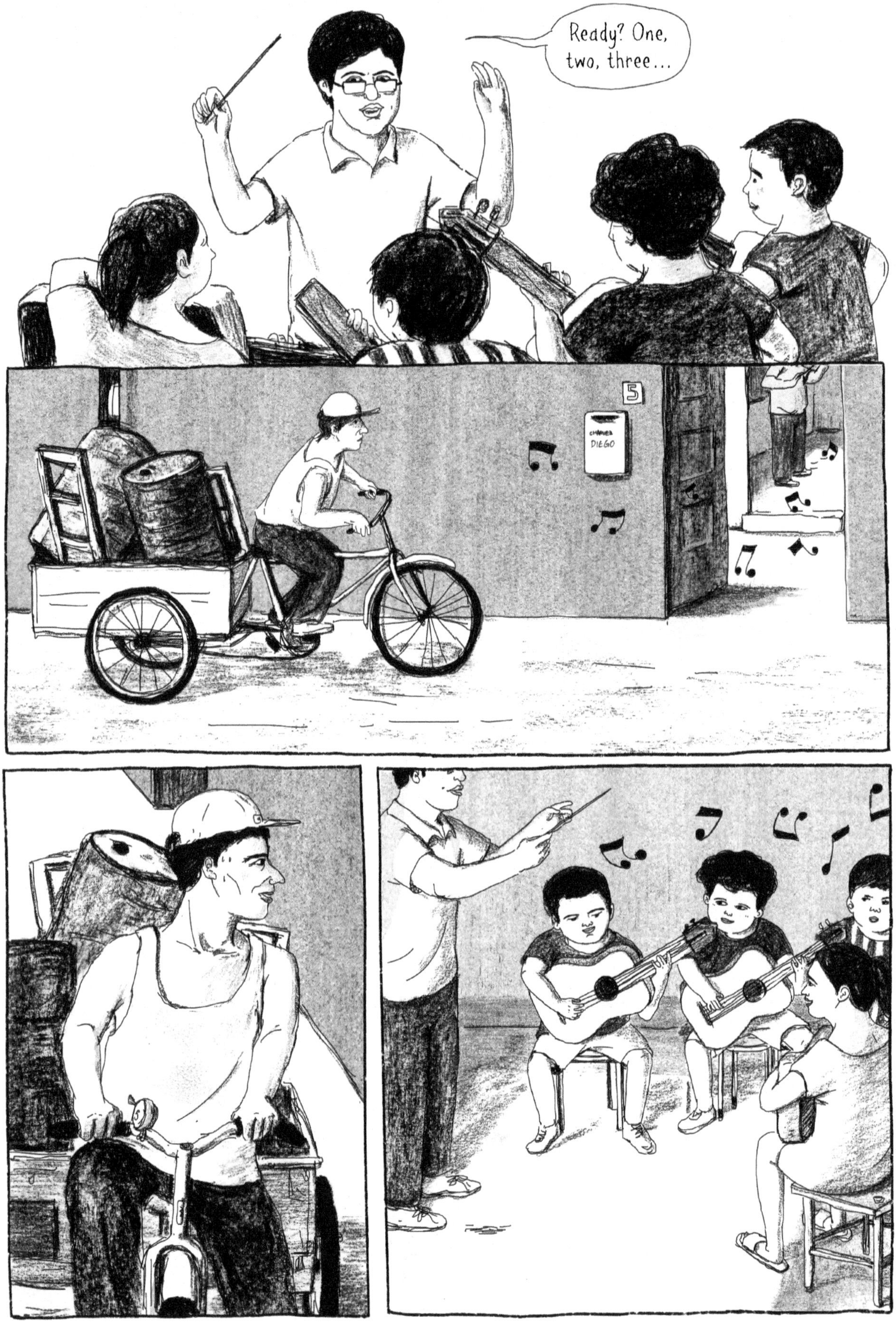
Ready? One, two, three...
5
CHAVEZ
DIEGO

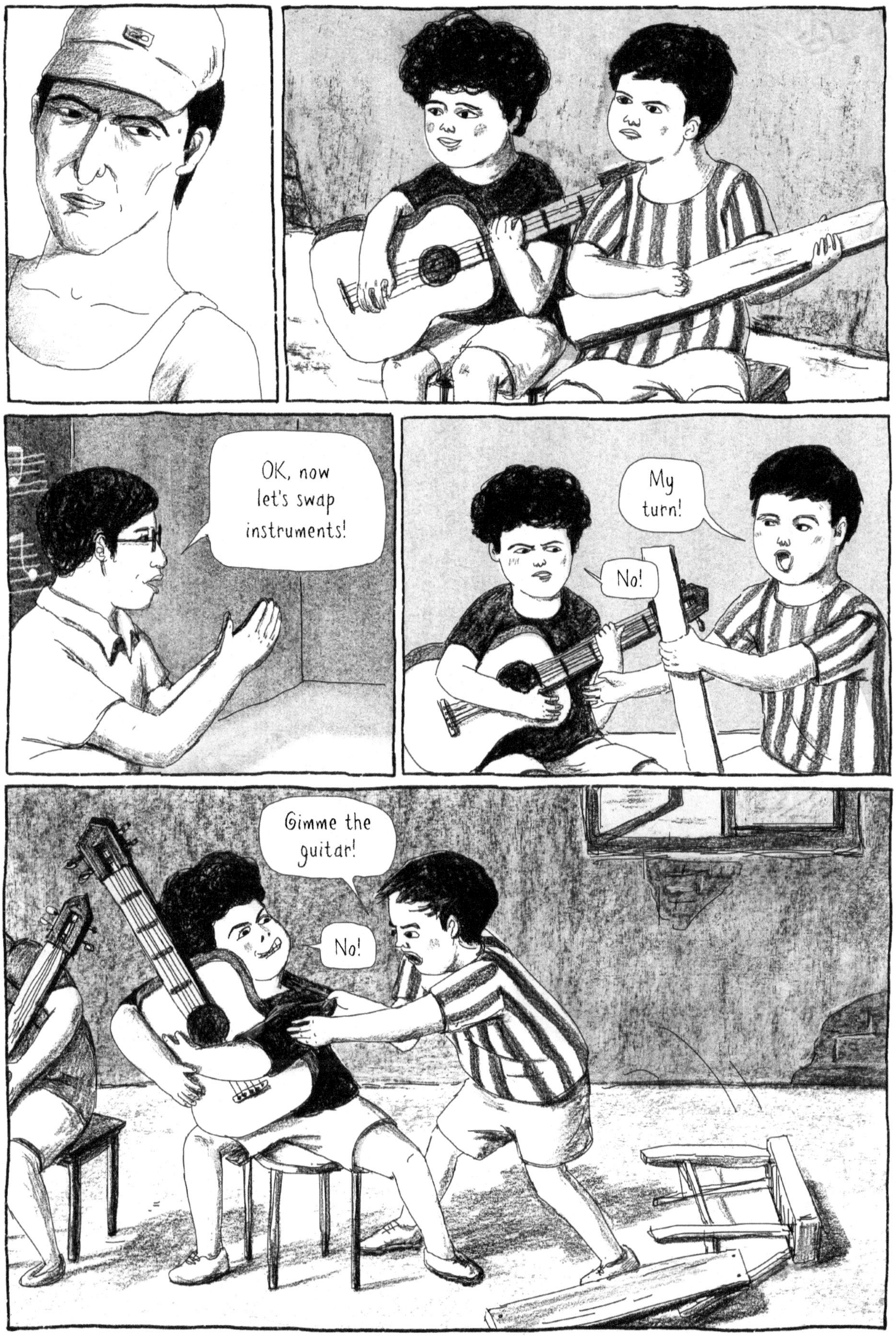
OK, now let's swap instruments!
My turn!
No!
Gimme the guitar!
No!

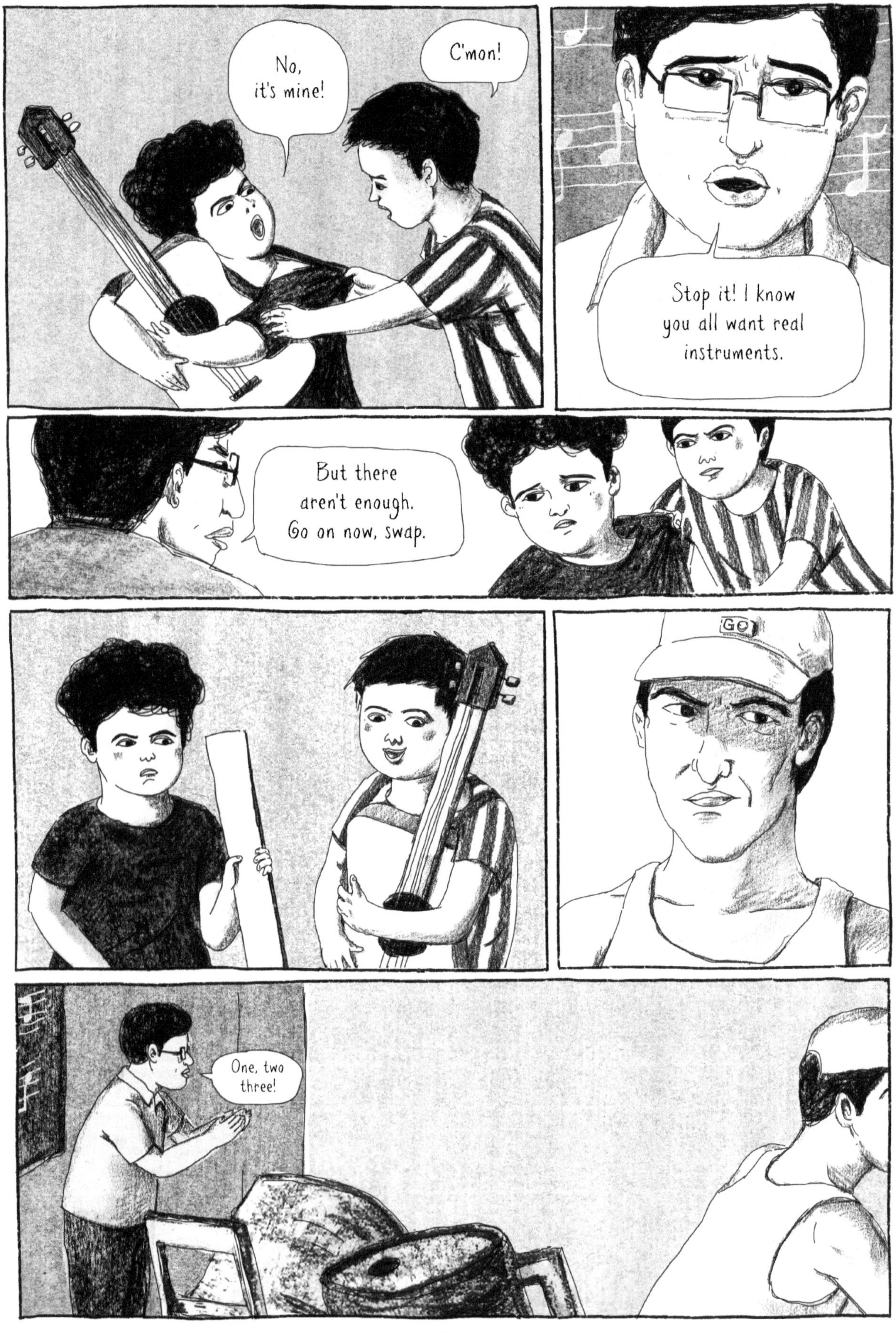
No, it's mine!
C'mon!
Stop it! I know you all want real instruments.
But there aren't enough. Go on now, swap.
GO
One, two three!

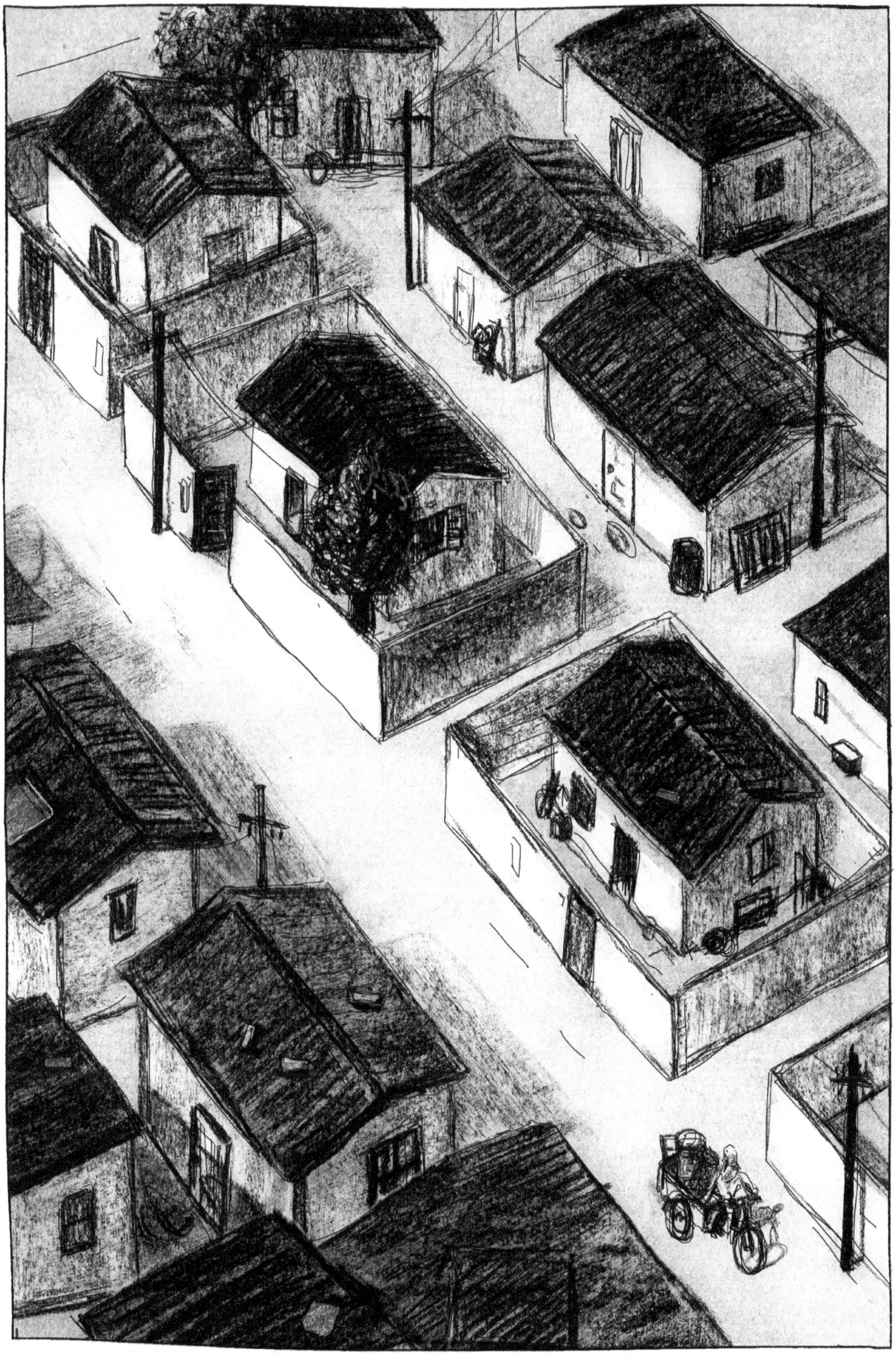

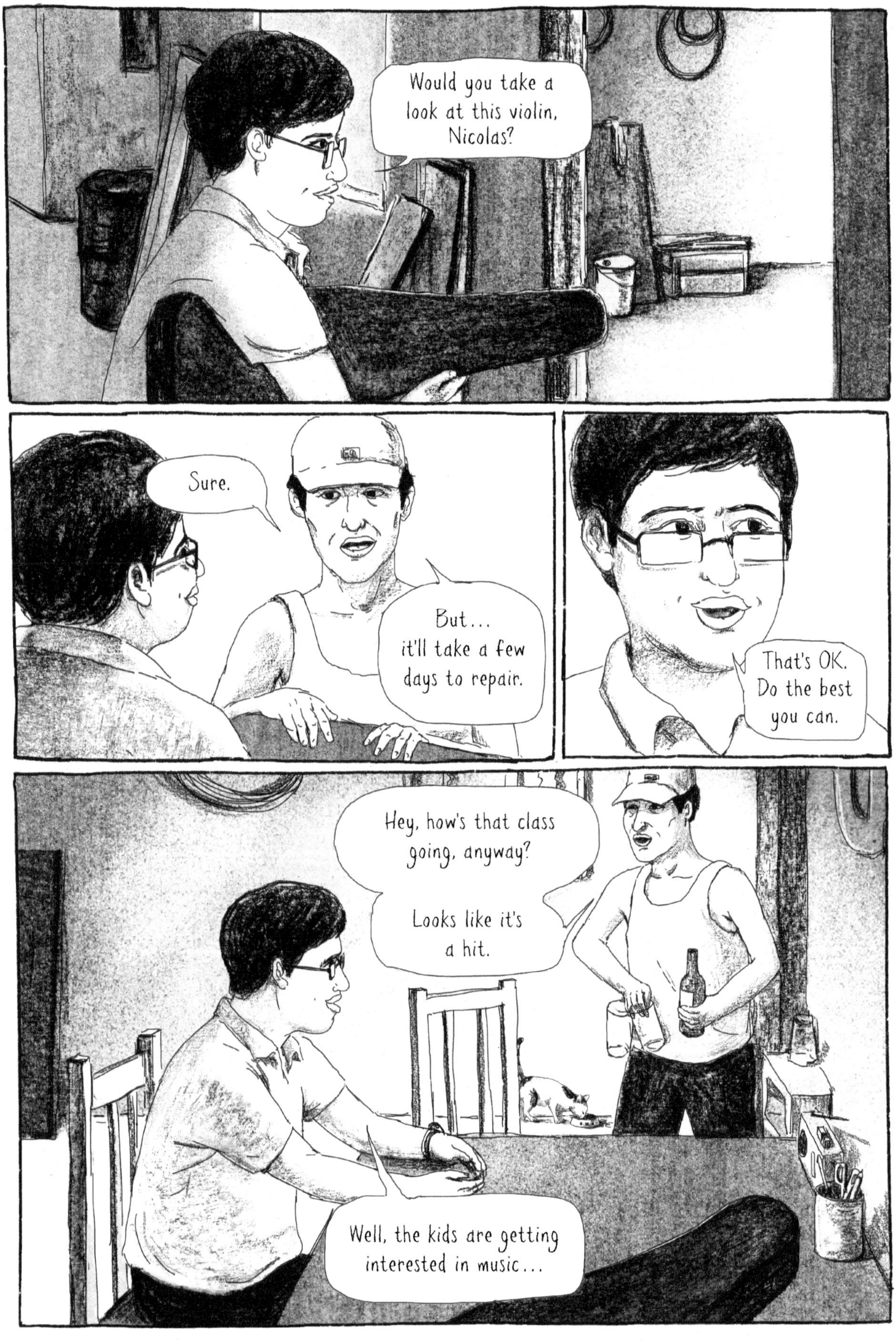
Would you take a look at this violin, Nicolas?
Sure.
But... it'll take a few days to repair.
That's OK. Do the best you can.
Hey, how's that class going, anyway?
Looks like it's a hit.
Well, the kids are getting interested in music...

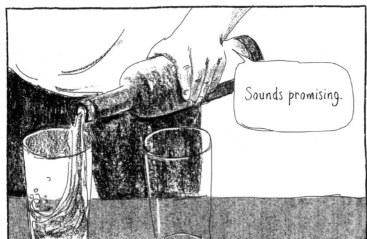

Sounds promising.

Thing is...

We just don't have enough instruments. Or the money to buy more. In the long run, that'll be an issue.

What kind of instruments do you need? Maybe I could make you some.

That's a terrific idea! I've got a book about instruments. Could give you some ideas.

Yeah, let me see it!

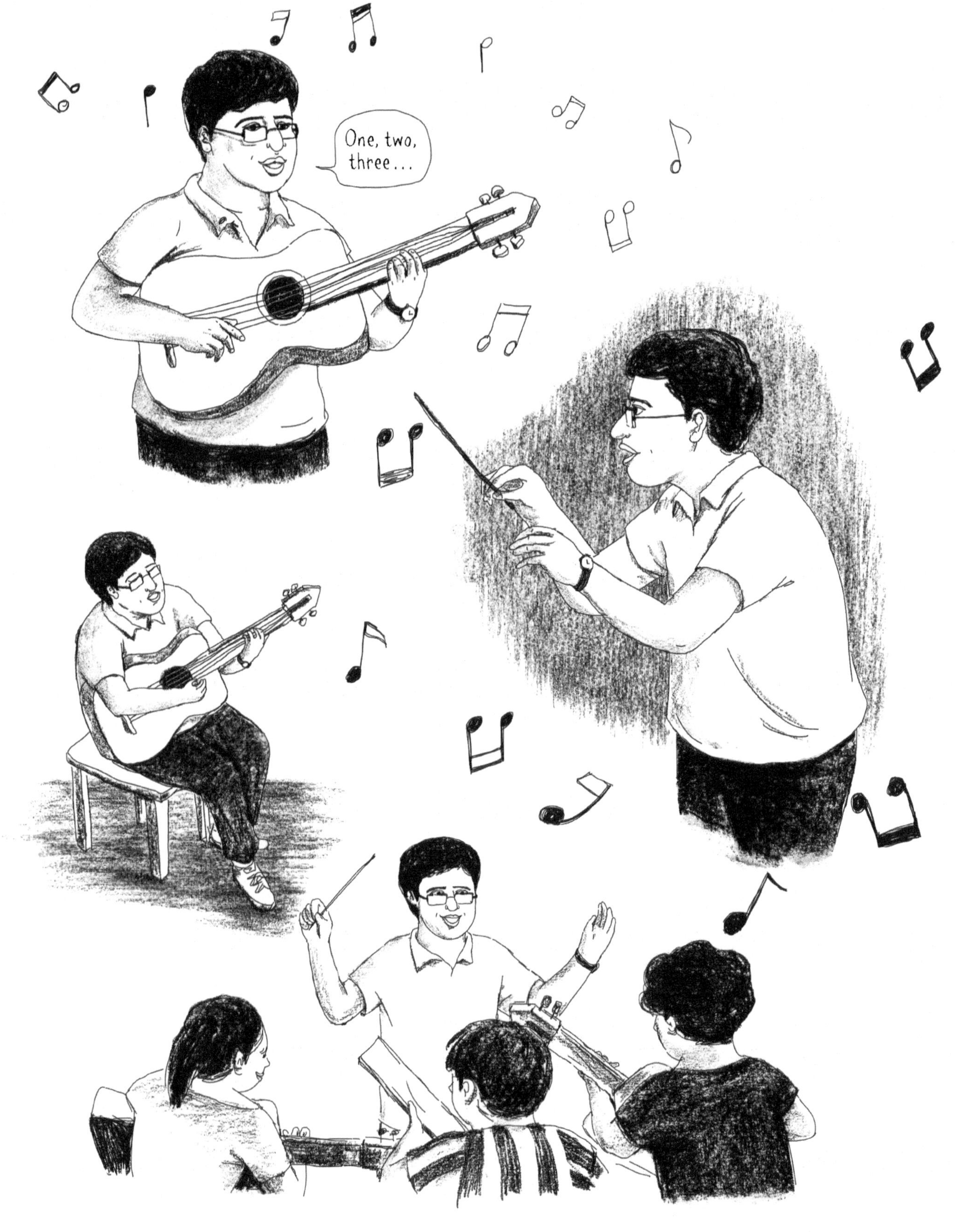
One, two, three...

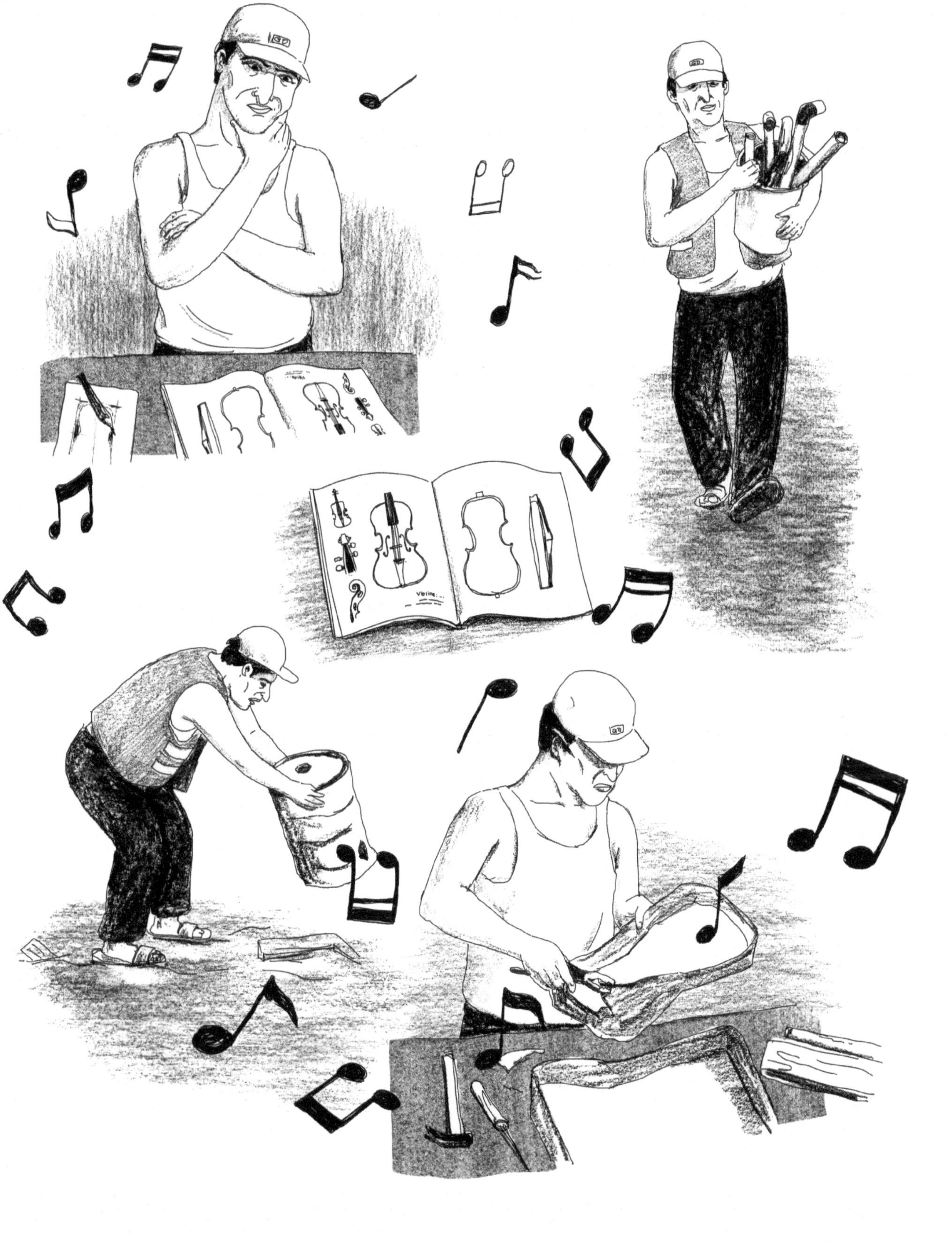

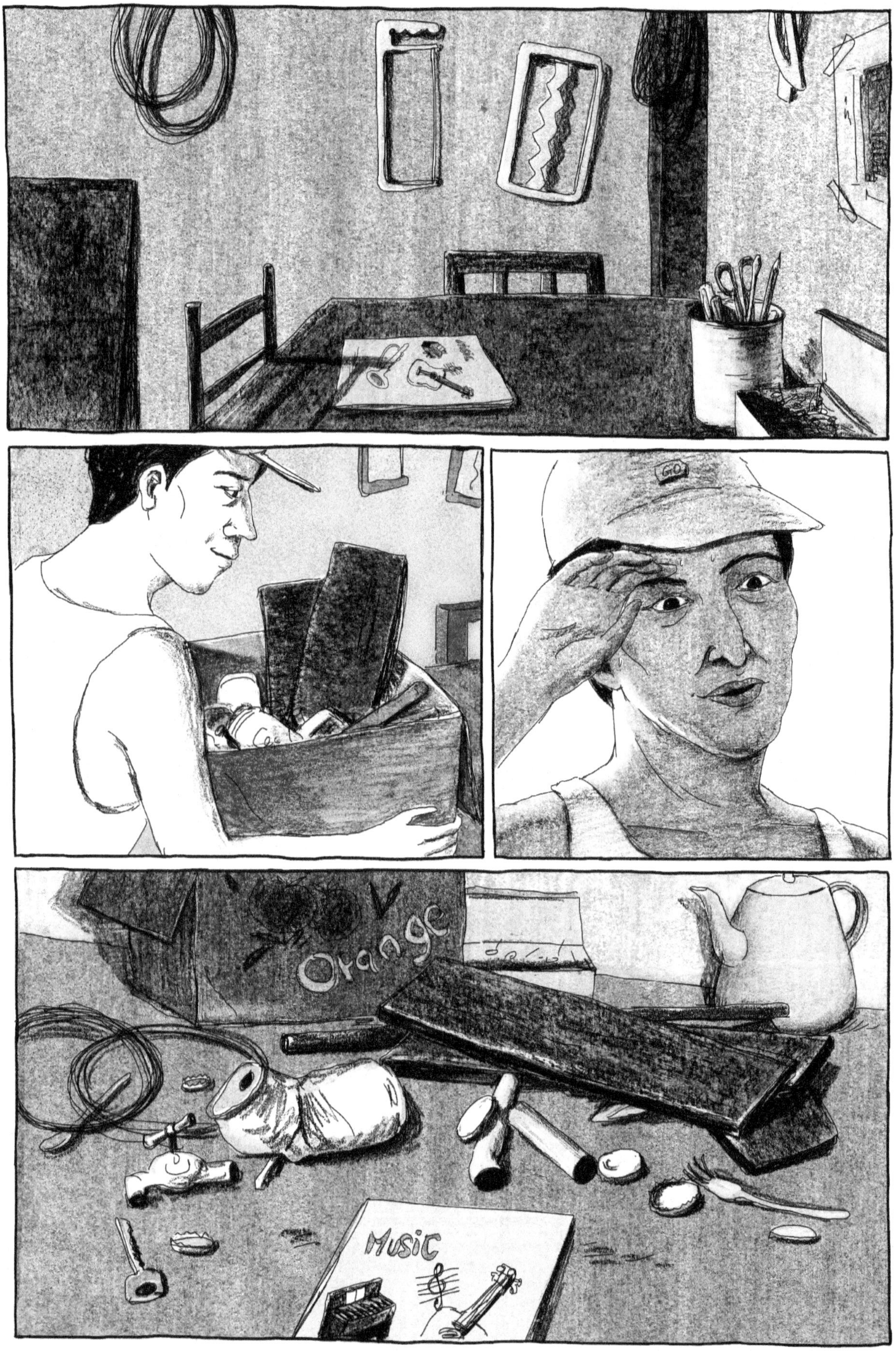
GO
Orange
Music

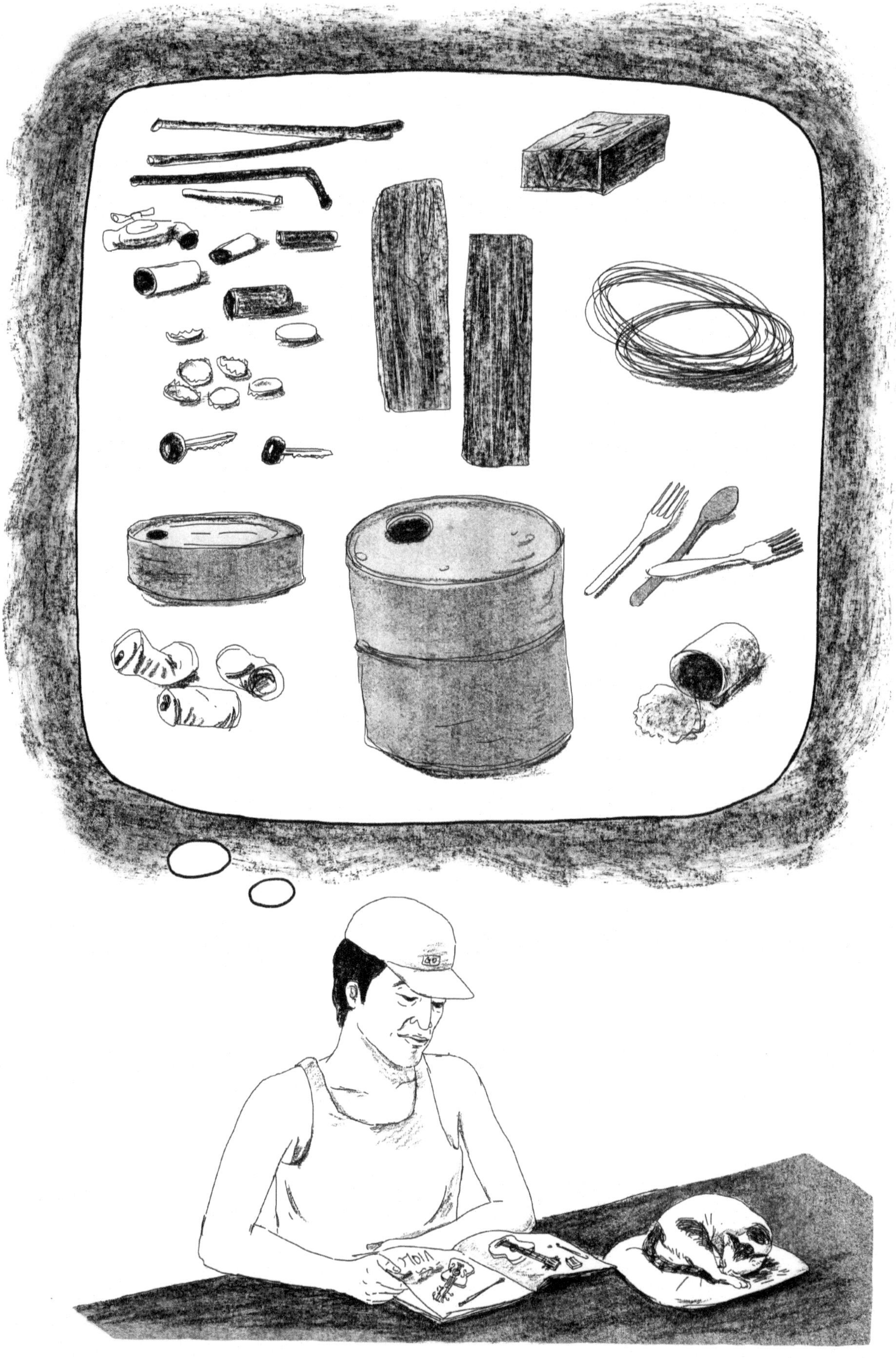

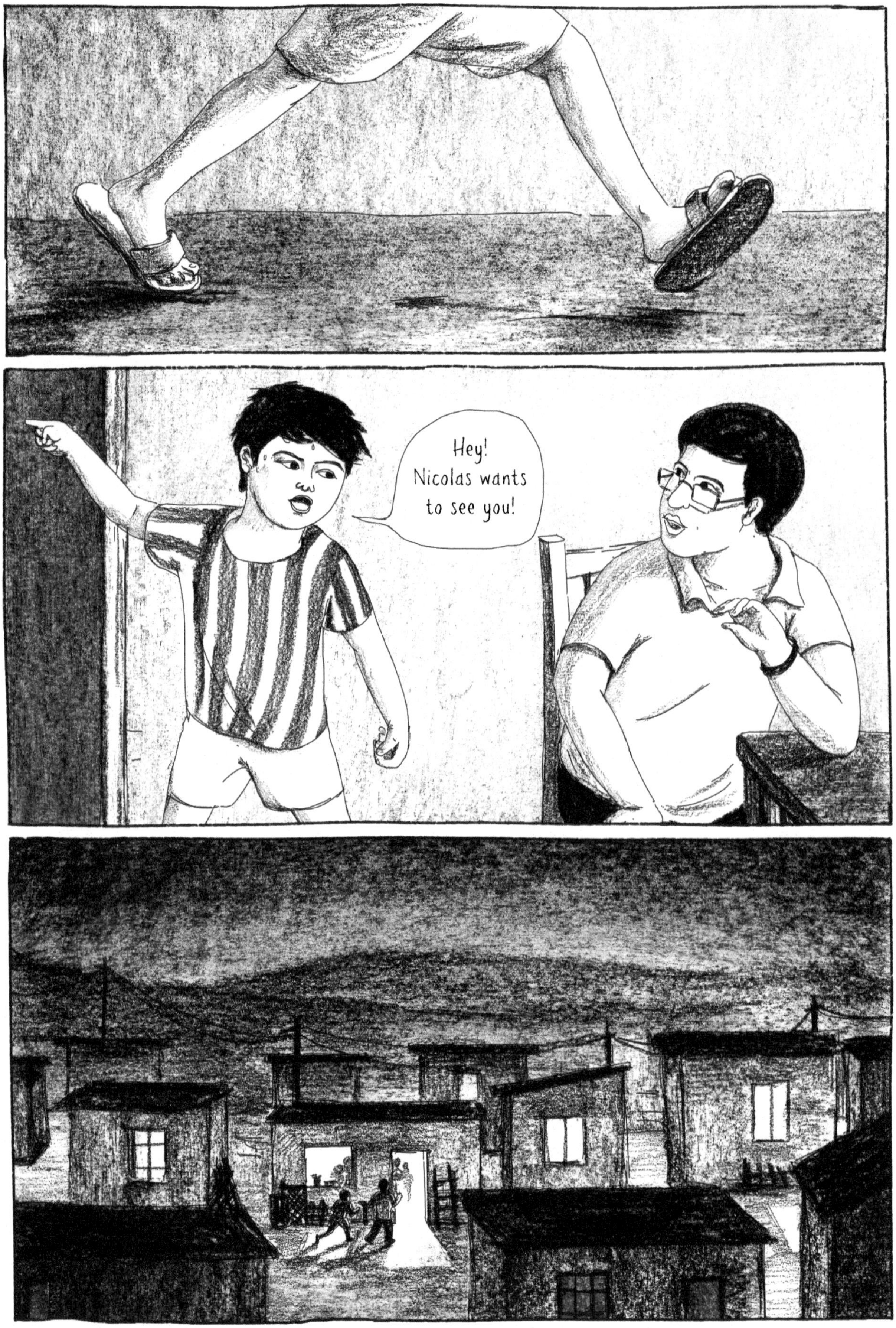
Hey! Nicolas wants to see you!

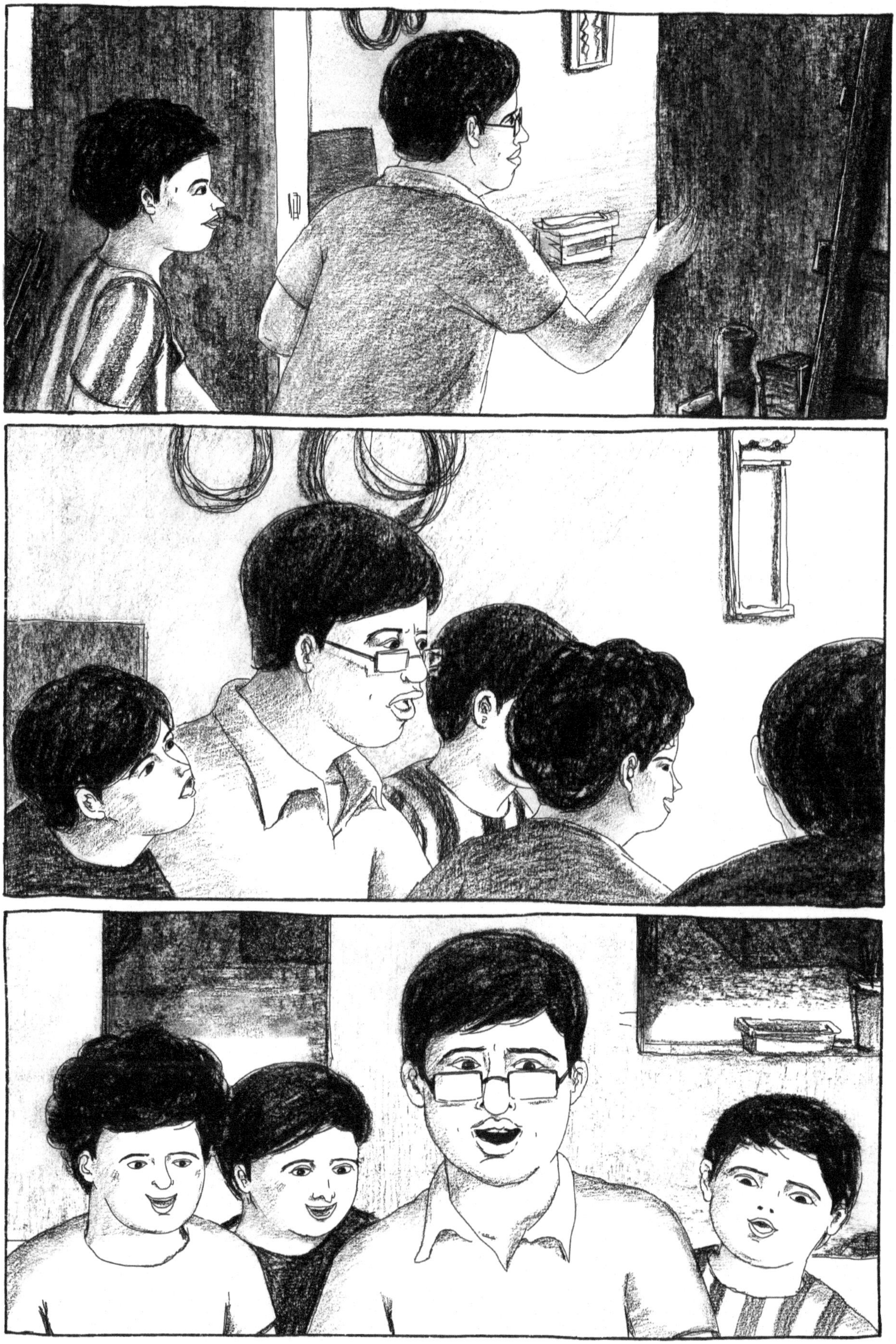

Wooden plank.

Paint can.

Faucet knob.

Kitchen utensil.

Aluminum pipe.

Fork.

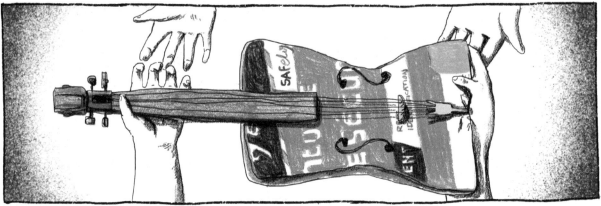

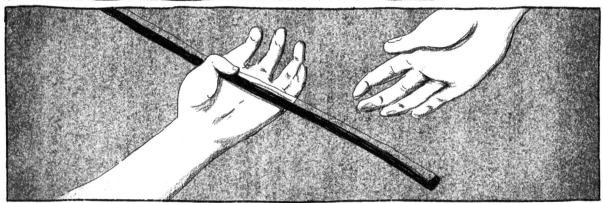

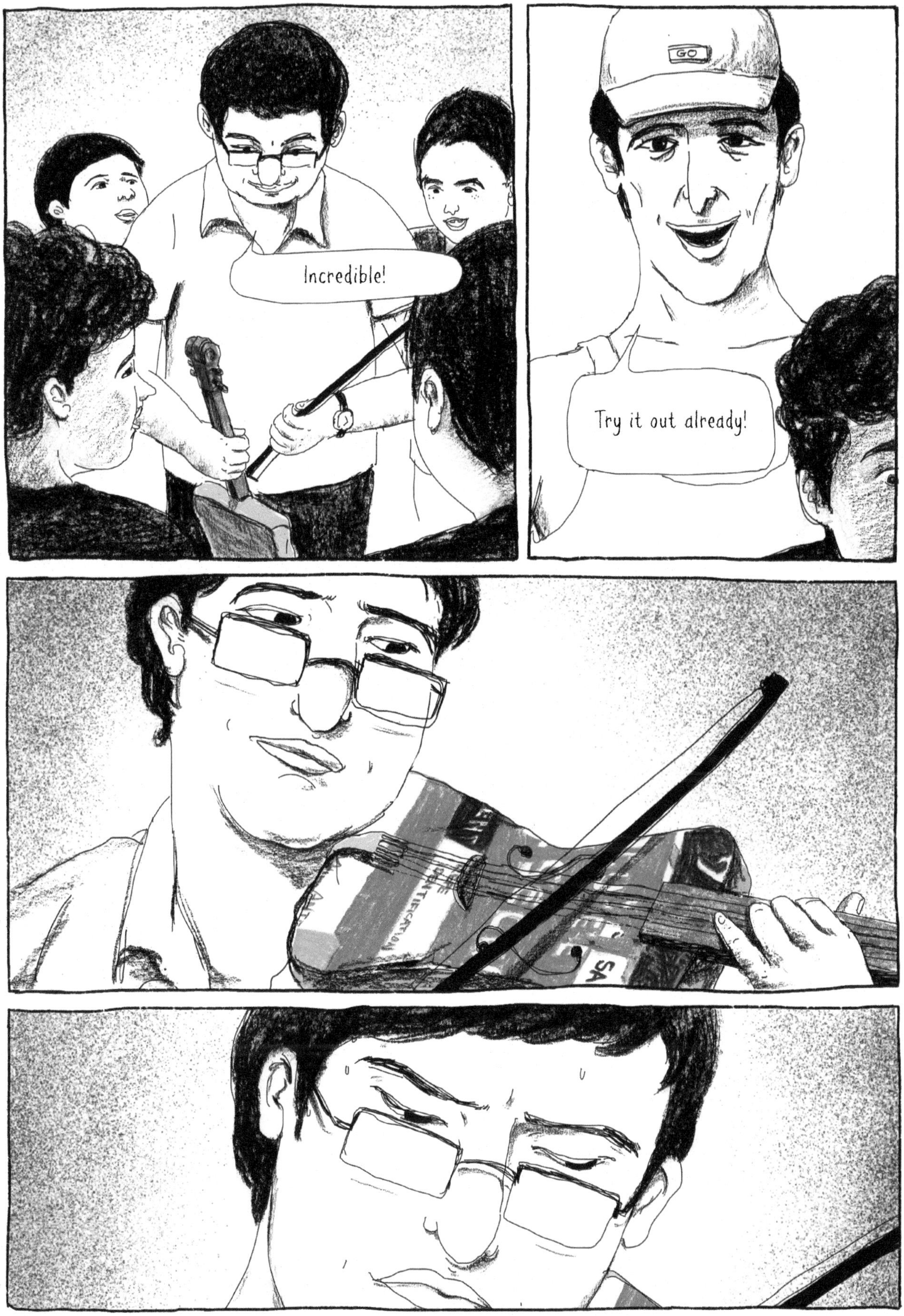
Incredible!
Try it out already!

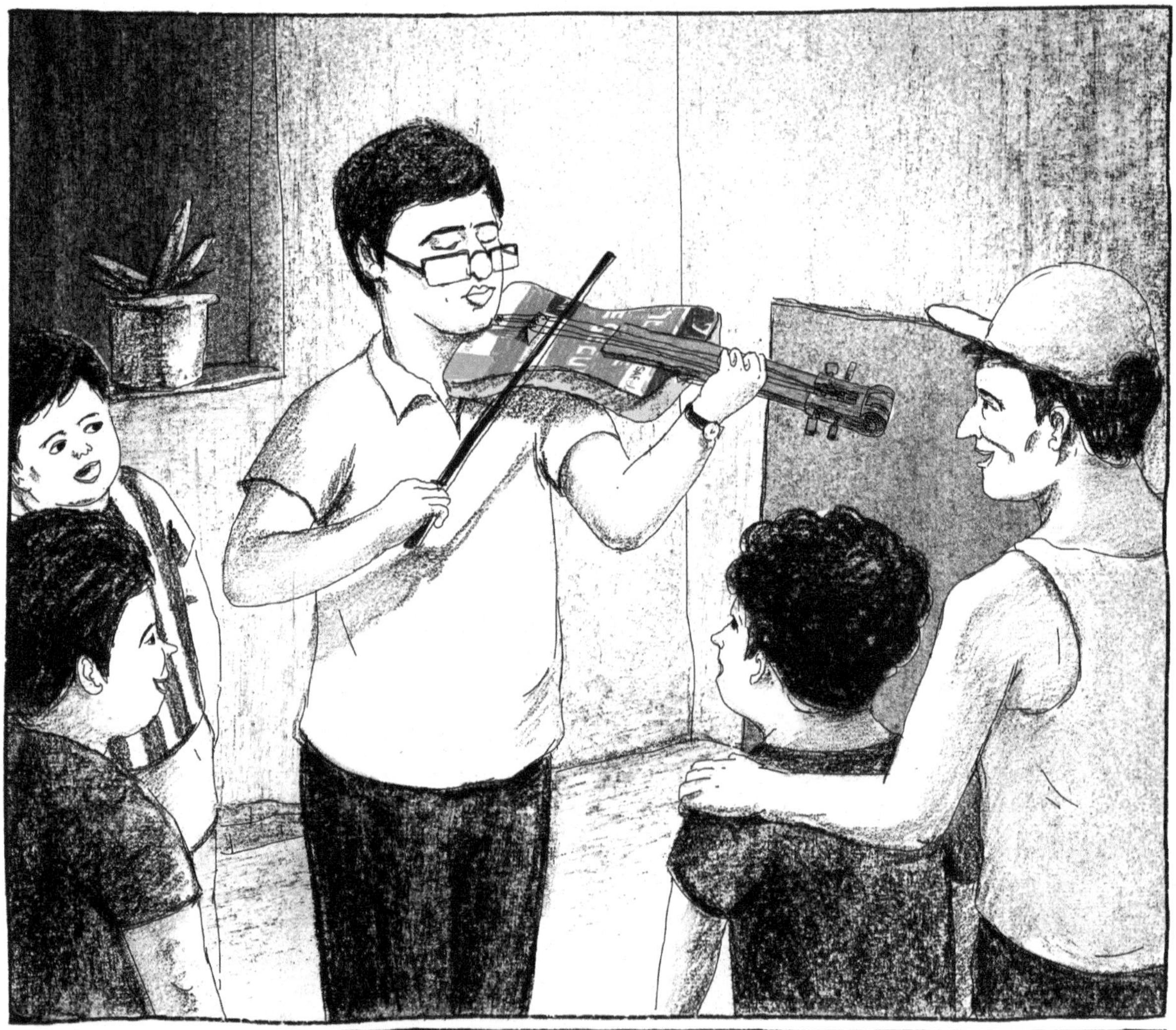

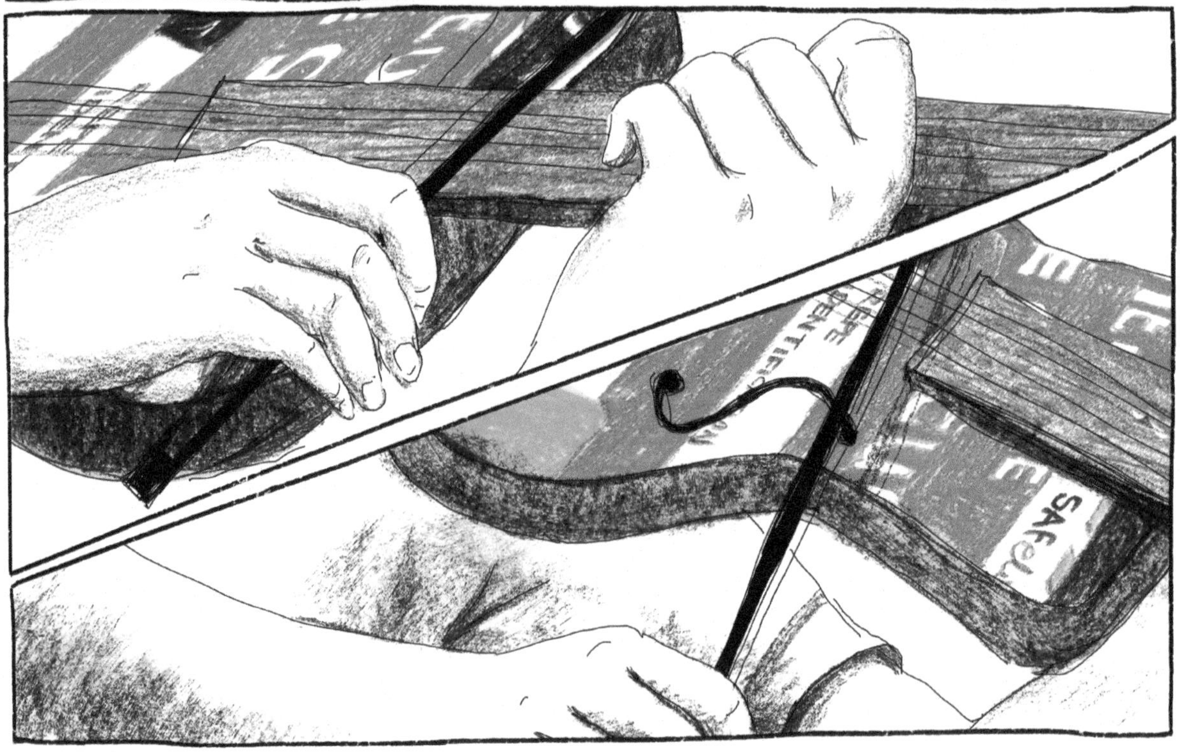

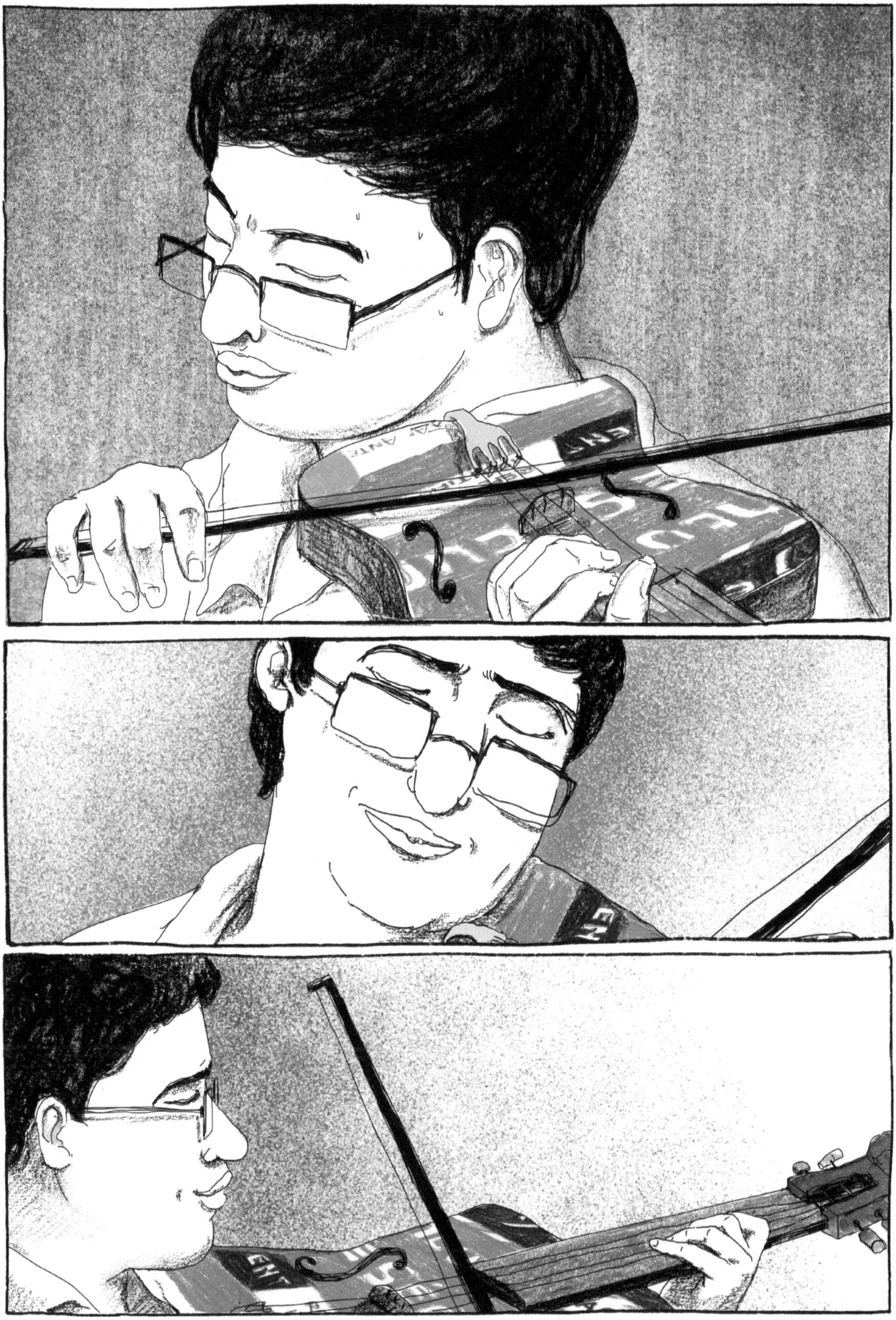

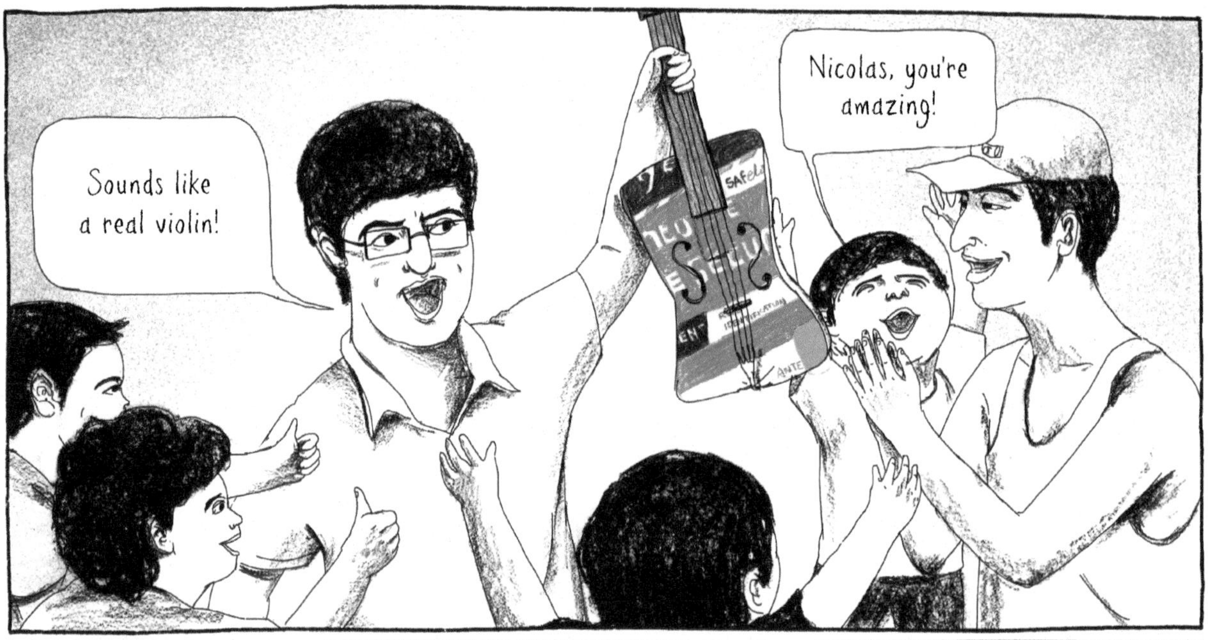
Sounds like
a real violin!
Nicolas, you're
amazing!

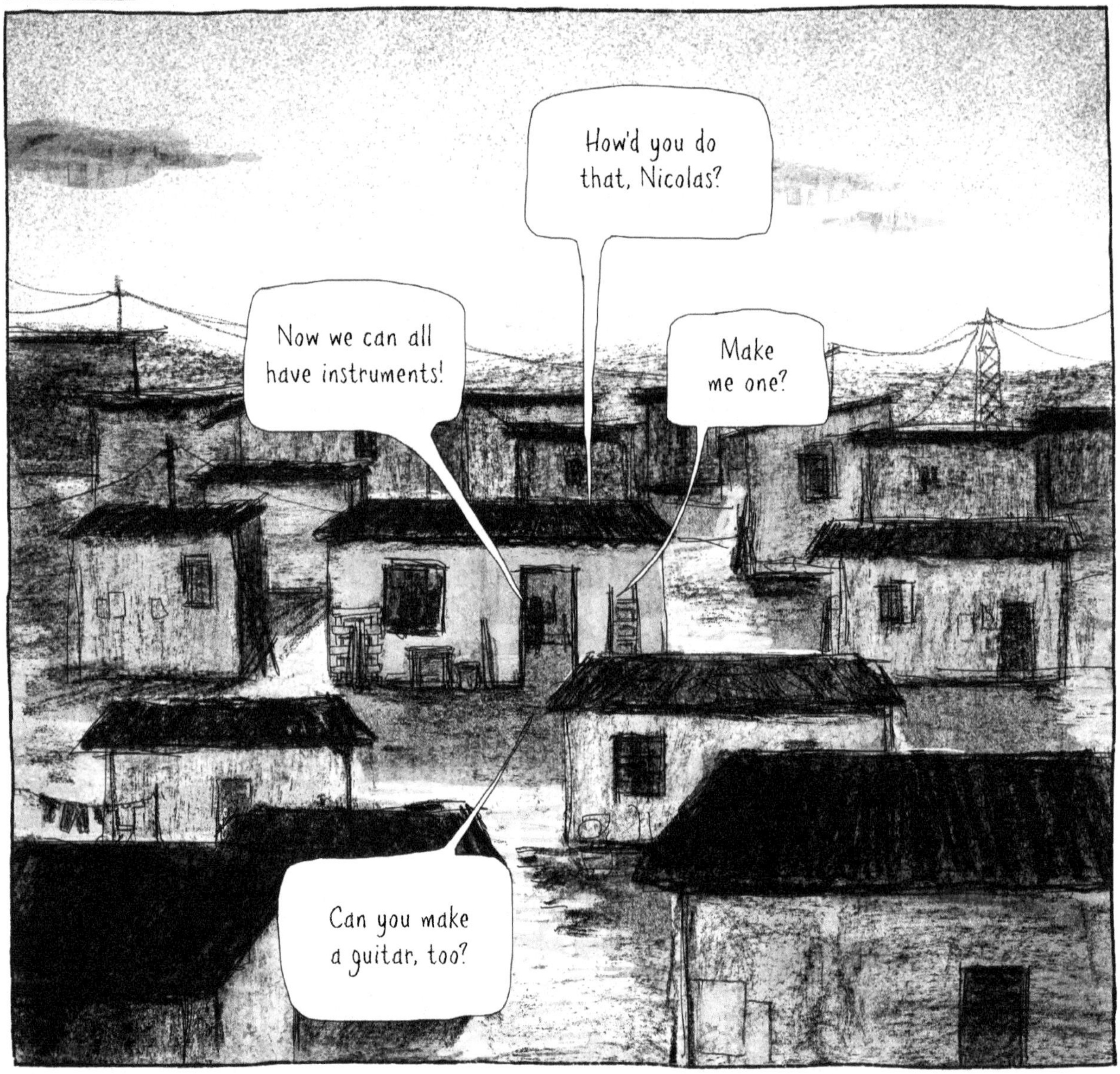
How'd you do
that, Nicolas?
Now we can all
have instruments!
Make
me one?
Can you make
a guitar, too?

5

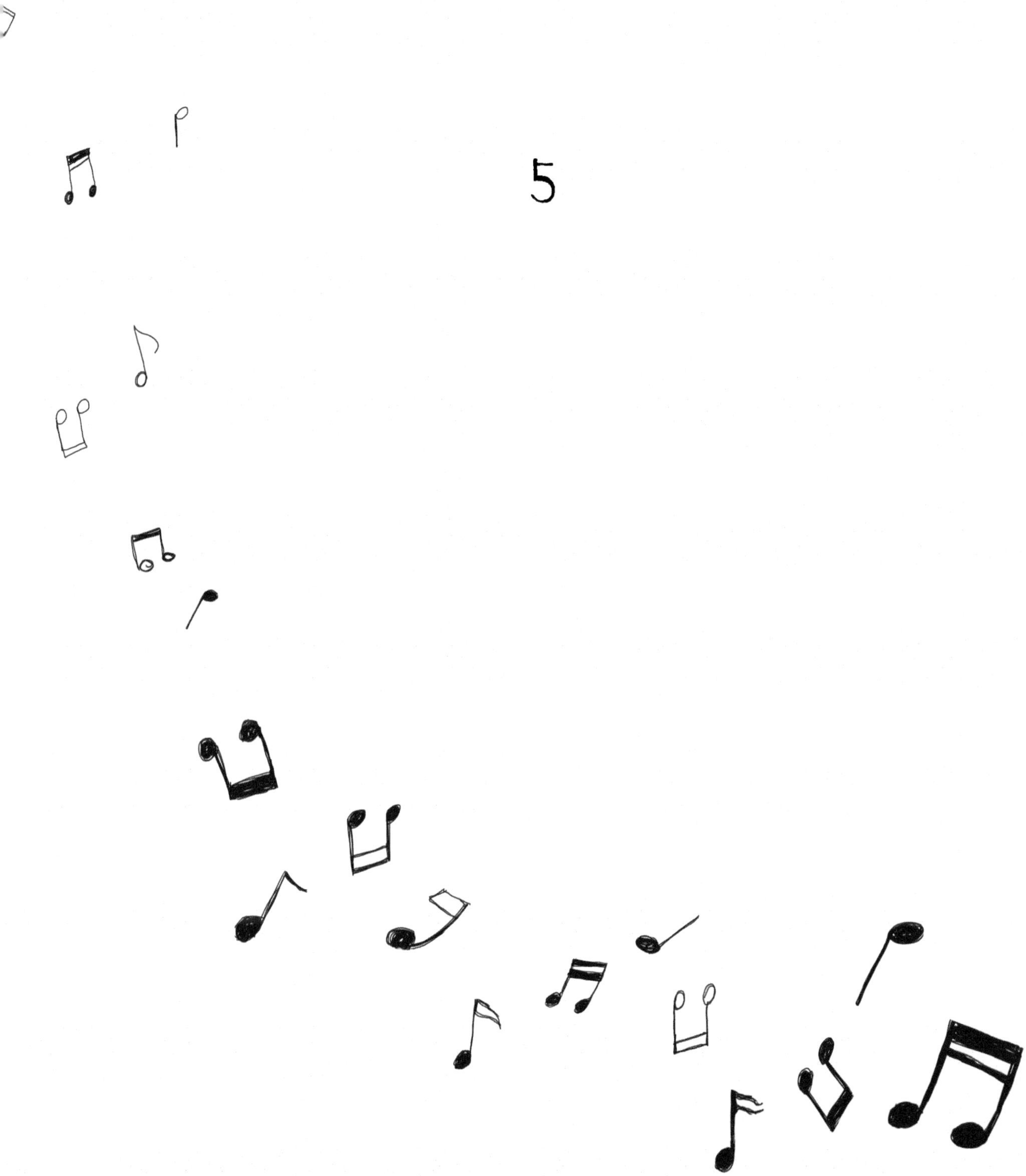

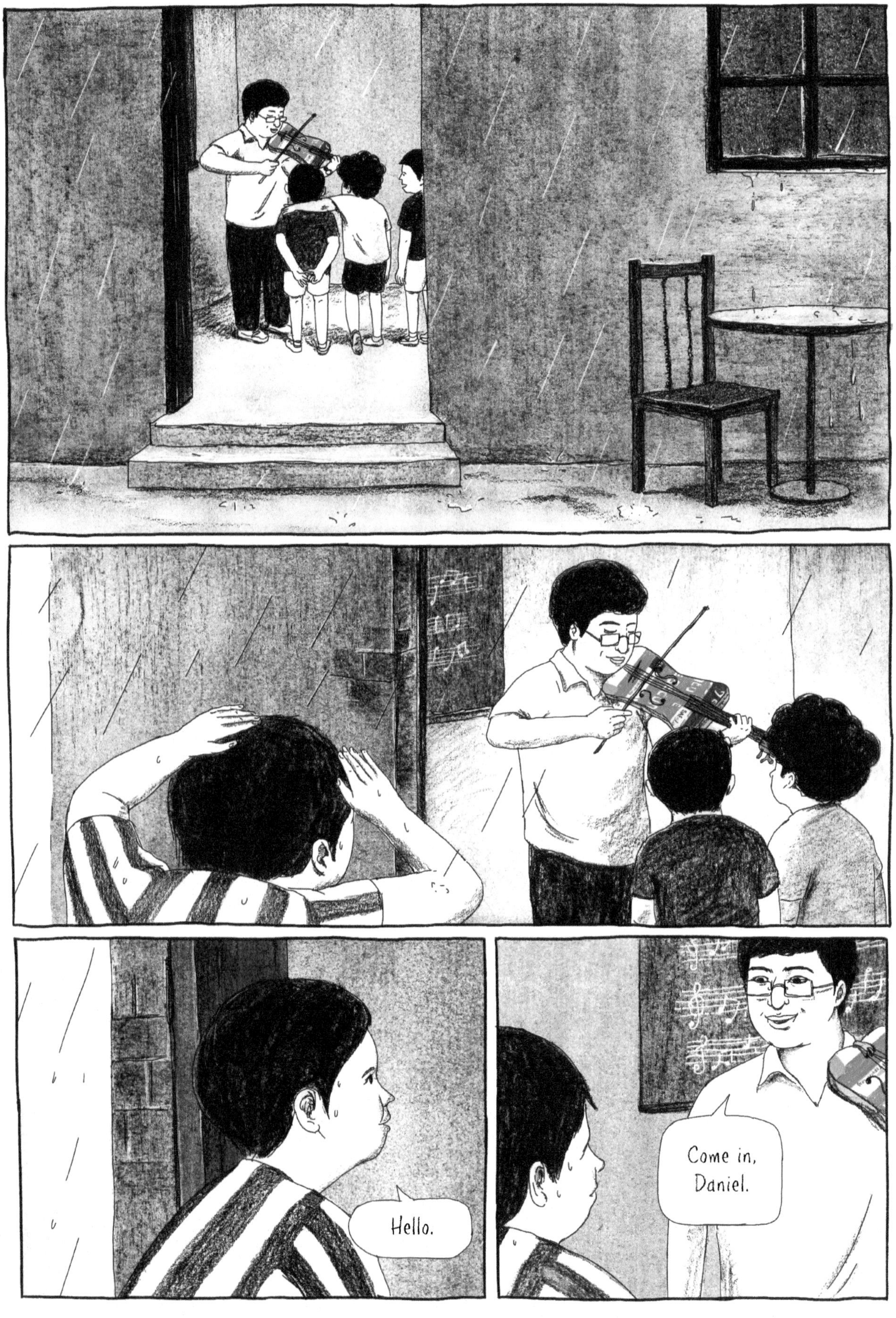
Hello.
Come in, Daniel.

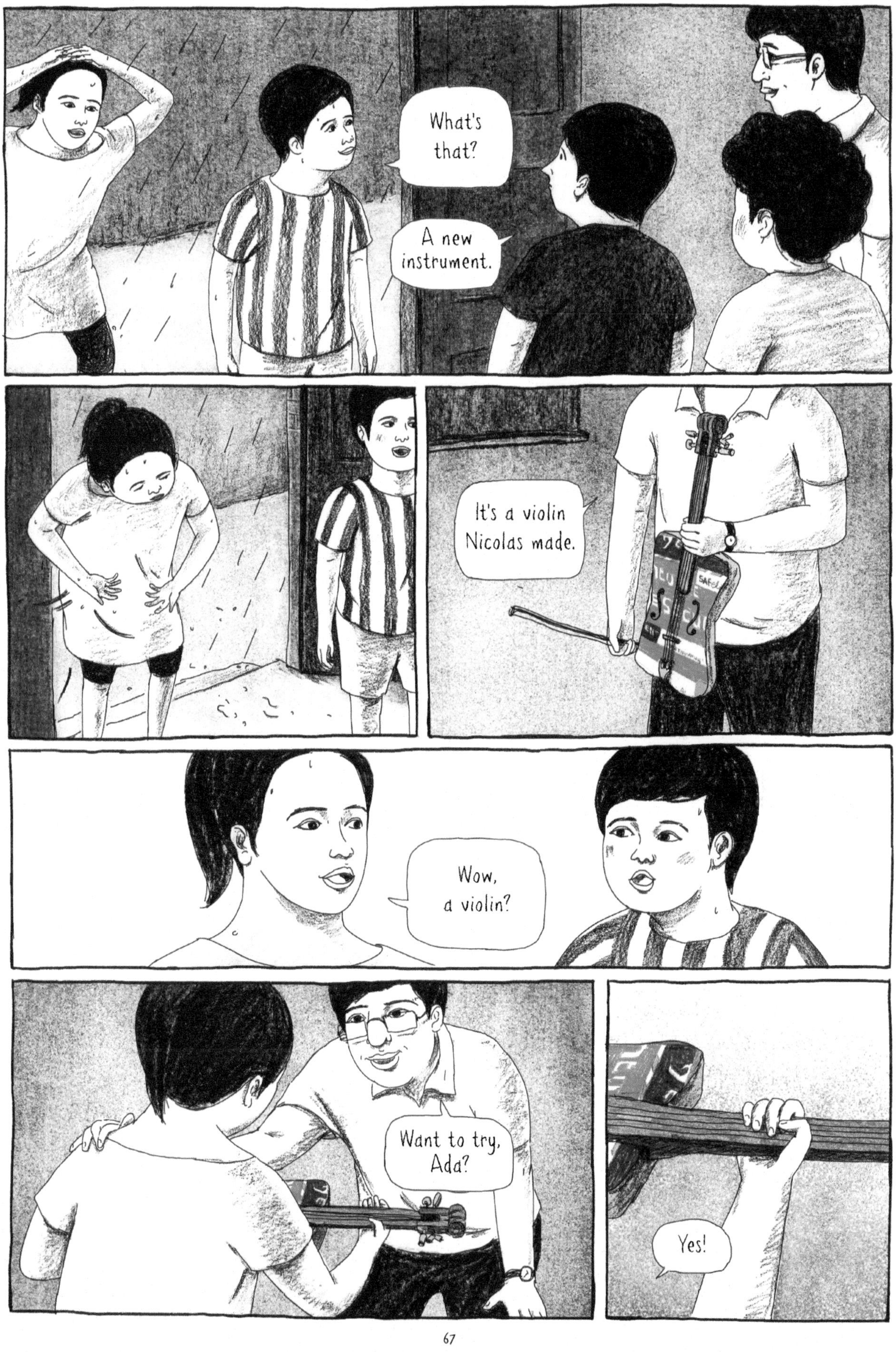
What's that?
A new instrument.
It's a violin Nicolas made.
Wow, a violin?
Want to try, Ada?
Yes!

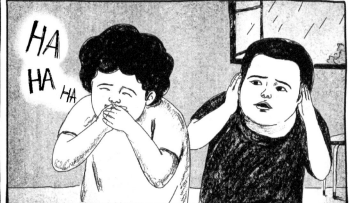

HA
HA HA

Shut up!

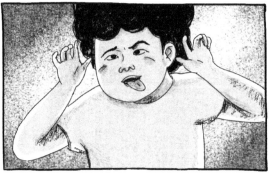

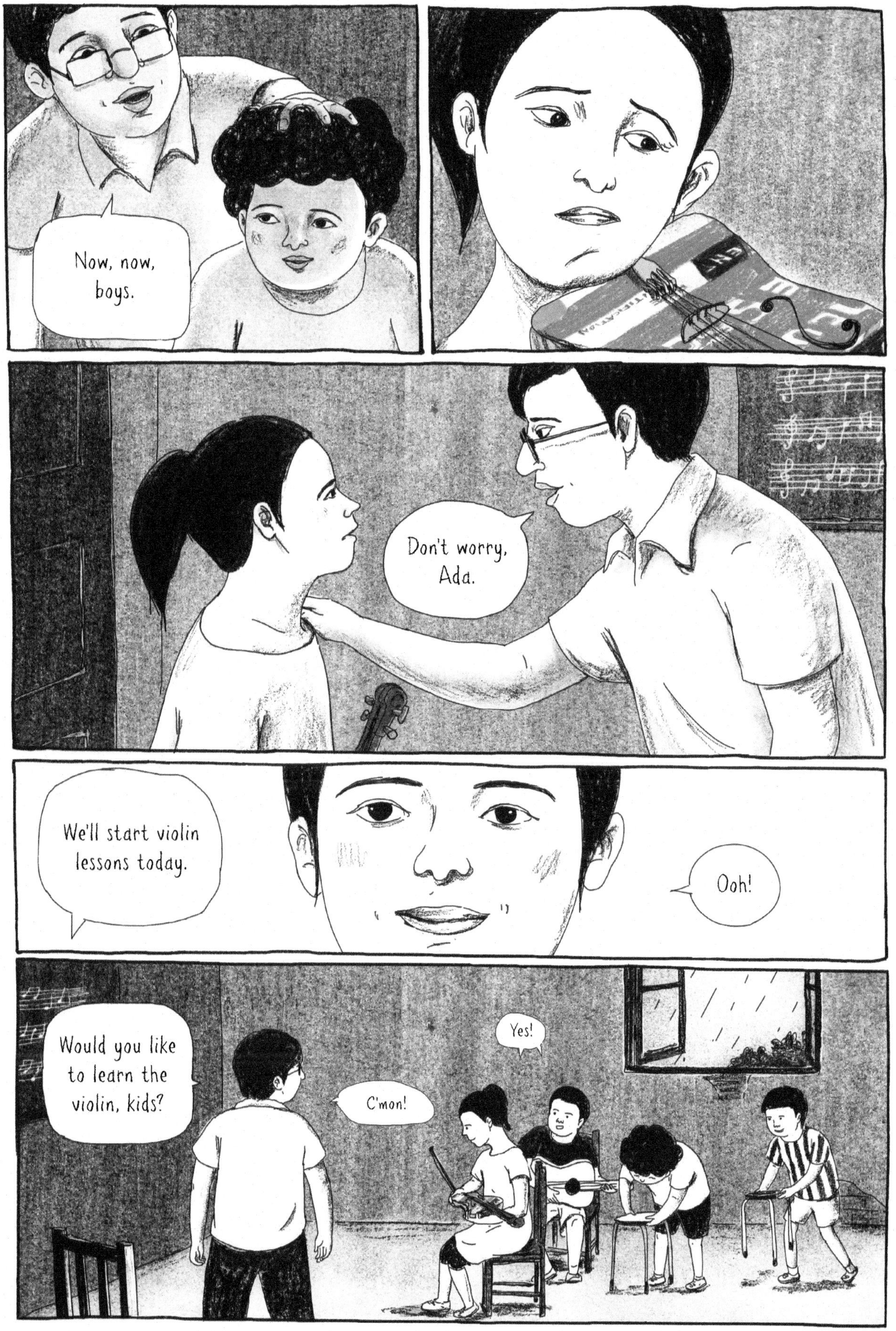
Now, now, boys.
Don't worry, Ada.
We'll start violin lessons today.
Ooh!
Would you like to learn the violin, kids?
Yes!
C'mon!

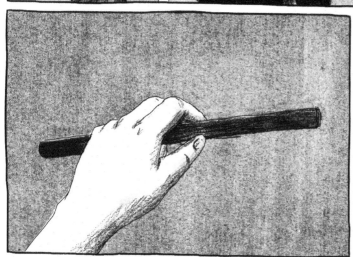

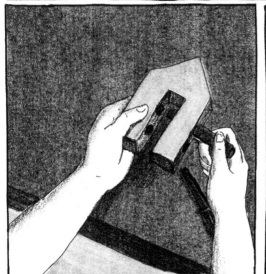

Morning...

I'm off to the dump. You stay here.

meow

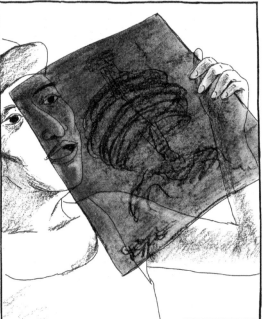

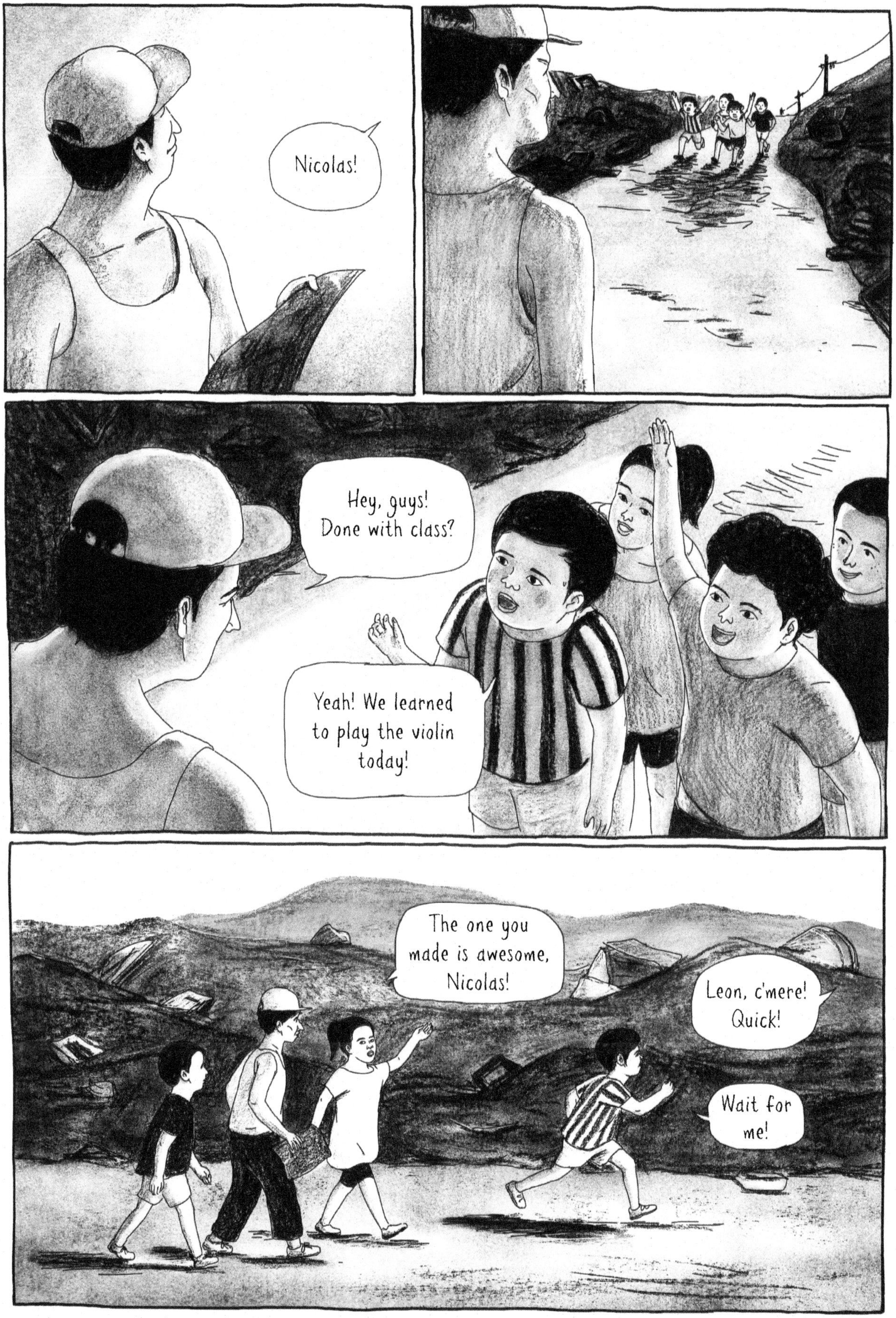
Nicolas!
Hey, guys! Done with class?
Yeah! We learned to play the violin today!
The one you made is awesome, Nicolas!
Leon, c'mere! Quick!
Wait for me!

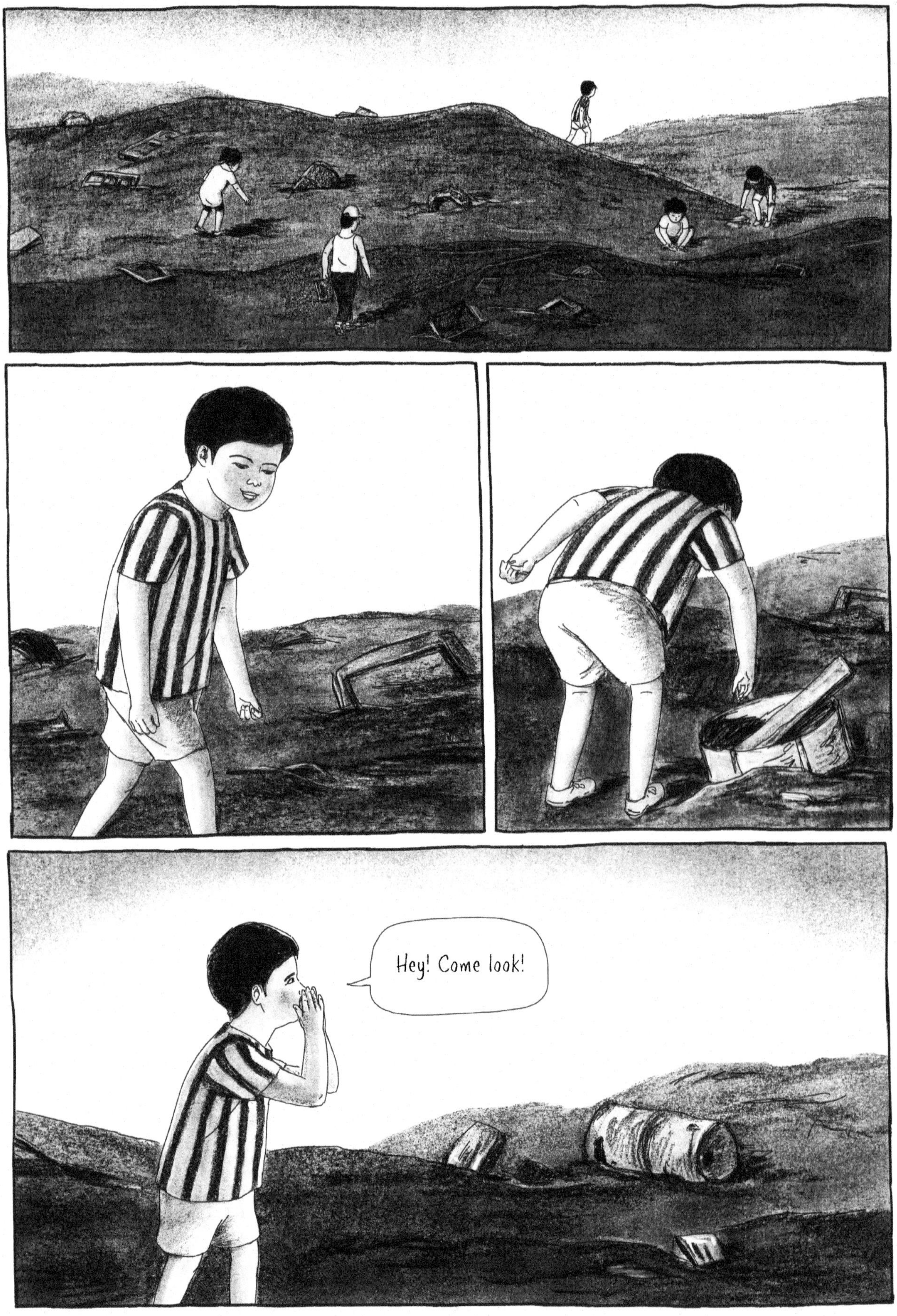
Hey! Come look!

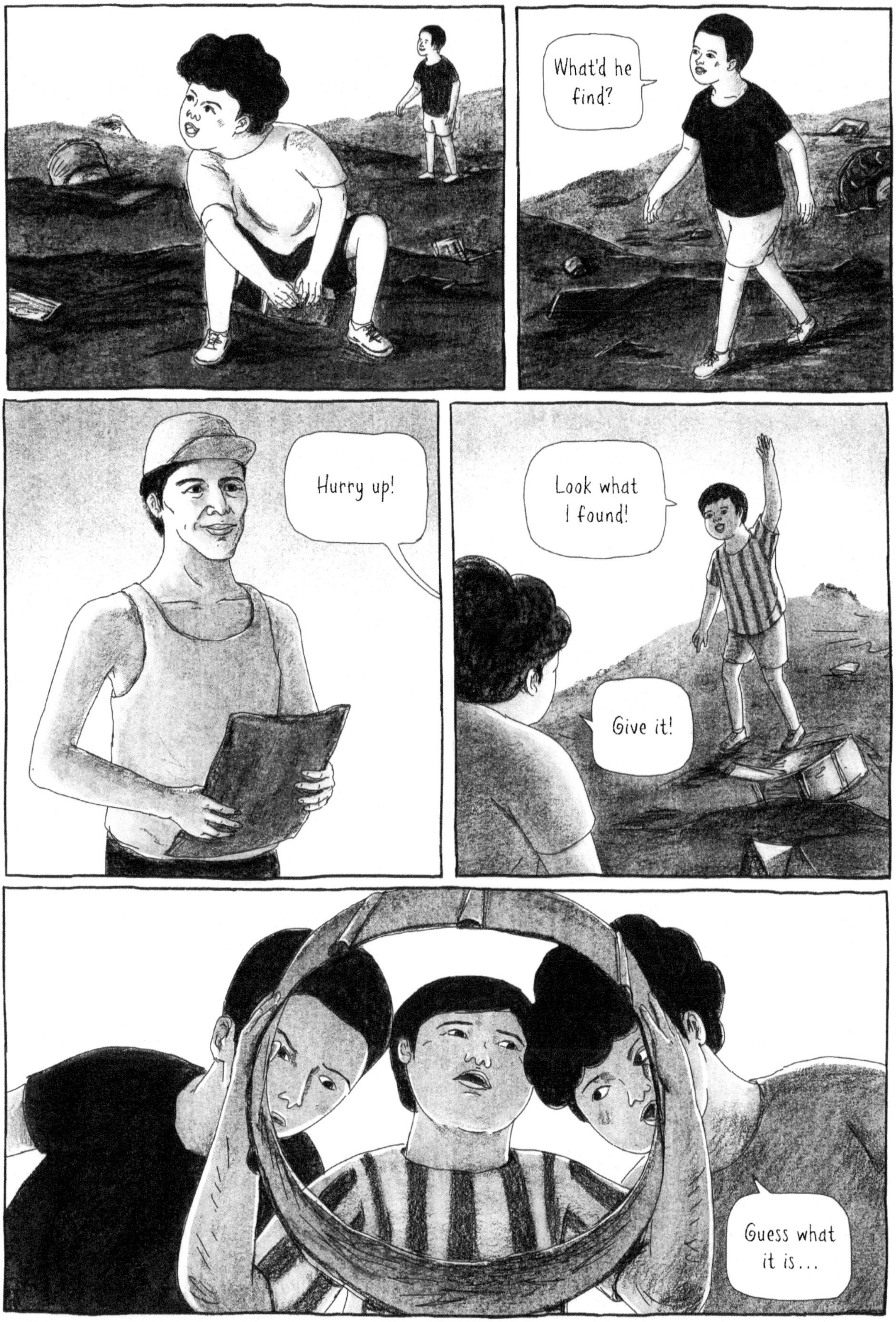
What'd he find?
Hurry up!
Look what I found!
Give it!
Guess what it is...

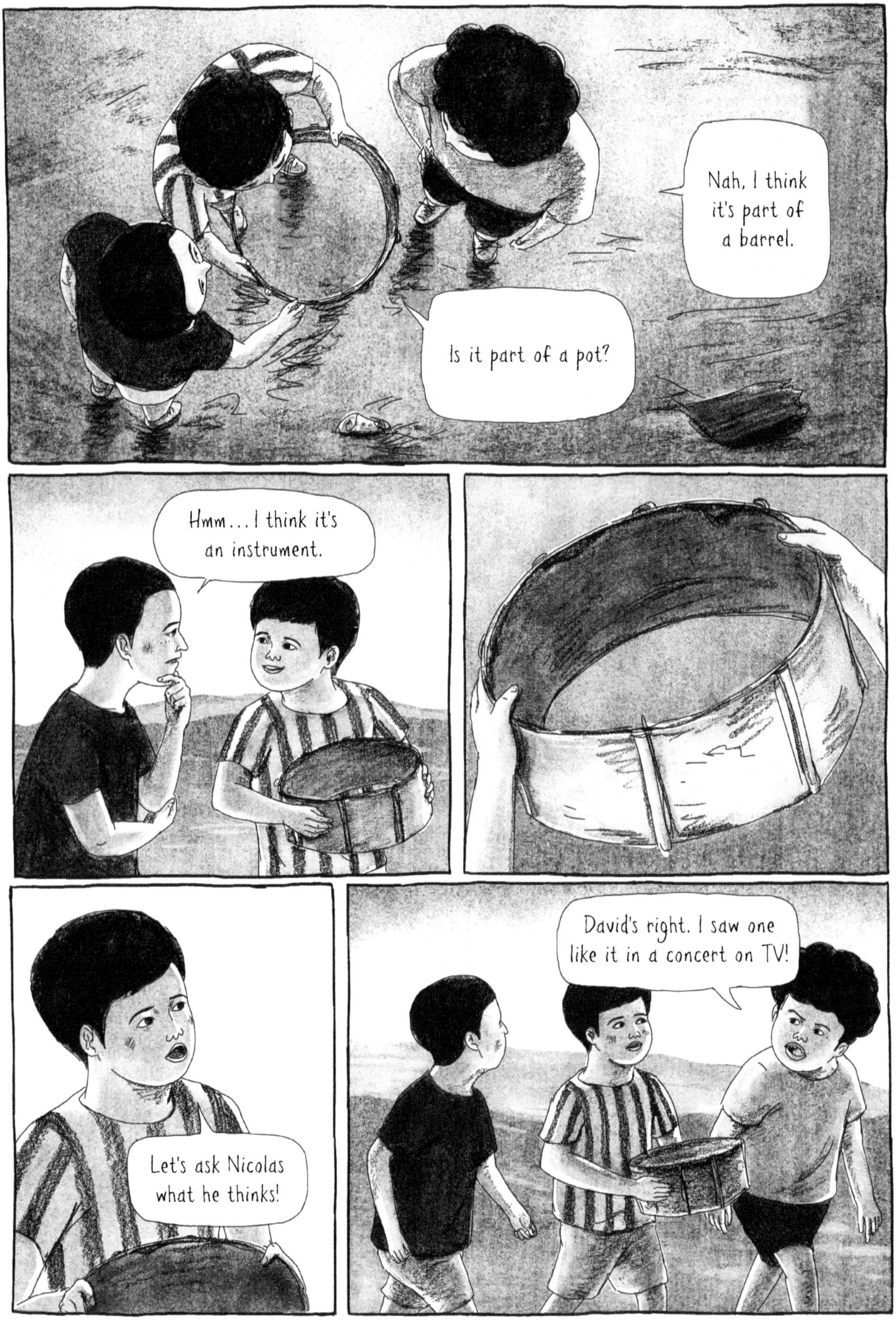
Is it part of a pot?
Nah, I think it's part of a barrel.
Hmm... I think it's an instrument.
Let's ask Nicolas what he thinks!
David's right. I saw one like it in a concert on TV!

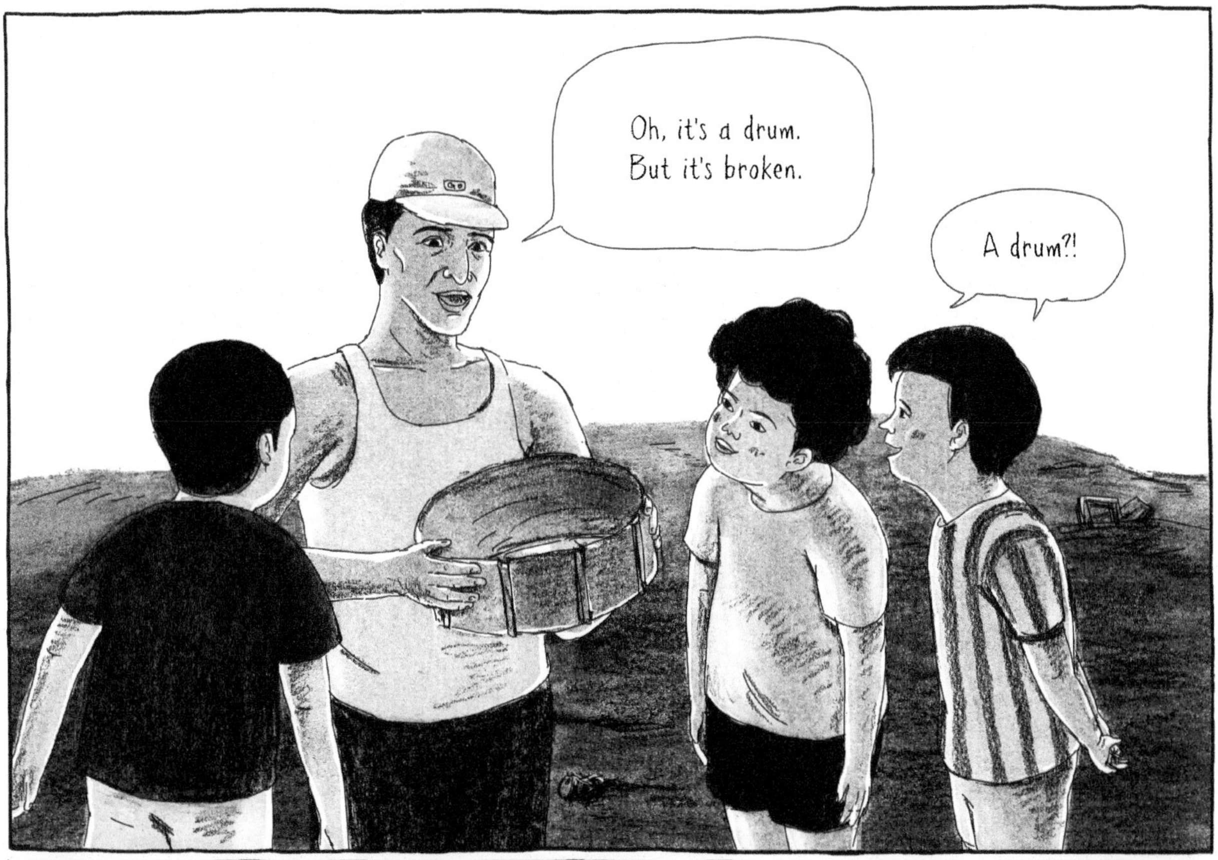
Oh, it's a drum. But it's broken.
A drum?!

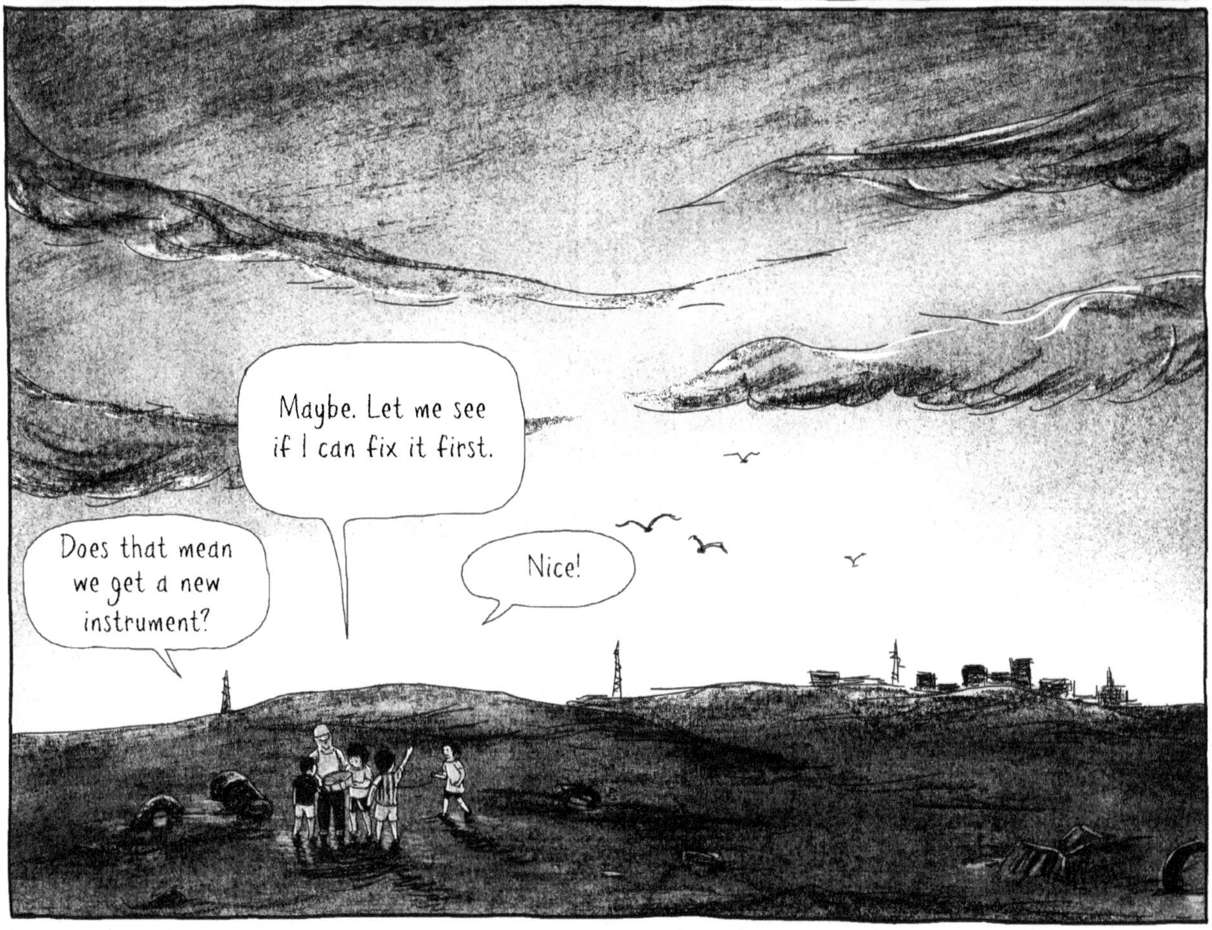
Does that mean we get a new instrument?
Maybe. Let me see if I can fix it first.
Nice!

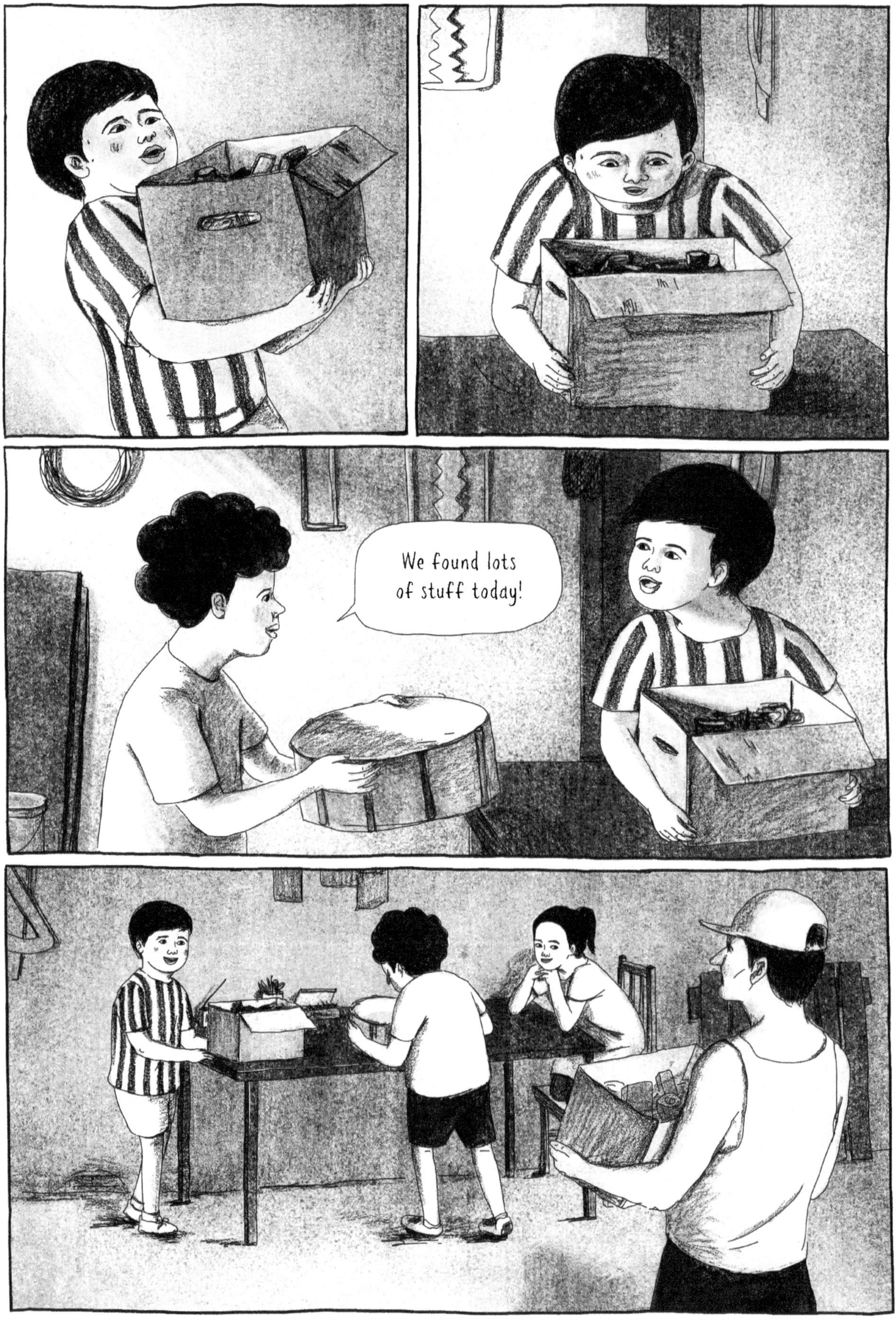
We found lots
of stuff today!

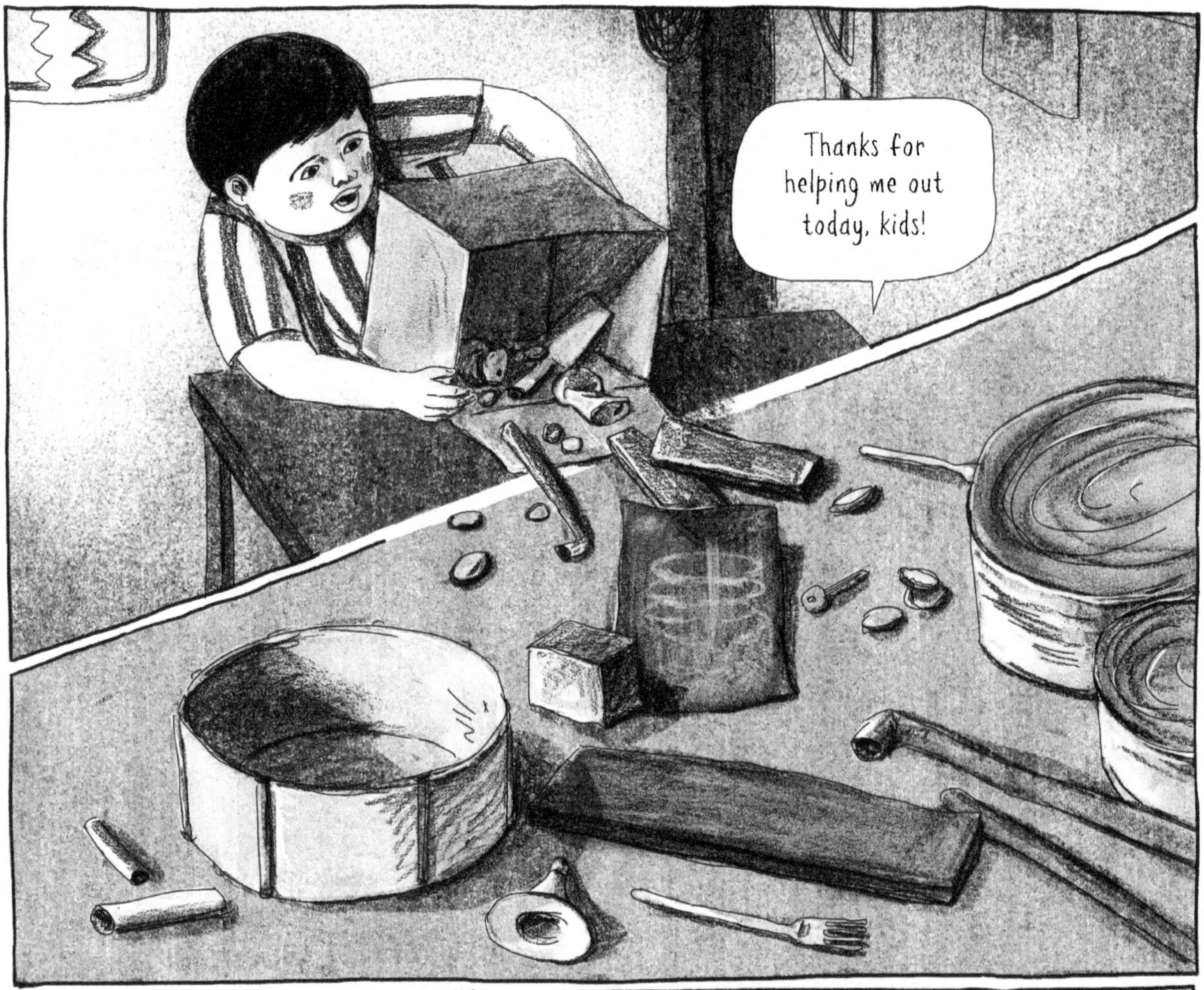
Thanks for helping me out today, kids!

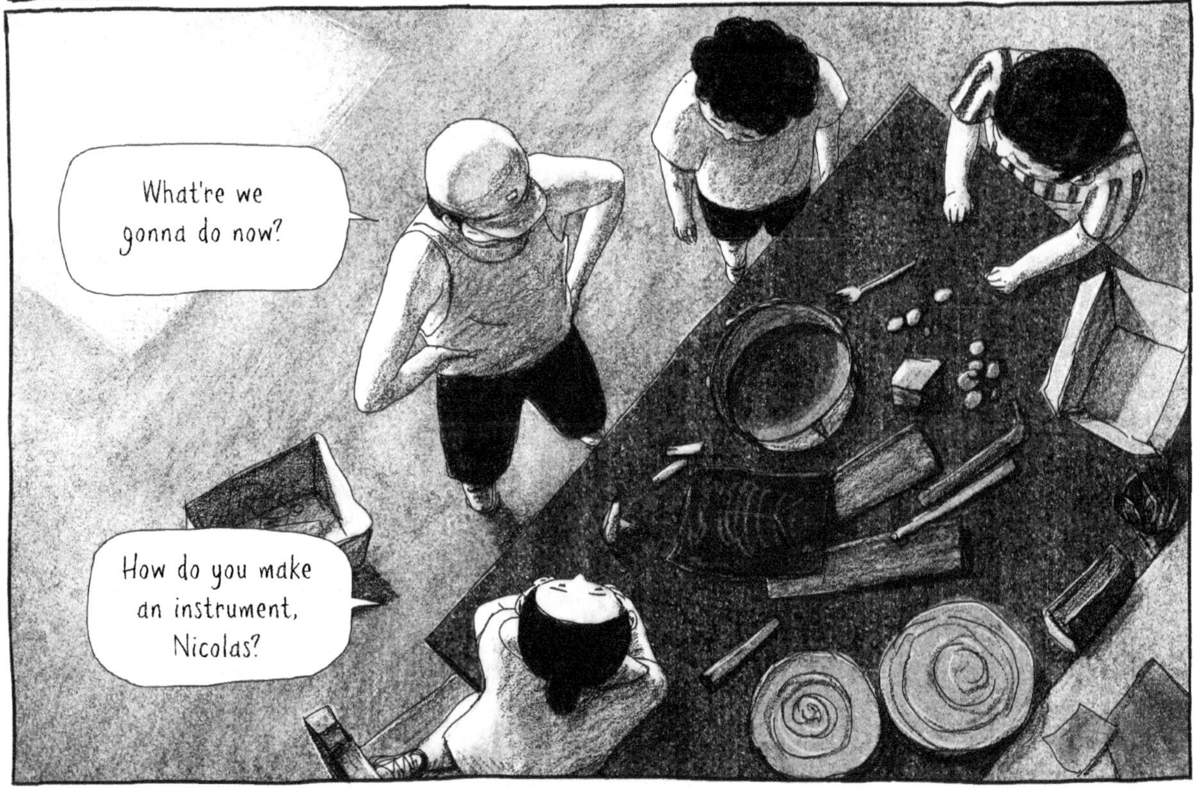
What're we gonna do now?
How do you make an instrument, Nicolas?

I've got an idea. Let's try this...

What's that?

It's an X-ray.

How can that help us make an instrument?

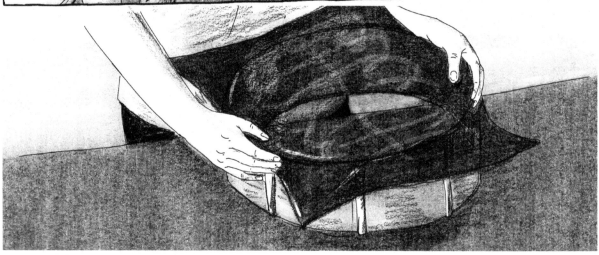

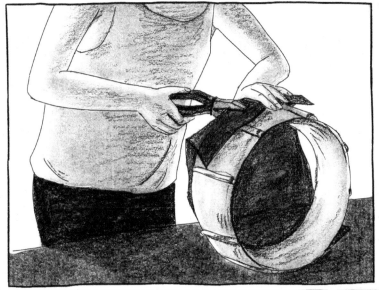

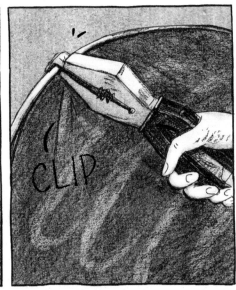

CLIP

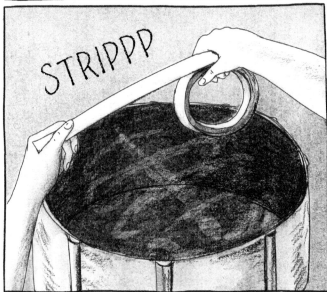

STRIPPP

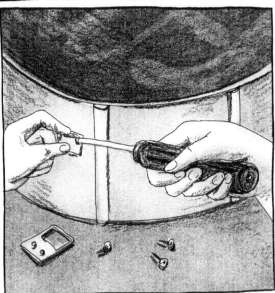

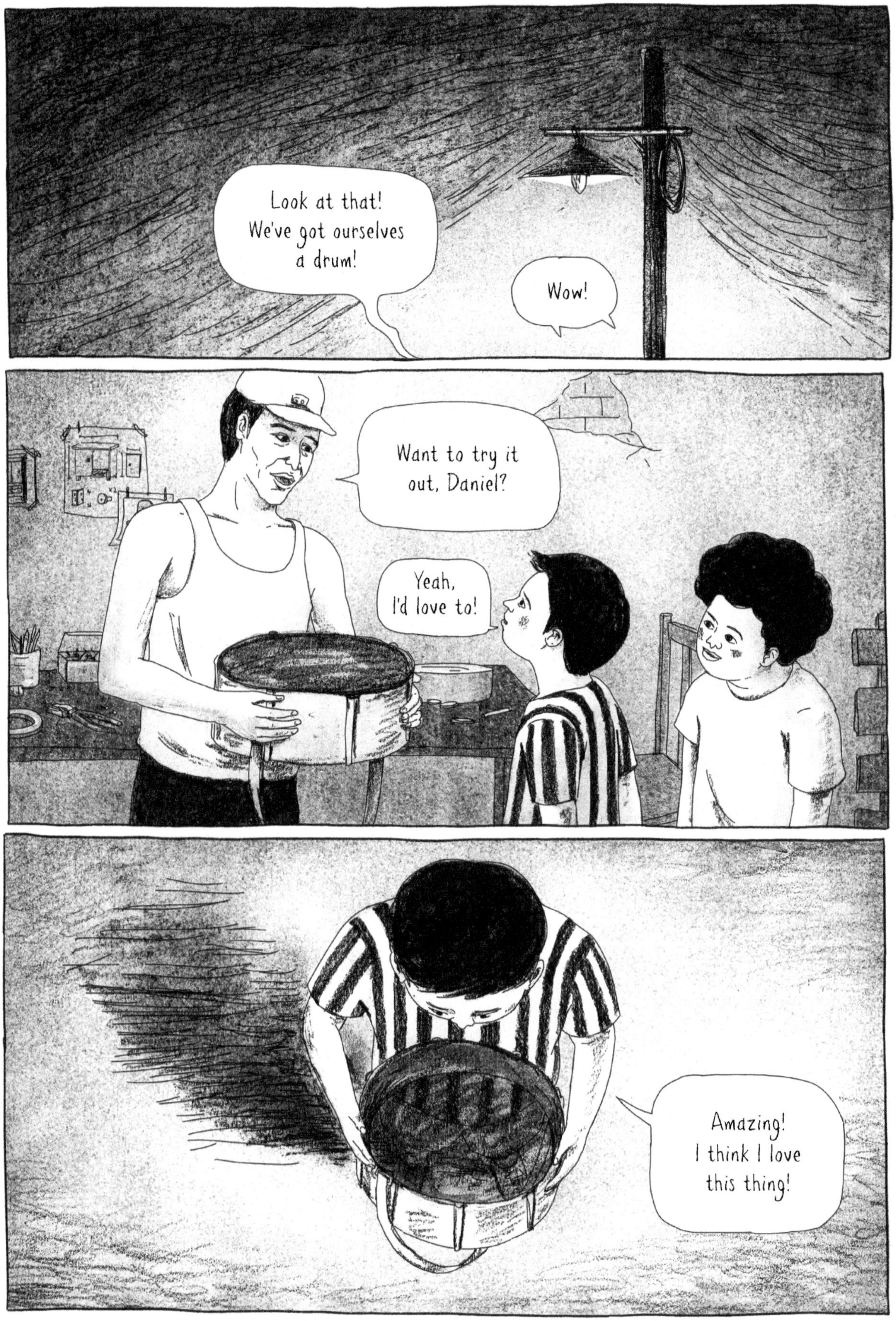
Look at that! We've got ourselves a drum!
Wow!
Want to try it out, Daniel?
Yeah, I'd love to!
Amazing! I think I love this thing!

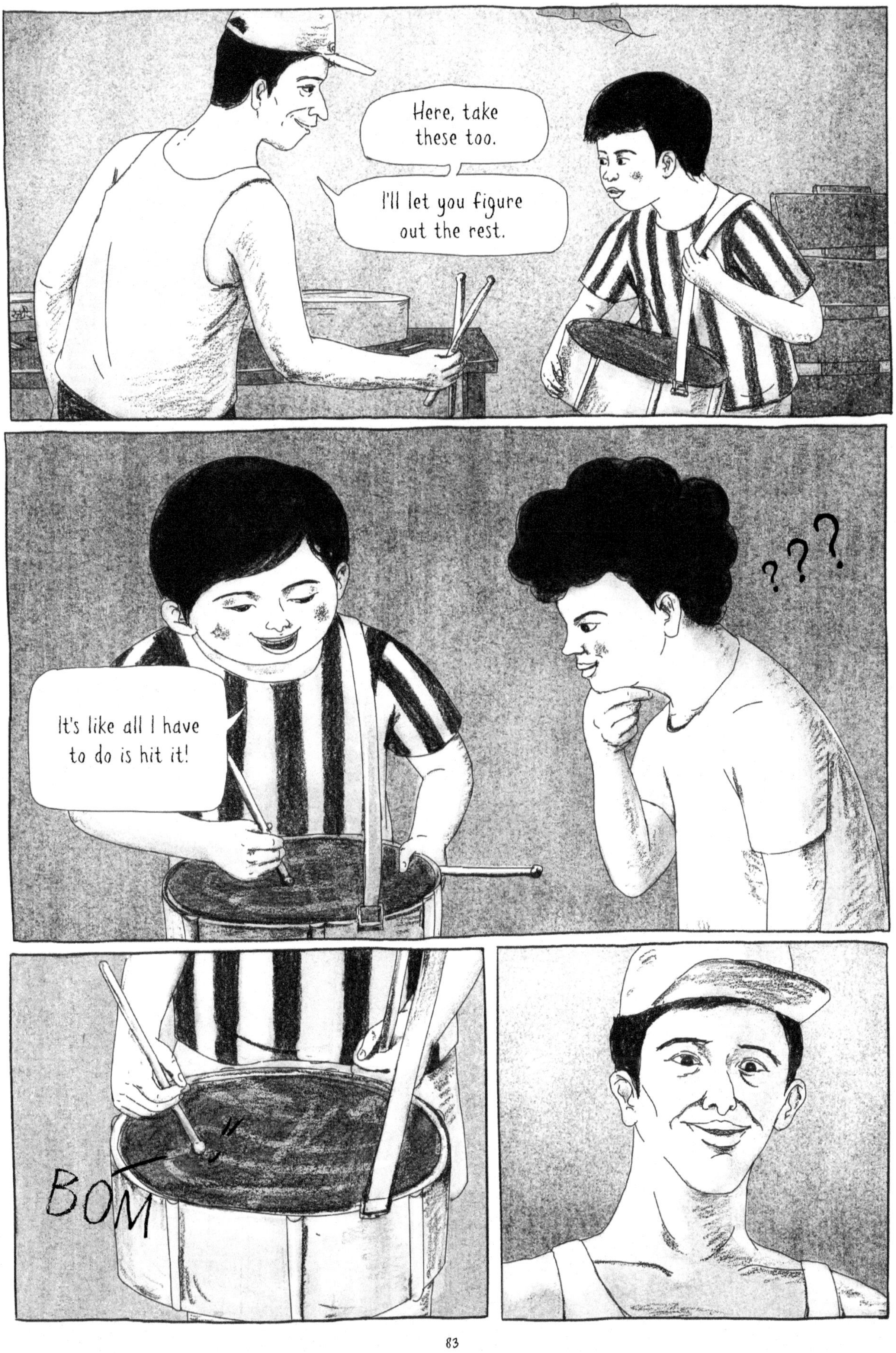
Here, take these too.
I'll let you figure out the rest.
???
It's like all I have to do is hit it!
BOM

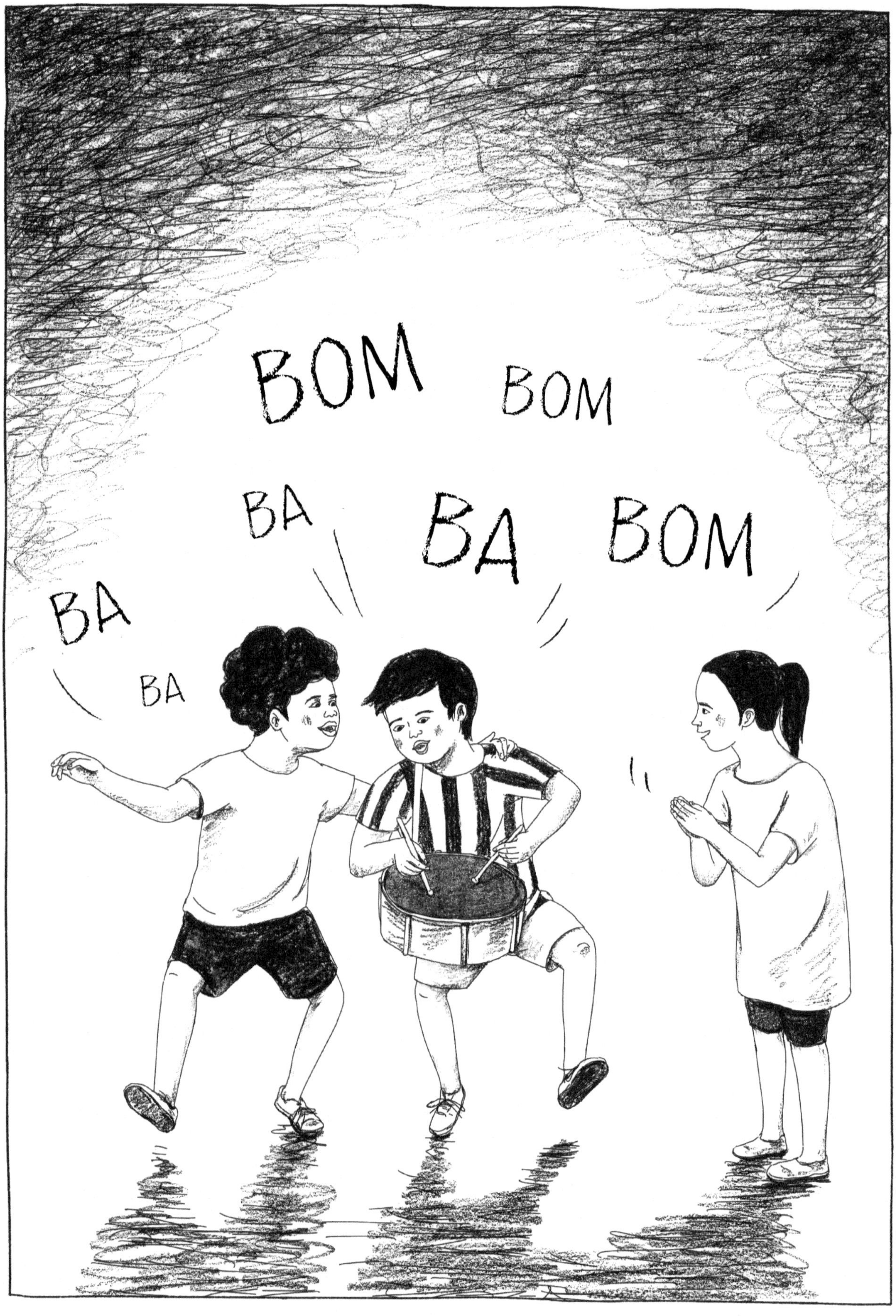
BOM
BOM
BA
BA
BA
BOM
BA
BA

6

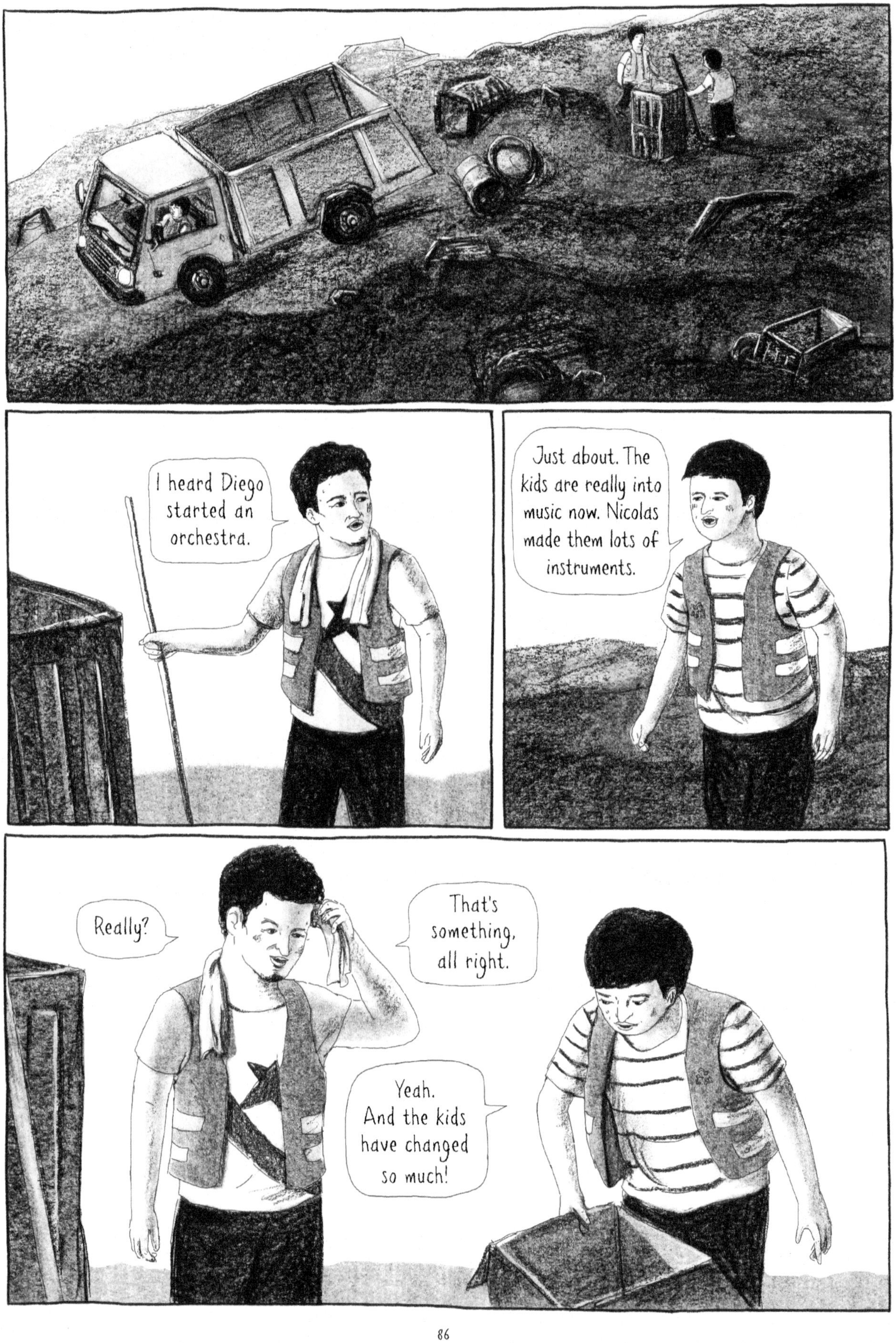
I heard Diego started an orchestra.
Just about. The kids are really into music now. Nicolas made them lots of instruments.
Really?
That's something, all right.
Yeah. And the kids have changed so much!

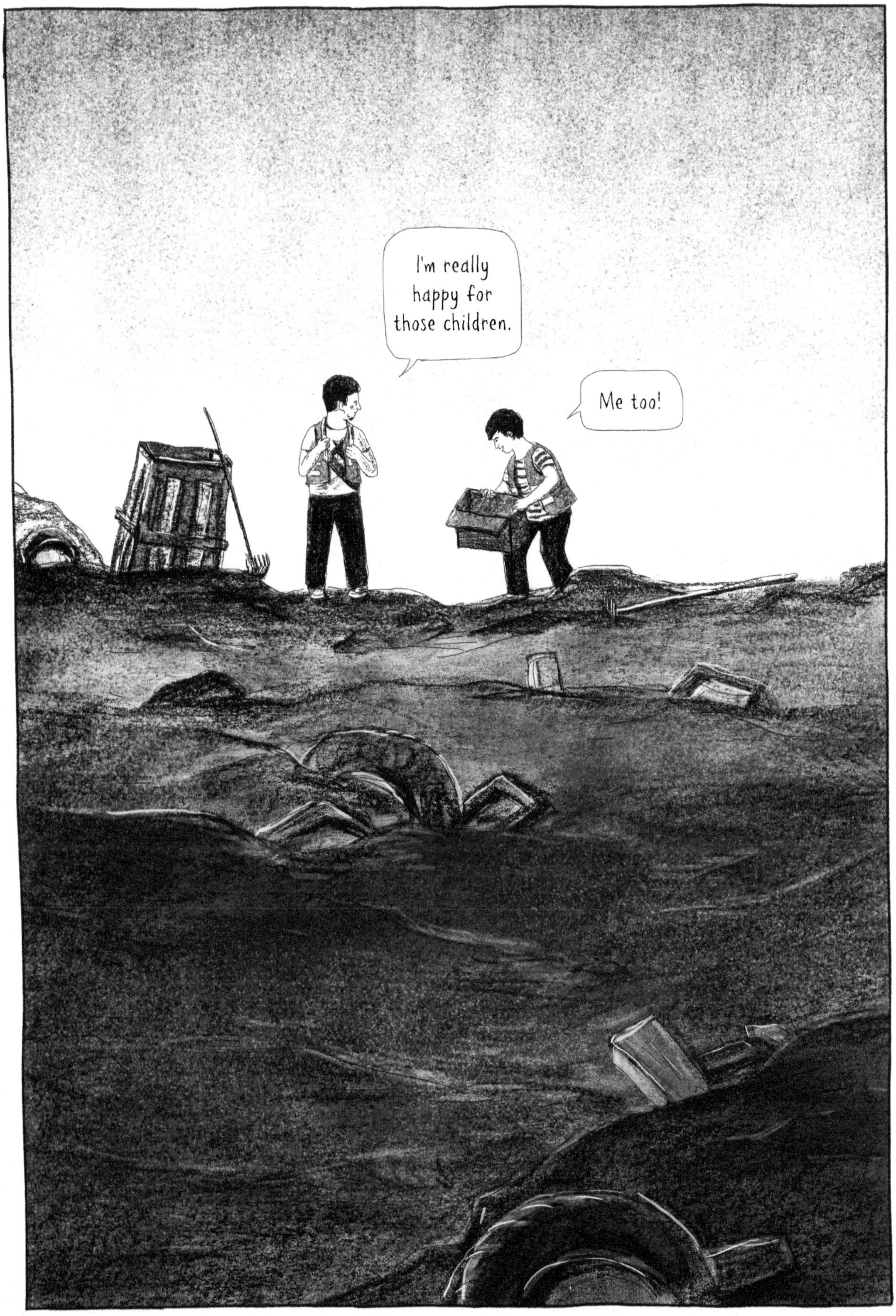
I'm really happy for those children.
Me too!

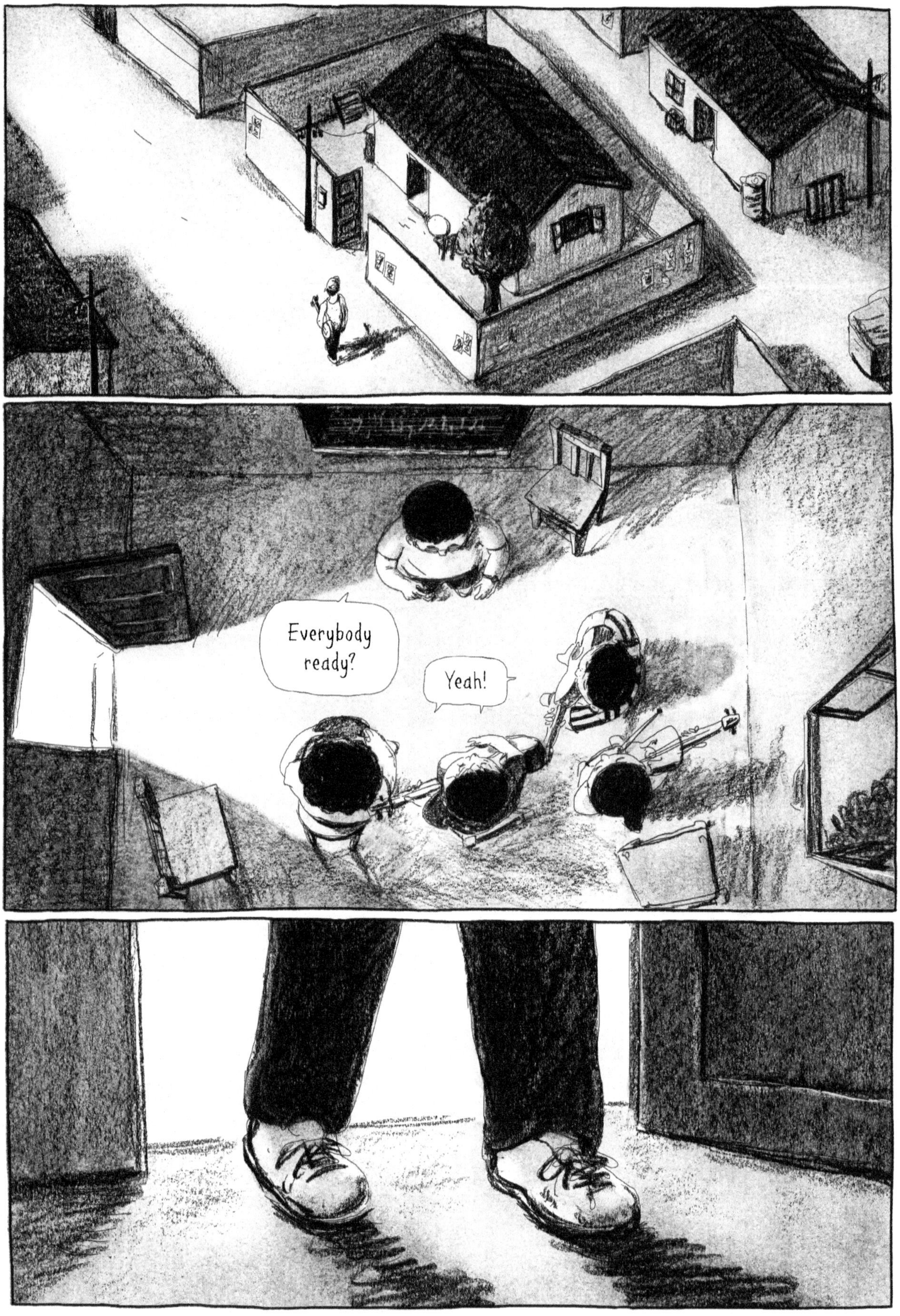
Everybody ready?
Yeah!

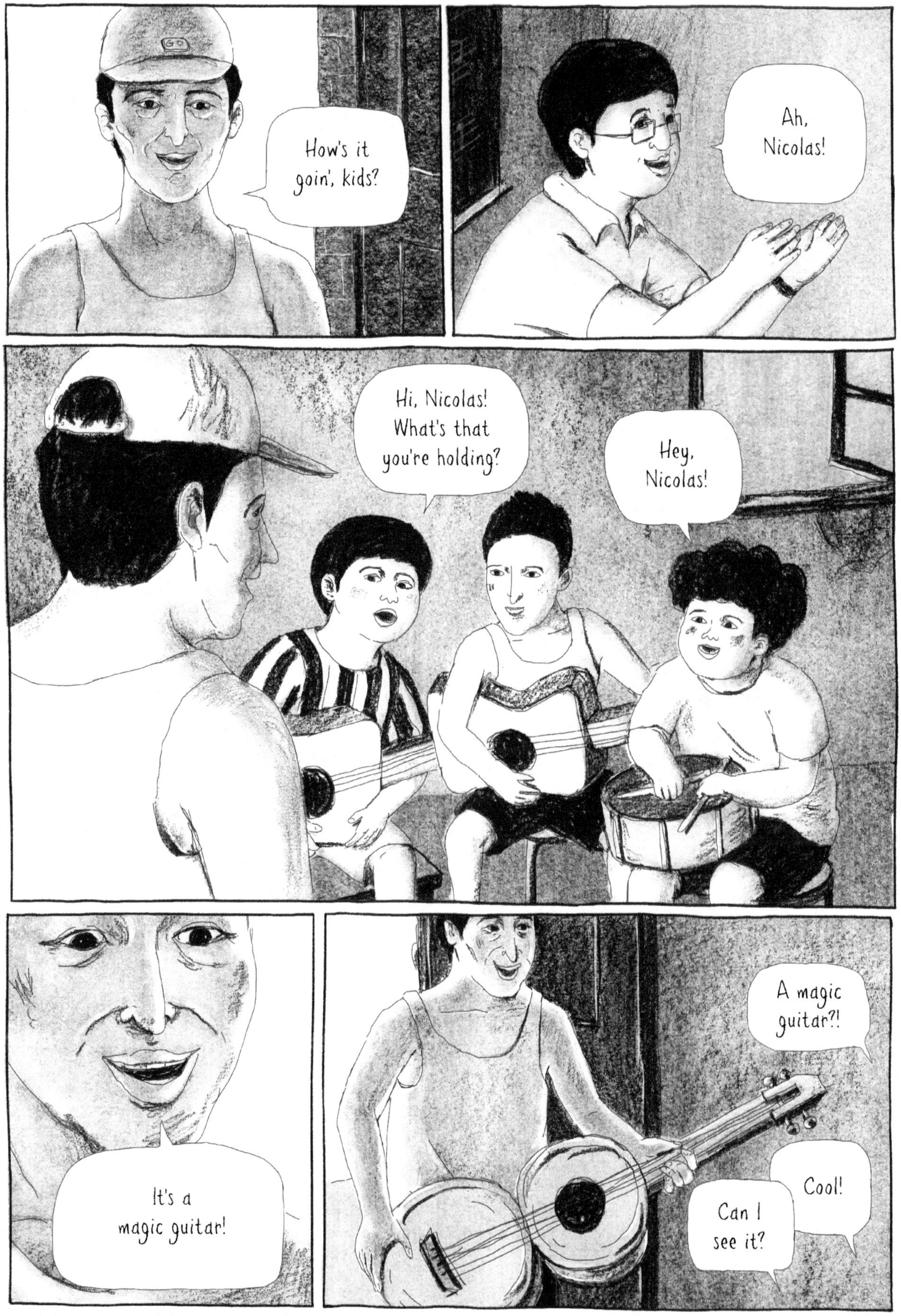
How's it goin', kids?
Ah, Nicolas!
Hi, Nicolas! What's that you're holding?
Hey, Nicolas!
It's a magic guitar!
A magic guitar?!
Cool!
Can I see it?

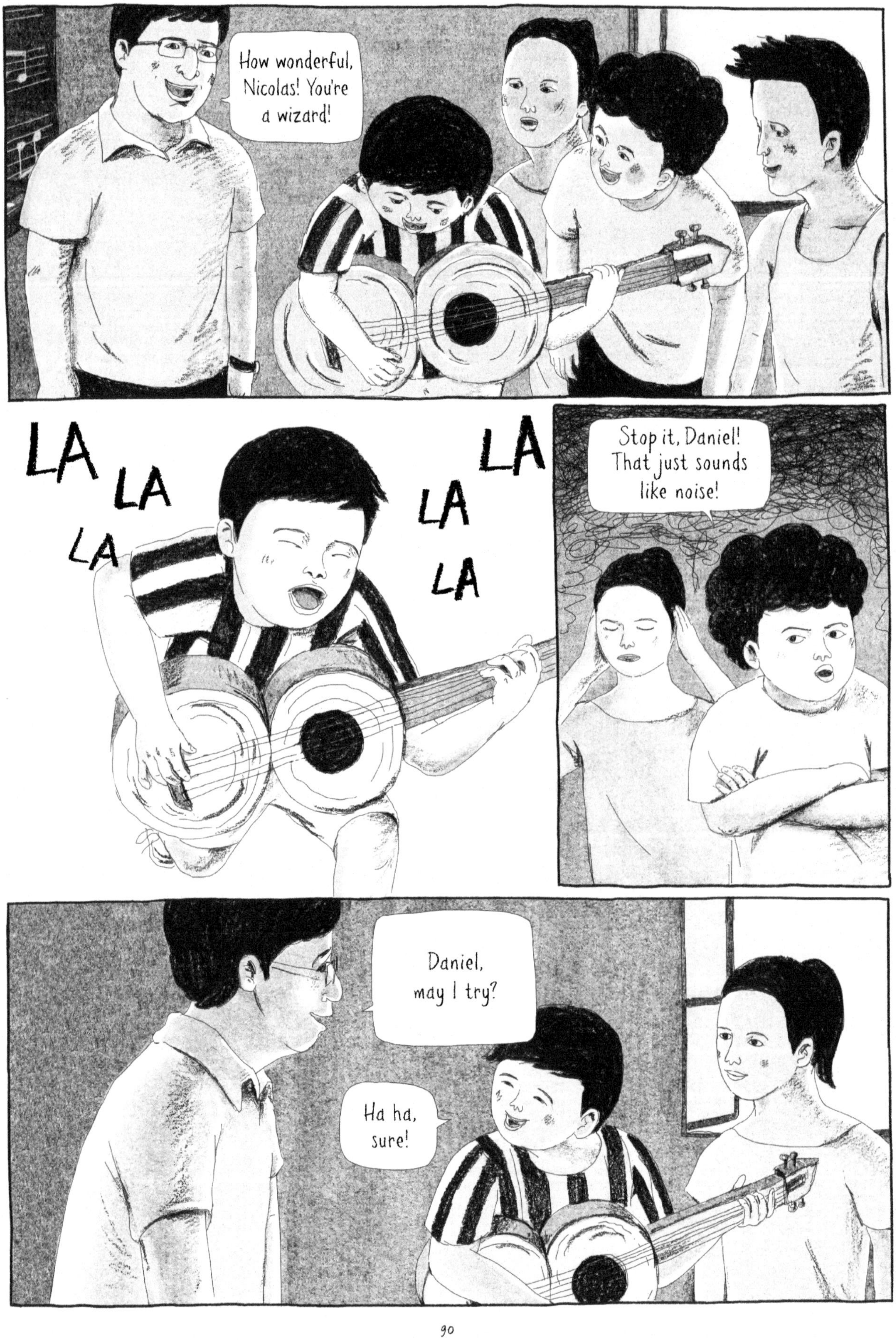
How wonderful, Nicolas! You're a wizard!
LA LA LA LA LA LA
Stop it, Daniel! That just sounds like noise!
Daniel, may I try?
Ha ha, sure!

What a pretty guitar!
STRUM
Wow, beautiful!
Can you make me one, Nicolas?

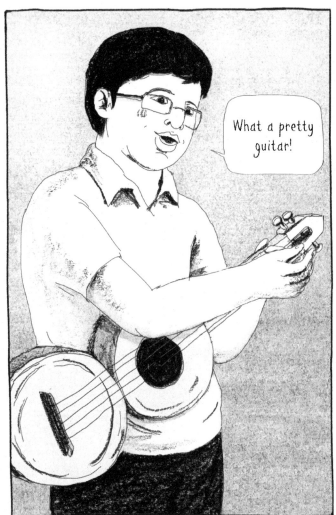

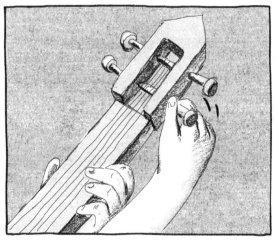

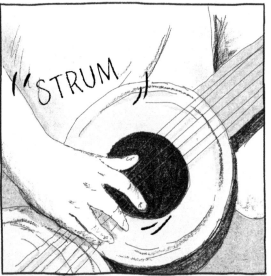

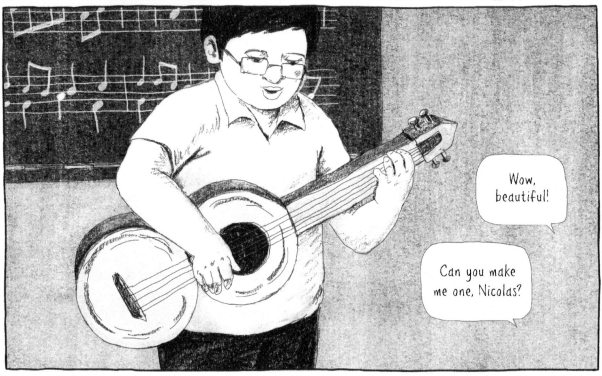

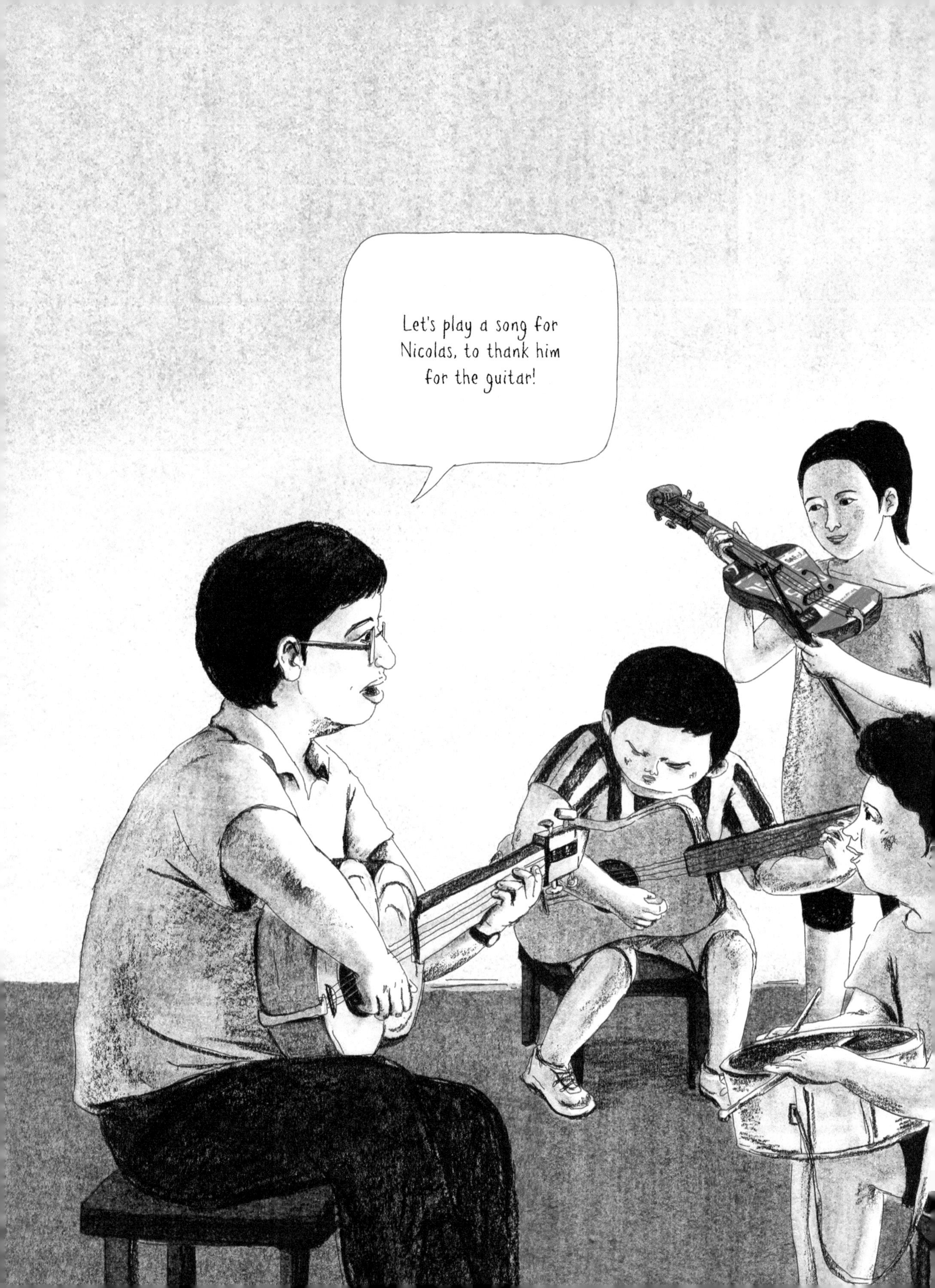
Let's play a song for Nicolas, to thank him for the guitar!

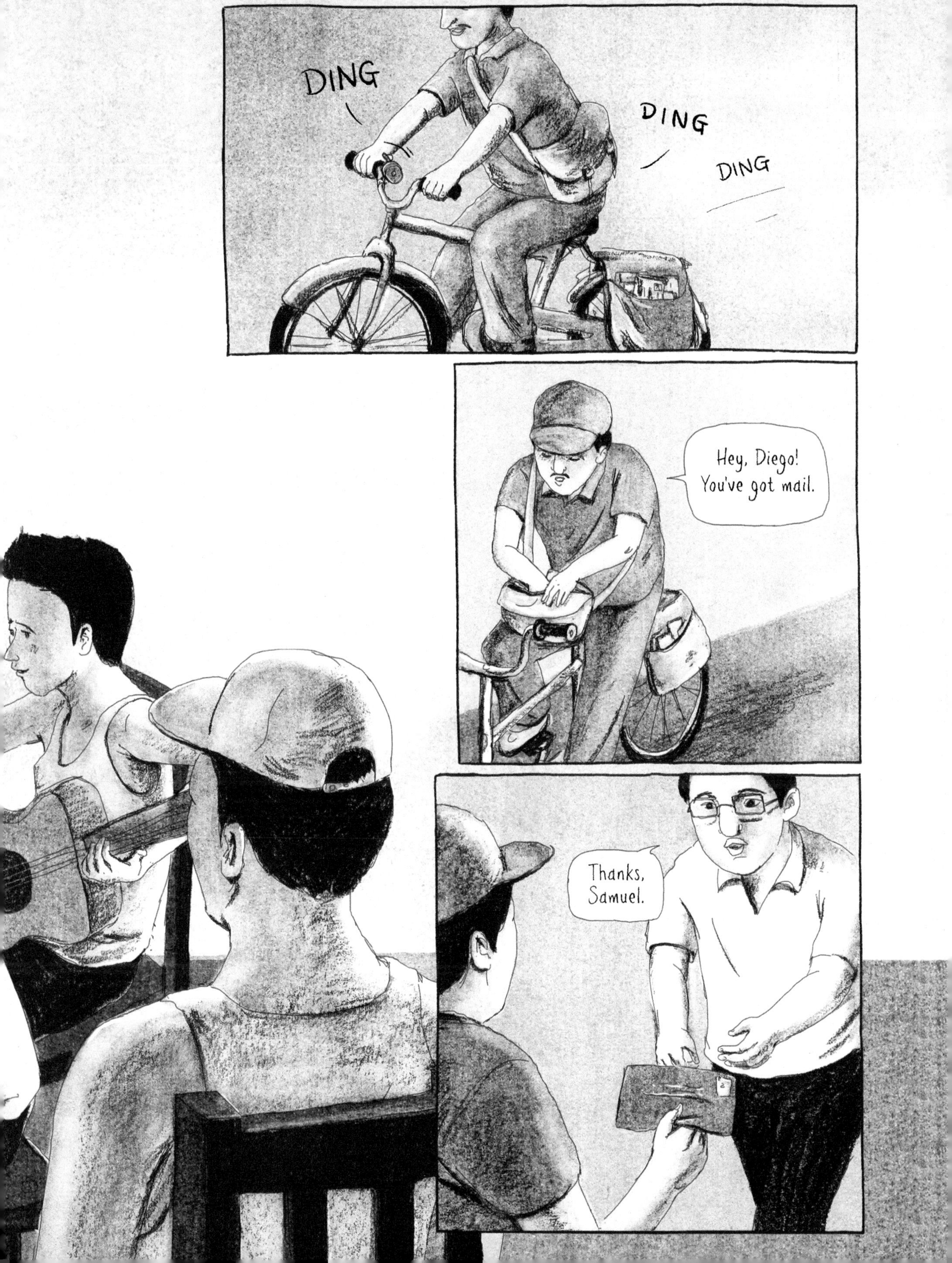
DING
DING
DING
Hey, Diego! You've got mail.
Thanks, Samuel.

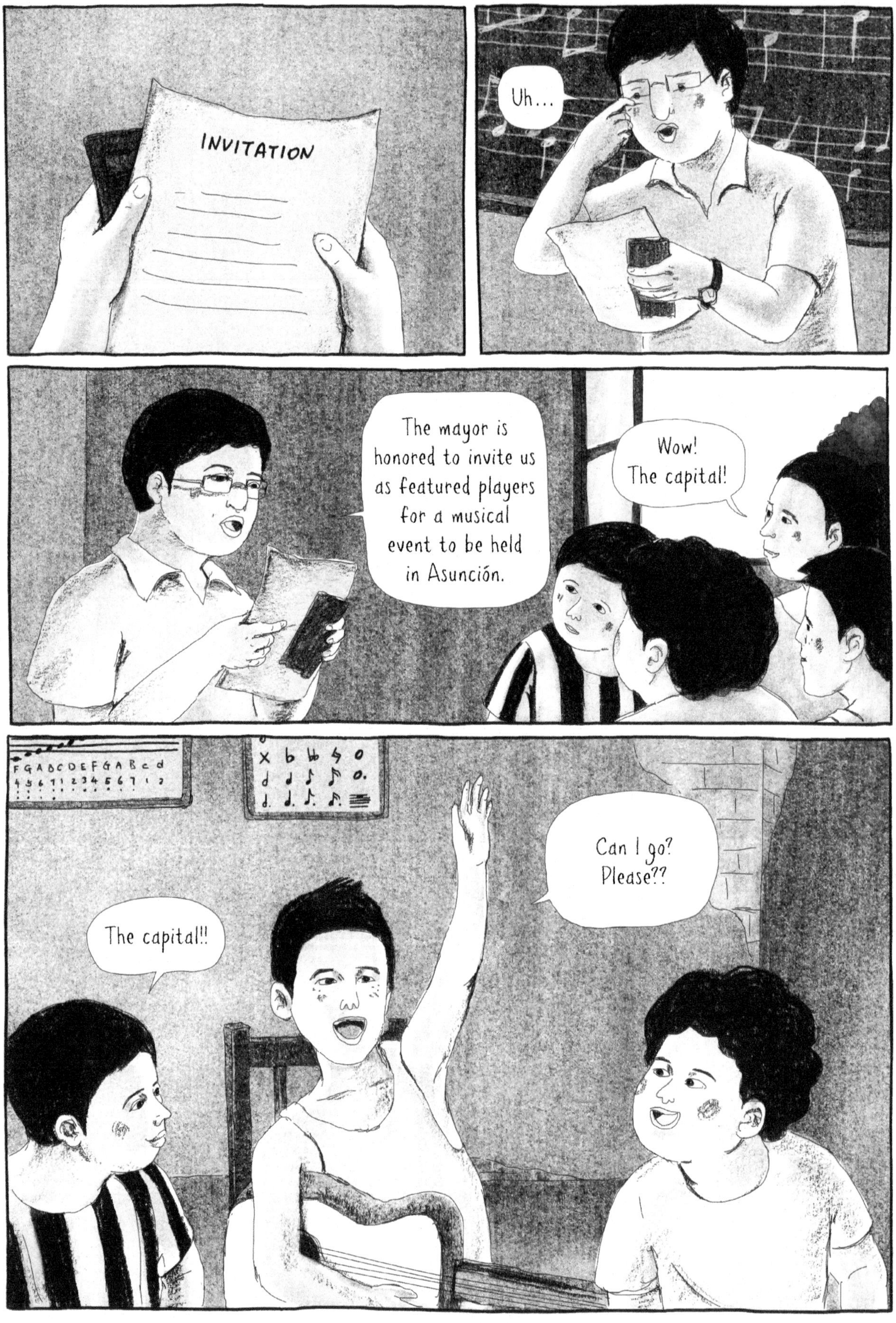
INVITATION
Uh...
The mayor is honored to invite us as featured players for a musical event to be held in Asunción.
Wow! The capital!
F G A B C D E F G A B c d
The capital!!
Can I go? Please??

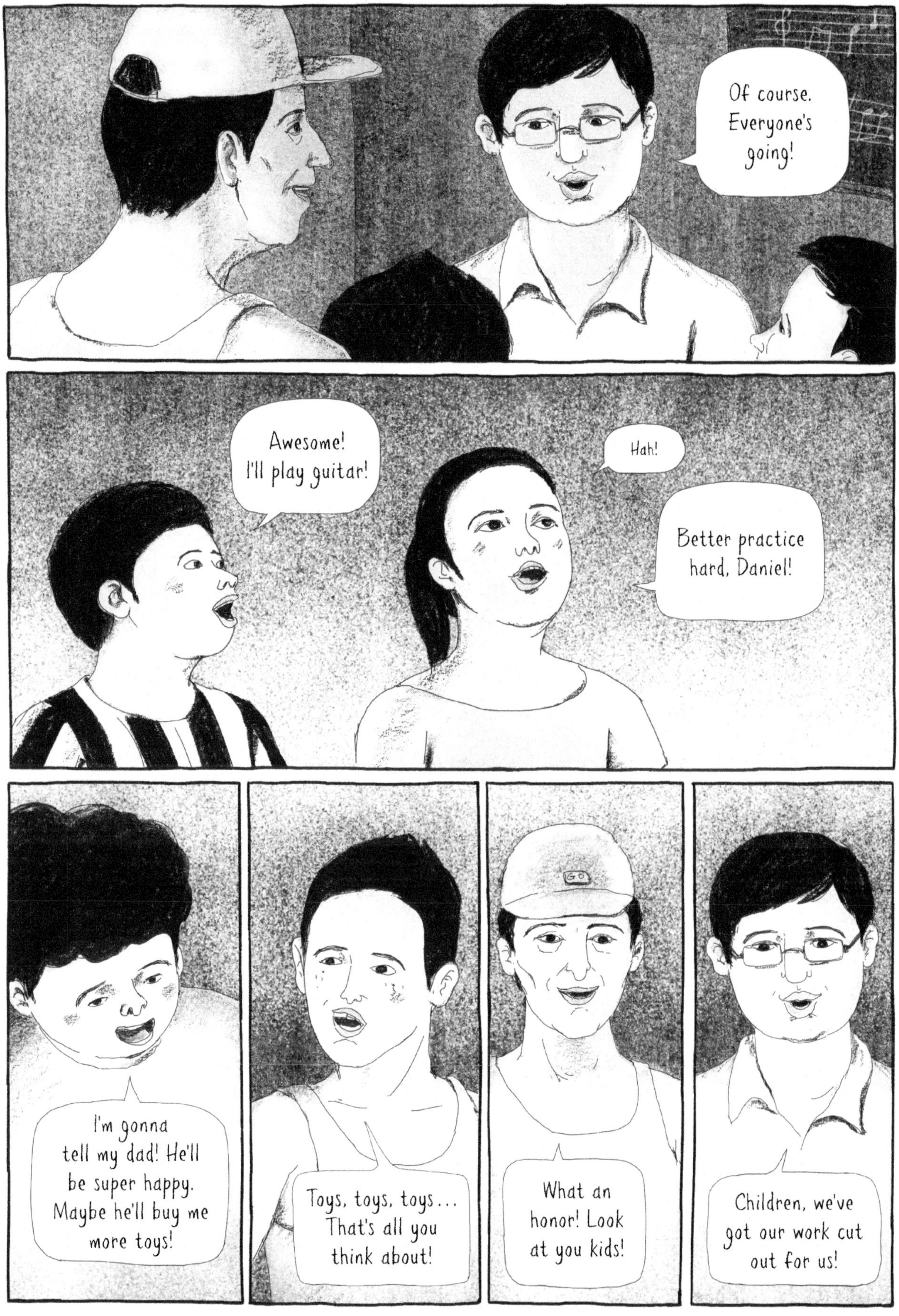
Of course. Everyone's going!
Awesome! I'll play guitar!
Hah!
Better practice hard, Daniel!
I'm gonna tell my dad! He'll be super happy. Maybe he'll buy me more toys!
Toys, toys, toys... That's all you think about!
What an honor! Look at you kids!
Children, we've got our work cut out for us!

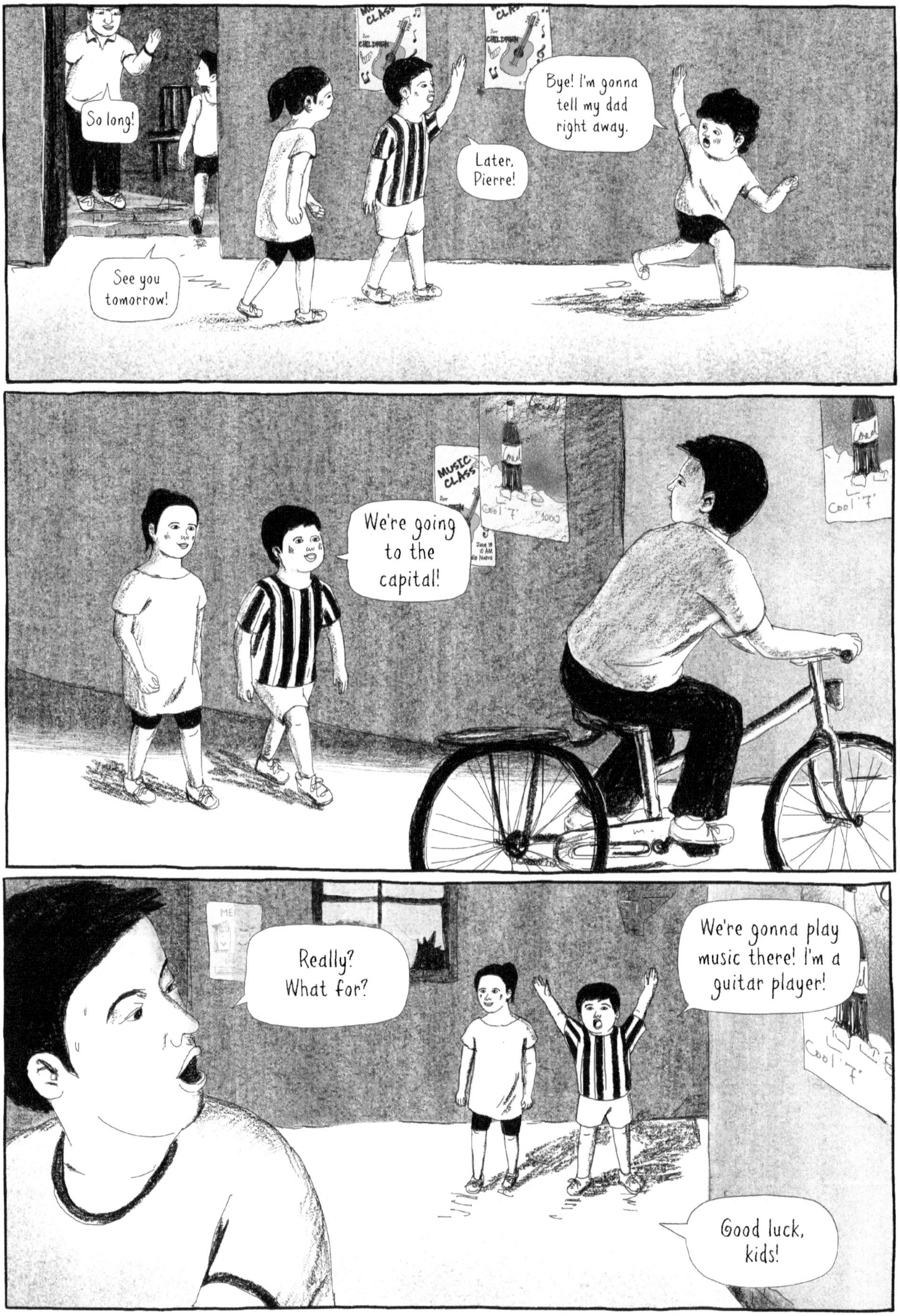
MUSIC CLASS
CHILDREN
So long!
See you tomorrow!
Later, Pierre!
Bye! I'm gonna tell my dad right away.
MUSIC CLASS
We're going to the capital!
Cool 'F'
Really? What for?
We're gonna play music there! I'm a guitar player!
Good luck, kids!

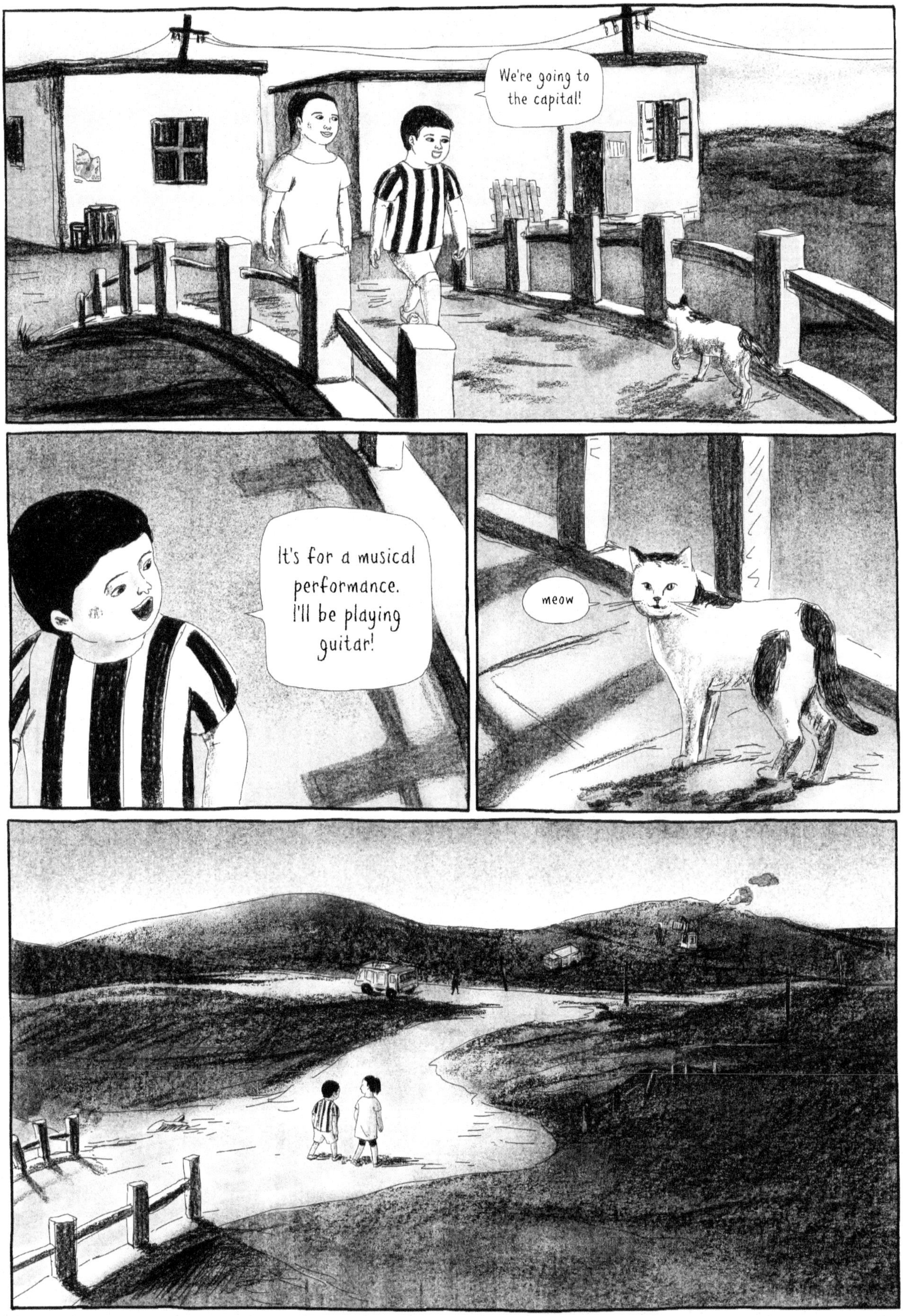
We're going to the capital!
It's for a musical performance. I'll be playing guitar!
meow

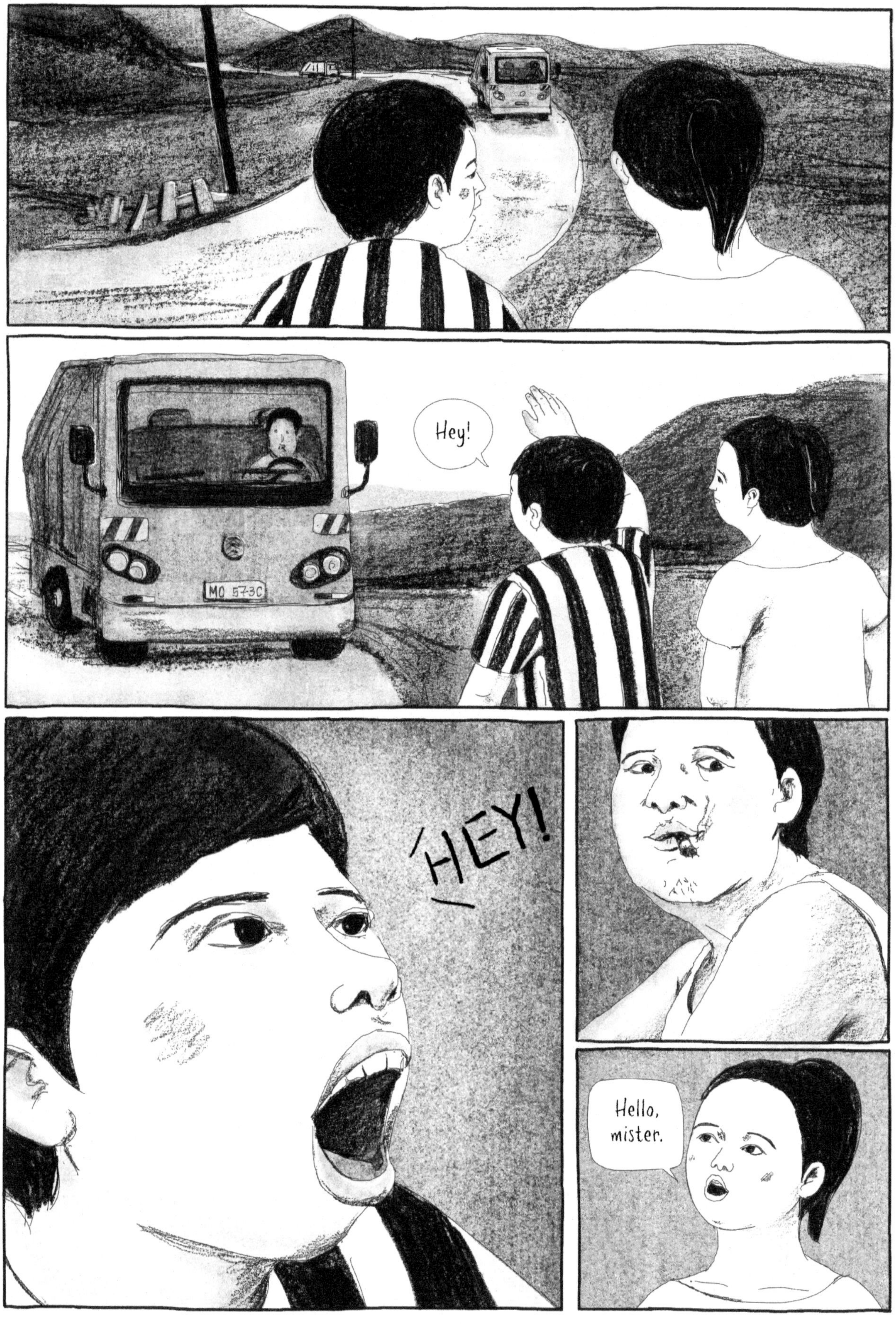
MO 573C
Hey!
HEY!
Hello, mister.

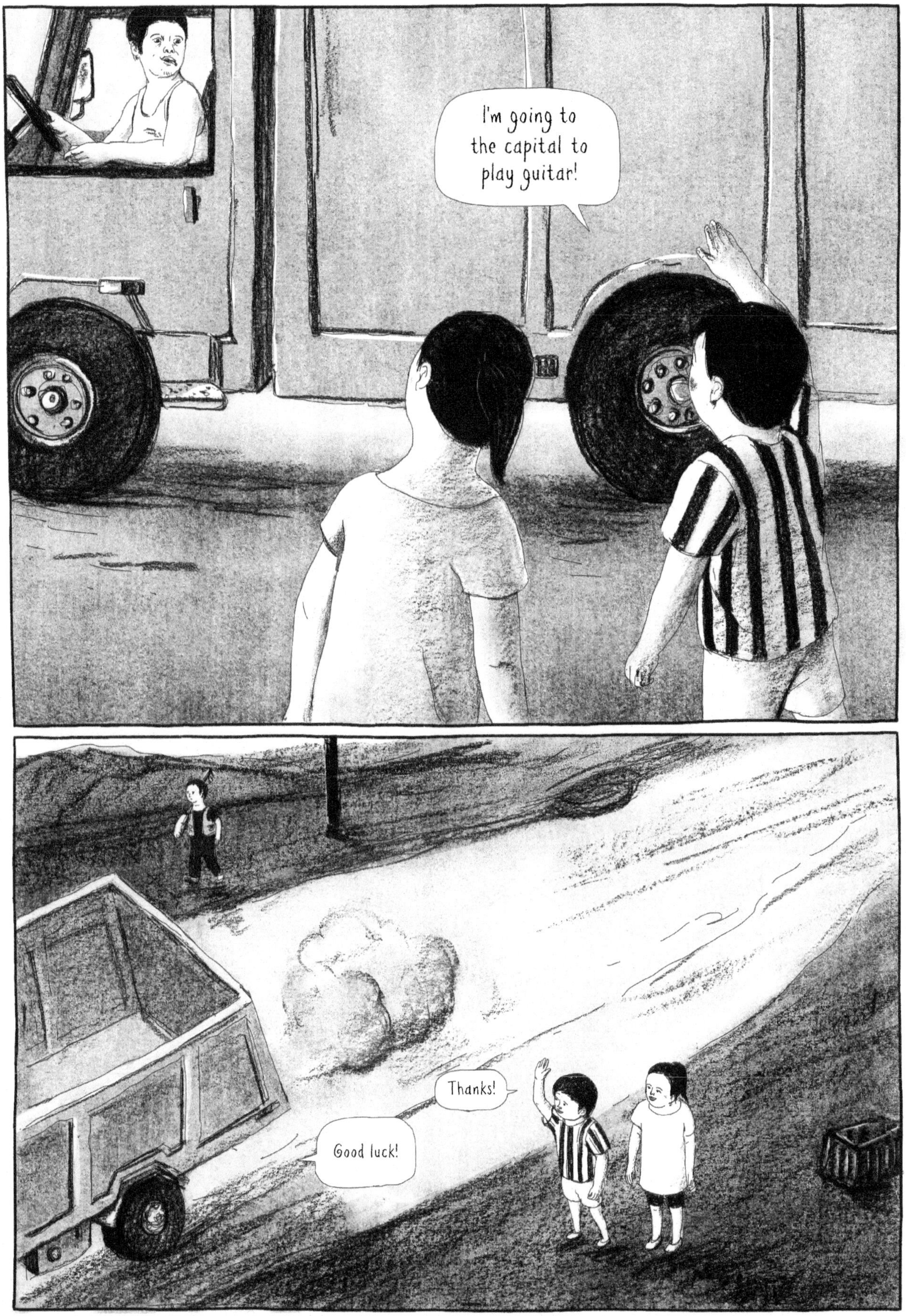
I'm going to the capital to play guitar!
Thanks!
Good luck!

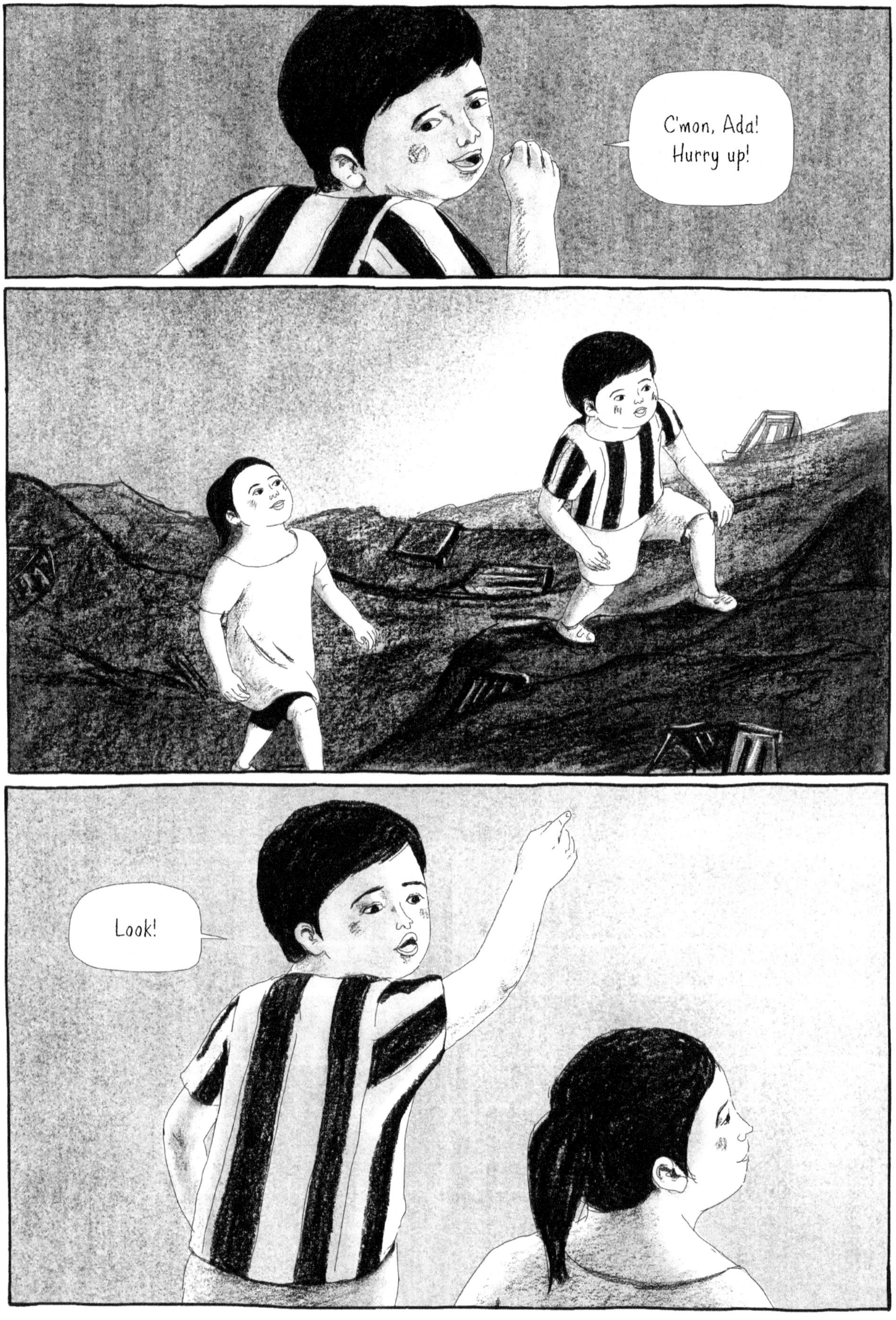
C'mon, Ada! Hurry up!
Look!

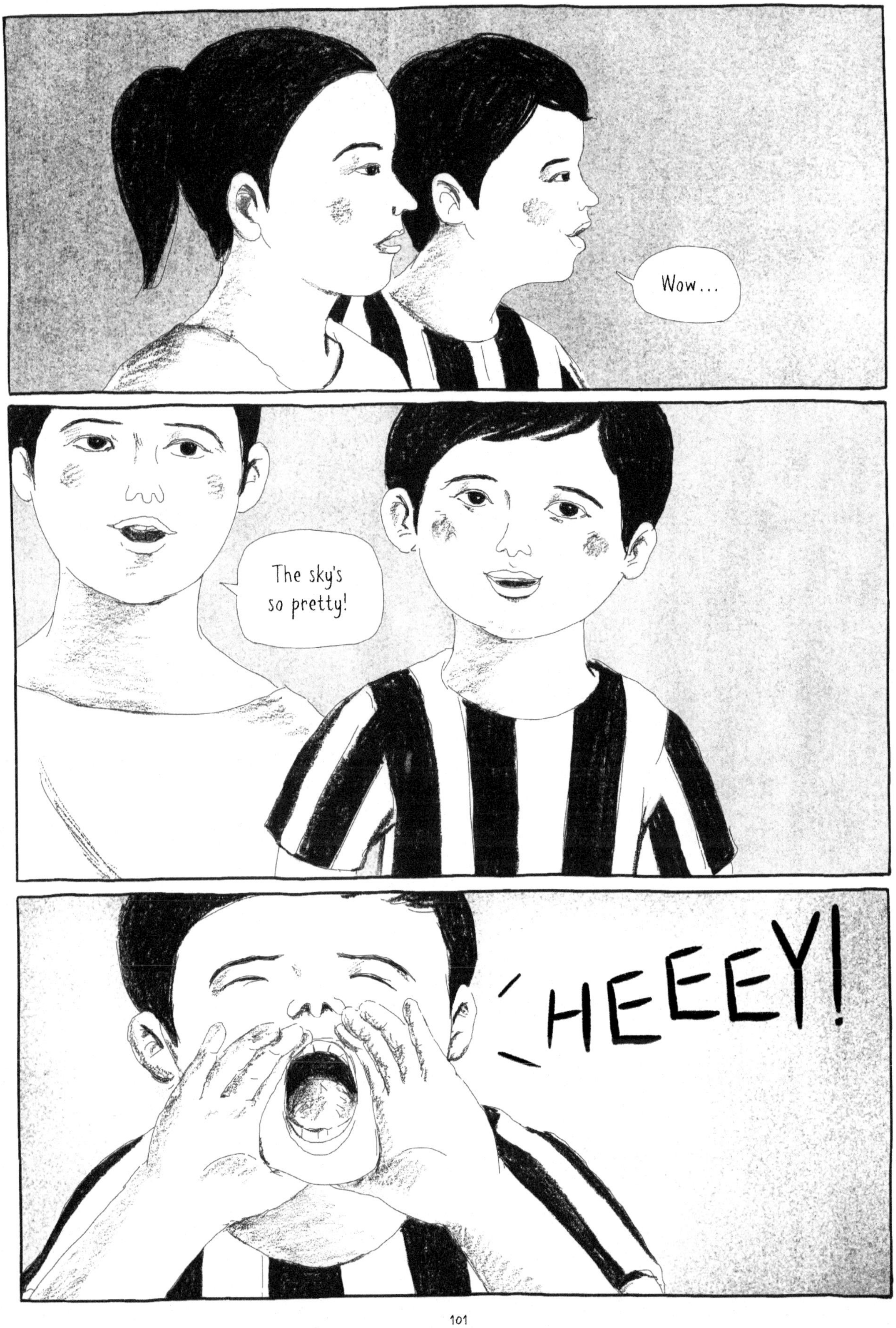
Wow...
The sky's so pretty!
HEEEY!

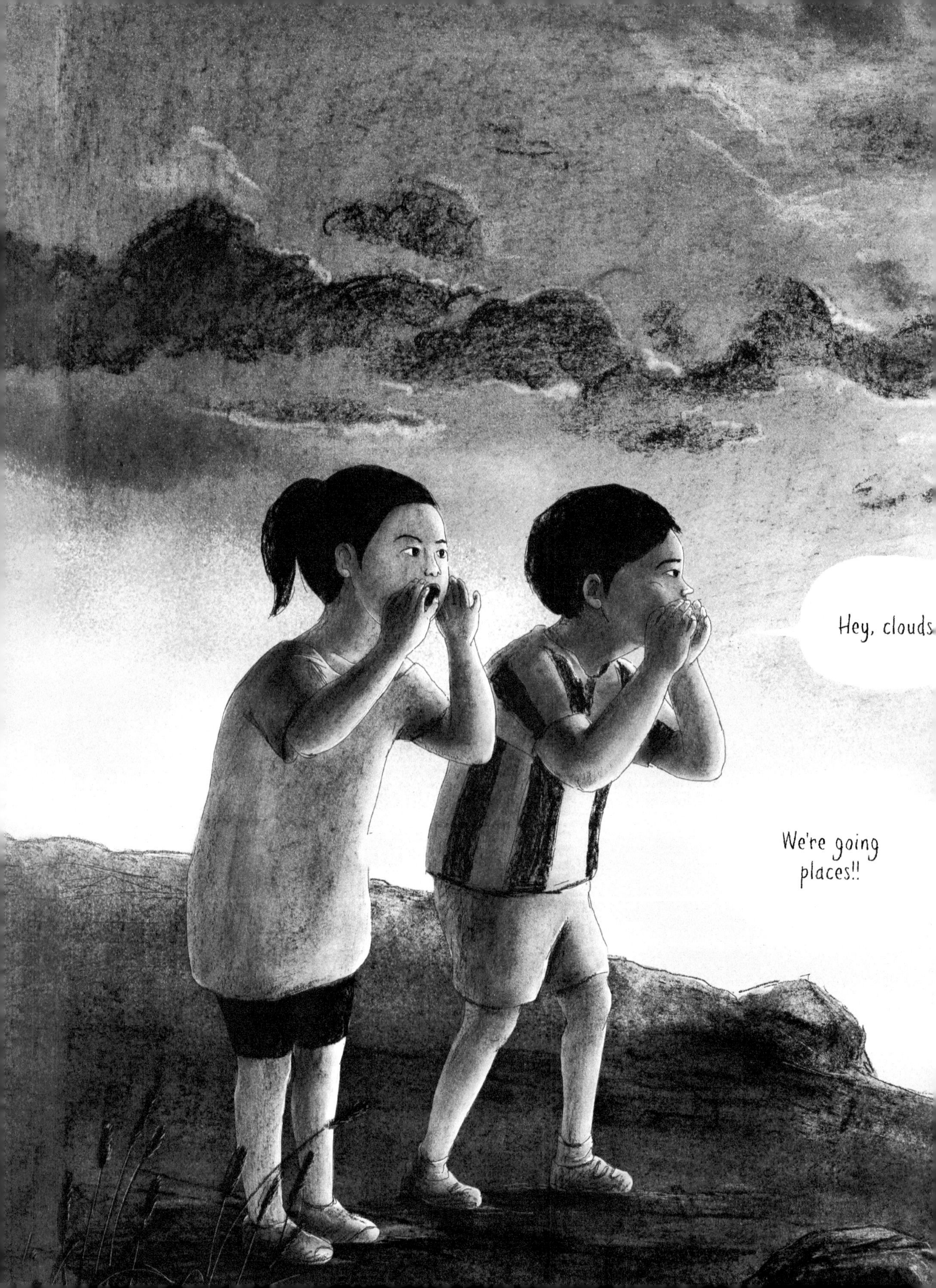
Hey, clouds
We're going places!!

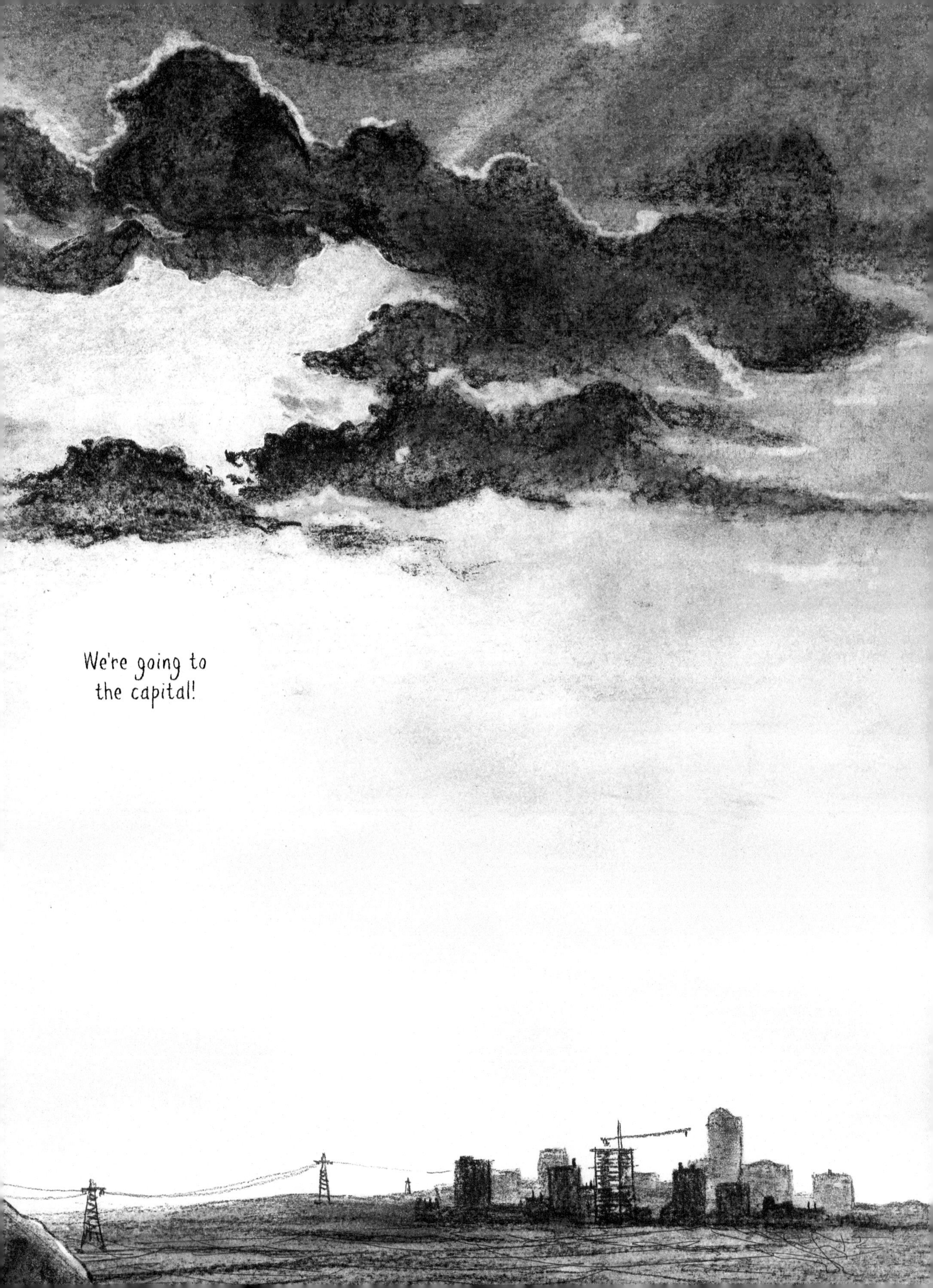
We're going to the capital!

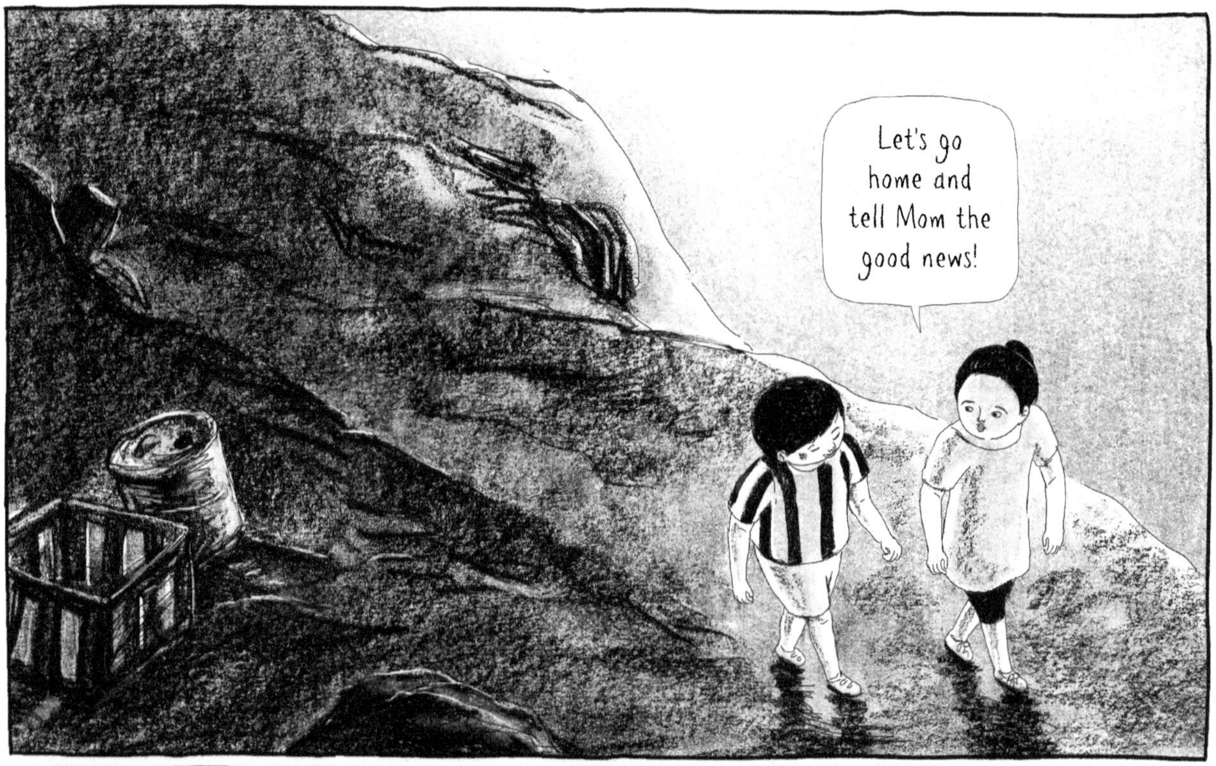
Let's go home and tell Mom the good news!

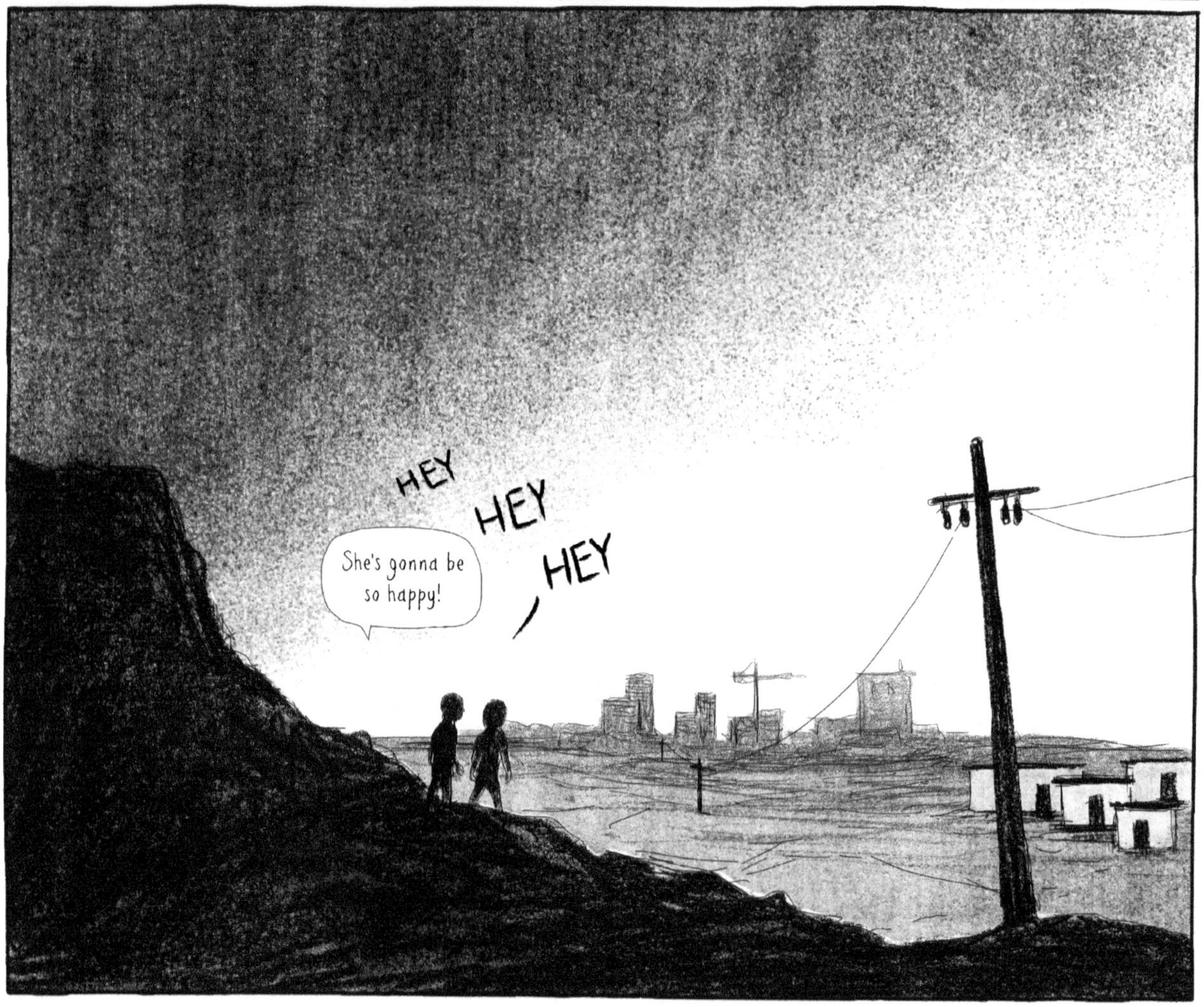
She's gonna be so happy!
HEY
HEY
HEY

7

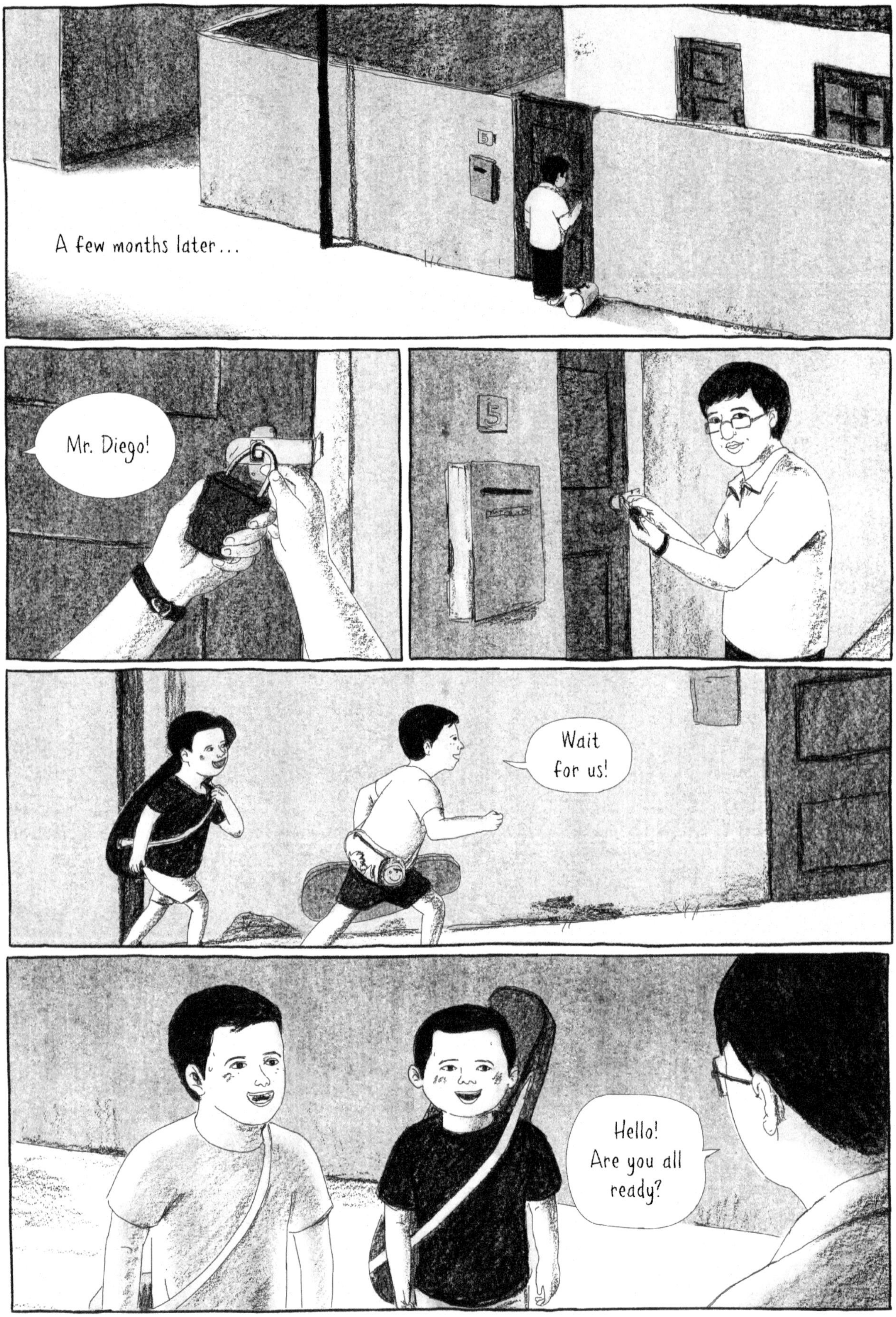
A few months later...
Mr. Diego!
Wait for us!
Hello! Are you all ready?

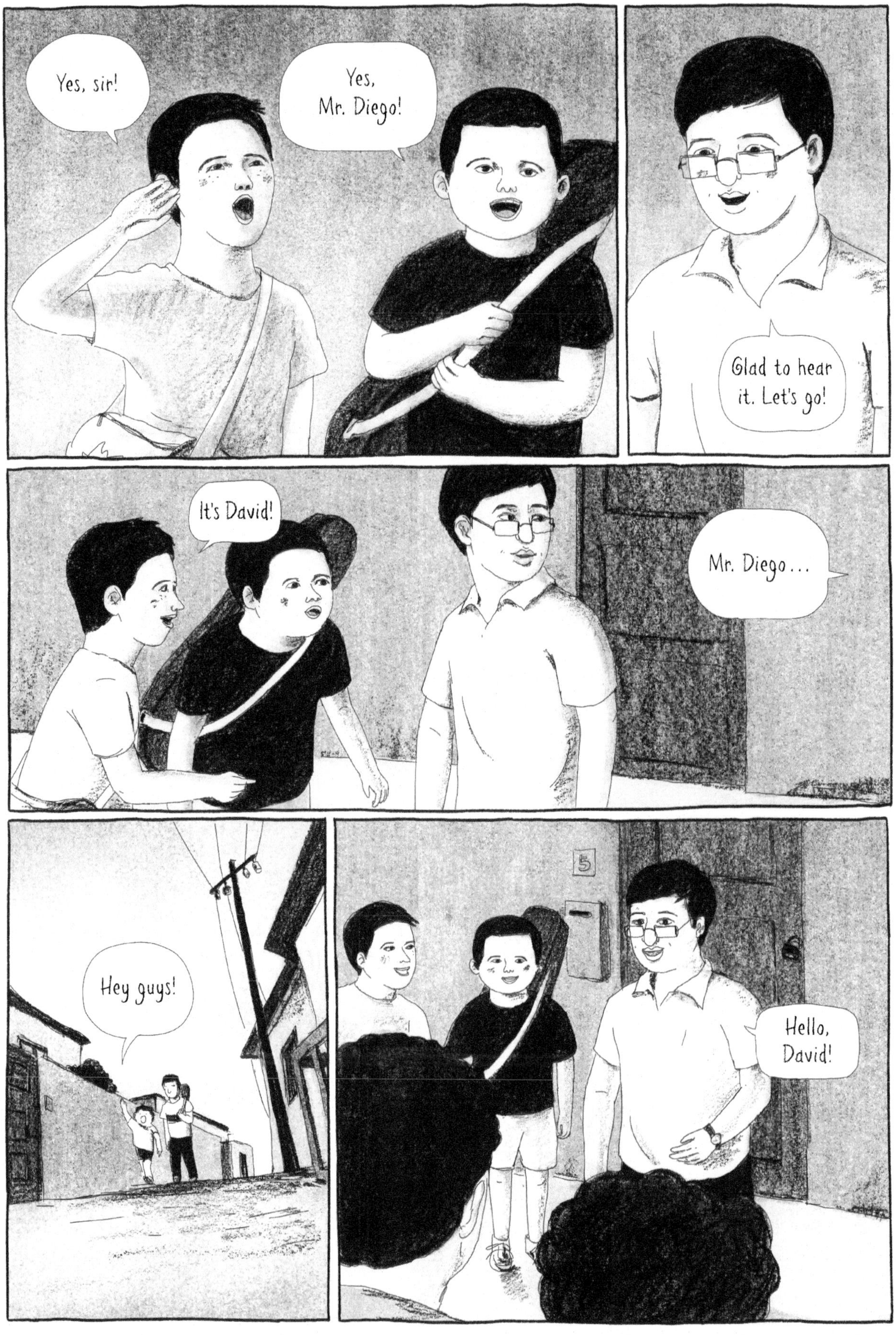
Yes, sir!
Yes, Mr. Diego!
Glad to hear it. Let's go!
It's David!
Mr. Diego...
Hey guys!
Hello, David!

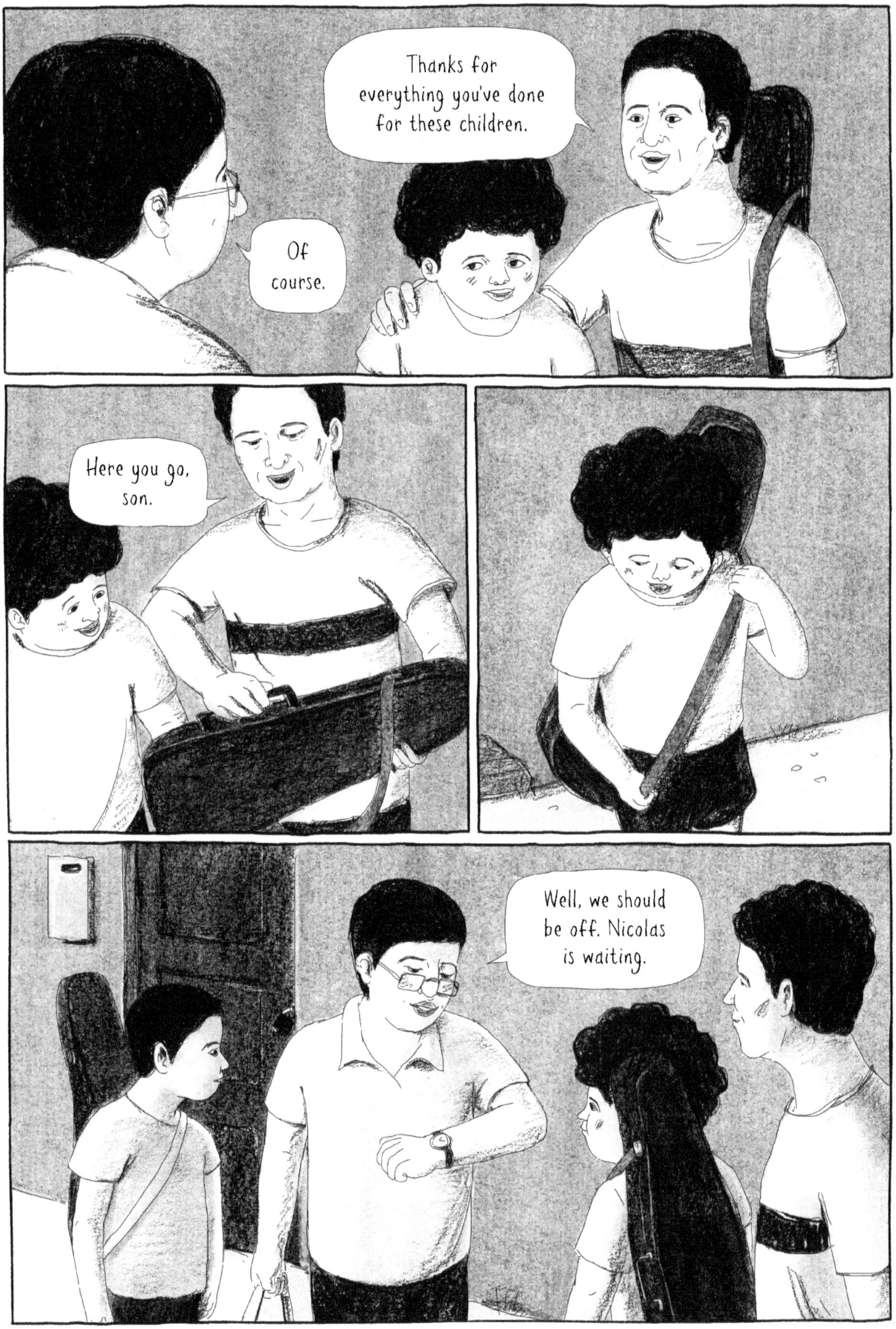
Thanks for everything you've done for these children.
Of course.
Here you go, son.
Well, we should be off. Nicolas is waiting.

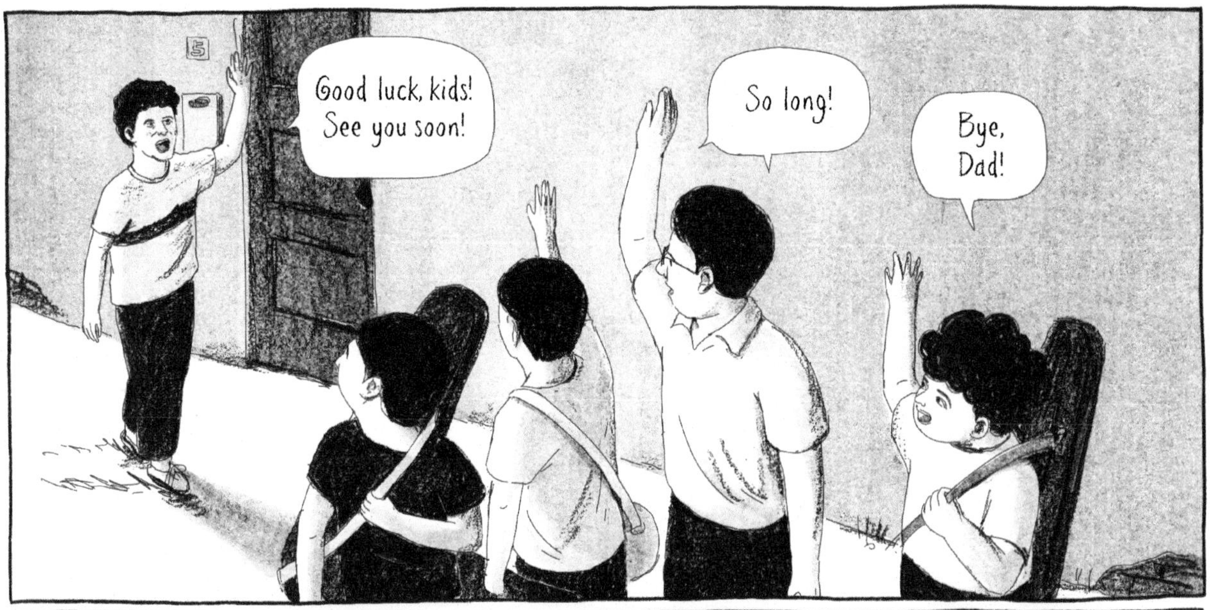
Good luck, kids! See you soon!
So long!
Bye, Dad!

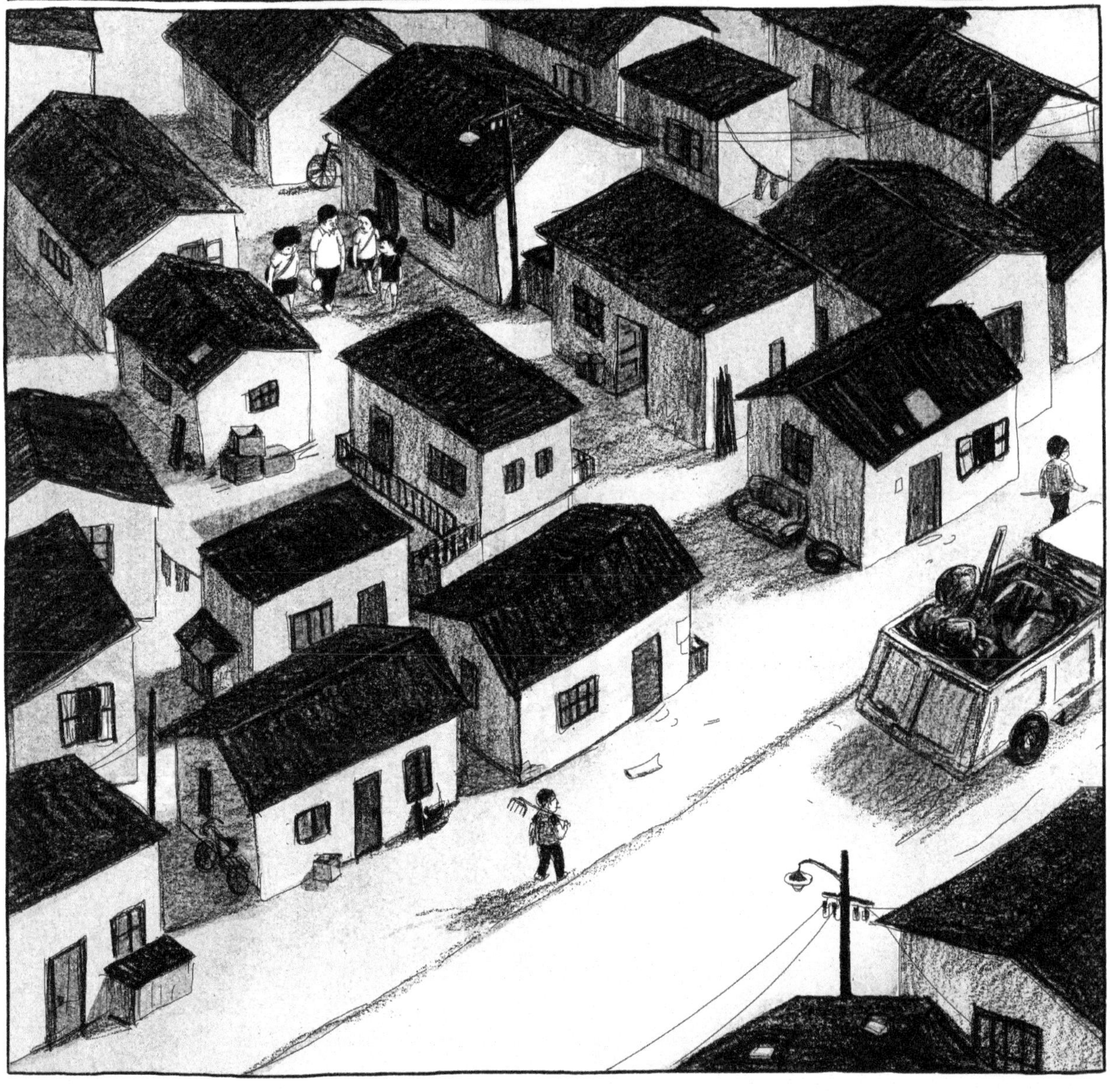

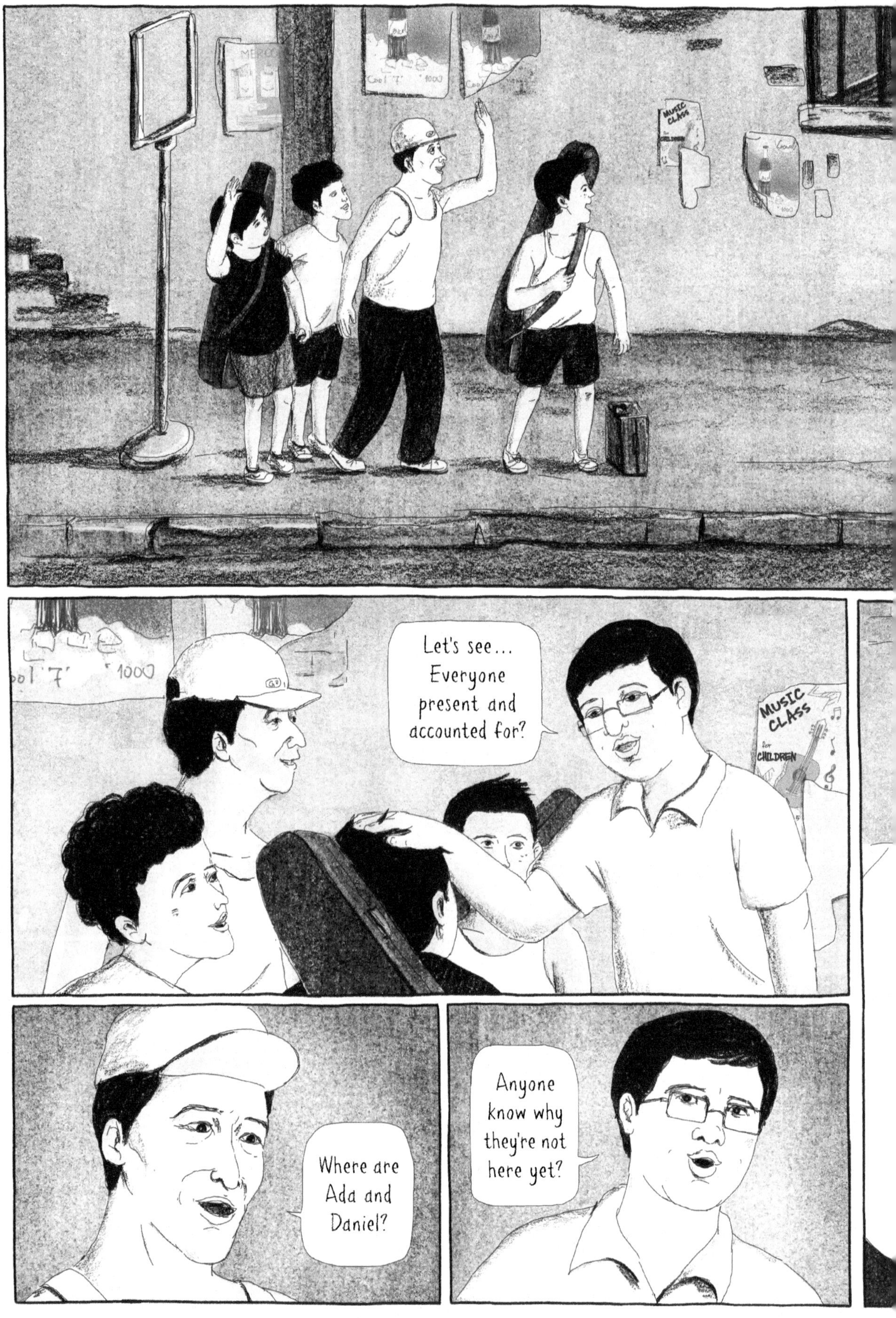
Cool '7' 1000
MUSIC CLASS for CHILDREN
Let's see... Everyone present and accounted for?
Where are Ada and Daniel?
Anyone know why they're not here yet?

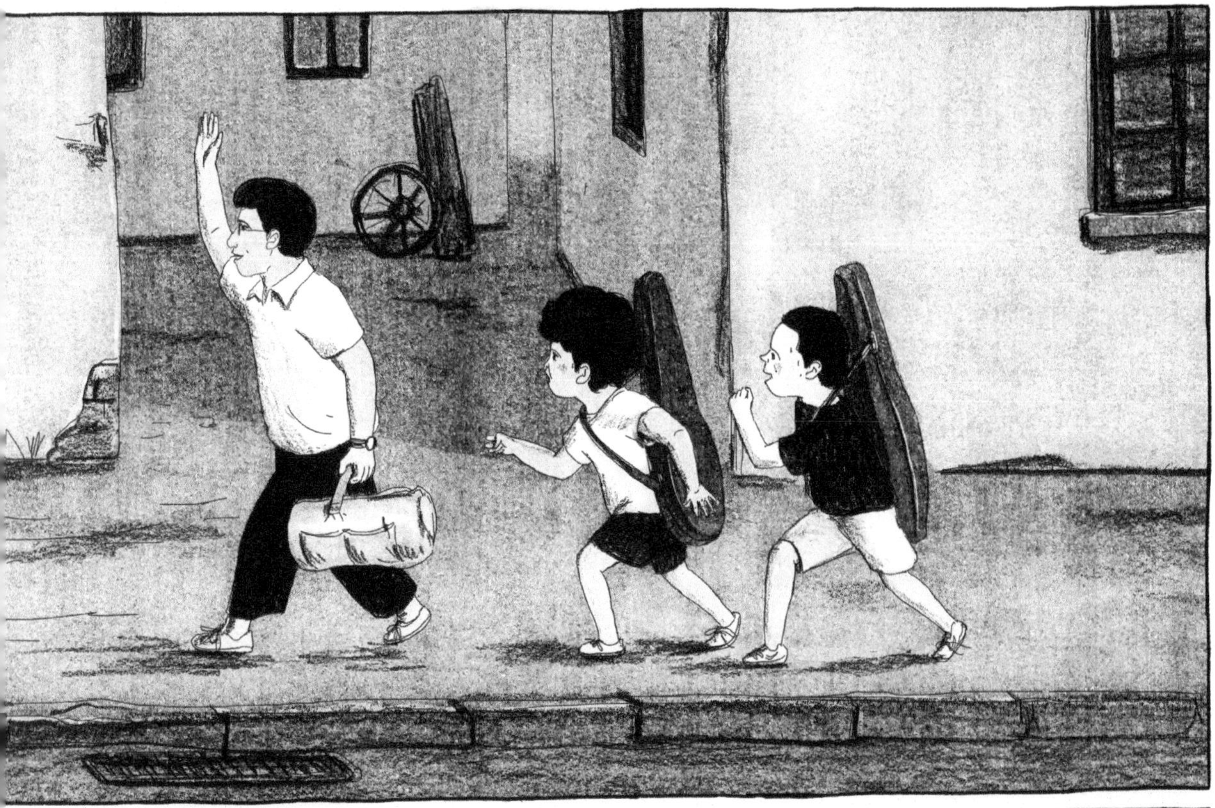

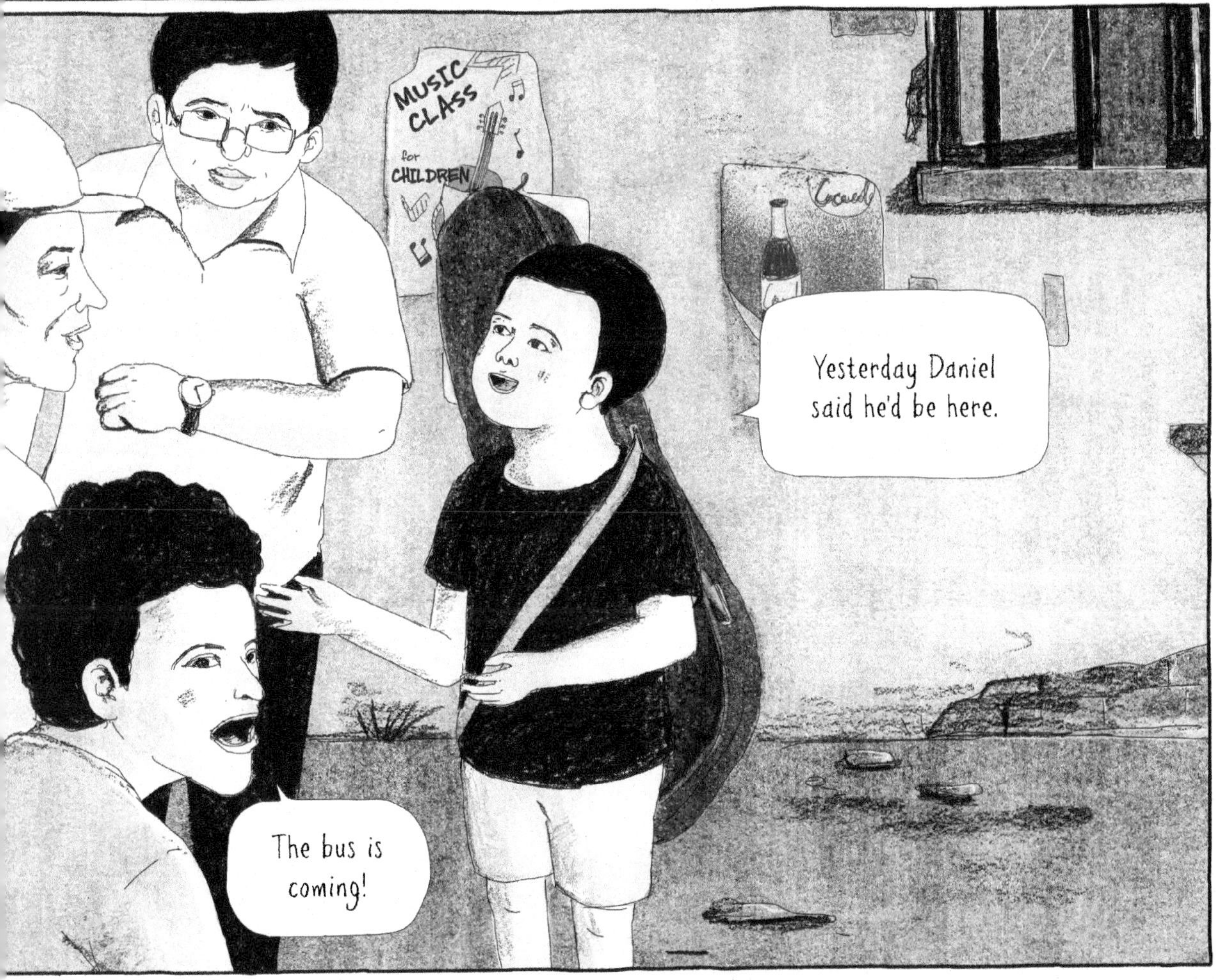

MUSIC CLASS for CHILDREN
Yesterday Daniel said he'd be here.
The bus is coming!

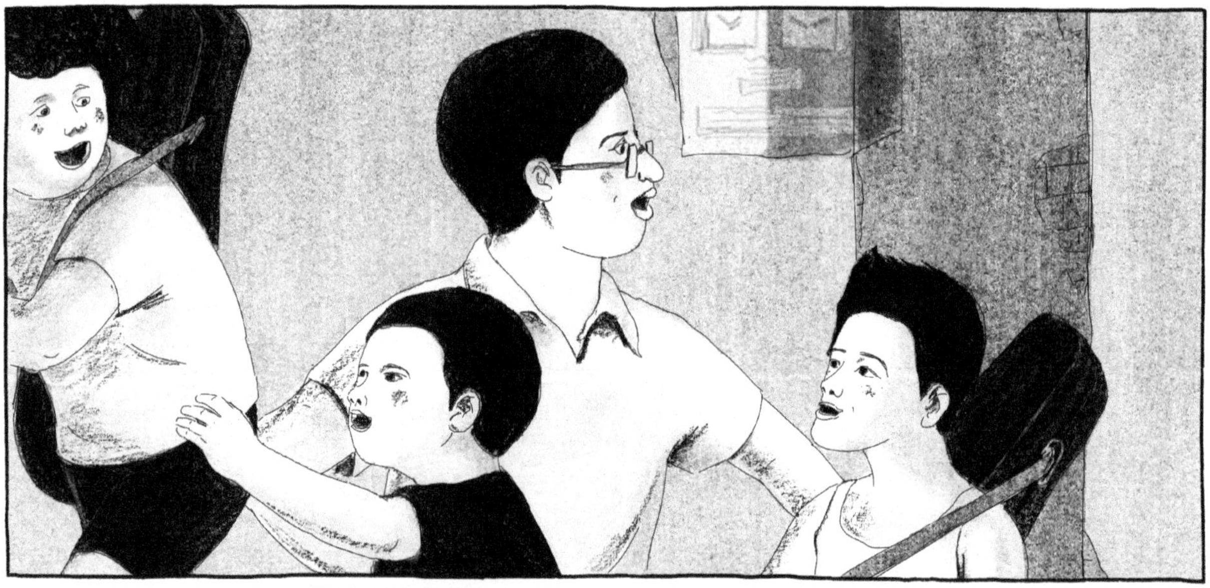

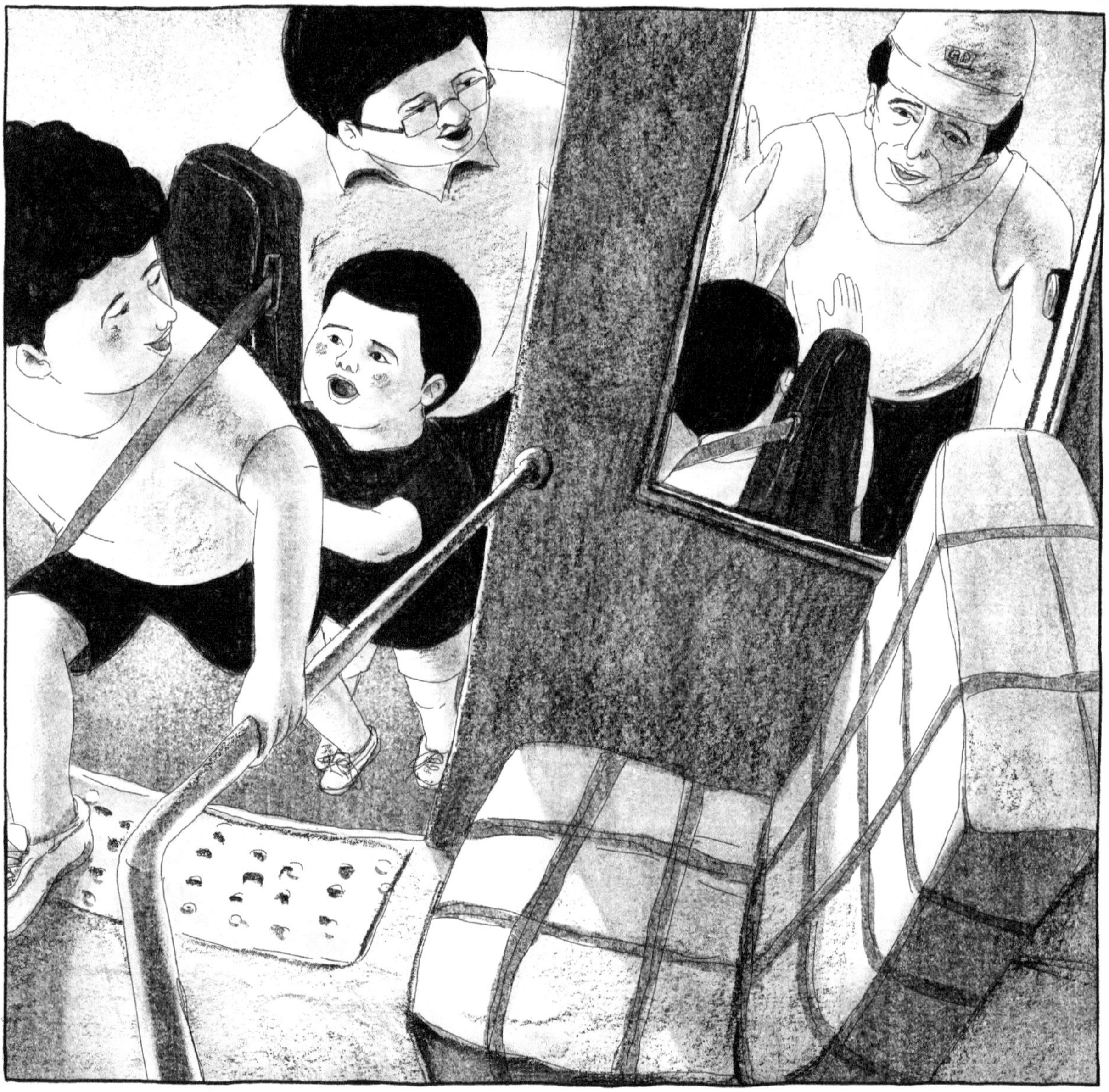

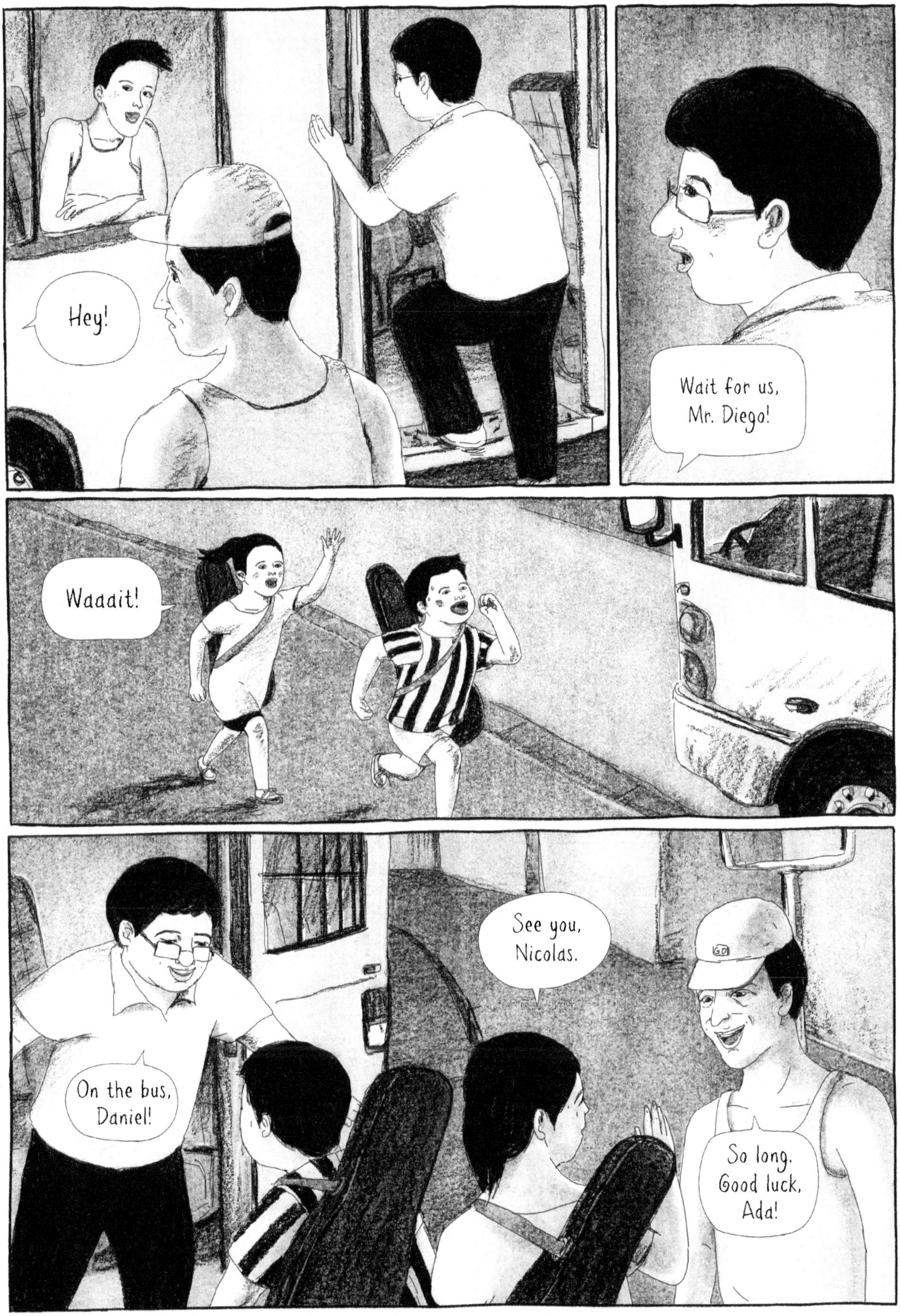

Hey!
Wait for us, Mr. Diego!
Waaait!
See you, Nicolas.
On the bus, Daniel!
So long. Good luck, Ada!

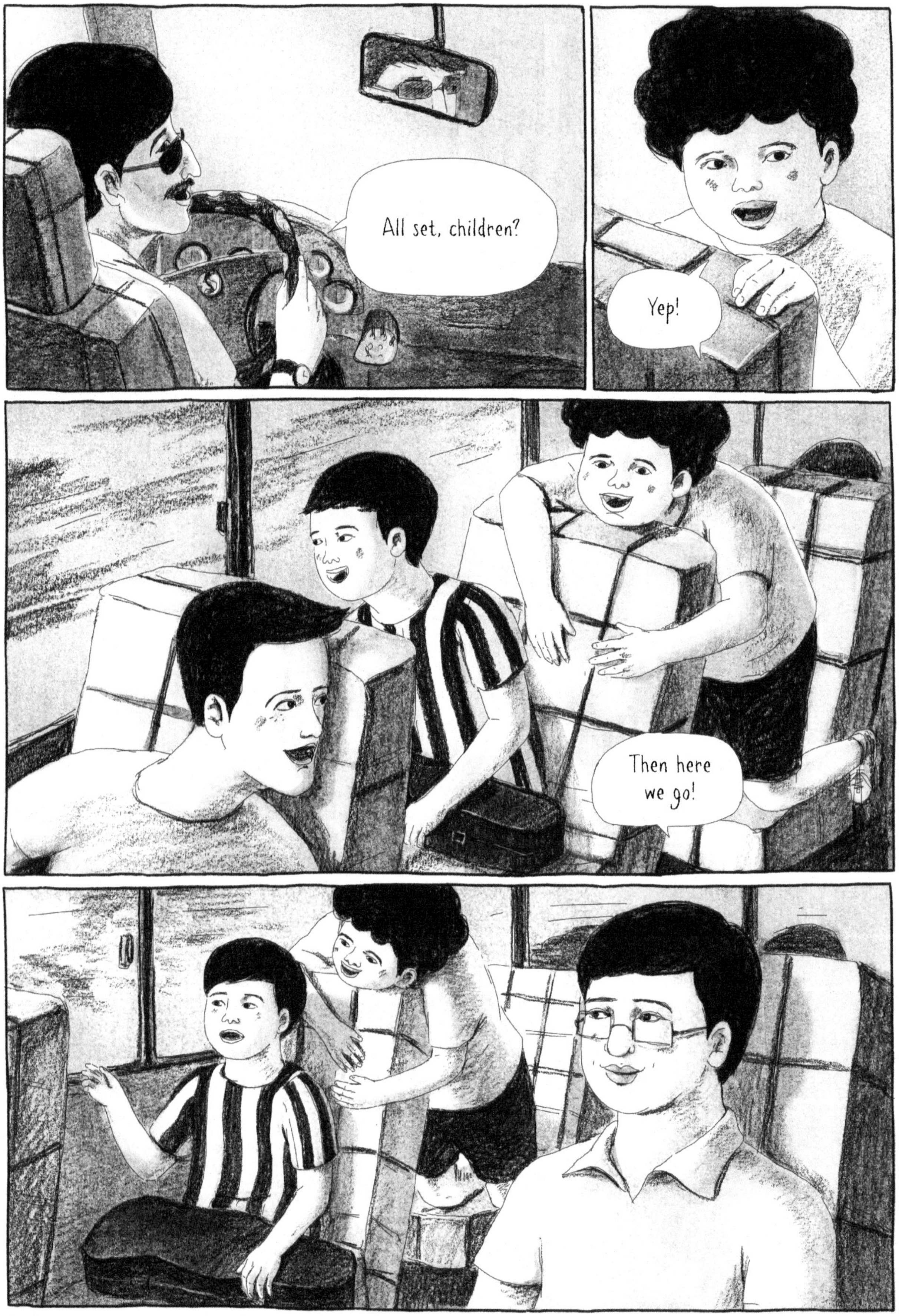
All set, children?
Yep!
Then here we go!

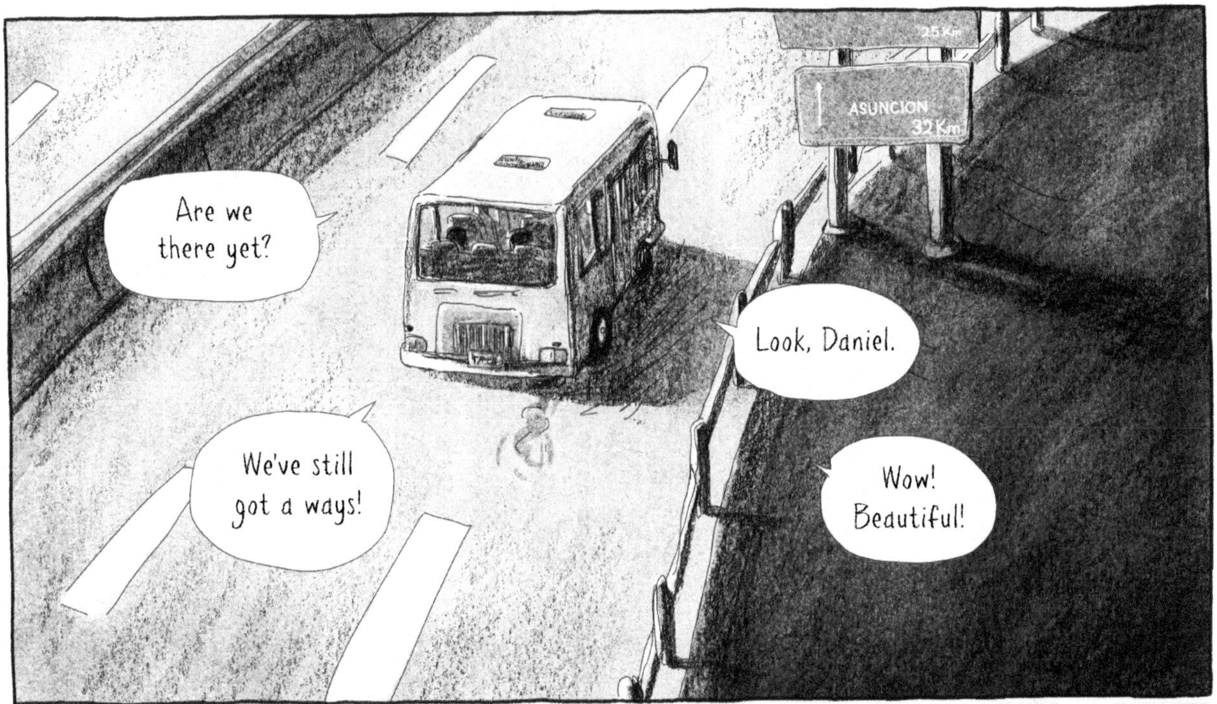
25 Km
ASUNCION
32 Km
Are we there yet?
Look, Daniel.
We've still got a ways!
Wow! Beautiful!

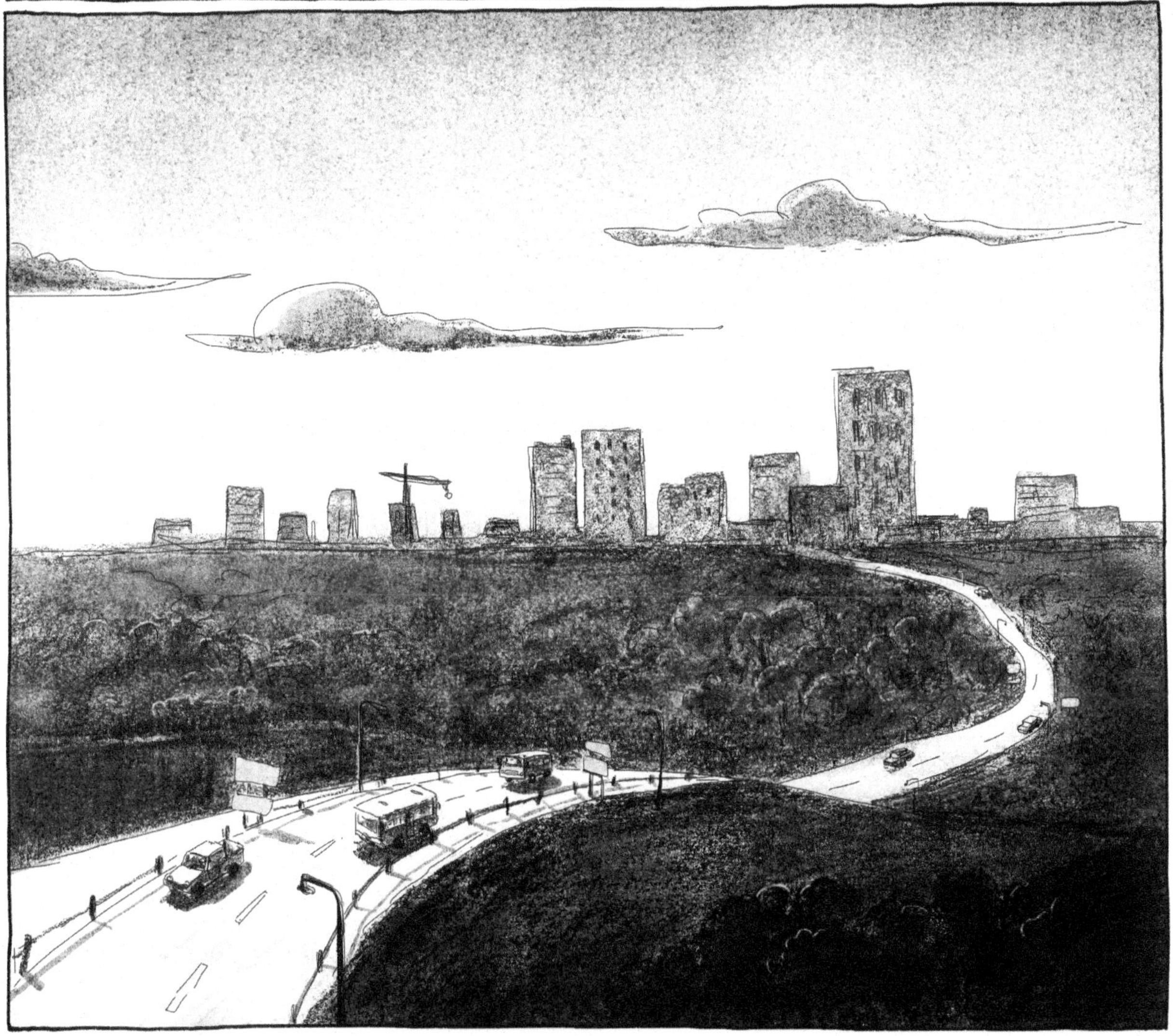

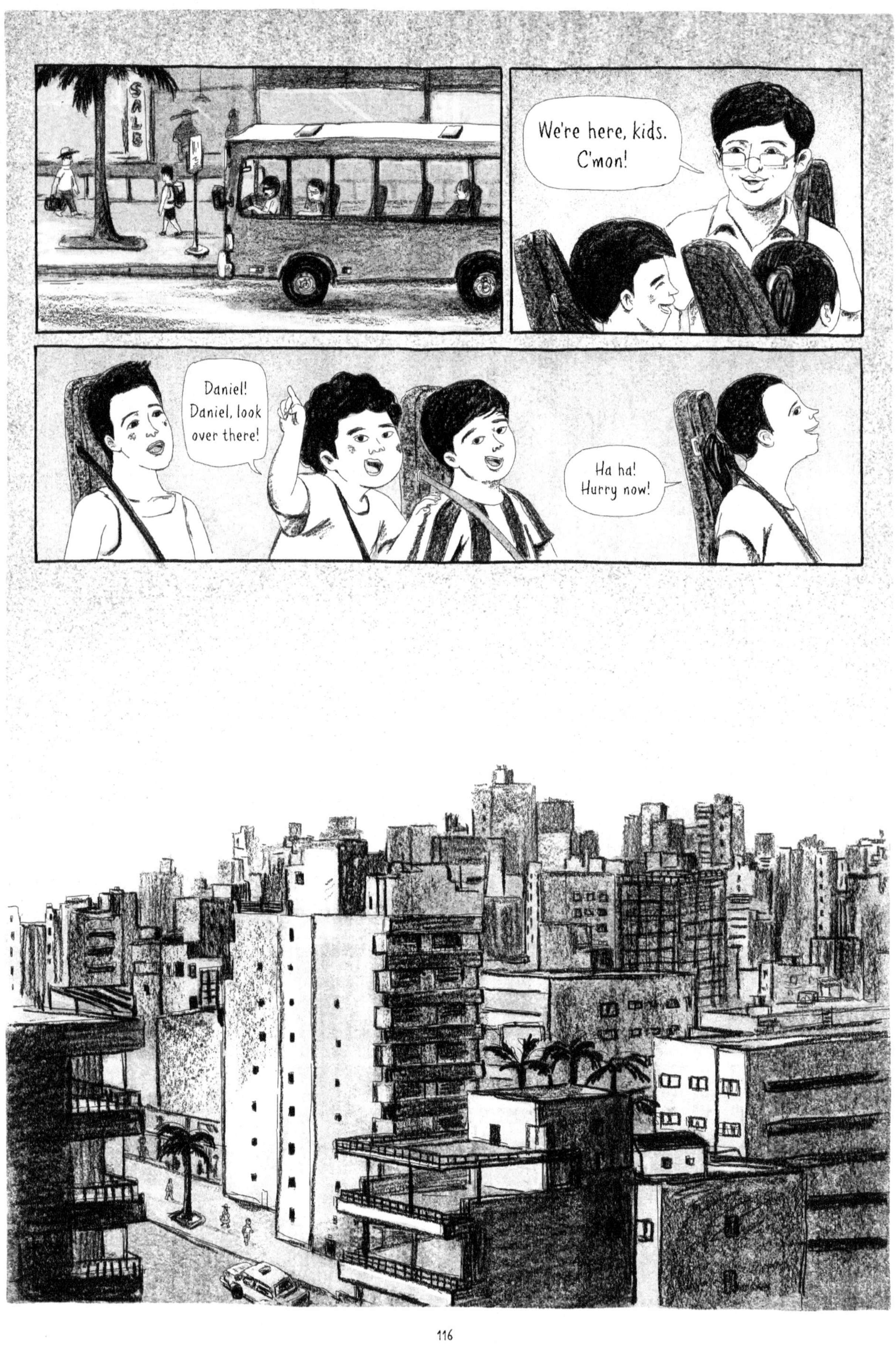
SALE
We're here, kids. C'mon!
Daniel! Daniel, look over there!
Ha ha! Hurry now!

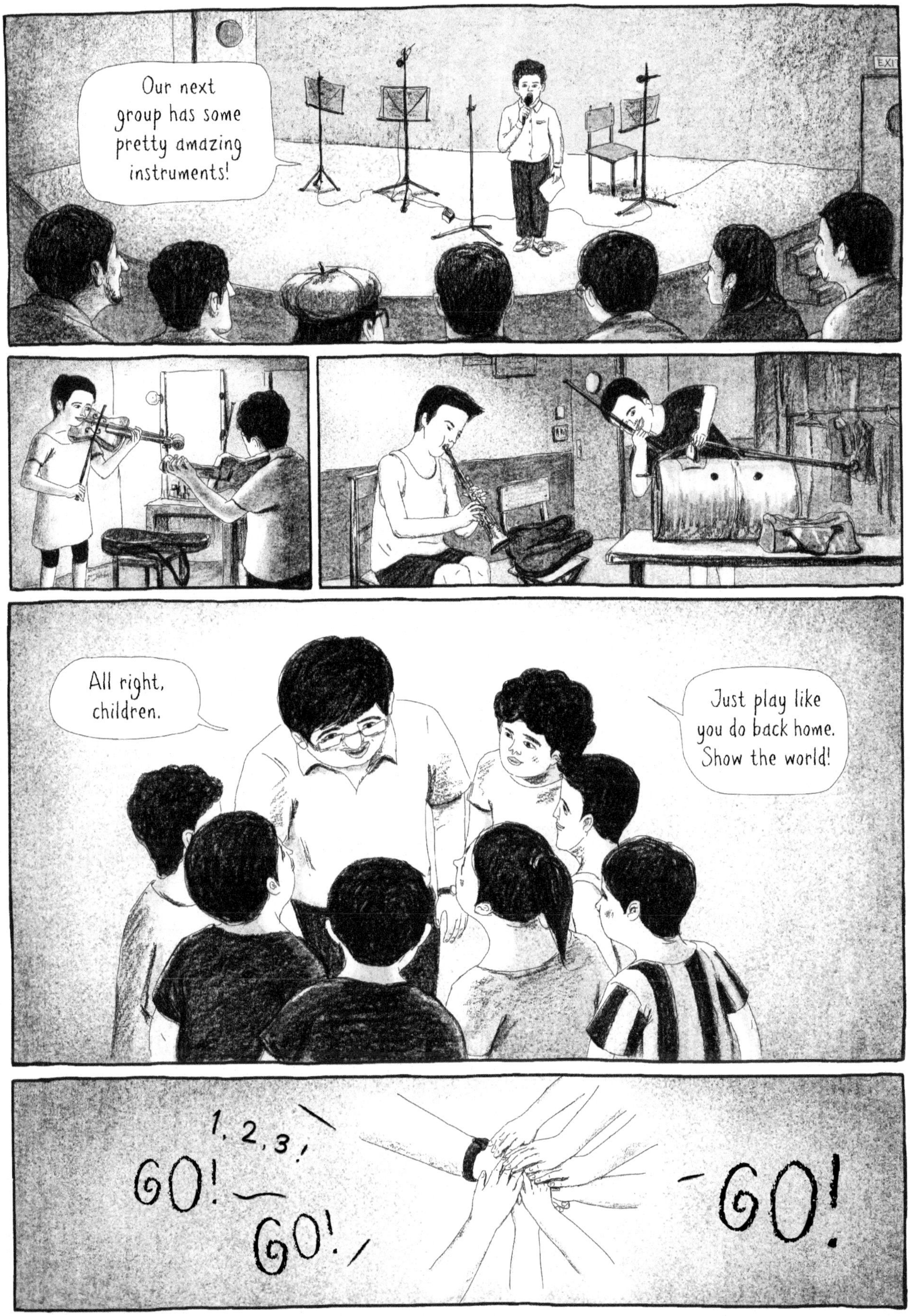
Our next group has some pretty amazing instruments!
EXIT
All right, children.
Just play like you do back home. Show the world!
1, 2, 3!
GO!
GO!
GO!

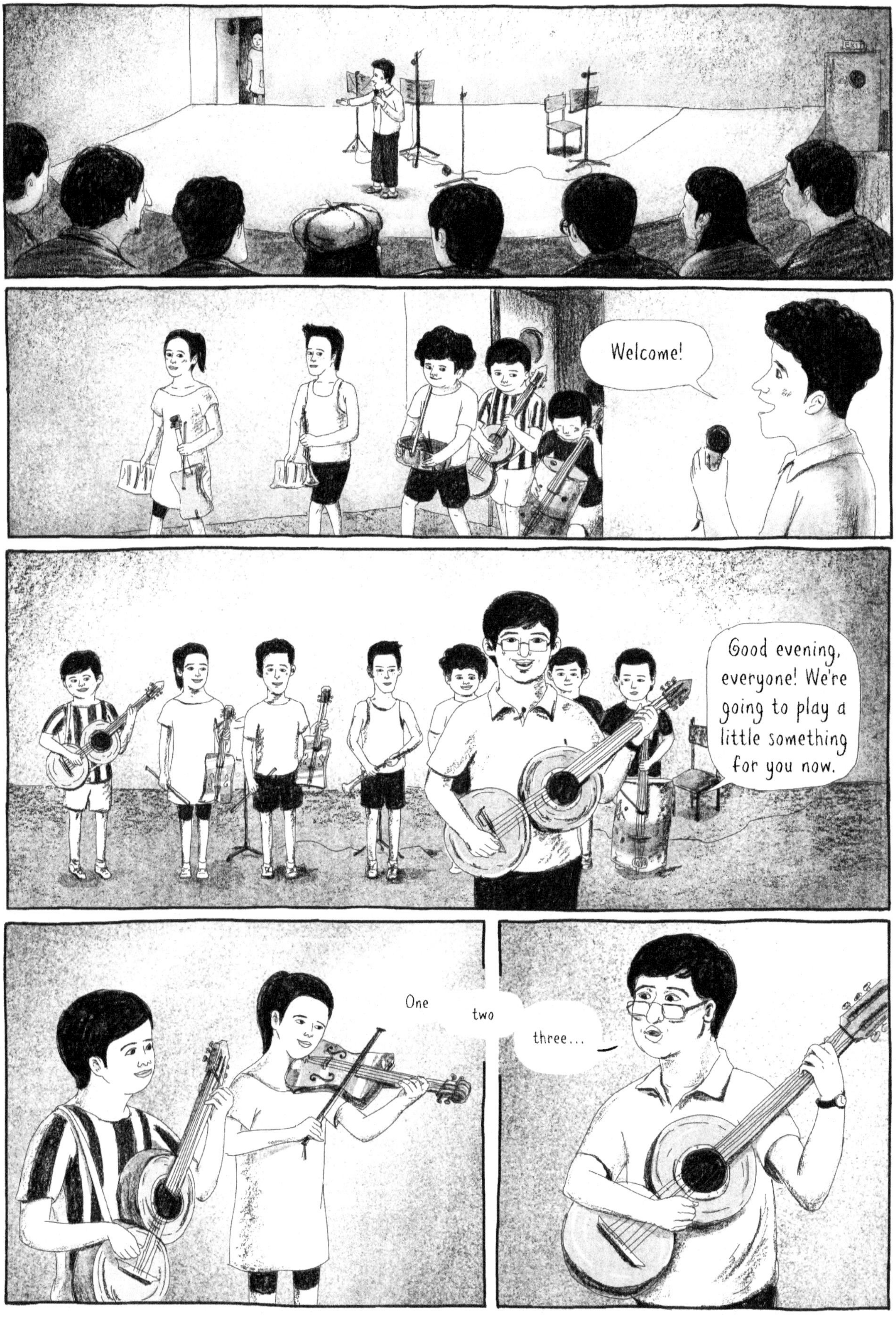
Welcome!
Good evening, everyone! We're going to play a little something for you now.
One
two
three...

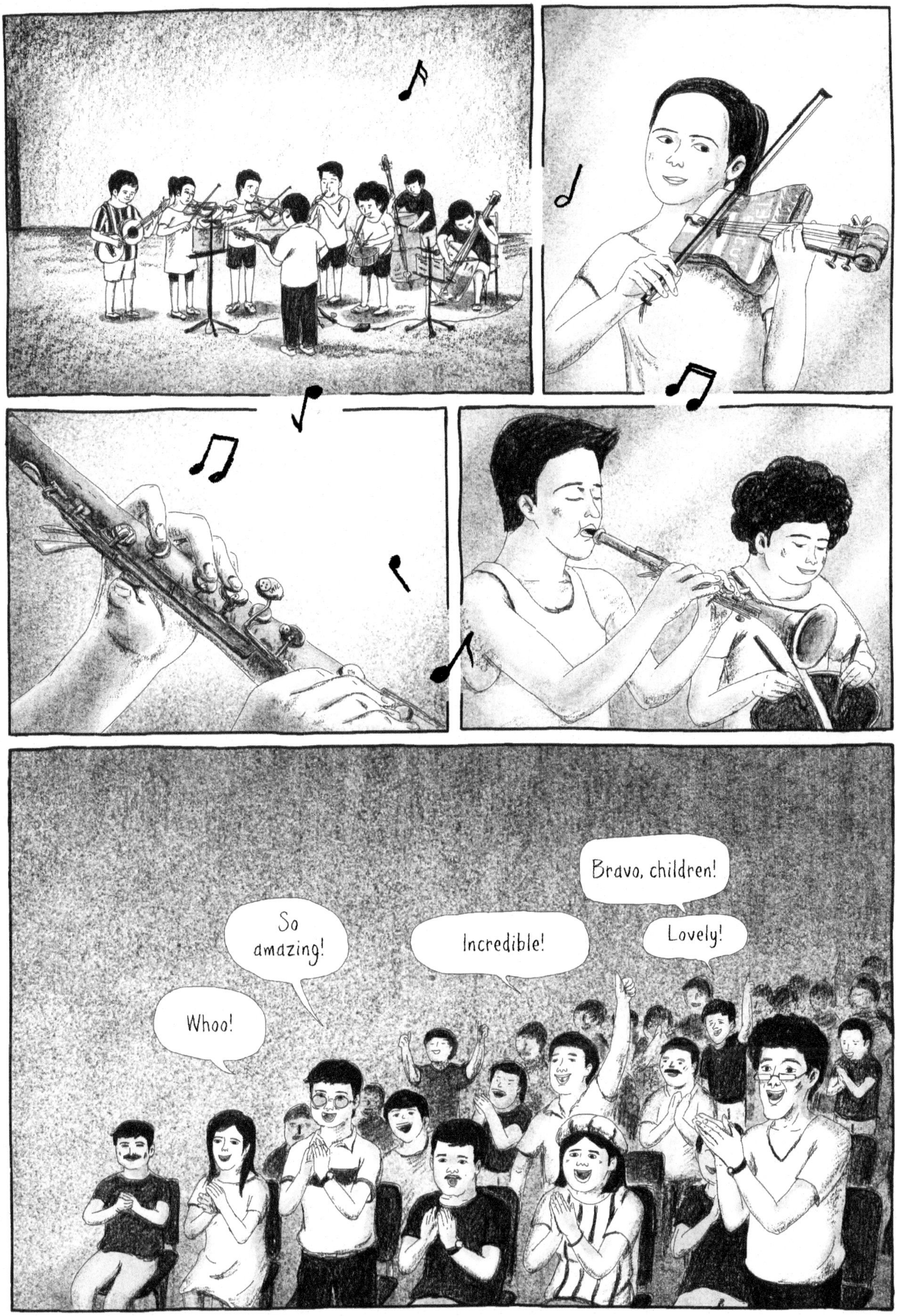
Whoo!
So amazing!
Incredible!
Bravo, children!
Lovely!

Thanks to this performance,
the musicians' story became known
far and wide.

The Recycled Orchestra went on to
play all over the world, changing
the lives of the young people born
near the landfill. More and more
people became invested and involved
in this project, even founding
a music school.

Diego and Nicolas never
stopped believing in the group.
They're still a part of it today.
And the story goes on.

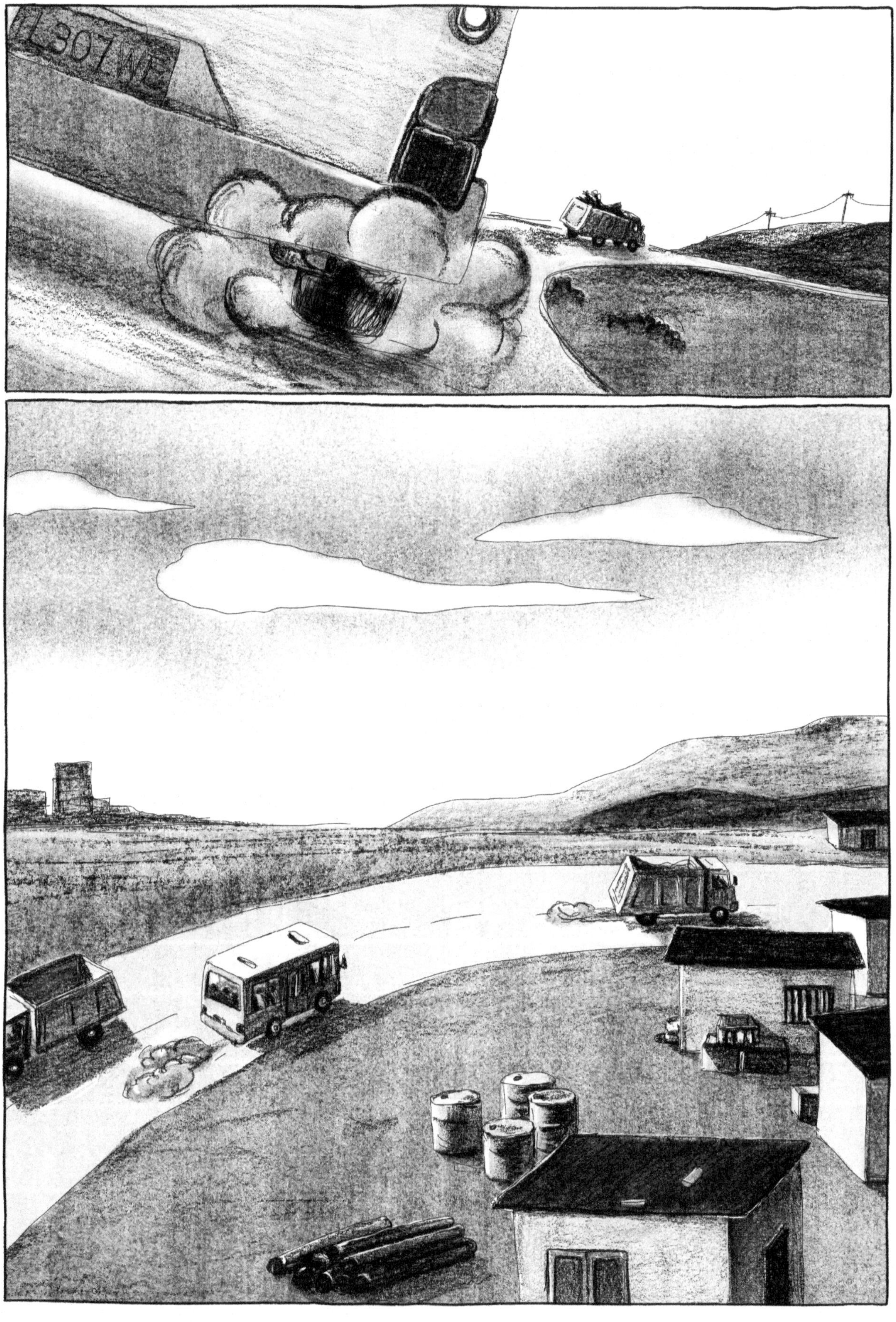
L307 WE

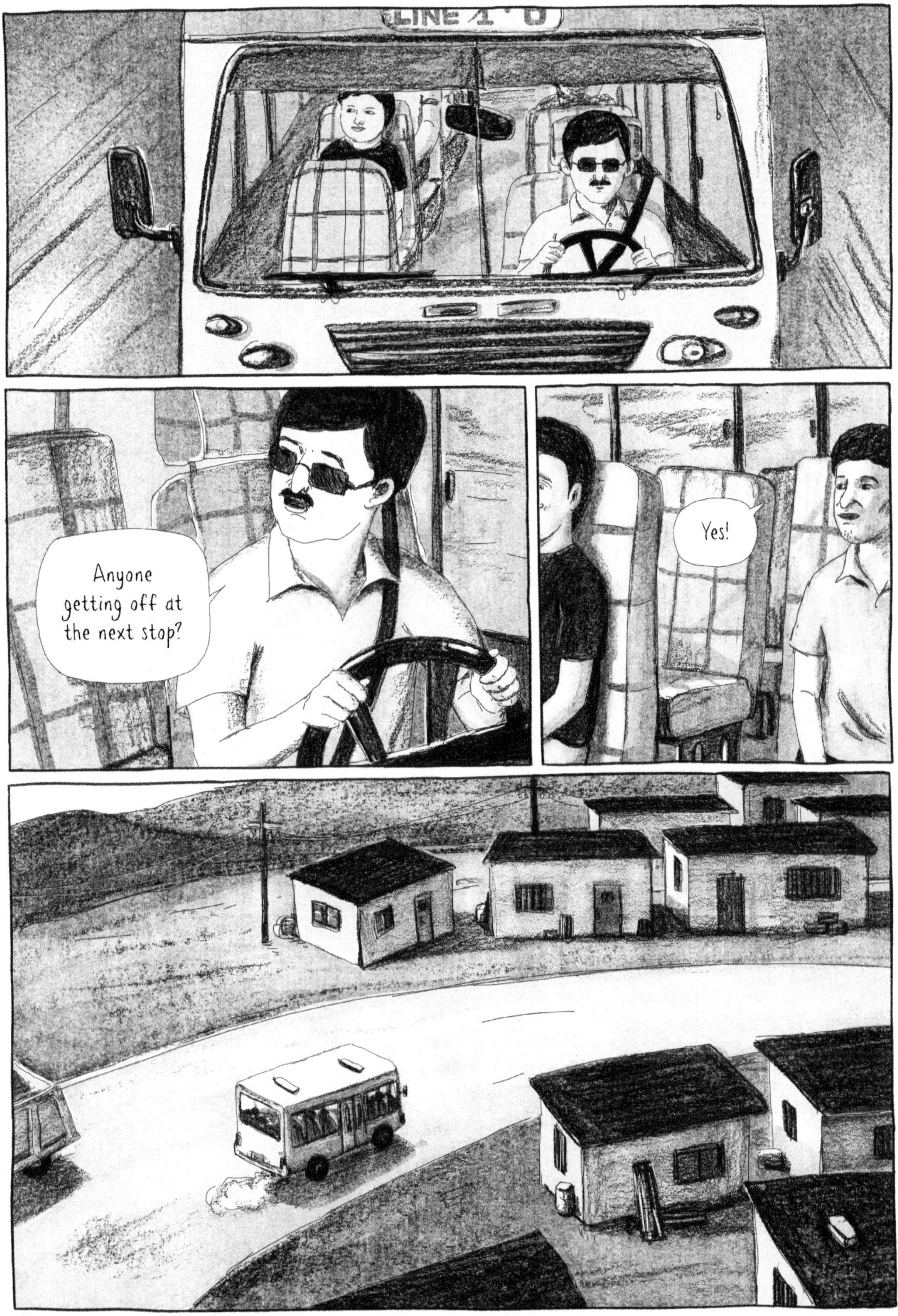
Anyone getting off at the next stop?
Yes!

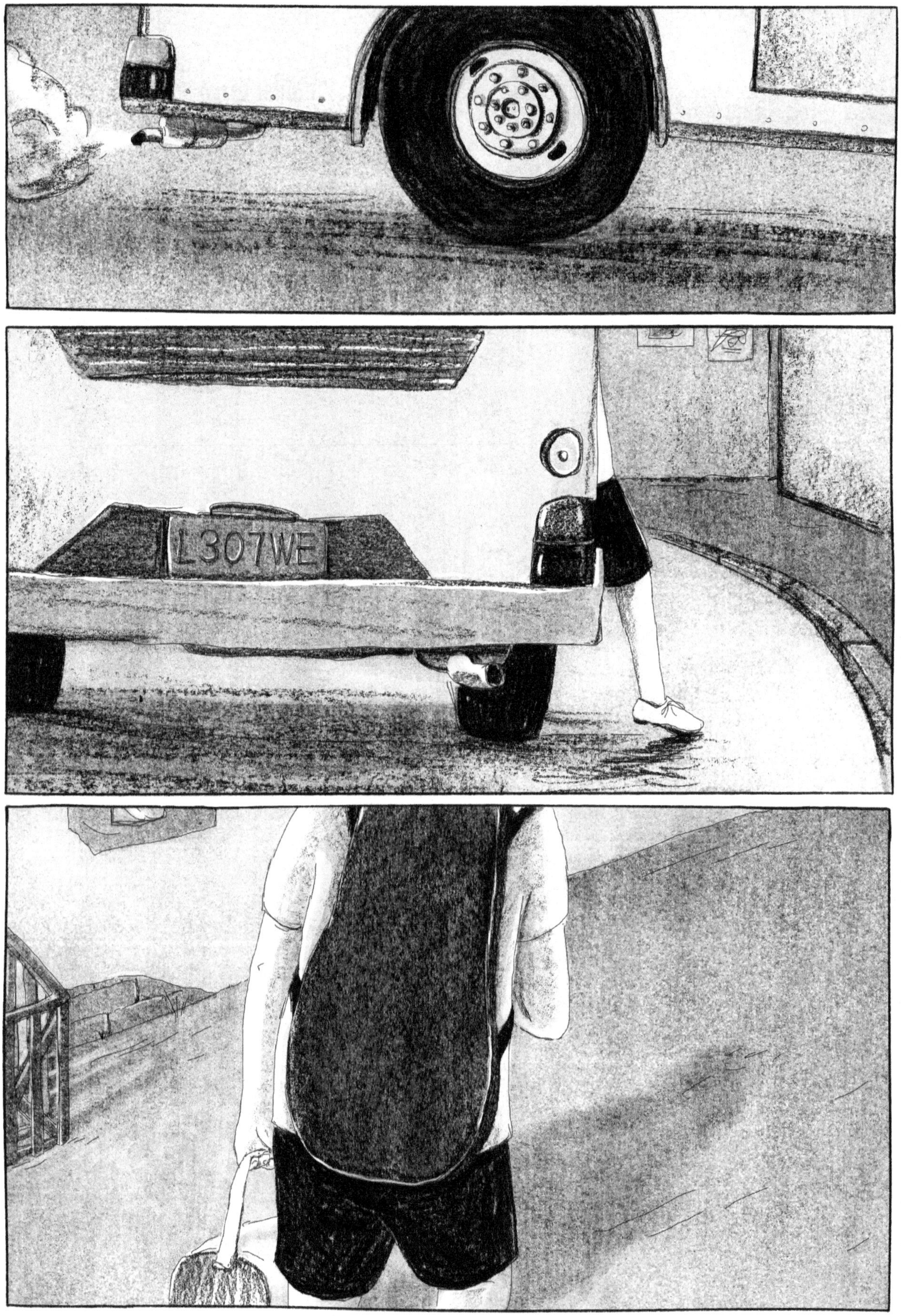
L307WE

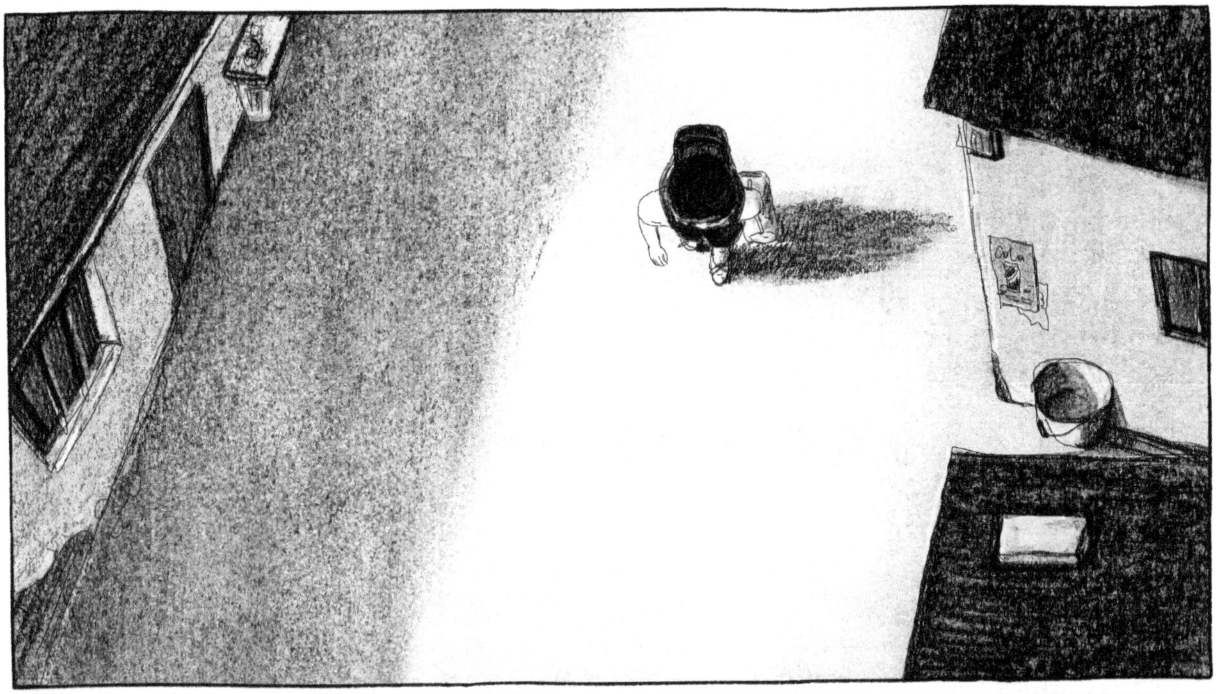

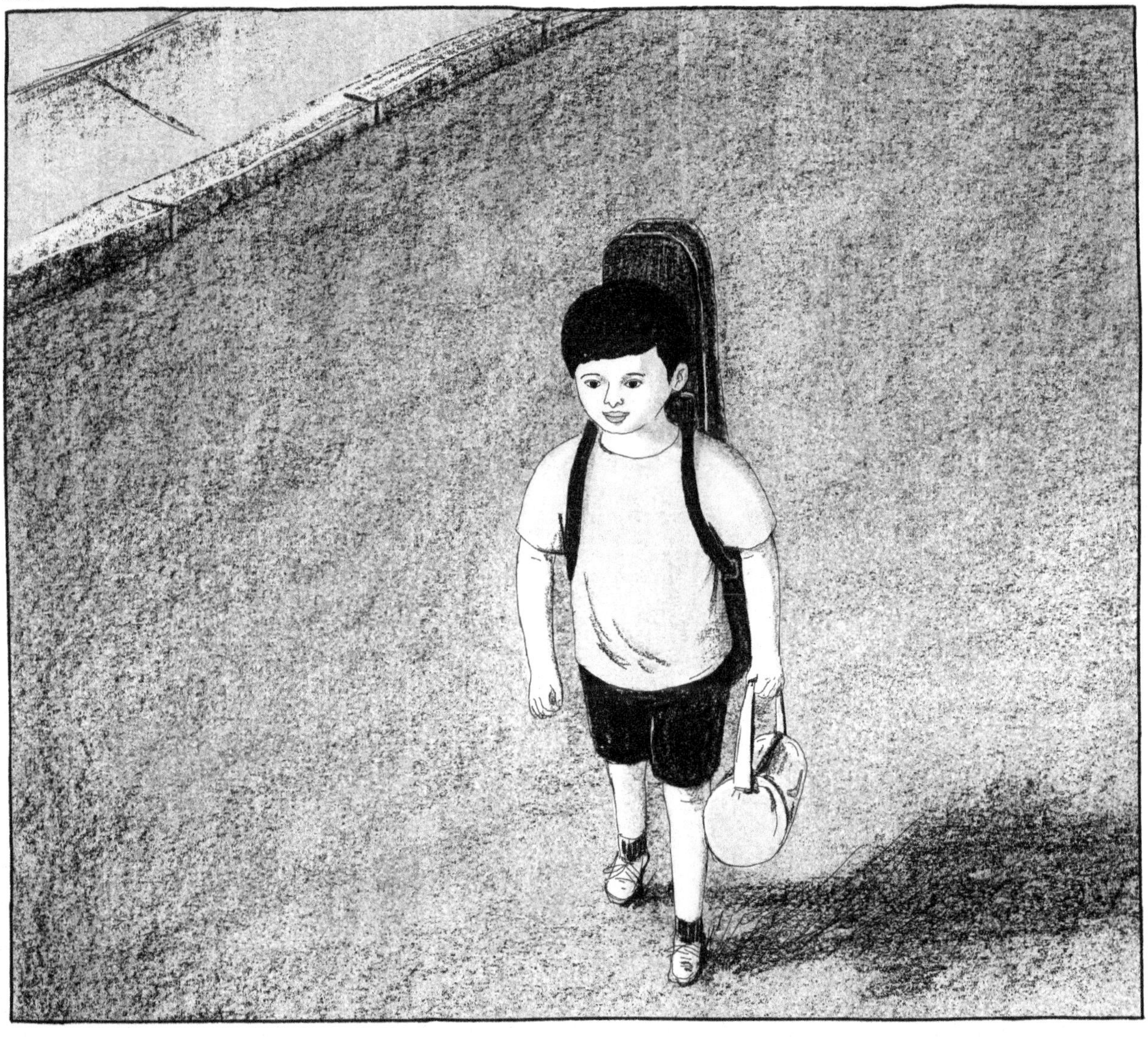

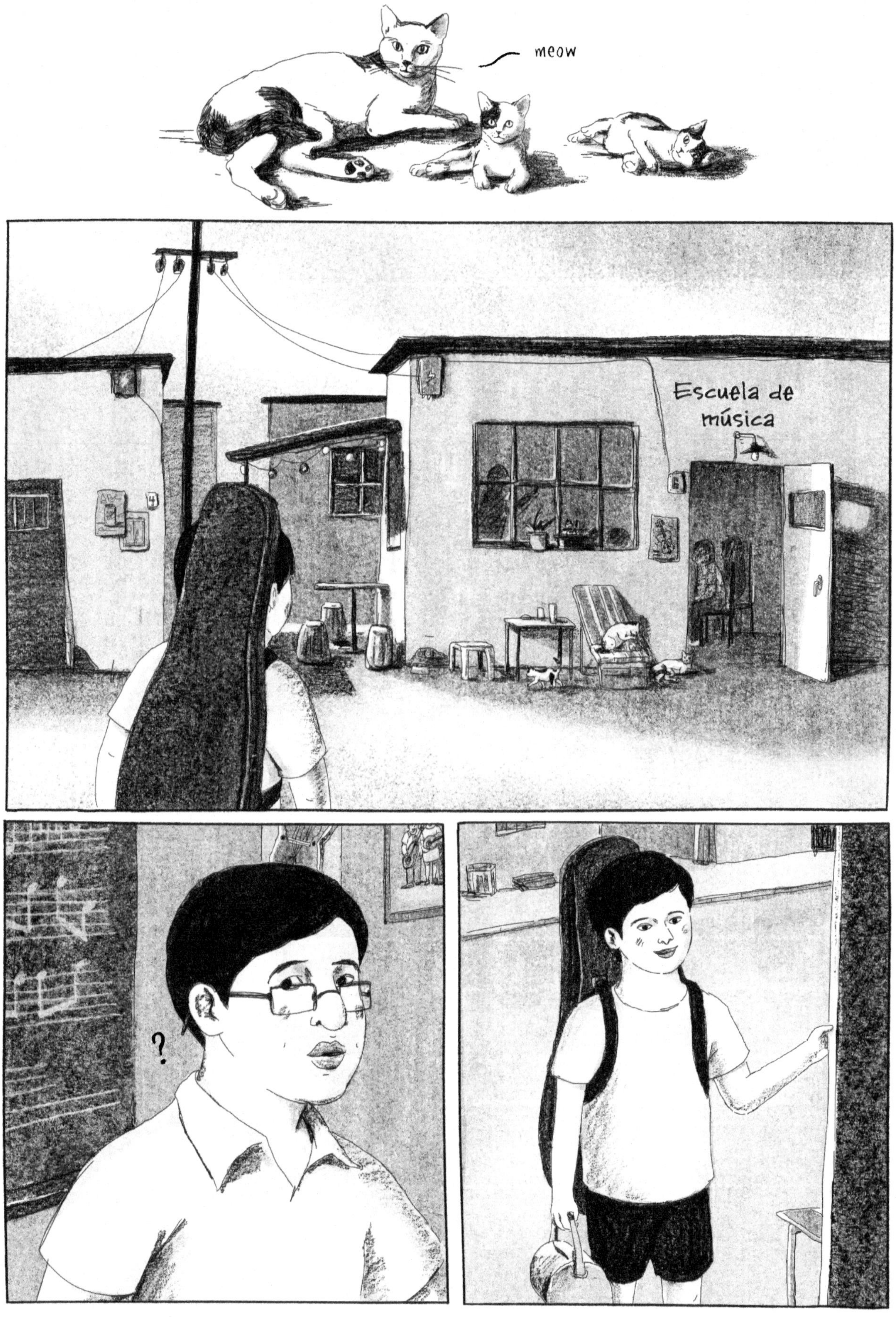
meow
Escuela de música
?

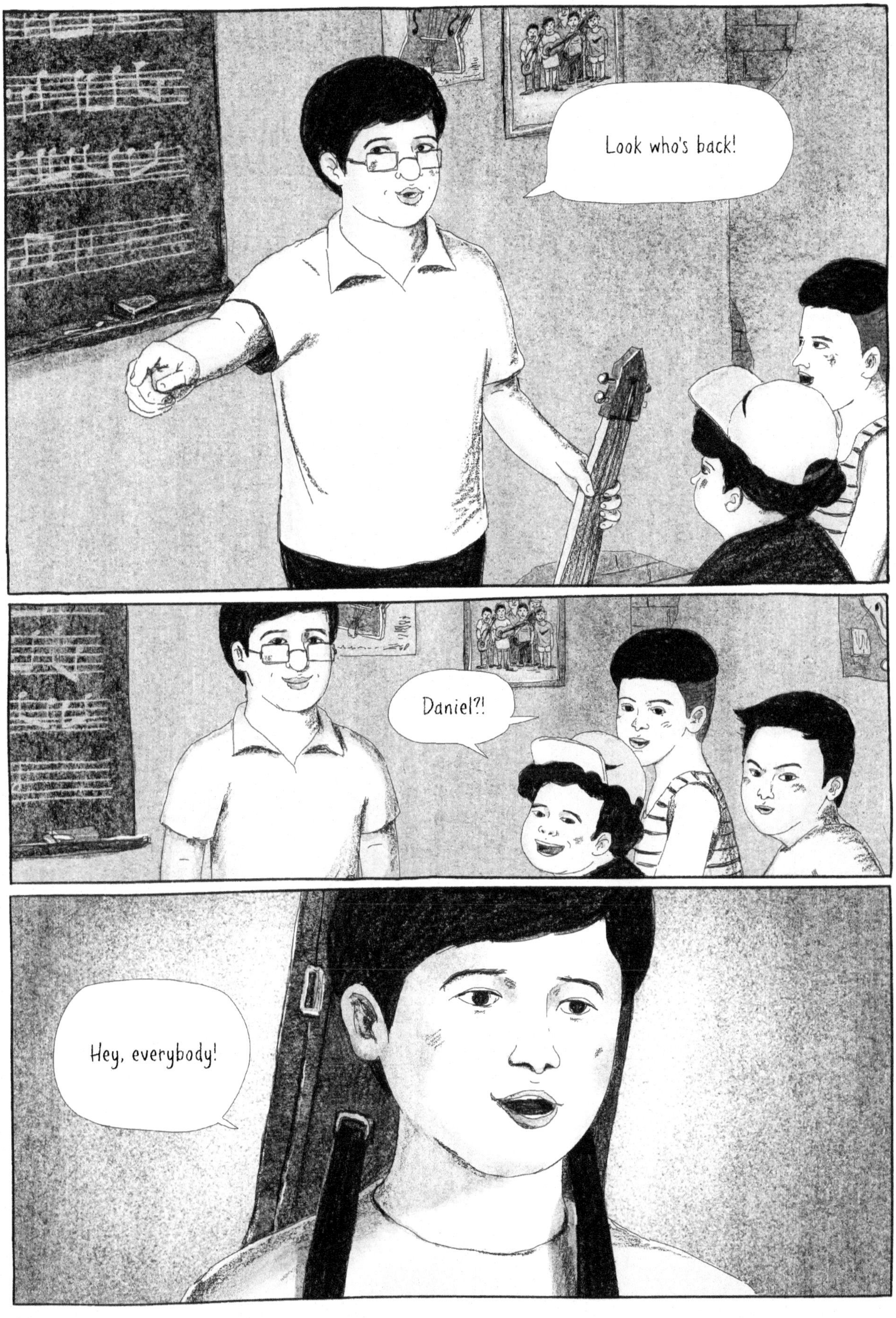
Look who's back!
Daniel?!
Hey, everybody!

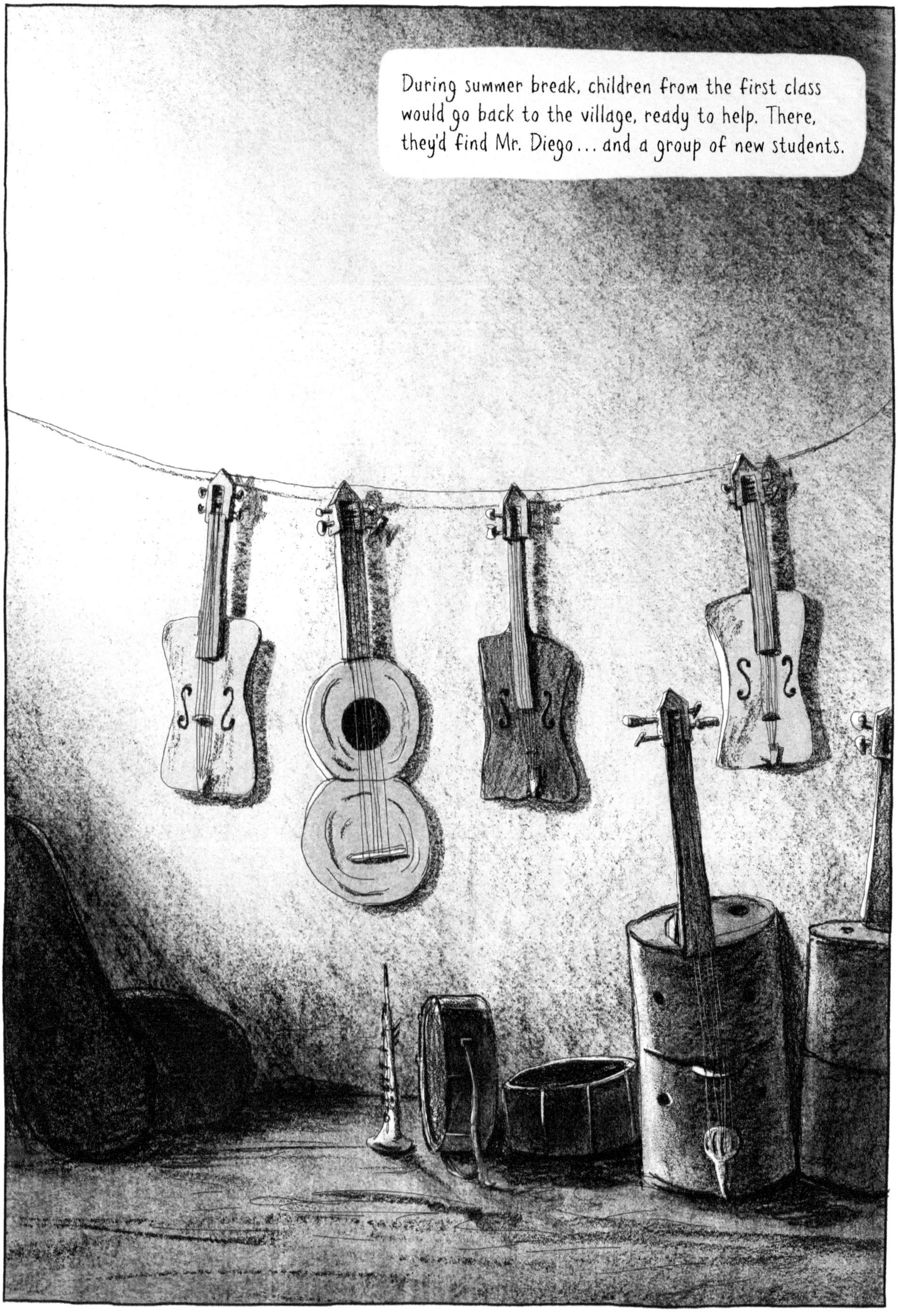
During summer break, children from the first class would go back to the village, ready to help. There, they'd find Mr. Diego... and a group of new students.

"The world sends us its garbage. We give it back music."

—FAVIO CHÁVEZ

This book was inspired by the story of Favio Chávez,
a musician and educator who founded, in 2006,
La Orquesta de Instrumentos Reciclados de Cateura
(Recycled Orchestra of Cateura), which has gone on
to play concerts all over the world.

www.recycledorchestracateura.com

ABOUT THE AUTHOR

Hua Lin Xie studied art and animation in Beijing, China, for four years before continuing her studies at the Émile Cohl School in Lyon, France, where she currently resides. *Another Band's Treasure: A Story of Recycled Instruments* (first published by Steinkis as *Sous les déchets . . . la musique*) is her first graphic novel.

ABOUT THE TRANSLATOR

Award-winning translator Edward Gauvin specializes in contemporary comics. As an advocate for translators and translated literature, he has written widely and spoken at universities and festivals. He is the translator of more than 425 graphic novels and a contributing editor for comics at Words Without Borders. His collaborations with Lerner, ranging in setting from Lebanon to World War II France to modern-day Beijing, have been honored by the American Library Association and the Eisner Awards. The ukulele is his fidget spinner. He has been playing for four fun years. Home is wherever his wife and daughter are.

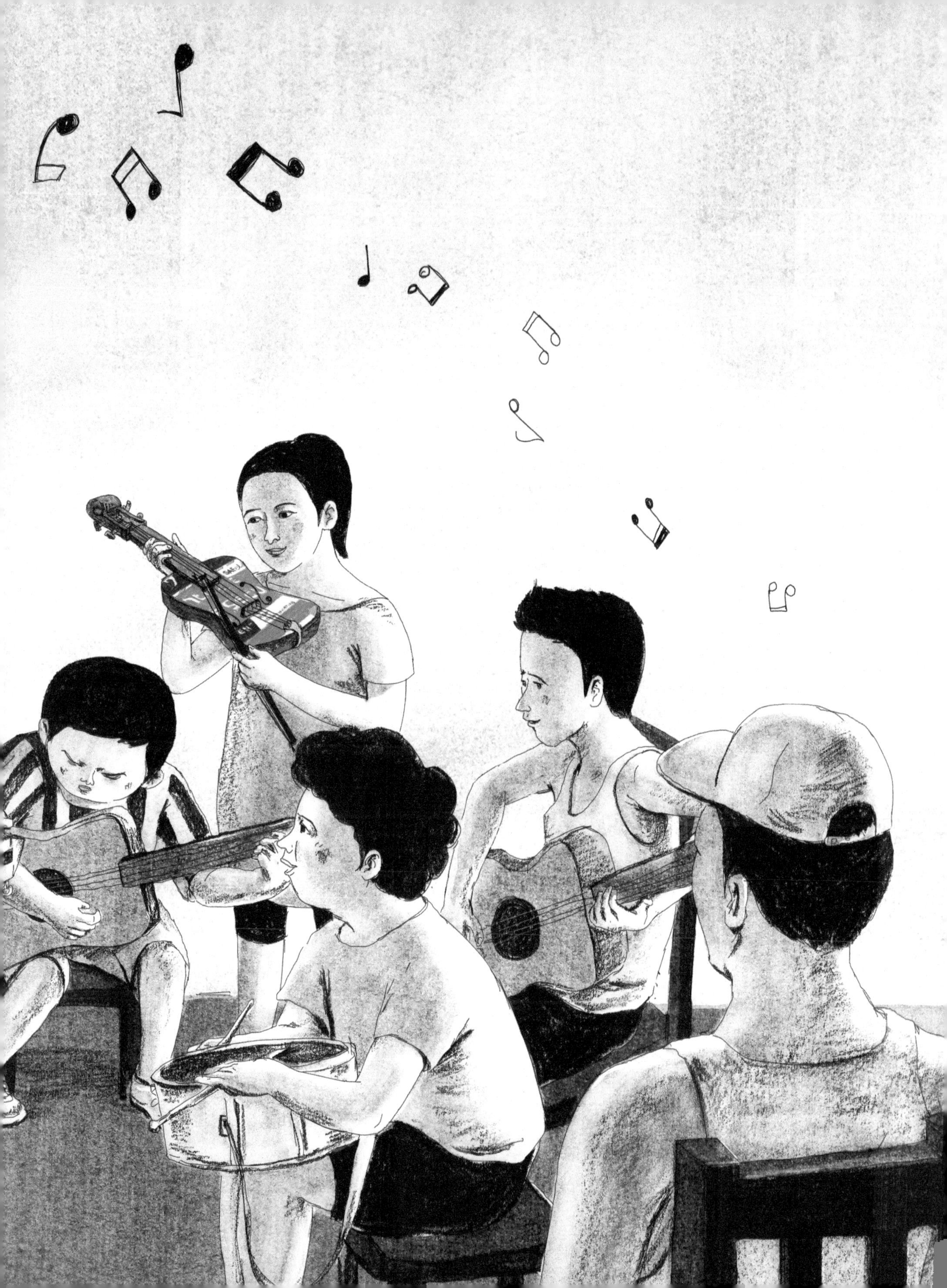